LOST ISLAND

LOST ISLAND

PLUS THREE STORIES AND AN AFTERWORD

BARBARA NEWHALL FOLLETT

farksolia

Lost Island (plus three stories and an afterword)

Cover design by Resa Blatman • resablatman.com

Cover photo by Ekrulila, generously shared on pexels.com

For more BNF, please visit farksolia.org

ISBN: 978-0-9962431-4-8 (softcover)

First edition, February 2020

CONTENTS

For E. A.

[1]

Not even a cat was out. The rain surged down with a steady drone. It meant harm to New York and everyone there. The gutters could not contain it. Long ago they had despaired of the job and surrendered. But the rain paid no attention to them. It was bent on an errand of hate against the city.

Windows were gray and tight shut. There was one window fronted with a box of pansies, and behind the pansies, rather than behind the window, Jane Carey lived. There was nothing outside, this morning. Nothing but gray curtains hanging between the sky (was there really a sky?) and the flooded streets. Solid gray curtains, sometimes swaying ominously in the gusts of wind.

In New York people never lived in houses or even in burrows. They inhabited cells in stone cliffs. They timed the cooking of their eggs by the nearest traffic light. If the light went wrong, so did the eggs. All the cliffs were alike, and even all the cells. Unless there was some personal reason for knowing a particular one, it could never be distinguished from the others. A gigantic beehive.

Opening her window a little wearily, Jane took the pansies in out of the lashing rain. Her face at first might seem like thousands of others that peered occasionally from cells in stone cliffs. Her plain brown hair was drawn back severely, and there was no light in it. But, on a second glance, there was something rare and haunting about her, perhaps her bold forehead in contrast to the wistfulness of her mouth, perhaps her dark brown eyes and the secret laughter in them—something intangible that was Jane Carey.

"I don't like civilization," she said, to the rain.

Millie Carson's voice answered sleepily, in the tone of one who had discussed the subject before. "Well, s'pose you could chuck Manhattan out in the Indian Ocean as you'd like to, it still wouldn't stop raining. Be a lot worse, too, out in the wild, woolly woods you're forever ranting about."

"Out in the wild, woolly woods," said Jane, "you'd stay snug in your own shack, or cave, or tree, as the case might be. You wouldn't go out to work till it stopped, whereas I—"

"But you'd have to lug home a lion to eat—if it didn't eat you first, that is." To Millie, "woods" and "lions" were practically synonyms.

"Oh, you'd pick yesterday's lion-bones," Jane told her. "And lion soup—delectable!"

Things like that were beyond rational consideration. "Broadway for me, gal, work or no work," Millie said.

"And the wild woods for me, lions or no lions," Jane echoed.

"What I can't understand is why the hell you don't beat it back to that one-horse town in Maine where you were raised."

"Some time I'll tell you."

"It would leave a job for somebody in little old N. Y., Janie. Worth thinking over. Always thought you were kind-hearted."

"If I left my job," Jane retorted, "there'd be a revolution. A hundred thousand people would fight for it." She flapped into her raincoat.

"Toodleoo!" Millie sang out. "Don't get drowned, kitten." And she promptly went to sleep again.

Outside, the rain was a wall. Jane made a dash into it. She lowered her head and struggled with it. At last, the blue light of the subway station, a dim but welcome symbol of hope.

She stood on the platform and let two roaring, jammed expresses hurtle by. Jammed was hardly the word, either. Millie wouldn't mind piling into them, being squashed to pulp. Perhaps she even enjoyed it. Millie and her absurd lions! Jane smiled. An elderly, stern-looking lady with a vast expanse of bosom and a string of cheap pearls noticed the smile.... Millie had never been off the pavements in her life. Didn't want to, either. No two persons could be more different, or fonder of each other. Millie's needs were snappy clothes, plenty of war-paint, and boy friends. She was a chorus girl in a cheap show—not very near the footlights, but on her way, perhaps. Jane was shy and retiring. She looked severe and plain by contrast, and a little old-fashioned, like something carved in oak. She idolized woods and hills and bright pastures. To her the city was purposeless and tyrannical. For months these two girls had shared the small uptown apartment. Jane was out all day, Millie most of the night. When they were together, they were a never-ending source of bewilderment and amusement to each other, which was perhaps why they got along so well.... Jane was still smiling. The dame with the pearls lifted her eyebrows and sidled up. "Do I know you?" she challenged, with immense haughtiness.

Jane quickly reassured her. "Oh, no! I was just smiling to myself, and—well, you got in my way."

The downtown local pulled in, its four yellow lights suggesting the feelers of some great dashing worm. Jane stood at the very rear of the train, and absently watched the tunnel lights. With a spurt, yellow meteors jumped up and arranged themselves in a row behind, one end of it growing, the other fading away in the tunnel. Sometimes a blue one flew into the row. Once the red eyes of an express train behind loomed up, a monster roaring past out of the dark. It was sinister but impersonal. It didn't care in the least whether or not Jane liked civilization. It *was* civilization—efficiency and machinery. The engine maintained a frightful pace, and you had to keep up with it or get crushed and mangled.

Everywhere now the engine was victorious. Even at sea. Jane did not know much about the sea, except that it held a nameless magic for her. But she was conscious of its transformation. No more sleepy galleons with purple and gold sails, moving on in a leisured sway. Even the fine old tea-clippers were too slow. Sails had to surrender to the propeller and the steam-engine. The world couldn't sit around waiting for the wind to blow in some special direction. But why think of ships and the sea? They were more intangible and unattainable even than woods and hills.... Here was Times Square—people nearly killing one another in their frenzy to get somewhere or other, as if it mattered. But you had to keep pace. Philosophize till doomsday; a lot of good it would do if you didn't keep pace. No chance at all for trees, sailing ships, or philosophy.

Jane worked in a very dark little office. Not a ray of sunlight could penetrate there; hardly a gleam of honest daylight. After three years, working without daylight was still torture to her. Otherwise, it could be said that she had an enviable job, particularly now, when jobs, as Millie put it, were scarcer than thousand-dollar bills. The truth seemed to be that one could starve to death on an enviable job—for mountain wind, for stars among pine trees, or the call of a wood-thrush to his mate.

No one knew precisely what the business of that little office was. Jane knew only that it was intensely scientific. Professor Myers was in charge of whatever it was that happened there. He was an aged and kindly soul who directed by correspondence mysterious researches in entomology, and wrote articles about them for which he was never paid.

Professor Myers amused Jane, and seemed to her always a trifle pathetic. He was so wrapped up in entomology that he never noticed when anyone laughed at him. People were forever laughing at him, though gently and affectionately. He never remembered his appointments. Sometimes he forgot his overcoat. His glasses were perpetually lost.

"Good morning, Miss Carey, good morning." He beamed. He was always in the office by the time she arrived at nine, and he worked there till all hours of the night. There were other members of the staff, but he and Jane were the only ones of any importance. They worked in a world by themselves. She was his secretary; upon her devolved many duties which seemed irrelevant, such as buying his railway tickets when he went out of town, keeping on hand a supply of cigarettes and pipe tobacco, and finding his glasses.

"The *Coleoptera Review* took that article of mine," he said, with another beam. "Let's write to them."

Jane fetched her notebook and settled down opposite him at his desk. He dictated in a leisurely way. Between sentences he seemed to be carrying on scientific researches, and Jane did her day-dreaming.

"To Dr. Carl Unger," he began, "Editor of—" Jane nodded. "I am very glad that you have accepted my article, and I shall be glad to make the changes you suggest. I was glad to hear—Oh, no, no, I don't want to be so darn glad. Take out some of those glads, Miss Carey."

He began floundering among the papers on his desk. "Have you seen my glasses?" he asked. "I had them a minute ago." She walked around his desk, and presently fished them out of the half-open drawer into which they had fallen. He thanked her gravely. "It's not so much whether you *lose* your glasses, Miss Carey, as whether you find them again." You couldn't laugh at

Professor Myers when he said such things so solemnly. He invested them with deep meaning. That remark could be applied to the whole of life. Not so much whether you lost your glasses —it was the finding that counted....

When Jane had first come to New York, only eighteen years old, alone, with little money, and less idea of where she would go or what she would do, old Professor Myers had taken her into his office for half-time work, while she went to business school and learned typing and stenography with the energy of desperation. He bothered her with no questions; he simply approved, advised, watched. Deep down he was a practical soul, but it was deep. Many people who thought they knew him never suspected it at all.

At least there was no great hurry in his office. Stepping inside his door, Jane temporarily stepped into an oasis in the desert of the steam-engine and the dollar symbol. She knew she was lucky not to be in the rush and whirl of industry. Furthermore, she was fond of the old man. But she hated his four dark walls. And his monographs on butterflies' antennae irritated her —as if you couldn't appreciate a butterfly without knowing all about its antennae!...

That day was over. Nothing was left of it, no one remembered it, when Jane stepped out into the street again. The rain had abated, but the air was still dank and cold. She stood still a minute, struggling with her umbrella. She was tired, but comforted to think that the week was almost over. From somewhere a voice seemed to be hailing her. It couldn't be real, but it was persistent. "Janie! Oh, Jay-nee!"

"Why, Bob!" (It *was* a real voice, then.)

He hurried up to her, and they shook hands gravely. His shape was vague in the rainy mist. He looked very tall, a bit piratical. That was the effect of his felt hat covered with mist. "What are you doing in this end of town, Bob? And where have you been hiding yourself anyway?"

"Right here for the last half hour; I thought you'd emerge some time. Janie, I need the proverbial shoulder."

"To cry on?"

He nodded. "Ellen's given me the go-by."

"Poor devil," said Jane, into the mist. And in the same minute she wondered why so many of her friends seemed to need her shoulders, whereas she— But she had not yet succeeded in convincing herself that the enigmatic person before her was Bob. He shouldn't look piratical; he ought to be young and boyish. The rain and her mood had changed him.

"You thought she would, didn't you?" he asked.

"I was afraid of it, to tell the truth."

"And you'll probably say 'good riddance.' And I wonder if you aren't right."

She squeezed his hand. "Come on up to my little hole," she invited, "and have some supper. We can't stand here forever, you know," she reminded him, as she might have reminded Professor Myers. "How about a steak-'n'-unyuns? Where's your car?"

He tucked a hand under her arm, and they vanished into the rain like two ghosts.

That steak did help matters. Jane hustled about her kitchenette in a green dress with ruffles and flowers on it, a sort of symbol of springtime. That helped, too. "Sit down," she commanded, when everything was ready. "I bet you're half starved. You'd never remember to eat if somebody didn't remember for you." She brought to the table a large platter of steak, and a bottle of red wine. "And don't sigh like a willow tree, old man. Never liked willows much. Spruces and firs have more the right idea."

Before long she had him almost laughing. He looked infinitely improved, then. Just a young thing, after all, who didn't know where he was bound, and who liked to pretend that he was grown up. He wasn't a man yet, but she felt that he was trying hard to be, that he would be very soon, and that he was struggling against heavy odds; for he was the son of a widowed millionaire who pampered him. It was only with Jane that he forgot this other life. With her he could be natural and spontaneous. She was a cold clear spring in the midst of a too languid garden.

"I wish," she said abruptly, "you could go and plough a field. Awfully good for your backbone, ploughs are. But with those damned button-hooks of your father's being such a success—"

"Fish-hooks, Janie—"

"I don't care if they were harpoons. They've made life too easy for you.

"You brute!"

"A really first-class backbone has to be developed in the face of resistance," Jane solemnly intoned.

"D'you suppose Ellen saw the flaws in mine, then?"

"I don't know; but it'll take a good one to hang on to her. She's a—fly-away. A sprite, sort of. What have you been doing to her?"

He smiled ruefully. "Well, I did look out the window once or twice," he admitted. "You know how it is. Just natural, Janie. No harm meant. But when somebody strenuously objects, the things we see out the window look better and better."

Jane smiled slowly. "No girl on earth wants to believe such things," she said.

"Jane, you understand, don't you? Couldn't you see Ellen, and explain to her? I can't; I've tried."

"She'd curse me for a confounded old meddler, Bob."

"No, I think she'd take it from you. She thinks of you as kind of an older sister who knows life, and all that stuff."

"That's ironical, to say the least," Jane chuckled. "Must be because I ran away from home. That always gets you a reputation of one kind or another."

"Jane, I wish you would see her."

"What can I say that you couldn't say better?"

"She won't see me. She won't talk to me on the telephone."

"Give her time."

"It's hell to wait. And I think she's going around with some other fellow."

The hurt look in his eyes persuaded her. "All right," she said. "I'll try." Old Professor Myers' words about his glasses rang in her mind again, and she added: "Don't look so worried, Bob. It doesn't matter so much if you lose her—just as long as you get her back again."

"Janie, I don't know how to thank—"

"Don't bother!"

She made coffee. They talked and laughed, discussed dreams and plans. "You haven't said a word about yourself, Janie. What are you going to do this summer?"

"Oh, work," she said casually.

"No vacation?"

"Couple of weeks. I may go to Maine—climb a mountain or two—have a swim."

"You like that job of yours a lot, don't you?"

She dared not flinch at that, for her usefulness to her friends lay in giving them the firm conviction that she herself was content with life. "Sure," she answered steadily. "I'm lucky to have any job, these days."

She was even trying to shrug her shoulders with appropriate nonchalance, but the doorbell rang, and that gesture was never finished.

Out in the hall stood a small, dim person. Jane stared. "Mary Rogers!" She grabbed both the girl's hands. "You're frozen, and drenched!" she exclaimed. "Come in.... No, nobody here except Bob Graham—you've heard of him."

"Janie," the other girl whispered—her teeth were chattering —"could you possibly put me up for the night?" She was a shy, gray, frail young person, with hungry but innocent blue eyes.

"Did you ever know me not to put you up for the night? Will you have the bed that lets down or the one that unfolds?"

"I'd be glad to sleep on the floor. The truth is, Jane, my job is gone and I haven't a cent—and you know I can't go home, after leaving them so proudly."

"Oh, Lord, how we all do seem to be in trouble! Well, come on in and meet Bob. Have some coffee. Help yourself to my elegant wardrobe if you're wet. And do let's try to be gay."

Millie came in late, with a scuffle of high heels in the corridor. Jane met her with one finger across her lips in warning. "Mary's here," she said. "Lost her job, and all upset. So don't fling the rough language too much, and don't be hard on the kid even if you don't think much of her.... Sa-ay! What you been doing? How come you look so pleased with yourself?"

"Oh, I've been getting engaged again, that's all.... Well, let me have a look at your little lame cat. I won't hurt her." Millie was not derisive, only mocking. To her, Jane's out-of-luck friends were always "lame cats." There were usually a lot of them around. Jane was too soft and easy, Millie thought—allowed people to prey on her. People would prey, of course, if they had the chance, or thought they had.

Millie's own ideas were different. Live for yourself first; you got on much better. Good things don't come of their own accord. They had to be fetched, and then hung on to. All that took energy. But it was the best way to use one's energy: for your own advancement and not that of lame cats. Jane was a darling, of course, but unpractical. She lived on dreams and ridiculous fancies. Always talking about the woods, or sometimes the sea. Living with her eyes half closed to the world around her, and a dream in their depths. Millie didn't understand that. She lived in the present. Get the most out of today—fun, clothes, money, laughs; get as much as you can. Tomorrow you may be dead....

Bob was just going. "Thanks, Jane," he said. "I feel improved."

She went to the door with him. "Good boy. Don't worry over Ellen or the fish-hooks or anything."

"Try not to," he promised.

"I'll telephone her in the morning, and ask her over."

"You're grand, Jane. And—say! You tell your nice little friend Mary to come and see my Dad next week. He's been thinking about firing his secretary."

"Bob—could you fix up a date for her to see him?"

"Sure—I guess so."

"Corking of you!"

"Well, we've all got to help each other out," he said. "You help morally, I help materially; everybody can, some damn way, and the world wags on."

"Keep it up," said Jane. "You're almost a philosopher."

Mary was vague and indefinable, Jane thought. But then, she was tired tonight and rather frightened. Millie was louder and ruder, and her world remote from Jane. And yet Millie was infinitely more real, more vital. She was colorful, with her bush of black curls, her snapping eyes, her gorgeous painted mouth. Mary tried to talk about industry, the lack of jobs, the sad condition the world found itself in. But that was an unfortunate subject. The world was going to the dogs… and conversation languished.

"You're tired," said Jane. "I think I'll put you to bed. You can have the contrivance that lets down, and Millie and I'll berth together."

Mary looked suspiciously at the swinging bed. "I won't wake up in the closet, will I?"

"Well, no one has yet. But you never can tell, you know. You might wake hanging upside down, like a little bat."

...A little shy gray bat which she had brought in from the woods and made friends with, years ago. Luna moths and bats;

thrushes at dawn, wild roses, butterflies, and the smell of pines —all these had been part of that "one-horse town in Maine," where she had spent her first eighteen years, and which she had always thought of with delight.... In those days New York, new friends, a job and money of her own, had been in her mind unattainable and romantic fancies.

The three girls were at last comfortably installed for the night. Jane became aware that Millie was nudging her under the sheet. "Kitten!" she whispered. "Coming to my wedding?"

"It won't go through," said Jane.

"He's a swell guy," said Millie. "Plenty of money, good looker, dances like a house afire." Those were the three ideal virtues.

"That's what you've said about all of 'em," Jane reminded her.

Millie's idea was to catch a man before you knew him too well and were disillusioned about him; then, when you began to see his faults, drop him like a red-hot poker. That was the way to get the most out of affairs of the heart. All the fun and none of the tears.

"You know," Jane confided, "I almost got married once myself."

"For Gawd's sake! I didn't think you'd even been kissed. And you never told me, you wretch!"

"Well, it missed fire."

"It would. You're so idiotic, kitten."

"Well, I got to the altar."

"Didn't he turn up, or was the ring lost, or—"

"Nothing like that. It was all quite proper. Horribly proper, in fact. So I skipped, that's all. Ran for my life."

"For Gawd's sake!" Millie commented again. "Honest, I didn't know you had it in you."

Jane shut her eyes. It had been a whale of a day, and tomorrow would be another. Time to sleep. But she had evoked a ghost, and it was not to vanish easily.... Not that Charlie had ever meant very much. He had been a jolly soul, and a pleasant companion. He could make a violin tell you of sunsets and far places, but he himself never lived up to the things his violin said. He had money, within reason. A college boy, too—very eligible. Nothing to worry about if she married him, her tyrannical widowed father affirmed. Well, nothing to think about, either; or to dream about. But she had accepted her fate. In that town, it would have been unthinkable to refuse. Furthermore, she was willing to believe that she was in love. Everyone assured her that she was, and there was nothing to compare it with. There were vague dissatisfactions, but she never analyzed them. That was dangerous; besides, it wasn't customary to worry about matters so obviously well arranged.

She had felt idiotic marching up that church aisle to the strains of the wheezy old organ. A heifer going to sacrifice; and not half so glamorous as if she were an Aztec maiden before the temple of the god of harvests. This sacrifice was all in the best manner, of course. They had invited the aunts and cousins of both families, people of whose existence she had not been aware—squeaky old ladies, mostly, in rustling purple and gray.

And then the face of old Father Benton, kindly and benign. God's right-hand man. That church was awfully stuffy, too—full of aunts. The whole thing was unbearably proper, anyway. She would have liked to be married out-of-doors, in sunlight.... Charlie seemed to be actually enjoying it. There was a beam on his face. Well, then, Charlie was an ass. The thought made her start.... "Dearly beloved brethren..." Father Benton's hands caressed his book smoothly, benignly.

Jane's resentment had surged up. They were not going to put this over on her! Without taking time to think what the consequences would be, she raised her voice high and yelled: "Fire! FIRE!" Then she gathered up the trailing gown, and tore down that church aisle like a wild deer let loose in a city street. Once in the open air she had simply kept on running—and she had good wind and strong legs....

The actual Jane, lying in bed in her New York apartment, smiled faintly. Well, her life had not been utterly void of adventure. Spectacular, at least, that had been. Saved for a far more glamorous doom, she was. A real Aztec temple? Not cut out to be hostess at dinner-parties for Charlie's friends. Even New York was better than that. A lucky break, that imaginary fire. New York at least was a going concern. It was tyrannical, but rather jolly, if you were in the mood. Chanting wheels of progress—maddening, but busy. You couldn't see much of God, though. Too much progress. God was like the woods—quiet and old-fashioned.

[2]

Jane awoke with a feeling that everyone in New York, perhaps everyone in the world, was unhappy or in trouble. It had been so long since one of her young friends had come to her with news of happiness and good fortune. There were two exceptions, and on them she counted more than she knew—Millie, Broadway flapper; and Professor Myers, contented scientist.

The worst of it was that nothing seemed to be leading anywhere. You might struggle up a mountainside, tired and aching, thirsty and scratched with brambles, your packstraps cutting into your shoulders as if they were red-hot; but the fight was to a purpose. You would win, stand at last on the crest with triumph. You would unsling your pack and feel light and free as the wind, and go joyfully about the chores of making camp for the night. Stars in the depth of an ice-cold little spring.

Here was never-ending struggle, with no aim in it; nothing more noble than the brute, beast maintaining of life. You were fighting in the dark, for no reason that you could see. To be happy in New York your whole scheme of life had to be in tune. Millie was in tune. But the things which made Millie joyful or disgusted never touched Jane at all. Her life wasn't cut out of the same pattern. Some people thrived on ten-cent diamonds. Others had to have stars. The star-people were not superior. They were in some ways less fortunate.

Jane knew mountains well, but the sea and she were strangers. She could not help wondering about it sometimes, when she heard the whistle of an outbound liner. There had been someone back in the Carey family: an Irish sea-captain?—a South Sea trader? No one remembered much about him. Nothing was left of his adventures except one fine old shell with the poetry of running tide in its heart. There must be peace at sea, if it could fashion a mysterious quiet thing like that old shell.... But the sea was unapproachable. On a ferry you could cross the harbor and see ships—rusty freighters and tall liners. But they weren't really ships. They were symbols, intangible and ghostly. If you looked twice, they were likely not to be there.

Awaking with nothing ahead but another day of the crabbed routine.... Even Professor Myers, absorbed in his entomology, seemed restless at times. "Good morning, Miss Carey, good morning," he greeted her. "Nice weather."

"Yes, it's a vast improvement over yesterday."

"Days like these"—reminiscent tone—"I get to thinking about—well, going somewhere."

"Collecting butterflies?"

"Butterflies, and other things. I get to thinking of all the men I know doing it, while I just sit here and tell 'em how. As if I was an old man—I'm not so old.... The West Indies, now—here's a letter from Dr. Schultenberger down there. Wonderful place for insects. Why, there are spiders *so* big!" He gestured significantly, measuring the air. Outside, a hurdy-gurdy was quavering a song about spring.

"I know," Jane said with a sigh. "Personally, I prefer butterflies to spiders, Professor Myers, but it's really all the same."

He nodded sadly. "Yes, it's all the same," he repeated, as if that were very important.

"Why don't you rig up an expedition and start out for somewhere, with all your bottles and nets and things?"

"Ah, you collect the money for me, Miss Carey, and I will.... And now let's write to that man—Schultenberger, or whatever it is. I want to tell him that the grasshopper he's so proud of is quite ordinary, only he hit on a deformed specimen. He thinks he's really discovered something."

Her thoughts hovered around that deformed grasshopper in the West Indies. It was very sad. He thought he'd really discovered something, and it was only a cripple. Must have hurt the feelings of the little thing. A grasshopper certainly had feelings. That one was dead, though.... The hurdy-gurdy was frantic in its efforts to sound like springtime....

Sales everywhere: bankrupt sales, final sales, over-stock sales, super-sales. Everyone frantic to sell, sell, sell. On the way home Jane stopped at a small bakery. Over its counter hung loud signs summoning the whole of New York to come with an enthusiastic rush because a three-day sale on doughnuts was now in effect. A solitary German leaned meditatively over the counter; otherwise the place was empty.

"So you're having sales, too!" Jane burst out. "Aren't we all funny?"

The German raised his head and broke into a long laugh. "You said it, miss!" he exclaimed. "Ve are! Ve are! You said it!"

Jane liked Germans. You could always get a laugh out of them, and a laugh was more important than anything else in the world, when you were fighting to keep your head above water. It was all right, as long as Professor Myers had a chuckle about his grasshoppers, Millie about her long line of boy friends, Bob about his fish-hooks, and the baker about his doughnut sale. She herself? Well, she could smile at the whole bunch of them.

There was the world to smile at, after all. But it was pretty lonely.

For, in spite of her many friends, acquired easily and quickly wherever she went, she was always, in the last analysis, alone. Perhaps she would be alone till the last star set. Perhaps everyone on earth was surrounded by an impassable barricade of aloneness, doomed to stay inside its walls forever, only they didn't know it because they didn't think about it. How could you tell? It didn't seem as though Millie had such a wall, for instance. Yet perhaps she had. It was a delicate subject. You couldn't talk about it—too intangible. Fancy going up to someone on the street and saying: "Beg your pardon, ma'am, but have you a wall?" Jane grinned: it was grand to be naive sometimes in the privacy of that wall.

When people were in love, were they still alone? Hard to tell. They liked to pretend they weren't, but really weren't they still paddling around in their own little orbits like the stars and comets—orbits which now and then coincided deceivingly, only to diverge once more? But in front of questions like those, you had to give up. One man's guess wouldn't mean a grain of sand more than another's.

The best solution to everything, perhaps, was just to go on and not think about it. That was Millie's idea. Just go on. Take what comes, have as good a time as possible with the materials on hand, and don't ask questions about it. That way, Jane supposed, you could in time kid yourself to think that even mud was beautiful. That was a horrid thought, that eventually you could lose your own standards, adapting them to what was around you! It might be a comfortable way out, but it was cowardly. Letting ugliness triumph...! The answer, then? Get away from it, move on—if you can.

"I think I will," said Jane, aloud. "I think I'd better, before it's too late."

Her hand was at her own doorknob. Physical habit had taken

her there, while her mind was away drifting on a confused sea. One lighthouse stood out sharply above that sea. The thought: "Move on!… I think I will."

"Oh, hello, Mary. Thought you might be still asleep. You were snoring like an old volcano when I left, this morning."

"Not like a little bat?"

"No, there was nothing bat-like about it."

"Bob crashed through," Mary said. "I've got a date with his father, for tomorrow."

Jane tapped her gently on the back. "Patience, and you're all set. Always takes a lot of waiting around."

Mary sighed. "Patience! That seems to be the one virtue on earth that counts."

Jane was looking at her now with sudden eagerness. Maybe it was fortunate that Mary had blown in upon her the night before, out of the wind and rain. For even if you'd had a message from Gabriel himself ordering you to leave the city and move on at once, there had to be a certain amount of arranging. You couldn't just drop everything in the middle. There were frazzled rope ends which had to be cleaned up. And Gabriel couldn't clean them up.

"Mary, how do you like this little hole of mine?"

"Adore it, Janie."

"Would you like to live here with Millie?"

"But you…?" Mary protested with bewilderment.

"Oh, me!" Jane's smile was not her usual everyday smile. Not the shopworn one she used when she handed Professor Myers his glasses. "Well, I think I'll be going away."

"Where, Jane? Going to get married, or—?"

"I don't think so," said Jane. "I really don't know much about it yet; it's very nebulous. Only, I've got a bit of money saved, and—spring is coming."

"Lucky!" Mary said softly.

"Oh, I don't know. Maybe I'm just plumb foolish. But how about the apartment? Want it?"

"Sure, if I get a job. But Jane, are you going right away, or what, or how?"

"Next week," Jane said convincingly.... And now, she thought to herself, perhaps the next thing was to find out where.

How did you find out, when the wind and the stars had told you to go? They gave the command, but left the road unmapped. That was why so many never went at all. Hadn't the courage to swing out into that void, or the strength to make a footprint upon it. You could stand on the verge and say: "If I only had the chance!" But when the chance came, either you never saw it at all, or you let it slip. It was a subtle thing. You had to grab it before it was there. And even after you had taken it firmly by the hair, it was likely to elude you.

It wouldn't have occurred to Jane to scan a newspaper for reports of tours and cruises, or to telephone a steamship office and be deluged with catalogs and folders, written in words which said "glamour" without meaning it, empty shells of words, a vain and futile mockery, trite and languid, savoring of hotels and deck sports. That she had long ago abandoned as a useless quest. You could find nothing there except words and hotel rates. The adventure to which she had been summoned was not like that. This adventure was not a separate thing, beginning on one day, ending another. It was a continuation, a going-on, of the life-long adventure. It was the next phase. It had no ending, and its beginning was vague. Whatever purpose it might have it kept a secret. Jane felt it there, but she knew nothing about it, except that it was likely to begin as an escapade to the hills and lakes of Maine—the country and the way of living with which she was most familiar. Pack, tent, cooking-kit...

"I feel," she said to herself, "as if this is going to be more than just a summer vacation. But maybe I'm crazy. Maybe I ought to stand by things here—ignore the whole idea, shove it away on a dusty shelf, call it an illusion and a dream. But that isn't common sense—is it?"

The two other girls aroused her out of this revery. They were getting ready to sail out upon New York and demolish it. Millie would doubtless do most of the demolishing, and Mary would follow obediently in her wake, finishing up odds and ends. Then Jane remembered that Ellen Green would presently be arriving. They had arranged by telephone in the morning. Another difficulty to be cleared up.

She had the apartment to herself for a few blessedly quiet minutes; then the bell jangled. "Hello, you old turtle," said Ellen, pouncing. "Always with your head well inside your shell! Same as ever, Janie? Well, don't be such an old iceberg. Gimme a kiss."

"Turtle and iceberg all in one breath," Jane laughed. "Wonder what I'll be in another five minutes!"

Ellen was an odd contrast to her friend. She was little and soft. Her curling golden hair was silky, and shone. Her small face suggested the conventional ideal fairy-tale princess. Limpid hazel eyes, and long curved dark lashes. Jane, who was tall and had strong shoulders, sometimes tended to wonder if Ellen were real. She seemed a helpless silken creature, calling up Bob's young chivalry and masculine desire to protect. This annoyed Jane, because she knew Ellen just a trifle better than he did, and recognized that silken helplessness for exactly what it was—a deliberate illusion.

"How's things, Ellen?"

"Terrible. Unspeakable. Life is a colossal bore, and all that stuff."

"Oh, that's just a state of mind."

"Don't you ever get bored yourself, Jane? Should think you would, taking dictation day after day from that old fogy."

"Oh, I have an occasional adventure. For instance, whom do you suppose I met night before last outside the office?"

"Moses, maybe."

"Somebody you know; a rather nice young chap of your acquaintance."

"Not Donald!"

Jane was startled at this give-away, but did not show it. "No, not Donald. Bob. He had supper with me."

Ellen endeavored to look hard and stern. "You can have him," she said, and lowered her eyes so that her innocent lashes were magnificently displayed. "And how's he getting on?"

Jane refused to admire the lashes. "He doesn't seem any too happy, either," she said. "I imagine he finds life a colossal bore, too."

"Oho! So he doesn't like it! Well, let him have a taste of his own home-brew, that's all I can say."

"Oh, come! Does he really deserve all this systematic torture?"

"Try him yourself," said Ellen. "If you think I'm so awful, just try him yourself. And what's more, if you think he's the only one hurt around here—"

"He's an honest soul," said Jane. "He told me a little of what it was all about."

"He doesn't like me any more," said Ellen.

Jane was conscious of a desire to scold her, as though she were a recalcitrant younger sister. But she was also very conscious of intruding into someone else's life. She had a horror of meddling people, well-intentioned or otherwise. Still, she had fairly promised Bob— He had made it her business. Promises like that were dangerous. The pain she remembered in his quiet eyes nerved her.

"Whoever is Donald?" she asked.

"I won't see Bob gadding around with other girls, and not pay him back. You wouldn't either, Janie." There was rising fire in Ellen's voice. "You wouldn't stand for it. No one would. Oh, Jane, you don't know! Bob's filled you up with his side of the thing. Now you just try to understand mine a little."

"I think I do," said Jane. "You're jealous. And nothing is more stupid or more forgivably natural."

"You'd be jealous, too, Janie. Nobody but a damn cold-blooded lily-white angel wouldn't be; and I'm not one, thank God, and neither are you."

This situation was hard to handle as an infernal nightmare. But she had promised, rashly enough, and now something had to be done. There was Bob, with the young pain in his eyes....

"Ellen, try not to be jealous of so little. It may be hard, next to impossible. I'm not denying that. But try. It's worth it. And I wouldn't say so if I didn't feel pretty sure you're worrying over wispy nothings. That's perhaps why you *are* worried: there's nothing tangible to get hold of and look at. Those girls you're upset about are like snowflakes; each one has its flash of life as a tiny and lovely crystal, and then melts. Bob's young and alive and interested, and—you'll have to face it—male. Naturally he has to look around a bit, see what's going on. Doesn't mean anything. Let him look all he wants. He'll love you more for it.... Oh, Ellen, 'scuse me for being an old Dutch aunt; but I've seen you happy together, and it was rare, and good—too good to lose. You know that better than I. Don't be jealous of snowflakes; not worth it."

Ellen drew a long sigh. "If I could believe that—" But she caught herself. "I *don't* believe it, you old orator!" she snapped.

Jane scented victory. She wasn't sure whether she had won her point, but she followed up fiercely, with the battle-light in her eyes. "Don't forget," she said, "that Bob's in the middle of a social whirlpool. He's awfully good-looking and entertaining, and—well, *rich*; and he must be run after a lot by all the young debs and especially their ambitious mammas."

Ellen turned her head wistfully to one side, and said in a very changed voice: "I was ready to make up, you know."

"Sure, but he didn't know, because you wouldn't show him."

"If he loved me, he'd have known anyway."

"You're trying to make him out a woman," said Jane. "Men are inclined to be rather dumb."

"Yes," Ellen said, "dumb about things that count." Her voice was extremely gentle now, and the eyelashes were more and more in evidence.

"He's longing and longing for you to make up."

"If he wants to make up, he can come to me."

"He *has* come, and you've always repulsed him."

"But he might have known," Ellen wailed, "that I didn't mean it."

"You're so subtle," said Jane, "how could he know?"

This was the lucky touch, the magic wand, this precious bit of praise. Ellen smiled.

"Forgive me for meddling?" Jane asked anxiously.

"I wouldn't forgive anyone else under the sun," Ellen confessed. "But somehow you're different. And oh, Jane—" She broke off suddenly, and giggled.

"Well?"

"Jane, I can't help wondering about you—if you'll ever manage a love affair of your own as neatly as you manage other people's."

"I've done some wondering about that myself, lately," Jane chuckled. "And, you know, I think I'll presently abandon other people's and concentrate on my own. So weep your last on this solid shoulder!"

The next day was Saturday, a free day. Professor Myers carried on his researches alone over week-ends, and to all intents and purposes the office was closed. But Jane knew that he would be there, poring among dusty old records, classifying butterflies' antennae and beetles' wing-cases, losing his glasses....

How did one begin an adventure? Almost any road you took would lead there, if only you went on far enough. Now that she had a ghost in sight, she would follow it. Maybe it would lead to the reality. Ghosts couldn't stay too long away from bodies to which they belonged.

So she crossed the Hudson in a ferry. It was a feeble beginning, she admitted to herself; but she would roam around in the woods of New Jersey and try to think out what she wanted to do. From the bow of the ferry, she listlessly watched a little tugboat snorting down-river, and wondered where it was bound. She might have been excited if she had known that it was heading for a lumber schooner becalmed in the harbor below, where old Captain Maynard was pacing his poop with impatience, anxiously watching his idle flapping sails, and cursing the lumber yard for being so slow with their miserable tug.

"Infernal, blasted nuisance, Davidson; that's what 'tis. They must think I've got a couple o' turbines, or something."

Davidson, the helmsman, merely glanced at the cracking sails. His answer was a sage smile that never came to the surface. You have to be fatalistic about these things. He shrugged his shoulders. It wouldn't have mattered to him that at the very moment Jane was watching it chug down the river with that quaint dignity tugs have—the dignity of a solemn snub-nosed dwarf, a coarse and common-sense philosophy of life. It was fun to watch three or four of them butting ridiculously into the immensity of the *Rex* or the *Ile de France*, handling the liner with such determination. She had often seen them after dark on the river, coming up with a string of three, four, five huge barges; or on some dignified errand alone, a light high astern, looking like a small cat with its tail in the air. Resolute and staunch, and with an air, too, of mysterious purposefulness, as if it knew all about the sea and the beyond, even if it was only a tug. This particular one, on its way down-river, seemed to say quietly: "I know a lot of things you don't know." She could almost imagine that it winked at her.

Up-river they had built a new bridge—a new perpetuation of the skill and strength of engineers. Men had given dreams and love to that structure, built their visions into its very fiber. Sleepless, someone had paced the floor at night, over complex blueprints. Now the leap had been dare; two gaunt dark gray towers supported the slow curve of the cables. There was a haze over the Hudson, and nothing beyond the bridge could be seen. It was obscure and mystic. Those pillars might be the gateposts to purgatory. They were unearthly and aloof. Their strength was remote, with the remoteness of dreams....

There were woods along the river, if you knew where to look. Jane was always at home in the woods. She could understand the language of young leaves, as they poised in the sun, letting gold-green sparks of light play upon them and flick off them. She dreamed of mountains she had known—the gods of forgotten but powerful religions. She had labored up their steep sides and ponderous brows; beaten through storms and clouds along their giant backbones.

And by evening, when she came down to the ferry again, she had nearly decided that as soon as she could decently leave the office, she would go back to those mountains once more.

Then she saw that out in the river lay the symbol of all adventure, gray and still in the dusk, peaceful as a seagull come to rest—a schooner anchored. She was dreaming there, wings folded. Up into the river she had brought with her an atmosphere of untroubled calm, mingled with a touch of the old-fashioned, as if not belonging to this world of engines and industrial turmoil. She was aloof as a little Chinese goddess, and as tranquil. As Jane gazed at her four straight masts and graceful hull, the sparks of her riding lights suddenly pricked out like a friendly signal, a beckoning.

Jane was suddenly overwhelmed with curiosity. She wanted to get closer to that quiet ship. She wanted to know the people aboard her, who lived in this old-fashioned world apart; and she wondered whether such a visit could be arranged. Her friendliness and curiosity vied with shyness. "Maybe morning would be better—" And then a new thought, devastating in its excitement: "Maybe I could sail in that schooner. What an adventure that would be! Maybe *that's* the way to get out of New York!" But she brought herself up sharply. "You silly dreamer, you know things like that don't happen...." Getting out, once you were rooted, took some doing. You had no courage, nothing except a few hazy and romantic longings which were doomed anyway....

She stood still a minute, lashing herself with scorn; then made her way down the river road, mud-flats on one side of her and factory yards on the other. A dirty and slovenly world. Slovenly people, too. Well, how could they help it, surrounded by this? Here was an existence where there was literally nothing but mud and squalor—a rather striking contrast to her own. Well, some had to have stars. Others could get more pleasure from sitting on grimy doorsteps and surmising who was the father of the landlord's niece's baby. They wouldn't see anything worth while about a mere star.

The lumber yard at last. Its gate was closed. The schooner herself, if she were real, lay somewhere behind, out in the open river. Jane hailed the watchman, an old man who sat inside the gate. "I want to find out about the ship. She came to your company, didn't she?"

The old man looked at her with suspicion, and pushed his cap back on his forehead. Obviously he was annoyed at this disturbance of his somnolent peace. "Ship?... Oh, you mean that old scow in the river? Yeah, she brung in some lumber."

"I want to go aboard her," said Jane.

"That old scow? Aw, there ain't nothin' there for you, girlie."

Jane flinched, but refused to be daunted. "I've never seen a ship like her, and I'm interested. Do you know the captain?"

"Yeah, I seen him once or twice. Too old to go to sea in a reg'lar ship, so they give him that old boat. Don't matter if he do wreck her, see?"

"How do you think I could get aboard?" Jane persisted.

But this ugly, leering old man apparently had no desire to cooperate in Jane's escape. "Swim, girlie, swim," he muttered peevishly, and ambled off into the gloom.

[3]

The river was smiling surreptitiously in the bright morning. And there lay the schooner of the evening before, as though she were trying her best to be real, perhaps for Jane's sake. There was not much doing at the lumber yard across the river, but at least the old watchman had gone. She found an efficient-looking person at last, who was apparently about to start off somewhere in a dirty launch. "That ship?" He waved an expansive arm. "Why, I'm just goin' out to her. You kin come along, young lady."

She looked him over again swiftly, and decided that he was harmless, in spite of the noisy alacrity with which he chewed and spat, in spite of the great red and green dragon tattooed all around his arm in spirals, and the swaggering coarseness of the atmosphere he inhabited and carried with him.

"Fine!" she said. "Do you know anything about this ship?"

"Sure. Whaddja want to know about her?"

"Well, what's her name, who's her captain, and where'd she come from?"

"*Annie Marlow*, Captain Maynard, Nova Scotia," recited the other, with a grin. "I can tell you more'n that, too. I'm goin' out now to get old man Maynard's order—for provisions, you know—doin' business even if 'tis Sunday; and I bet I can tell you what he'll get. Beans, mostly."

"Have you ever been to sea?" asked Jane.

"Wal, not farer than Coney Island."

They were making a circle around the stern of the *Annie Marlow*, her gangway being on her starboard side, and her bow pointing up-river. Jane was feasting now—devouring every line and curve of the trim ship ahead: her slate-gray side, bulwarks and taffrail; her masts, weathered purple-gray; the white crosstrees, and the rigging that led aloft to them, narrowing but straight, through which Jane could imagine the wind singing as through harp-strings, and where she could imagine salt spray freezing in fantastic patterns, like frost feathers on a mountain peak. "I love that ship," she said. "I don't think I ever loved anything so much." As they drew nearer, rigging and masts shifted stealthily, magically.

"*Annie Marlow* ahoy!" sang out the launch skipper. His chest swelled; he felt immensely nautical. "Cap'n Maynard!" He shut off the engine. The sound of a door opening aboard, and someone emerged from the companion and came over to the taffrail. "Ahoy yerself!" he answered.

Jane looked up into a pair of genial blue eyes surmounted by shaggy eyebrows and a shock of steel-gray ruffled hair. The master of the *Annie Marlow* was rugged and gnarled. His face was weathered as the masts of his schooner. His powerful shoulders were bowed a little. The sea had marked him, in every line and fiber; and there was something about him that was more than dignity. It was the unconscious majesty of the sea.

"Ahoy yerself, Jones!" Even his voice was gnarled, but pleasantly. "Come aboard, come aboard. Glad t' see ye, glad t' see ye."

Jane smiled. "I'm just an ordinary landlubber, Captain Maynard," she called up, "but I'd love to see your schooner if you'll let me."

"Come aboard!"

She climbed the wooden gangway, stepped airily upon the poop deck, and looked around with one enraptured glance. Then she shook hands with the captain. "There are a few real ships left, aren't there, Captain Maynard?"

"Oh, sure—one or two, one or two."

They were immense friends. Jane had never before looked into such eyes; in spite of the nests of laughter wrinkles in their corners, they might have caused a typhoon to hold off in hesitation. She waved an empassioned hand around her. "I've fallen in love with your ship," she said.

Now Jones was aboard, and proudly greeting the captain with an irreverent clap on the back. "Wal, what sort of a trip didja have comin' down, Cap?"

"Oh, one o' them wet, sloppy, nasty trips, with a dirty roll going," the captain drawled amiably. He lingered over the words, and Jane could distinctly feel that "dirty roll going."

The ship was neat and trim from stem to stern. The big wooden wheel was newly varnished, and the binnacle and bell were shining. Jane glanced at the big spanker boom overhead, with the neatly furled sail. The hemp lines, the blocks, even the belaying pins were steeped in romance—a peaceful, unostentatious romance, like that of a pine forest. Things smelled pleasant, too.

Jones was talking again. "And now, Cap'n, about this matter of provisions and all that. Might as well get to business, even if it is Sunday. Beans, I suppose?"

"Beans, nothing! Got so many beans aboard now I don't need no ballast. Let's see: how about some eggs?"

Jones jotted on a pad in a business-like manner. "Eggs, eh? About six dozen? Wal, do you want 'em fresh or cold storage?"

"Fresh, you bet! I don't want none o' them affairs with chickens in 'em. I buy my chickens separate." And so they bantered, while Jane looked about the ship only half hearing their voices, making the most of her adventure while it lasted.

Jones was ready to go. "But you'll be stayin' aboard, won't you, Miss Jane?" asked Captain Maynard. "Sure! One o' the boys'll pull ye ashore in the skiff tonight. Stay aboard 'n' see my li'l old *Annie*."

"Is she very old, Captain?"

"Not turrible old, but oldr'n you at that, Miss Jane."

"And you've been in her a long time?"

"No. I just took her over couple o' years back. Before her I was in a barkentine, the *North Star*. I tell you I loved that ship. Ten years I had her. Sometimes I see her little white ghost now, risin' out o' the sea."

"Was she lost?"

"Aye, broke up on the Maine coast. 'Twarn't I that lost her, though. I was sick ashore that v'yage, and my first mate took her down east. Told me afterwards she was cranky from the start. He didn't understand her. Ships take a powerful lot of understanding."

"Perhaps she missed you."

He nodded wistfully. "I been at sea forty-five year, Miss Jane, and you'd think I'd oughter know the ways of ships, wouldn't ye now? Well, I'm tellin' ye, I don't. But she was a sweet ship." He spoke with tenderness. "She would do anything but talk, and she tried hard enough to do that."

Jane was silent, sharing his reverence for the little ship that had tried so hard to talk.

The *Annie Marlow*, this present and more tangible ship, seemed deserted. "Well," explained the skipper, "here it is Sunday, and all the boys is off ashore a-larkin'. Sundays they jist skip like rats off a sinkin' ship."

"Do rats really leave a ship that's going to sink, Captain?"

"Well, some say that's jist an old yarn o' them stupid sailor-men; but I seen things as would s'prise you, Miss Jane. One time I was out in mid-Pacific, and we met up with the *Nellie Ross*, a bark I knowed. There warn't no wind, we was both flat becalmed, and Cap'n Walker 'n' me wanted t' compare notes, like, on the longitude. So I pulled over t' the *Nellie*. Well, would you believe it, 'bout a score o' rats off her come back with me—clumb down her side, they did, right into my boat. But the *Nellie Ross*"—he paused dramatically—"she warn't never heard of no more. Them Rosses allus was a unlucky tribe, anyways. There was five ships, all same fambly. The *Martha Ross* was the last and the finest. The Rosses lost their hull blasted fortune in her."

"Ships are perverse creatures at times, I guess," said Jane.

"Perverse t' break your heart, like old women," said the skipper; "'n' then agin just as gentle 'n' lovable as young ones."

He showed her about his schooner. "My, but it's good to have some livin' being to talk to, besides Barnacle the cat. Us old sailor-folks gets amighty lonesome at times.... First I want to show you my little flyin'-fish. That's what I call her to myself." He walked to the very stern of the ship, where a sizable life-boat hung. Peering down between life-boat and taffrail, Jane could see part of an ordinary small row-boat.

"Don't look like much, maybe," the old man chuckled, "but she's my pride and joy, she is. And she's a sail-boat, too. In her bottom is a mast and boom I made myself—jist for the fun of it. Sometimes I take her out, all by my lonesome—have a little sail like I used to when I was a kid. And I keep water and biscuits in her, same as in the life-boat."

They walked forward, and he described each line of the complex rigging, telling her its purpose, the subtle part it played in the total harmony of his schooner. After a while she gave up trying to remember their names, but she never tired of craning her neck to look aloft into the grandeur of the masts. She tried to understand how it came about that at this minute she was so far away from New York—what this magic could be, that had whirled her so powerfully away. This mystery was unfathomable. That made it infinitely tormenting and soul-satisfying, all at once. It was the old eternal romance of the sea and sailing ships, that was all. It had no other name. It could not be torn to pieces and put under the ruthless and scientific microscope.

They had reached the galley up forward. The cook, a small, dark man with a warm smile, was starting up his coal fire. The galley seemed to be the very quintessence of compactness.

An intriguing ladder led up on to the fo'c'sle deck. Jane climbed it, curious to look over the bow. A man was sitting motionless on the schooner's very shoulder, buried deep in a book and smoking contentedly. A big yellow and gray cat (Barnacle?) lay in his lap, asleep. The man looked up when Jane came to the top of the ladder. "Good morning," she said, with a friendly nod.

He was a little embarrassed, and laid the open book, face downward, on top of the cat. "Same to you," he muttered with a shy smile. Then he seemed to remember that his shirt was pretty far open at the neck, and perhaps something had better be done about it. Fumbling for a button, he was secretly chagrined to find it missing. Buttons were intangible things. Defeated, he picked up the book once more, with the air of one resigned to the fact that the world and its buttons were too much for him.

"Have you found something worth reading?" asked Jane, curious.

He held it up, backbone toward her: Conrad's *Lord Jim*. She was startled and delighted, and burst into enthusiasm.

He nodded. "Well, Conrad is the only one who ever wrote about the sea and knew what he was saying."

His voice was graceful and refined. "What a good lot these sailors are!" she thought. Shy, that was all. Needed a little friendliness. "If you wrote about the sea," she said, "you'd know what you were saying."

He smiled a little. "I wouldn't have anything to say. It's my life," he explained simply.

"It was Conrad's life, too," Jane reminded him. "Well, I'll leave you in peace." Obviously, he wanted to be alone.

His eyes were gray. All seafarers had something in their eyes that was honest and peaceful and deep. He had fine shoulders, and his strong brown hands, holding the book, were rough from handling hemp and canvas. Hands made to endure and accomplish the work of the sea. She wanted to say: "You look as if you would last."

He made an odd contrast to the people whom Jane met every day. It was hard to imagine him on Fifth Avenue, with the slow, rolling stride he doubtless had acquired from pacing many decks. But she had a feeling that he was much more worth while than Fifth Avenue. Why think about Fifth Avenue, anyway? It was only a feeble dream, already dead after these few hours of absence from it. This schooner, these people: here was a dream that would outlast a thousand such futile scurryings.

She looked back at the sailor on the forecastle deck. Doubtless she would never see him again. Look while she could, for he, like Captain Maynard, had the sea's wisdom in his gray eyes....

"Been yarnin' with young Davidson?" asked Captain Maynard.

"Not so much yarning," said Jane. "He's a very quiet chap."

"He's a very good sailor," said Maynard, "'n' ye don't see so many these days. All the smart young fellers go in for engineerin' or somethin', or if they go to sea they head straight for a steamer's bridge. Davidson's a reg'lar deep-water man. He'll be second mate this trip.

The two walked aft again and down into the cabin. "Watch your head!" the skipper sang out in the companionway, and Jane ducked just in time to avoid a shining brass clock. The small chartroom and library, which also served as a living-room, had a pleasant mixed smell of varnish, tar, lumber, and pipe smoke. It was paneled in golden-brown maple. Here and there on the walls were gimbals of well-polished brass, for lamps. The room was lighted during the day by the skylight, under which a compass hung. "See that? Wal, that's how I keep track of all them absent-minded young greenhorns that steer her. Same's if I was lookin' right into the binnacle over their shoulders. Got another o' them telltales at the head o' my bed."

The bookshelves held an odd assortment of pipes, modern fiction, navigation books, and tightly rolled charts. "Well, you're fixed up here in great style, captain." He chose a pipe from the shelf, and carefully packed it. Then, settled down in a leather armchair, he answered her:

"Oh, 'tain't so bad, but a'mighty lonely at times. This goin' t' sea"—he shook his head sagely—"ain't nothin' in it. What would you be a-thinkin', now, Miss Jane, with tons o' green sea a-smashin' down into this cabin, and you achin' for a wink o' sleep, but couldn't stay in your bunk? Can't have flyin'-fish weather all the time," he added.

"Well," Jane put in, "people don't *have* to go to sea."

He chuckled. "You wouldn't think they would," he agreed. "We sailors are a stupid lot. Everybody says so, 'n' I guess it's so. Y'know, many's the time I been workin' ashore, 'n' bound I'd stay there. Why, one time I went out to a ranch in Montana —thought I'd git off from the wharves, the sight 'n' smell o' the shipping—fur away's I could git." He shrugged his shoulders, shook his head again. "Well, the joke was on me. Less'n a year, and I was headin' for 'Frisco fast as I could go."

"You wouldn't make a good cow-puncher," said Jane. "Anyway, it seems to me that whatever you're doing, there's always a lot of discontentment thrown in. Otherwise, there wouldn't be any adventures, would there? Captain Maynard, do you know that just coming aboard this schooner today, and talking with you, is the grandest adventure I've ever had?"

He smiled, delighted but a trifle bewildered, and still in serious mood. "Y'know, it's almighty queer, this business o' stickin' to the sea. They jist can't git away from it. They hate it 'n' cuss it and 'd give a lot to set up a barber shop or run a chicken-farm or somethin', but leave it they can't. Or if they do, back they come in a little while. Get in their blood for good'n all, I reckon. Well, it's all right fer an old feller like me. I got my ship, and I'm a bit of a philosophy, if you know what I mean. I'm contented enough now. Got over all the rearin' and cussin'. But take a young chap like that Davidson, or lots of others, they hadn't oughter be here a-reefin' sails. They'd oughter be tryin' fer a steamer job if they're bound to go to sea. Because, Miss Jane, there ain't no more ships to speak of, now." He spoke with deep wistfulness.

"Have you ever been in a steamship, Captain Maynard?"

"No, I ain't never been in one; I don't reckon I will, neither. I got my ship, and I ain't a-goin' to live such a whale of a lot longer, so I'm all fixed. But a young feller's different. I reckon as he'd oughter get an eddication, ye know. 'Cause ye can't git nowhere without it, these days. Men ain't what they used to be. No wonder—ain't nothin' fer 'em to do. Sailors ain't what they used to be. Well, I'm askin' ye, is that any wonder? But there—things change, that's all. Nobody can't say if it's worse or better. But I mind me o' the old deep-sea ships at times, and wish they was back in style. That was a rotten hard life, Miss Jane—nothin' at all to be said fer it, ye wouldn't think—but there was somethin' about it—I dunno." He pointed over to the cabin wall, at the picture of a full-rigger tearing before a hammering sea. "See her? Lovely, ain't she? Well, she was my first command, Jane, more'n twenty year ago—my first command."

Jane sighed. "I never before wished so much I were a man," she said. "Yes, I'd go to sea tomorrow."

And then a bell rang from the messroom. "Come have a bite of lunch," said the captain. "Then I reckon we'll both be better off for deciding what's wrong wi' the old universe." The mess-room was small and cheerful, the table spread with a red-checked cloth, and the usual bright array of little bottles and shakers in one corner. "Ain't nobody aboard but us," said the skipper. "Mate gone off on some 'social function' or other; that's what he calls 'em. Second mate paid off last night."

The cook waited on the two of them efficiently and smilingly, if not gracefully. It was regal. "How's that pepper-sass comin' along, steward?" the skipper enquired.

"Well, sir, I shook it up good an' plenty. Oughter have some spice to it."

"That's jest about the most—most *unexpressive* pepper-sass I ever did see," the captain observed, shaking it vigorously over a plate of beans. "An' I been goin' t' sea for forty-five year."

"You said fifty-five, last time." The voice came from behind Jane. She started, and turned her head. A stout man with scant gray hair, a large cold grin, and blue cold eyes, was standing in the doorway.

"Hello! There's my mate," said Captain Maynard. "Back from your social functions, eh, Stevens?"

"Don't you see I am?" said Stevens, with the same inscrutable grin.

The captain ignored the retort. "This young lady," he explained, "come aboard this morning to see my li'l old *Annie*. She thinks *Annie*'s about the best ship she ever saw."

"I guess she hasn't seen many, then," said Stevens, grinning still more broadly. Jane began to understand him now. The purpose of the grin was to allow him to say ironical things and get by with them by making them appear genial. A clever dodge. He was doubtless the sort of taciturn person who liked to make every word do double or triple duty. He would have that cruel knack of demolishing an argument, distorting the whole point of a story, by a few well-directed words. Yet he would do it with a smile, and there would be no satisfactory retort.

"Don't you like the ship yourself?" she ventured.

He thought a moment. This was a delicate question—mustn't commit himself in any direction. "Well, yes—and—no," he said slowly, with pauses between the words. Then he withdrew his immense frame out of the doorway, and Jane and Captain Maynard exchanged a smile.

After lunch, they went on deck again. Jane was too happy. It was dangerous. It was more than happiness. It was wild and feverish. She felt that she could not hold her own heart any longer. It had become too light. There was golden mist around her, and she could not feel the deck under her feet.

Captain Maynard was glancing aloft. "Well, Miss Jane," he said, "s'posin' I was to tell you to run up there—to loose them topsails, maybe; think you could do it?"

The challenge, unconscious on his part, came at the nick of time. To Jane, already walking on high clouds, the ratlines and shrouds of the schooner's rigging looked very solid. "Sure I could!" she sang out, and was over the bulwarks with two long strides.

"Hey! I didn't mean that!" he called, startled.

She waited tremulously, one hand on the shrouds. Her neatly arranged brown hair was loosening in the wind. "Can't I, Captain?" she pleaded.

"Well, go ahead, go ahead. But hold hard and watch yourself."

She looked upward, and saw the clouds rolling past over the tops of the four tall masts. It gave a curious illusion of speed, as if the ship herself were rushing on against the wind. The tense wire shrouds thrilled in her hands. Ratline after ratline she climbed into the wind, with the sensation of entering the upper reaches of a cloud-swept hall of sky. She kept her eyes upward, and saw the trucks of the masts coming closer; but once she looked off to the east, and caught a fragmentary glimpse of New York pinnacles and turrets. She was climbing out where they could not reach her. She did not even stop to draw breath until she had pulled herself on to those white slender crosstrees, that had looked from below so insignificant and perilous. She trembled with excitement; her heart was pounding. She closed her eyes, to shut out that swift illusion the clouds gave. Dizzying even to think about it. The stalwart base of the topmast was a welcome friend, after a trip up a ladder through far reaches of space. She put both arms around it, and leaned her cheek against the weathered varnish, and held tight, while a great river of wind fell past her.

When she found breath again, she looked into the sky through a crowd of lines, and saw gulls veering and calling. She waved to them. She was on equal terms with them now, and their white wings. Perspective had altered weirdly. It was hard to believe that the toy hull she looked down upon could support these colossal masts. The cook, standing outside the galley with his apron on, craning his neck to look approvingly upwards, was an absurd little figure. She waved to him, laughing.

When she came down, she was nearly blind with excitement. "Well, well, you are a sailor for sure," said Captain Maynard.

She had hoped he would say just that. But she could not speak. Every fiber of her body still vibrated to the speed of the clouds, the supreme beauty of that schooner's rigging. "I love this ship—I love her," was all she could find to say.

The old man understood that. "To tell you the plain truth, I do myself," he said. "If I go away from her, jest for a day or two, I begin to feel homesick right away." He chuckled. "Want to go down and wash?" he asked, glancing at her coal-black hands. They strolled toward the companionway. "How would you like to be up aloft there with a Cape Horn gale for comp'ny, 'stead o' them little gulls, when the wind was like a wild demon to shake you off? Sails splittin' like thunderbolts, sleet and hail peltin' you like lumps o' broken glass, and the whole sea black-green?" They were settled once more in the cabin. "Yes, the sea's a cruel ol' mistress, sometimes, Jane. But—git out in the South Pacific trades, with them little flyin'-fish a-flitterin', an' the sun on their little wings; or take it at night, moon on the sails, an' everything so quiet an' peaceful like, seems like you kin hear the ol' earth a-spinnin'—seems like you could see God."

"Oh, Captain, there's nothing in the world I want so much!" Jane exclaimed. "If only I could sail with you! I'd give up all the rest of my life, and die happy!"

The wire shrouds vibrated in her hands, the clouds tore past, New York was a lost inferno, staring upwards at its escaping prey. White friendly wings brushed by. She was excited and stirred beyond endurance. He looked in astonishment at the great fire of longing in her eyes, and wondered at the strain of desperation in her young voice. "Why, bless your heart," he said slowly. "I'd no idea, Miss Jane! Why, come along, to be sure! Glad to have ye go along with me!"

She leaped to her feet, like a wild bird breaking into flight. "You don't—really—mean it, Captain Maynard!" She was challenging him.

"Why, to be sure I mean it," he said gently. "To be sure I do!"

[4]

Jane sang as she fried the eggs for breakfast. The world had suddenly changed from a drab, exhausted mud-puddle into a rainbow. She sang ridiculous songs. Why, even the eggs had changed! They were positively smiling now, instead of presenting a wrinkled scowl. Literally the weather was desolate, but that was to be expected on Monday. It was probably trying to deceive her into thinking yesterday was all a dream. But it couldn't deceive her. A tingling sunburn was on her arms and face. There was no mistaking that, or the haunting vision of rigging and white clouds.

Millie's voice drawled sleepily from the bed, with a yawn in the middle. "Why all the operatics, Janie?" she protested.

"I'll tell you when you get up," Jane caroled. "But I won't confide in a lump of bedclothes.... Millie, you make me quite tired lying there under the bedclothes on such a grand day."

"Grand day, you nut! 'S raining cats and hot dogs!"

"Oh, it's clearing up fast. Do get up, lazybones, and let me tell you about yesterday."

"Why didn't you tell me when I got in last night, if it's so important, kitten? I can't get up. I was working till three-thirty. Jeese, have a heart!"

"Oh, Millie, I'm not the same old flub-dub any more. I feel as if I could sleep in a buttercup bowl or any other little stunt like that. I feel ten thousand years younger."

"Gee, Grandma, you must feel prehistoric. What's up? Fallen in love?"

"That's exactly it," said Jane. In love, yes—with a ship."

"A what?"

"You heard me."

"Janie—now listen here—you crazy, insane—"

"I'm sailing in her. Never was saner in my life."

"Gawd!"

"It's all arranged," Jane went on gaily. "Mary's going to take over my share of this little joint, when she gets a job. I'm going to pay a month's rent in advance, so nobody'll get stuck."

"Hey, wait a minute, wait a minute. What is all this? S'pose I don't want to bunk in with that little lame cat? And when did you get all this doped out, anyways? Jeese, kitten, I didn't know you could move that fast. What's the big idea?"

"I'm only following your precious advice," Jane said. "I'm going to visit my lions. I wouldn't be surprised if I turned into a lioness, would you?"

"Not a bit! But come across with the story, can't you? When are you going?"

"About a week."

"Well, where?"

Jane frowned—wanted to laugh, but was too overwhelmed. "I don't know," she said.

The other girl whistled sharply.

"You seem to be rather less sleepy now," Jane remarked.

"Gawd, I think I'm sound asleep and having nightmares. What is all this you're trying to hand me?"

"It's straight goods," said Jane. "I forgot to ask." After all, she thought to herself, it was not so surprising. In the hilarity of the adventure, facts simply did not exist. The destination of the *Annie Marlow* was a mere earthly detail, of no consequence. Whether she were bound for tropic waters of peacock blue, or for the iceberg-haunted seas off Greenland, mattered not at all. An adventure like this had to be taken one fragment at a time. They were to be outward bound in a week or so; that was enough.

It was futile even to try explaining any of this to Millie, of course. Millie had simply abandoned the whole subject, as something out of which it was impossible to form a connected sequence which an intelligent and rational being could comprehend. "I don't suppose you happen to know, by any chance, when you're coming back, do you, lioness?"

"Of course not," said Jane lightly. She heard Millie swallow hard, and added considerately: "Oh, next fall, probably."

"What'll all the busted backbones, bleeding hearts, etc., do?"

"Oh, you'll look out for them."

"Will I! They'd better look out for me!"

"They're one of the things I'm taking a vacation from," Jane explained.

"Yeah, and from your own brains, looks like. Out to bust your own backbone, huh?"

"That's the idea. Don't you want any breakfast?"

"Nope."

"Will you miss me, Mill?"

"Aw, nothin' doin' on the sentiment, kitten."

Jane walked with an air of triumph, on her way to work. Daylight was ahead, above. She had made the first step to get out of the pit. The kindly grasp of old Captain Maynard's strong hand, the wind-swept rigging of the schooner, the gray eyes of the sailor reading Conrad on the fo'c'sle deck, the quiet calling of the sea and far places—these were her weapons, and New York was swaying perilously on its false throne.

But another feeling was mingled with the bright swirl of her thoughts. A curious sense that she might really be going away forever, instead of a few weeks; that the sailing of the *Annie Marlow* out of the Hudson River would mark for her the beginning of more than the voyage itself, as though she were about to step into a new life, adventurous and unimaginably beautiful. "I'm going to be disillusioned, of course," she told herself, with mixed sternness and sadness. "I'll have to come back, and when I come back things will be much the same as now. But I won't think about that." Let the illusion persist, for it had beauty. Let it persist until cursed old civilization had driven it out, if it dared.

Instinctively as she walked, she clutched at fragile wings, perishable branches of iridescent trees, elusive shimmering fruit that a playful wind jerked from her, the jewels that the sun trailed across the sea. There was a small cold fear around her heart—fear of the return, fear of the dreams she had allowed herself to dream. "Maybe I can stay with the schooner indefinitely, on and on. (I'll work. Captain Maynard shan't complain that I'm a nuisance.) Maybe there'll be other schooners." Fragile wings, perishable branches of iridescent trees....

It should be satisfying to think no further than the immediate adventure. But no one with a sane mind could always do that, Jane thought. You had to look ahead. Hers was a bothersome sort of mind. It often got in her way, poking too far into the future, where it had no business.... Now she was off on another train of thought. Her old and must futile question: what did life mean? What was it for? Once she had believed it was for happiness. But happiness was as ethereal as the colors on a bubble, the powder on a butterfly's wing. Often if you looked it square between the eyes, it was gone. It could not stand your gaze. Surely there was something brighter and firmer to hold. Beauty? That was what they called it, said Jane, for want of a better word. The thought annoyed her, for it savored of cosmetics and manicure parlors. Movie stars, too. Some time, when there was leisure and peace and the sea, she might invent a new word. This one was frazzled and worn out.... She rammed herself into a downtown subway....

At about the same time that morning, on the deck of his schooner, Captain Maynard was talking with Mr. Stevens, who had paused in his supervision of the stevedores long enough for a smoke. The schooner was now tied up at the lumber company's dock, and was unloading her cargo of Nova Scotia spruce. The captain was happy. He had been pacing the poop that morning with a light tread. He felt almost like a young man. Jane's visit aboard, her headlong love for the ship, and her "romantic notions," had made him laugh to himself more than he had done many a year. He was keenly looking forward to having her sail with him, and as he walked his deck, with an air of prideful possession of his schooner, he pictured to himself how intense her delight would be at the bright blue mornings and soft nights with moonlight on the great sails.

"And then, Stevens," he recounted, "she throwed her arms up and said if only she could come along of us she'd die happy. Well, I ain't made o' steel."

"So she's coming, eh?" Stevens appeared none too well pleased, but his face was imperturbable. "Seasick females!" he muttered.

"Stevens, d'you believe in that there old yarn 'bout it bein' bad luck to have women aboard of a vessel?"

All questions of this nature Mr. Stevens answered with caution. He said he took no stock in any old superstition whatsoever, and followed this announcement by recounting a tale in which a woman had brought exceedingly bad luck upon a vessel.

"Bad luck or good luck, she's coming," said Captain Maynard. "And I don't mind sayin' as I'm glad of it. Don't often have comp'ny, Stevens."

"Passengers are a damn nuisance, Cap'n. But I'm not saying

anything, you understand. I never saw a woman yet aboard of a vessel that didn't get into hot water o' one kind or another. But I'm not saying anything." He continued to say nothing for a fairly long time.

The captain was annoyed. "This gal ain't goin' to get in no hot water," he said, with a little curtness. "'N' if she's seasick that ain't your fun'ral, is it?"

"No," Stevens admitted, "that's between her and the fishes, Captain."

"'Sides, I've a fondness for Miss Jane," the skipper went on. "She brung to mind my own daughter—poor little girl."

"Was she the one that died, Cap'n?"

"She was the only one," the old man said, with reverence. "Born at sea, lived at sea, died at sea—poor little girl."

"Well, Cap'n," the mate morosely answered, "I don't know about being born, but lots of us live at sea, and expect to die at sea."

Jane was walking into Professor Myers' office. It occurred to her that she would have to tell him. He would be surprised, and perhaps such short notice wasn't fair. But fate had taken it out of her control. She would have to tell him, that was all. He would be concerned, too, when his questioning disclosed that she did not even know where the ship was going. He was fatherly and conservative.

"Good morning, Miss Carey, good morning." He had not changed; he never would. Subconsciously she had expected him to share the radiance of her own heart, and it disturbed her a little that he did not. Wasn't her adventure written plain as print upon her face?... "Allen has cornered a brand-new cricket," he announced. "South Seas. Quite a beauty." (That elusive word again.)

"Well, I'm glad he's cornered something at last."

The old man chuckled. He had a good spirit of fun. "I

imagine the Foundation was beginning to wonder what on earth he was doing with his time and their money."

Jane had often wondered how it happened that some foundations were so eager about latest styles in crickets. She had never solved the puzzle. But just now there was something of far more importance to talk about, and it was hard to begin. She plunged bravely. It ought to be done before the two other members of the staff arrived.

"Professor Myers, I'm going away." It sounded brusque, and now she wished she had said it differently.

He took off his glasses and looked up quickly, but otherwise betrayed not a quiver of surprise. His life had not been without adventure. There had been scientific expeditions into the recesses of the Malay Peninsula. He had very nearly been poisoned once, for the Malay gods were not altogether friendly. He had faced a typhoon in the China Sea. Tigers he had met, on one or two occasions, face to face in the wilds of Burma. He had learned how to encounter the cataclysmal, and keep his face as passive as any Oriental's.

"Away, Miss Carey? Tired of this little dry, scientific place of mine?"

"No—tired of New York, that's all. I'm sure you can understand that!" She paused, smiling, and he nodded encouragingly. Her words sounded stilted and uneven. Her forearms glowed with sunburn, and the sound of wind about a schooner's rigging haunted her. "I'm afraid I haven't exactly played fair," she went on bravely. "I'm leaving in about a week. You see, I didn't even know until yesterday."

"Going traveling, Miss Carey?" Characteristically, he never commented on the shortness of the notice at all.

Her eyes shone, but she merely nodded her head. She didn't want him to question her too closely. It would sound idiotic to say: "No, I don't know where. I forgot to ask." Although, if the worst came to the worst, she could invent a destination for the

Annie Marlow. Let's see... No, every port of call that occurred to her sounded absurd. A dream ship bound for nowhere.... Professor Myers crashed in again.

"Well, traveling is great experience, any way you look at it, Miss Carey, whether it's beetles you're after, or original Old Masters, or just a glimpse of life. Broadens the outlook. May we expect you back?"

In spite of his naturalness she was troubled. "I don't know just how long—Perhaps you'd better not count on me, Professor Myers." She felt, indeed, as little to be counted on as though she were bound for the moon or one of the planets.

He smiled reassuringly. "Well, here's a word of advice from a seasoned old traveler. Don't do too much work or studying while you're abroad. My entomology almost ruined my good times." He was talking in a confidential tone, with a sly smile which, from him, was startling. "Tourist third cabins are fine in the Cunarders, but the food's best on the new German boats. Trust the Germans for a square meal every time."

Jane visualized the schooner's little messroom, its red-checked tablecloth, and the captain's bottle of "unexpressive" pepper-sauce.

"Well, I certainly hope you enjoy yourself, Miss Carey. And I also hope to see you back here some day." He began groping patiently about his desk. "By the way," he said, "have you seen my glasses, by any chance?"

That day Jane's work was done unconsciously and mechanically. Some kindly god of chance kept her fingers from writing, on the big typewriter, curious sentences which were burlesques of the ones Professor Myers had painstakingly dictated to her. She wanted to mingle a nautical flavor with the entomological atmosphere of his letters. "The peak-halliards of your new cricket are doubtless spliced differently from those of any other which I have examined through the sextant.... I see her little white ghost now, risin' out o' the sea. It is orthopterous and saltatorial. She would do anything but talk; but, having modified fore wings, makes a low humming sound by rubbing them together."

The two other members of the staff came in later. There was a sallow-faced young man who did the dustiest of the classifying and arranging of specimens; and a tight-set woman of indeterminate age, who attended to—well, it was never altogether clear what she did attend to. She was a trig but unattractive little person, whom you could never catch napping. She irritated Jane sometimes by her air of knowing a great deal which she would never under any circumstances divulge, and of being perpetually very busy. Miss Perry prided herself on her knowledge and practice of modern business efficiency, although Jane suspected that Miss Perry's efficiency was no better than it should be. Her manner was nearly always cold and detached. She had a reputation for coldness, in fact. And in this she gloried.

Jane had never thought much about her until today. She had been too preoccupied in her own first job. But now, with the secret knowledge of sudden release, she could glance in a more leisurely way over the long carriage of her typewriter, and see what was going on. No wonder Miss Perry was slightly inhuman! Jane felt a wave of compassion for her. Why, she had been right there, behind that very desk, for some nine years. Would she ever be anywhere else? It was not likely now. Did a sense ever sweep over her of the utter futility of all this small toil? And if it did—well, no wonder then that she gloried in her detached manner, her little coldnesses. They were all she had.

A vision of lofty rigging obscured Miss Perry. Lines leading aloft, slender and poised, free of perspiration and money, created to a purpose and a beauty. Perhaps the loveliest happening of the afternoon had been the seagulls, so close and seemingly so friendly. She and they had understood each other, and flown on intimate terms. Glorious white wings brushing by, in the sunlight....

"I'm going away, Miss Perry," said Jane. "In about a week. I've told Professor Myers. And by the way, I know a simply corking girl who could come in right away if you'd like to have her. Mary Rogers, a friend of mine."

Miss Perry looked up from her broad ledgers, and it seemed that her eyes, of an indefinite blue, were friendly. She had hired a great many stenographers from right there behind that desk. She had dismissed some of them with equal imperturbability. Jane was merely one of them. But the indefinite eyes were friendly. She nodded.

"Yes, send Miss Rogers in. You look very happy. Glad to be getting out, I suppose."

No need of dissimulation, Jane realized with relief. "Well, I am," she answered as frankly. The gulls' wings brushed by. "I'm going on a sea voyage, Miss Perry. It's been a dream for a long time, though I didn't realize it. Now it's suddenly come true." She watched the other's eyes closely, but they were inscrutable. Had she said too much? Were dreams banned from conversations with Miss Perry? Did she indeed believe in dreams at all? It was doubtful.

"Dreams," said Miss Perry slowly, "are half one's life, and the most important half. Take them away and—what have you?"

Jane could only nod in reply. Miss Perry went on, in her noncommittal voice. "It isn't so much whether they come true, either, because in a way a dream *is* true if you have it."

And this was the crass little materialist in her rut! Strangely, it was Jane who said: "They're so much more satisfactory if they do come actually true, realistically true."

"I doubt it," Miss Perry said with conviction. "Often I think it's better if they don't. Because the reality is never as good as the anticipation. Not by a long shot."

"Never?" Jane protested. She felt herself on unfirm ground: Miss Perry seemed to know all about dreams.

"I don't know about 'never.' All I know—and you may not

believe it—is that I had one once myself." She smiled. Jane was sorry for her—liked her, all of a sudden.

The spell broke then. Miss Perry remembered her beloved reputation—impersonal, unaffectionate. Jane was a mere stenographer. Miss Perry settled down over the ledger with immense energy.... Jane's seagull wings flashed against the rays of a friendly sun.

It was noon. Jane stood on the steps of the building, uncertain whether to go east or west. Nothing much in either direction, for that matter. As she stood undecided, she glanced down at her very sober gray dress, her calm black shoes. That dress was utterly impossible, all of a sudden. There was no use even considering it. How on earth had she ever got into that thing this morning? For the most part she was not concerned with clothes, but the drabness of this was more than she could bear. She hurried off down the street, longing to get rid of it—bury it somewhere, cast it off forever.

All out of breath, she hustled into the nearest store. "I want a red skirt," she announced. "Right away, if you want to save my life."

The salesgirl looked at her in cool amazement. "Red, miss? I'm afraid we have nothing in red today. How about this little navy blue one, or a beige? These are the very newest tints."

"Newest or oldest," said Jane, "red I must have. Why do you talk fashion when my soul pines for red?"

That was New York. Prating of newest tints. No wonder people were melancholy, in the clothes that prevailed this season. Like being in mourning. As though a little gaiety were against the rules.

In the next store an old lady with white hair waited on her. "A red skirt, my dear? Why yes, of course. Here you are. This russet is very smart, my dear."

"Is that the reddest you have?" Jane asked, with great irony.

It was. She fled.

At last, in an obscure little place on a dingy street, she unearthed a blazing creation with a flare and a general cockiness that won her.

"And a blouse, too," she commanded. "Some soft little white thing. With ruffles. Yes, *ruffles*," she repeated, sternly.

When she walked out she left the dress of gray tweed behind as a present to the astounded salesgirl. It was a symbolic gesture which stood for the denial of New York's hold on her. She was climbing into space on the mesh of a schooner's rigging.

[5]

The *Annie Marlow* glided ahead evenly, obedient to the small snorting tug that was taking her down-river. Gulls veered around her, as if they were glad she was outward bound. They would escort her gracefully down to the open sea. The wake glimmered with their wings, flashing gray and white, beating strongly and softly, in a shifting, weaving crowd. Their yellow beaks glinted now and then, and their cries surrounded the ship. She herself was light-footed as she walked on the waves of the broad Hudson, as she swung down between the wharves and immense bright liners on either side of her. She was quite willing to follow the tug wherever it might be taking her, but, in spite of her patience, she was only waiting to show her own free strength, when they would give her sail and she would forge lightly ahead alone.

"It's a sweet day," said Captain Maynard, surveying the vault of sky like one who knew its whims and weaknesses. "And there'd ought to be a fair breeze once we get outside, Mr. Stevens."

The mate nodded. He was pacing the poop deck slowly, keeping an eye on the tug ahead. "You can't tell, though. It's likely enough to baffle all round the compass and then leave you flat becalmed. Or, it might last for days." He never committed himself with the breezes. His own personal opinion was doubtless quite definite, but he would never divulge it. No one should claim that *he* was wrong in his judgment of a piece of weather.

Jane stood in a corner of the deck with her hair blowing. She saw that the sky was blue and white and windswept, and the sun gleamed upon gaudy smokestacks of big passenger ships. The gulls feathered back and forth astern, a soft cloud of wings. Beauty—that was what the whole world was starving for, and she had found it.... She closed her eyes in rapture, and the young wind played with her hair.

The river broadened out. Mammoth turrets and pinnacles arose tumultuously astern, the skyline of the city. Jane had seen that skyline before, and she knew its grandeur. But she gave the receding city only a couple of swift glances—glances in which there was a touch of fear that the roaring monster might snatch her back before escape was complete.

Captain Maynard, eyeing the wind, called out through a megaphone to the stalwart tug ahead. Jane heard the answer come back faintly: "All right!" And then, the skipper's voice again: "Start your engine, Mr. Davidson! Mains'l up, boys!"

There was a rumbling up forward, and the whole schooner began to tremble as if she were profoundly excited, as if her heart were pulsing. There were creaks and rattles, sounds of wood and hemp and canvas. The schooner was shaking herself hard. And the mainsail, like an immense white wing, lifted before Jane's eyes—crept up the mast one hoop after another. It rippled and billowed like grass on a windy mountain top. Straining and aspiring, it came to rest at last, and as the sailors close-hauled, it filled with wind and curved outward, lifting. The schooner stepped faster, and the tow-rope slackened ahead now and then.

To Jane this setting of the *Annie Marlow*'s mainsail meant far more than the beginning of this particular voyage. She knew that nothing would ever be quite the same again, after she had stood on deck and watched great sails rise over her, and felt the tremulous shaking of the ship, impatient to be off into the waiting sea. She would be living in a dream after this, and her steps along New York pavements would be light as falling snow. She would move in a world of shapes and silences, things done automatically without thought. There would be strange little Miss Perry who believed in dreams; and Professor Myers, calm and fatherly, searching for his glasses. Bob and Ellen would doubtless quarrel again. She would glide among them, helpfully and not unhappily, and listen to voices of seagulls, and feel a schooner tremble beneath rising, yearning wings.

As the foresail, mizzen, and jibs followed the mainsail, finally the spanker, and the topsails, four small peaks aloft, the *Annie* gathered way and forged ahead with a louder chuckling and knocking of waters beneath her breast. She swung along almost airily, leaning a little on her side, every sail drawing well, jibboom pointing arrow-like into an eternity of sea. The tow-rope was very slack now. Much to the captain's delight, his schooner was gaining on the squat black tug ahead; gaining on her, surging up alongside her, with ivory castles at her bow.

"We'll manage now!" the captain shouted.

The line was let go. "O. K., Maynard!" The tugmaster leaned out of his small wheelhouse, spat genially, and signaled to his engine-room. "Good luck!" he sang out. The *Celia* became a receding black blot astern; the schooner, tall and slender and bird-like, settled down alone to the long sapphire trail under the noonday sun.

Jane felt an irresistible sleepiness. She was completely at home here. There was serenity in the swinging gait of the schooner, the sounds from her hull as she rolled a little to the incoming swell. She tossed up her bowsprit, and stepped gaily ahead, with now and then a whiff of spray that was white and ethereal and part of the whole dream. Jane sat down on the saddle of the spanker boom, and planted her back against the mast. It was something substantial and trustworthy to rest upon.

It had been a long, hard week for her. Swamped with the immensity of her secret, throbbing with its excitement, and always dogged by vague fear that something might still prevent her embarking—with all this, which was in itself as much as she wanted to bear, she had to keep pounding away at the office grind, unslackening. She had to finish up odds and ends of work. There were questions to be intelligently answered. She had to help Mary get started. Mary's job with Bob's father had not materialized after all, so she was taking Jane's place with Professor Myers. Jane found it unimaginably hard to be serene and polite to everyone, about multitudinous details which she secretly scorned. She was conscious of a desire to say: "Shut up! I'm thinking," and one day she had narrowly escaped saying to Professor Myers: "Oh, darn your old glasses!" But she had carried through without a single serious slip, and the strain had been overwhelming.

Leaning against the mast, she closed her eyes, and still saw only a restless shimmering horde of seagull wings. Her entire world was ceaselessly in motion—swells; horizon, which waved up and down like a blue flag; the schooner herself; the sun-trail on the water. The world had become a gigantic cradle. The wind was singing. And before very long the *Annie Marlow* had rocked Jane off to sleep, free of the pavements, free of money and perspiration, like the ascending taut lines themselves.

The captain found her there when he went down to lunch, and said to his cook: "Steward, I reckon as Miss Jane won't be comin'." The steward smiled knowingly, and his smile plainly said: "Something's up 'tween her 'n' the fishes, eh?" But, being a tactful steward, he said nothing.

Jane awoke with a little start, not knowing just where she

was. The schooner's great mast was behind her, and she felt an increased swaying, for the land was out of sight now, every last vestige of it. The sun blazed low in the west, a great smoky orange globe behind a film of cloud; and the sea shone translucent silver-blue, traced with darker shadows and lighter streams. The breeze was not so fresh, but the sails were still curved and steady. The sound of water at the ship's bow had changed to a faint murmur. Jane felt alone in the very center of the universe, which was nothing but sea.

Then a single disturbing thought occurred to her. She had not the faintest idea where the *Annie Marlow* was bound. She had simply forgotten to ask, that was all. At times during the week it came upon her forcibly that she must find out at once, but that week had been frantically busy. She had been to the schooner once, in the evening, to find out for sure when they were sailing. Everyone had seemed busy, and she had put off asking the question. There was too much else to think about. She was surprised at herself, and very much amused. It was all part of the adventure, dream-like and unearthly. The ship might be sailing off the edge of the map; quite likely that was it.

Mr. Stevens, the portly first mate, strode the deck with heavy tread and stern gaze. He was in command, now. He kept his eye on the sea and the sails and the nonchalant helmsman, all at once. Nothing could escape him, by Jove! Like many short men —he was an inch or so shorter than Jane—he made the very most of what height he had by standing stiffly erect. His broad shoulders and pompous waist gave him a squat, square appearance, like a cider-jug.

Somehow, thought Jane, he didn't look like a person of whom she could ask her question. "Mr. Stevens, will you kindly tell me where the ship is going?" It wouldn't do. You could twist the words around a hundred ways, but you could not make them sound sane. Some time she would have a look at the logbook, if she could discover where it was kept. Maybe after a while she would hear someone mention in the natural course of conversation where they were going. But, after all, for now it didn't matter very much. They were outward bound—enough for one day.

"Good evening, Mate," Jane greeted him airily.

But his dignity was not to be trifled with. He drew himself up portentously, and looked at her with his cold eyes. "My name is Stevens," he announced.

Jane considered an impertinent retort, but thought better of it. She climbed down on to the main deck, and strolled its length once or twice, looking up into the sails. They were arched and vaulted, and silent. They seemed to form part of some immense domed castle ceiling. In this silver-blue light that came just before sunset, they were purged of wear and tear and smudginess, and gleamed smoothly white. The ship was so still, except for the long slow swaying, that she seemed hardly to move at all.

Jane climbed the main rigging, on the windward side of the ship. The shrouds vibrated a little, from the straining of sails at the masts. They were living and tense. She climbed toward the sky on a gray mesh, and the marble slopes of the sails were her companions. As she climbed, the horizon broadened out a little, but it was all alike. The sea was almost imperceptibly heaving. You could not see where undulations began and ended, but they were there, because the schooner recognized them. Sometimes a suspicion of a silver ridge, scarcely more than a shadow, glided across—no more.

Even mountains, even woodland rivers, pine forests and moss and ferns, had never held for her such peace as this of the sea. It would rock to sleep all ambition, desire, grief, leaving only a great serenity, and a purpose of things. The ship, steering for one tiny but determined point in the quivering circle of the compass card; the great aloneness; the colossal importance, or the microscopic unimportance of her—these things twined themselves with a subtle possessing rhythm, into Jane's heart. And she desired no more than this tremendous symphony of sound and feeling.

Clinging to the topmast, she sat on the crosstrees, and swung her feet almost jauntily over eighty feet of space. She looked down through graceful sweeps of sail, and up to the peaked topsails. The sun had slipped into the sea without so much as a single hiss, and the world was unbelievably still. A smear of color began to glow over the west, and there were limpid pools of blue-green in the sky, with cloud shapes between, and small rose feathers trailing languidly across the zenith.

No telephones here, or jazz bands, doorbells, phonographs, alarm-clocks, typewriter clickings, or the roar of subways and the "L." It all had been cut clean out of the picture. Jane cried a little. It was too completely what she had longed for, and it had come before she was ready to believe in its reality. You couldn't bear a piece of beauty like this. Beauty.... Now that she was away from the manicure parlors and hair-dressing shops, that word did not seem so pitiful. It was adequate, now. It was God. The topmast, warm from the afternoon sun, felt alive in the crook of her elbow. It was companionable and strong. Her shoulders trembled, and a few more tears fell through the height, to land in the lap of a sail.

In a way this escapade was the direct sequel of another. Vaguely she wondered, there on a level with the ship's long gaffs, if Charlie ever thought of her any more. She had neither seen or heard of him since her wild dash from the church more than three years ago. Most likely his delicate sense of propriety had been profoundly shocked. Most likely he would be shocked all over again if he could know that she was at this moment sitting on the main crosstrees of a schooner whose destination she had had no proper chance to ask about. And she smiled to herself at that thought.

There was another person to be thanked for this adventure —Andrew, the old Scotch gardener, the one mortal in Jane's home town who had sympathized with that frantic dash of hers. He was a quaint character, half of whose words she usually failed to understand, though she knew they were friendly. It was to his cottage that she had run from the church, two miles away, across fields. She had kicked off her white slippers and run barefoot, leaping fences and brooks, tearing through fringes of brush, holding off the ground her white dress with its lace so carefully stitched by one of Charlie's innumerable aunts. During that run she had been conscious of almost hysterical happiness and relief, which refused to be dispelled by thoughts of uncomfortable consequences.

She reached Andrew's place streaming with sweat and out of breath. At first she had not been able to find the old man; but his pet duck, Heather, was waddling across the back yard, with its perpetual ridiculous expression of good nature. "Andrew!" she called, in desperation.

And then his youngest son appeared, John, a lad of about Jane's age, who had been her friend and playmate for years. He gazed at her wedding dress, and smiled slowly, approvingly.

"Well, I couldn't do it, Johnny.... I just spread my wings—came sailing over fences..."

"I wish I could ha' seen ye. Ye always did run grand, Jane."

"Where's your father? I want to talk it over with him."

John said, with many r's, that his father was somewhere about, but he didna ken just where. And then he glanced around the yard, and caught sight of Heather. "Why doon't ye pin a note on the duck, Janie? If Heather's aroond, Andra's no far awa'."

In his Ford truck, old Andrew drove her to Portland, where one of his married daughters lived. He demanded no explanation, and asked only one question—whether she had bolted just after the ceremony or just before it.

"It was a close squeak," Jane had answered gravely; and Jane on the crosstrees of the schooner trembled.

He told her she was a "verra wise lass."

"How so, Andrew?"

"Aweel, Jane, if tae rin awa' was hoo ye lo'ed Charlie, ye sairtainly couldna be cantie wi' him."

She would never forget this simple approval. How much she had needed it! His daughter, too, had been unbelievably kind, lending her a little money with which to start her proposed fortune-hunting in New York, understanding her silence, asking no questions. She wrote to Andrew a good deal, asking how Heather was and how John was, thanking him for all he had done for her, and giving the latest news from New York. To these letters he replied that Heather was well and John was well, and he wasna much of a hand at writing, and they all wished her luck. Also, he usually said that he had pleaded with her father as well as he knew how, and hoped he would soon come around and act human about Jane's escapade, but that right now he was determined to have nothing to do with his scapegrace daughter, ever again.

So Andrew had played his part in Jane's sailing for unknown places in the *Annie Marlow*; and she thanked him again from the crosstrees and the sails and the great peace of the sea....

The bell for supper jangled loudly from below, crashing into the calm. Jane twisted herself and peered downward, and caught a glimpse of the cook on his way aft, carrying his big "dog-basket." An aroma floated up, perhaps imaginary but very tantalizing, of baked ham, mingled with other undefinable scents. Carefully she lowered herself between the white arms of the crosstrees—a perilous moment, with the world gracefully swaying, before her feet rested on the ratlines again. Then down slowly on the stairway of the rigging, between tall sweeps and curves of sail.

Captain Maynard and Mr. Stevens were already at the table.

"Feeling a little—?" the captain began. But he stopped short, for obviously she wasn't. "Well, well! You look as though you were enjoying yourself, Jane. Thought you might be turnin' toes up afore now, maybe."

"Oh, no! You see, there's too precious little time for me to be wasting any of it."

"Little, eh?" he retorted. "What d'you think o' that, Stevens? She calls a two months' v'yage little!"

(*Two months!*)

"Huh!" Stevens commented, "she'll think different before it's over."

"Not that it'd amount to so much afore them new-fangled steamboats 'n' sich got to swallerin' the sea 'n' changin' everyone's notions," the captain resumed. "In the old days we'd think nothin' o' seventy 'n' eighty days." He interrupted himself to pour pepper-sauce generously into his soup, all the time shaking his head at the little bottle as if to say: "My, my, how can you be so unexpressive! Why, even pepper-sass ain't what it used to be."

There were no stars when Jane went on deck. The night was close and thick, and rounded sails leaned mouse-gray out of it. The only light was the coppery gleam from the binnacle lamp, which now and then touched the brown varnish of the big wheel, or sent up a ray to illuminate for an instant the helmsman's youthful face. The man whistled softly from the midst of a pool of mingled flickerings and shadows.

At first Jane thought he was alone there. When her eyes became used to the dark she thought she discerned another figure in the stern on the windward side; but if it was a man he was so motionless that he might have been cut in ebony. He leaned against the taffrail at ease, looking out ahead—jet-black against a sky of deep, deep gray.

He gave her a sense of absolute tranquillity. It was as though he had become part of the ship, like one of her masts, or the great curve of sail that faded aloft in the night. Perhaps he was holding subtle communion with the sea. There was strength about him, too. Not a dashing, valiant strength, but the quiet power of some splendid pine tree in a New England forest. He belonged completely to the sea and to the night; he was one with their aloofness and long silences.

It occurred to Jane that he was the only person aboard whom she could ask where the *Annie Marlow* was bound. She had considered Captain Maynard, but some intuition restrained her. He was more aloof and solemn now they were at sea. The colossal burden of guiding the schooner by infinitesimal compass points through an eternity of waves, had deepened and changed him. But the young man by the taffrail would understand. In the same moment she realized why he looked familiar to her. He was Davidson, the new second mate, whom she had found reading Conrad on the fo'c'sle deck the first time she had come aboard.

They said good evening gravely. "Have you finished *Lord Jim* yet?" Jane asked.

He nodded shyly. Jane was exploring the very innermost corner of his world, a corner which he had never mentioned to anyone. You couldn't, and be at the same time a sailor and one of your mates. Jane, of course, was not one of his mates. He could talk to her about Conrad and books. Yet he was not at ease, because he felt shy with her, instinctively afraid to infringe on alien worlds.

He admitted that for a long time he had known *Lord Jim* almost by heart.

"I suppose," said Jane, "you would rather read it six times over than read six other books."

A little surprised and vaguely pleased that she understood so well, he nodded once more. Jane tried to put him at ease. "You have to pick your books, though," she said.

"Oh, you pick them over just as you cull apples. But Conrad is safe, you know."

"A lot of people can't make head or tail of Conrad, and don't want to try."

"Well, a lot of people can't abide prairies, and a lot more say that too many trees clutter up the sky."

"And some," Jane echoed, "don't even like to look at the sea, while others are utterly unable to stay ashore."

He returned her quick smile. He wasn't afraid of her any more. "How did you find that out?"

"Your captain told me. But I think I knew it anyway. Has it got you, Mr. Davidson?"

He admitted, after a small silence, that he was "in pretty deep."

"Another thing your captain and I talked about," said Jane, "was the merits of sailing ships and steamers. 'I wish the old clippers was back in style,' was how he put it. Of course he admitted it was a rotten hard life, but there was 'somethin' about it'—he didn't know quite what, but there it was. It's positively uncanny, Mr. Davidson, the way you sailors feel about the sea."

"Well—" They talked it all over. But it left Jane as mystified as before. There seemed no answer at all, no consistency. It was a strange vicious circle of conflicting emotions that could not be broken or changed. Davidson was a true deep-water man, thought Jane. The true ones always got muddled when they tried to explain.

The breeze was just barely enough to fill the sails. "Are we going to get becalmed?" Jane asked.

He said he was afraid so; yes, it looked it, all right.

"What happens then?"

"Well, everything stops, except that the ship begins to tear herself to pieces. I don't like that, myself. Hurts."

"One gets to think of a ship as a living thing, I guess," said Jane.

He smiled and said he guessed that was true; anyway, you got mighty fond of a ship.

"Captain Maynard talks about his ships as though they were his children," said Jane. "It struck me as quaint at first. But now I really believe the *Annie Marlow* is alive."

They fell silent for a little while. That bothersome question Jane wanted to ask had been forgotten once more. She had again let it slip into oblivion, because she did not care. The ship herself, and the slumbering sea, were the facts that counted.

"I think the *Annie Marlow* is alive," she murmured again.

The mainsail, until now steady as though carved in ivory, drew a deep breath and sighed; and the schooner swung gently as a cradle over the domes of polished jet that slipped beneath her.

[6]

Jane was up early, and came on deck to feel the incredible blue of a young morning at sea. The wind was like the primrose wind that chases about fragrant pastured hills at dawn; only bolder and freer.

That day Jane decided she would make a determined and systematic effort to find out where the *Annie Marlow* was bound. She tracked down Davidson, and found him busily painting the interior of the small engine-room up forward by the fo'c'sle.

"Mr. Davidson, I've come to ask you the most astounding question anyone ever asked you in your life," she began.

He put down his brush and smiled. "The trouble is, I probably can't answer it, Miss Carey."

"So you've found out my name?" She frowned at him mockingly. "Well, that isn't my name. Not here. That's my Sunday-go-to-meeting 'longshore name. Here I'm known as Jane, just plain old plain-Jane, you know."

He gave her his shy smile again. "Then I haven't any 'Mr.' to me," he ventured, busy with the paint-brush now.

"Oh, I'm glad of that. I don't like handles. And now that

that's all settled so soon, will you please hand me that other brush?"

"Aren't you on vacation?"

"Oh, well, I have to earn my passage, you know. And—oh, yes! Now for that great question I was going to ask you. Get ready!" She lowered her voice apprehensively. "I want you to tell me where this ship is going. I didn't dare ask anyone but you; and I suspect it's time I found out."

He placed his brush quietly across the pail of white paint, and looked straight at her. She gazed back into his honest gray eyes. The moment would have been absurd if it had not also been a cosmic adventure. A miracle took place. For he understood, and far more completely than if she had told the whole story, with all its details, explanations, excuses, in hundreds of words. Words were a nuisance, and this no time for them.

"Valparaiso," he murmured. "Going after nitrates." And without saying anything more, he went back to his work. As for Jane, the swift silence of his understanding was even more exciting to her than the ring of "Valparaiso." She painted at his side without answering, but the big brush was unsteady in her hand....

At sea days slipped away fast, lost over the rim of space. They were born in a splash of gold, marched over in a blue arc, and vanished with a pouring of moonlight across the curves of sail. Jane spent many hours alone, walking the deck and day-dreaming. She walked in the early mornings, which were bright as new butterflies. Sailors would be washing down the deck, then, and one of the mates tramping about among them with a bucket of sea water. She walked on the poop at noon, when Captain Maynard and Mr. Stevens were up with their sextants, in ambush to catch the sun at the peak of its flight. She paced the long main deck in the afternoons, in the shade of the sails. She walked on those calm days when one languid blue dome after another rose up, gleaming subtly like moonstones, and the weary old schooner was beating her wings and yearning for wind. Sometimes she walked at night, almost alone with the magic of the ship—the ship southward bound across the dark—southward under those stars, all there was in the universe, and yet nothing.

Here, at sea, Jane was able for the first time to feel definitely that the earth was a sphere. Till now, she had accepted the fact only as something which she had trained herself to believe, but around which she had found it hard to wrap her imagination. At sea there was clear unobstructed expanse on all sides. She saw ships hull-down. Several times she had a distinct sensation of the *Annie Marlow* crawling on the outer rim of a huge globe, with nothing but a mysterious power called gravity to keep her from flying off into that infinite space which was another very difficult thing to visualize.

Sometimes Jane scrubbed dishes in the galley or painted with the sailors. The engine-room was finished now, and Davidson's watch had begun on bulwarks and waterways. Also, within a few days she had become the official sewer-on of buttons for this crew. Not that the men weren't able to sew on their own. They had done it for years, and would continue as they drooped into senility; but it gave Jane a grown-up, motherly feeling which she enjoyed, and also a good opportunity to talk with them.

On the first Sunday afternoon she held a session amidships, sitting on one of the long spare gaffs. Most of the men were out in the sun with their buckets, washing clothes in mountains of soapsuds with such energy and thoroughness that only the most valiant and time-tried specks and stains could withstand the strain; sometimes the material itself gave way first. In return for the buttons Jane sewed, they insisted on washing her blouses for her, with the result that everyone felt mutually useful.

They thought her an extremely good sport anyhow, not so much for the sturdy and seaman-like way with which she sewed buttons, as for her companionship, the eagerness with which she listened to their tales, and her laughter that mingled so naturally with their own.

"Bill, what were you all laughing your heads off about awhile back? Oh, I heard you! Why, it shook the whole ship." Bill was sitting beside her while she carefully sewed up a rip in his blue shirt, and between stitches admired the sleek brown shoulder under the torn edges of cloth.

"Why, the p'int was, Miss Jane—Well, tell me now, ain't ol' Barnacle a tom-cat?"

"Sure he is," Jane agreed, stitching away, and not having the faintest idea of whether he was or not.

"Well, doggoned if *he* ain't gone and had a hull fambly o' little Barnacles—five of 'em!" announced Bill, elated that Jane had fallen into the trap.

She received the momentous information in the proper spirit, laughing with the rest of them.

"The ol' man don't know yit," Bill pursued. "But he's gone t'have the s'prise o' his sixty years. Yessir!"

Young Jim took up the strain. 'N' tell her about the cook, Bill. You see, Miss Jane, the cook's a very superystitious sort of a chap, 'n' when he seed that the tom-cat had kittens he throws his hands over his head 'n' gives a whoop 'n' says: 'Then sure this ship's a-gone ter have the damnedest worst luck in the world.'"

"What do you think yourself, Jim?"

"Why, Miss Jane, what I figgers is that natur is natur, 'n' if we was thinkin' that cat was a tom the joke was on us. The ol' bitch! Think o' pullin' a stunt like that."

"Do you figger as them kittens was borned out o' wedlock?" drawled Pete—a signal for another general uproar. There followed an enlightening discussion of the love life of cats.

Jane enjoyed these gatherings. She had found out that the atmosphere of coarseness which often prevailed in the crew's conversation was unintended and unconscious, so that it was actually not coarseness at all. She liked their enthusiasms and their spirit of fun. She liked to have them show her their pictures and keepsakes, and to listen when they talked about wives and daughters, the son who ran a barber shop, and the gal friend who worked at a sody-fountain in 'Frisco.

Still more, she liked to talk about books and dreams with Davidson. He was one of the *Annie Marlow*'s crew, but at the same time he was mysteriously different from them.

"How about *Youth*: have you read it yet?" she asked him one evening.

He confessed that he had been saving *Youth*; that he nibbled at Conrad slowly, in order to make that shelf of blue-bound books last a long time. That was how she came to read the story aloud to him. She read it straight through from beginning to end one evening below decks in his little cabin. Mr. Stevens smiled knowingly to himself as he marched the poop on watch, as if to say to the broad expanse of sea and to the uninterested back of the helmsman: "See there? Didn't I tell you?" He and his imagination were so happy together that he could not for the life of him resist mentioning to Captain Maynard, later in the evening, that Jane seemed to be "in powerful deep with that six-foot swashbuckling second mate."

"Shucks!" said the skipper. "Swashbuckling" was the very last word one would ever apply to young Davidson. "Shucks! They ain't nothin' but pals, and why the hell shouldn't they be pals if they likes?" But he looked thoughtful, all of a sudden.

Most of the time the captain was busy with his ship, contemplating the horizons, studying his charts, all alone, with the weight of an entire world on his shoulders. But sometimes he came out of his aloofness as on the first day Jane had been aboard.

"Well, Jane, are you enjoyin' it as much as you thought to?" he asked her once.

She answered jovially that it would be all right with her if they never got to the Panama Canal or Valparaiso.

He lowered his voice, hesitated a little, and then asked: "That ain't—'cause o' young Davidson, is it, Jane?"

She was surprised, and if it had been anyone but Captain Maynard she might have felt a trifle hurt. But he was completely unconscious of this. He was asking a question, and only wanted an honest answer. "Oh, no," she assured him. "It's just—well, your schooner, and the old sea, and not having to worry about anything that's going on ashore. You know, I feel as if I'd never been in New York at all—as if the place didn't exist any more. You don't know what a grand feeling that is."

"Reckon I do know, maybe," he said. "Been to sea forty-five year." But he would not let her pass it off so easily. He leaned back in his leather armchair, glancing now and then from force of habit at the compass overhead. "I was thinkin' o' my daughter—poor little girl," he said quietly. "You didn't know as I had a daughter, did you, Jane? Well, I hain't, not no more. Her mother died when Rose was fifteen years old; and then I took her to sea along of me: happened so sudden-like, and I was that bewildered, I didn't know what else I could do with her. 'Twould 'a' all been fine, 'cause she liked the sea jist the same's you do, Jane; but—well, 'tain't a long story—it was a sailorman as shamed her and broke her heart; and—she went overboard half a year after, Jane, when I was beginnin' t' see what was wrong. Off Hatteras, one o' them cold, blowsome, dark nights.... Him? Jane, I'd 'a' killed that skunk, 'cept I knowed as it wouldn't 'a' done no good."

Jane was very still. The old man seemed to be talking to himself, as though he had forgotten she was there. "Rose.... She was as lovely as her name—poor little girl," he said tenderly. Then he struck the arm of the chair with his fist, and went on bitterly: "An' hadn't I been a-tellin' of her—hadn't I told her a hundred times to watch out fer sailormen, an' any other kind of a man? Only, she jist thought as *he* was diffrunt from the hull rest of 'em, ye see.... Aye, everyone thinks that, at one time or another, an' some is bound to get a rotten deal. So, ye see"—he nodded his head slowly—"God knows I ain't a-preachin', Jane, but—you remember 'bout my Rose—poor little girl."

Jane had heard that story, with variations, from many people; but never before had she felt so deeply touched. Perhaps that was because of her affection for the gray-haired master of the *Annie Marlow*, with his quaint ways of speech and his kind blue eyes. It seemed to her that no one could do him a wrong, or his daughter, or anything belonging to him.

But on deck once more, with sails like great caves half lit by the moon, and the sea eastward paved with silver, and her hands grasping the shrouds of rigging that beckoned her aloft to where the moon glanced upon one narrow white bar of the crosstrees —then this present world of beauty was all that counted....

Passing through the Canal was a hot day of contact with mankind, and then all was left behind again, and it might have been only a confused and noisy dream. As the *Annie Marlow* drew southward, mackinaws had been thrown aside, and flannel shirts had long ago given place to light blue ones, or to none at all. A flock of small brown and white albatross pursued the ship; "goonies," the sailors called them. Jane sometimes threw chunks of bread to them, for which they raced and quarreled. There were dolphins in the wake, iridescent and electrical; jelly-fish, too, which appeared suddenly all over the surface of the ocean in the middle of the day, and then vanished again.

"How do you account for that, Davidson?" Jane asked.

"Oh, well, you see, they just come up at noon to take their sights," he told her, with the familiar shy chuckle.

"And then go down, I suppose, to figure 'em out?" she retorted.

And days melted past, without a murmur, without a shadow. Sometimes when Jane awoke she smelled a strange deep-sea smell out the porthole, and heard a husky, gigantic breathing—a whale wallowing and blowing through the swells. Sometimes the captain told a yarn at the dinner table. He liked the southeast trades, even if they did make his course to Valparaiso a circuitous one. "I could *purr*, I'm so happy when there's a breeze," he said one day, rubbing his hands together as he came down the companion. Occasionally he spoke to the schooner herself: "Keep it up, lady! I'll hold ye to it!" But that was all. That was the way of the sea.

The friendship with Davidson grew. Jane had never experienced a comradeship so simple and so happy. That, also, was the way of the sea.

"Davidson, there's one more thing I'd love to do before we get to—Valparaiso," she said one afternoon, giving him her little one-sided smile as she mentioned that name. "I'd like to stand the mid-watch with you some time, if I may."

"The graveyard watch?"

She nodded. "The point is that I can't wake up, Davidson. I sleep too well at sea. What would you recommend?"

He reflected. "Of course," he teased, "I'd like to come and wake you myself, but—well!"

"Mr. Stevens would enjoy it if you did," said Jane.

He gave a wry smile. "Stevens has a habit of enjoying a lot of things that plain ain't so."

"Well, he gets a lot of free entertainment out of the world that way," Jane affirmed.

"It's a pretty kettle of fish," he retorted, "when there's so little fun in the world that you have to invent it out of your own imagination."

"Well, they say that to create is the most satisfying kind of self-expression," said Jane, laughing.

"You're a mighty arguer! I can't fool you, but we can fool Stevens. Let's see. Suppose you take some string, and tie one end of it to your wrist, or your ear, or something, and stick the other end through your porthole—the one that opens on to the half-deck. And then, you see, I come on watch at midnight, and I—well, psychic communication, and all that."

"Grand! You're a genius, Davidson." They chuckled together like grammar-school mischief-makers, and it flashed across Jane's mind that she had always wanted a brother....

When she came quietly on deck, a little after midnight, the trade wind was blowing hard, and the schooner darted lightly across a long sweep of black and silver waves. Nearly full, the moon was threading in and out of white clouds. It felt very late. The deck slanted weirdly beneath Jane, and her hair blew. Never before had she felt the sea and the night and the wind like this. She knew that, like Davidson, she belonged to them.

"It's grand tonight," she said.

"I know. But you get fed up on it."

"You all say that, but you all come back." She was very beautiful in the half-light, with her hair blowing straight back from her serious young face.

"Well, you can see why, can't you, Jane?" He made a sweeping gesture ahead somewhere, at slanting booms, dark tumbling sea, and wild white clouds. "You get ashore, you see, and you get flurrying around, backing and filling, and never quite sure what your course is—"

"Or how to steer it," she put in.

"They don't have charts with compass roses and all. And you sort of lose—well, you lose your sense of values, if you know what I'm trying to say."

"I do know. I've been there. You get to thinking a dollar bill's pretty important; or if you don't think so you miss your dinner."

"Yes, and you get stewed up in a lot of little frazzles that don't matter. And then one day you're disgusted and you—well, you go to sea."

He was not very articulate, but his words spoke eloquently of the thousand trivialities ashore, and the great restfulness of the much-cursed sea.

"I believe you're rather like me," Jane ventured. "I call it civilization, and I don't like it. But if I say so, everyone laughs in a gentle and superior manner."

"I don't."

"No, thank heaven. This civilization thing—it has its points, I suppose. But you get fed up with it. What's more, it looks as if God had got fed up with it, too."

"Do you believe in God?"

"Well, I don't know. I rather think not. Anyway, not when I'm mixed up with civilization. Nothing means much there, and if there is a God, He's all worn out, and I don't wonder. Here almost anything might be true; but here it doesn't matter. As far as I'm concerned, He's a failure anyhow; for when I need Him, I'm suddenly hesitant and skeptical; and when circumstances are such that I might believe in Him, I don't have any use for Him. What good is an elusive hide-and-seek sort of God like that?" She chuckled happily.

He was silent a minute, then said: "He gives it to sailors coming and going. We get driven back and forth between civilization and the sea, and can't decide which is worse."

"I think," Jane put in, "that probably sailors get the worst of civilization, too. You know—the back alleys and certain large tin cans."

He smiled in agreement. "But we always think we'll do better next time—and we don't. We flounder round a bit, get in no end of trouble, and—go to sea again. And the sea ruins us for anything else, because it's immense and sometimes peaceful, and because it unrefines our characters." Jane knew that he was speaking now from the standpoint of his shipmates, of the sailors of all the world; she noticed again how curiously he belonged to them and at the same time was very much alone and—a little lonely.

"Speaking of God," said Jane, "just what do you believe?"

"He and I don't always hit it off very well. But at least I'm not a wild, raving atheist."

"I'm glad of that, because it seems to me that atheists are—well, too impudently sure, perhaps."

"They're forever throwing stones at other people's windows," said Davidson.

"Because they haven't any of their own, probably."

"It may be too cold outside for the other people to live without their windows—if they aren't hard-skinned people. And, even if the glass is a bit fogged up—well, every man has a right to his own."

She liked the metaphor. "And then," she added, "isn't any window as good as any other? I mean, does anybody really know?"

He shook his head, smiling, and looked off to sea. His ideas had come from twelve hard years of this sea. Jane wondered quietly how it came about that he, whose life had been so apart from hers, should understand her so well, not alone in words, but in feelings and the subtle shades that are never put into words at all.

It was a night for companionship. They talked about evolution, the prehistoric ages, and the pathways of comets; and they laughed at themselves for incongruously discussing trilobites and dinosaurs in the small hours of the morning on the poop deck of the *Annie Marlow*. Four bells came with amazing swiftness, and the wheel was relieved.

"Let's go on a marauding expedition," Davidson whispered.

"What shall we maraud?" Jane whispered back, feeling very gay.

"The honorable and reverend night-lunch-box."

"I trust that the first mate sleepeth."

"He snoreth," Davidson assured her.

They walked cautiously down to the companionway, keeping

close together in the dark, and tiptoed into the messroom. A lamp burned there dimly, and the night-box bulked big on the table. Jane felt as if they were congenial ghosts, and as if a ghost was a pretty good thing to be. Her heart was thumping a little. She thought that was odd, and wondered if Davidson could hear it, or if it might wake up Mr. Stevens. She pictured to herself the first mate's surprise and secret delight if he should find her there.

"How Stevens would enjoy this!" she whispered.

Davidson just smiled. They went on deck again, as soon as the raid was over, and the wind came at them with a rush. "I wonder what's got into that cook," he said. "They never before put up such a good night lunch."

Whitecaps gleamed about the ship, and the wind was almost warm. It was not very dark, because of the moon; the light was gray and it gave Jane an eerie feeling, intensified by the schooner's slanting. Was it on a night like this—colder, perhaps, and darker—that Rose had thrown herself into the sea?

"Davidson, tell me, did you ever hear the story of the captain's daughter?"

"Yes, the old man told me all about it just a couple of days ago." He looked at her oddly in that light which seemed to come from the wind rather than the moon. A smile lighted his face then. They wanted to laugh, yet somehow affection and respect for the skipper prevented that. It was at once solemn and absurd that the old man should unroll to each of them separately the same subtle chart to guard them from reefs and shoals that still lay remote in another ocean.

"Aren't you awfully afraid of me, Jane? Don't you tremble for fear I may pounce upon you like a lion and devour you, at any moment?"

"Don't make fun of him," said Jane, smiling back in spite of herself.

"I wouldn't for worlds," he assured her.

Captain Maynard had woven still another strong thread into the fabric of their comradeship, contrary to what he had intended—a complete trust in each other.

To young Davidson, Jane stood for something fine and aloof and precious beyond measure. He had never known anyone like her—a companion, something of a rebel, and a fellow dreamer. They had come together out of worlds that were far apart; and each found in the other something much needed and beautiful. His simplicity and honesty were to her like a deep mountain spring after a long hard trail. There was no more shallowness or meanness about him than about the sea, and—unlike the sea—no cruelty.

He knew mostly the backwash of cities, and to his mind girls were painted gold-diggers to whom you paid casual attention, if you were in the mood, for obscure and unworthy reasons that you did not bother to analyze. Jane was not a girl. She was a friend.

He always seemed shrouded in mystery. His way of speaking, to begin with, could hardly have been taught by the sea. But he had read widely, free from the influence of all academic or pedagogical conventions. He contended that a great deal of Shakespeare was tedious, and that the last chapter of *Moby-Dick* stood even with anything in literature. Conrad was the supreme master, of course, head and shoulders above them all. He also liked the stern calmness of the Scandinavian writers.

But how had it all come about? Jane never knew. He remained a mystery. She had to take him just for what he was, and in a way that too was a relief. His gentleness and deep-lying sense of values were even harder to explain than his curious literary knowledge. But for her this did not need explaining. After all, a person was a person, at sea or ashore. Heredity—surroundings—they had a good deal to do with it, but not all. Davidson was there. And that was soul-satisfying. You didn't probe into the depths of a friend as though—she thought of

Professor Myers—as though he were an entomological specimen.

How lost he was! He realized it, and yet she was frightened for him. She admired his aloofness from the world; his way of turning his back upon it, paying no attention to its little cold realities. But some time he would bump hard against it, and it would receive him like a wall of granite—and it would hurt.

He was a man whose virtues seemed to count against him. He did not care to bow to the little gods, saw no reason why he should, and had the quiet courage to ignore them. He wanted to drift and be let alone. His virtues were elemental; the little gods were scornful, and so he gave them the cold shoulder. He wanted peace and solitude, and found them alone; he laughed cynically at nearly everything about mankind and civilization.

He was a true seafarer, and this instinct, together with his unconscious virility, directed his destiny. Life had been simple. He found peace, for the most part. Sailing ships were dying now, but he still pursued them. In them he had grown up and become a man, and they and the sea had laid the foundation of his life. And they were failing him, gradually leaving him high and dry. Ashore, in the thick of industrial competition, he was helpless. Probably, by dint of effort and struggle, he could have succeeded at something, but it was not worth while to him. So he remained a drifter, a man who was nothing, who belonged nowhere; and yet who was somehow stronger than the civilization that defeated him, grander, and immeasurably more romantic....

They conversed in low voices, and watched the phosphorus in the wake, knots of greenish light. Davidson told her how once, when he was first mate of a full-rigged ship some time ago, he had been on deck late watching for the lights of an expected landfall. He had been told to call the skipper out the minute they were seen. He had walked the deck, looking anxiously ahead, nerves taut. He saw at last a string of lights, twinkling along the horizon's dark rim. With a sigh of relief he called the captain. When they came on deck together the entire sea ahead was blazing, paved with fire. That row of lights, so like the harbor of a seaport, had been only first sparkles of the phosphorus.

He told her also about rainbows he had seen in the moonlight; and she described to him the "frost feathers" in her beloved New England mountains: frozen mist, delicately chiseled into feathers of lace, projecting outward from crags into the wind which had carved them.

It came three o'clock, with a chiming of six bells. Davidson asked, then, just how it happened that Jane had sailed in the *Annie Marlow*. "You never told me that story, you know, Jane, and I'm a wee bit curious."

"Oh, I just ran away from our mutual enemy."

"Civilization?"

"Yes. It happened like a flash. I smelled an adventure, and before I knew it—"

"You were at sea, and in such a hurry that you even forgot—"

"Exactly." They exchanged smiles.

"That ought to satisfy me, I suppose. But it doesn't. I want to know just what it was our mutual enemy did to you. There must have been something terrible—and terribly sudden."

"Only general disgust. It's all so little, Daveson, and so moneyish." She had unconsciously contracted his name. He thought the contraction very pleasing. Exclusively hers. "I worked for an old professor of entomology," she finished abruptly, as though that ought to be enough said.

"You wouldn't enjoy entomology. By the way, what is entomology? Birds?"

"No, bugs."

"You're the sort who gleefully runs away from anything you don't like, aren't you?"

"I am an awful runner-away," she admitted. "I ran away once

from such an important occasion that my deluded father never forgave me."

"What? A dinner-party, or something?"

"Thousands of dinner-parties!" said Jane, with a smile. "As a matter of fact, it was a marriage. Even that would have been all right, if it had only been someone else's marriage. The trouble was, it happened to be mine."

Davidson was terrifyingly silent for a minute. Then he asked: "You aren't married now, are you?"

"Didn't I just tell you I ran away?"

"Yes, but— By Jove, that was fortunate!" He sounded almost fierce.

"That's what I think. But what do you know about it?"

"Nothing—except that it was almighty fortunate."

Jane unconcernedly pursued the subject. "If I hadn't run away, I'd be there this minute—hostess at a dinner-party, probably."

Actually a tremor shook Davidson's powerful frame. "Imagine that!" he brought out, with terrible irony and indignation.

"He was sort of a fool," said Jane, amused by this display of vehemence. "He liked dinner-parties and such things. To tell the truth, it was my father who was in love with him, not I. The young man had cash, you see."

Davidson felt that never in his life had he heard of such rank injustice. "Trying to sell you—was that it?"

Jane admitted that her father had had dreams of luxurious senility. Davidson glowered. His black eyebrows were threatening.

"Why does my little escapade upset you so?" Jane asked.

"Just to think that they should try to put anything over on you, Jane. Of course, they didn't make the grade. But suppose they had!"

"Well, I wouldn't be here, that's a cinch."

"That's just it," he said. At that minute he wouldn't have traded her companionship for anything else on earth. Seven bells sounded.

"I suppose I'd better be going down," Jane said. "You'll be arousing Stevens pretty soon, won't you?"

He nodded, with some sadness, and reflected that never before had he found the graveyard watch too short. He strolled with her to the companionway. She glanced out once more over the gray waves, and up at the mysterious sails. The wind was strong and swift.

"Can we do this again, Daveson?"

"Yes." He paused a moment, and then said with sudden emphasis: "*Yes!*" She was inside the door of the companion. "You know," he said, "it's a curious thing that they should have made me second mate this particular trip—instead of next, say."

"You mean, that if you had been only the man at the wheel—"

He nodded. "Sometimes I wonder," he said slowly. "I wonder if perhaps there isn't such a thing as—Fate."

Jane smiled, and said with seeming irrelevance, knowing he would understand: "Daveson, you're a grand sort of brother."

[7]

The storm came with a frowning of the sky, and ponderous shadows over the sea's face. Jane sensed it, early one morning when she went on deck. Serenity was lost, cast away behind. The sea had no use for that now. The world was a gray color, unutterably gray. The wind was gray. It came in whorls, biting at the foam. The waves showed white hungry teeth.

Mate and captain stood together in a corner of the poop, but Jane could not hear their voices. The wind had set its heart upon transforming the two men into marionettes, animated but soundless. She moved a little closer, and thought she heard Captain Maynard say: "Dirty, by the look of it." Stevens solemnly nodded his head. All of a sudden Jane wanted to laugh, and wished Davidson were up there with her. Human beings had dwindled, and seemed puny and helpless. The ship was diminishing, too. Once, without any warning, she took a gaunt wave over her windward bow, and shuddered to it like some wild creature.

"Best get them topsails in, Stevens," the captain said. "Then they'll *be* in." The mate nodded again, somewhat grimly, Jane thought.

Breakfast was rather silent. The ship lurched a good deal, and shook herself when waves met her bows too hard. The captain was troubled. He felt that there was treachery in the sea. And he could do nothing about it. He must push on ahead into the ambush of the storm. And the burden was all his own.

Davidson was on deck when she came up again. He stood gazing out to windward. Jane met him with a question in her eyes. But he could not answer. He doubted the loyalty of the sea, that was all. You had to be fatalistic about some things. A storm was one of them. He hoped it would hold off, but if it came he was ready. As he turned to greet her, his eyes were very gray. The sea had darkened them.

"The *Annie*'s a staunch old girl," he said consolingly. "Well put together."

"If we do go down," Jane teased, "and you are the sole survivor, you might inform my deluded father and my ex-intended. It would be a shame for them to miss that pleasure."

"Shall I give them your dying affection, and all that sort of thing?"

"No, the dolphins can have that. But you may go shares with 'em if you like, Daveson."

"And suppose nothing happens at all? It may not, you know."

"Well, then the dolphins won't have to go shares with you. But if I should be the lone survivor, are there any little things of that sort I can do for you?"

"Just remember," he answered, "that in my case there weren't any dolphins at all."

By afternoon it was blowing half a gale. The sky sagged with ominous clouds, shadowing the sea, which swirled and heaved like boiling ink. The voice of the wind rose and fell, and its tone was resentful. Sometimes it shrieked triumphantly through the rigging, and then fell to low moaning. The *Annie Marlow*'s sails were storm-reefed, and she tore on obliquely before the wind, rising high over the piles of water, crashing down into innumerable hollows, while spray crackled sharply upon her decks. Her masts leaned at a weird angle against a frayed sky, and they looked tired and old.

Evening came, and the wind remained about the same. The captain began to be hopeful. "Perhaps we'll run out of the doggoned thing yet, Stevens." The mate, as usual, was taciturn.

Jane went to sleep in peace. She had no serious idea that anything calamitous might happen to the schooner. Shipwrecks belonged to adventure stories. She had trust in the old skipper, and perhaps in Davidson. She fancied the wind was going down a little. The motion of the ship was not uncomfortable, except for occasional jerks and plunges. Besides, the sea was her friend....

When she awoke it was with the sensation that her feet were jammed tightly against the foot of her bunk, and that she was almost standing upright. The universe gave a violent shudder; there was a rush, and Jane found herself in a heap in a corner of her room—which corner she could not tell. There was no great pain in the fall, and yet when she tried to get up she could not. "What have I broken?" she wondered. She clung frantically to something that was in her way, and recognized it as the small bench opposite the bunk. But she was still not sure which was up and which down. And something in her body began to ache. An arm, or a leg? She could not tell. Nothing was familiar, not even her own limbs. She wrestled to get up, but it was like struggling in pitch black with an unseen foe—like one of those nightmares in which all strength and control have vanished.

She looked for the porthole, but wasn't sure where to look. At last her eyes found it, a small gray piece of doubtfulness in the black wall. Then she knew where the floor was, and struggled up, clinging to the bench. Nothing broken after all, only she felt full of bruises. One arm was hurting badly now, but it was sound and she could move it.

She found it comical, this crushing of the world. Here she

was, groping for the floor, which had got so mixed up with walls and ceilings; relieved, now that she had found it, as though it were some inestimable treasure; thanking heaven because she knew where it was, and where the porthole was. She tried to get to that porthole, with the vague idea of looking out; made a desperate dash for the bunk which was somewhere up above her across the room. As she started to climb at it, she was hurled down upon it violently. She caught its edge and stood clutching that, while the world seesawed about her again. She chuckled a little. A feat of acrobatics just to cross her room!

She managed to peer out the porthole, just in time to see three or four big silver stars go flying up somewhere into infinity, while an immense black weight hurled itself with malevolence at the small pane of glass. When the sky came down again, there was only one star left, which went out as she looked, extinguished suddenly against its will.

Then she remembered a flashlight she had left somewhere about. Perhaps she could get a bit of light. It might help. A little flicker of light could cheer one's soul. But she could not even think of anywhere to look for it. There was nowhere. She concentrated her faculties into a reasonable studying out of where she had last seen it. As if in mockery, something hit her on the head and flew off across the room. What on earth was that? There was no way of finding out. Then she remembered the little row of books on the shelf above the bench. She groped over there, vaguely hoping to do something about it, but could find nothing except occasional edges which she held on to thankfully. No, she could do nothing about anything. The air might be full of flying books, but she could not help it.

The ship was plunging desperately forward, swinging back, leaping, staggering. Waves beat and hammered the decks with diabolical frenzy. The wind howled. Outside, the sea was black chaos gleaming now and then with fangs of white foam. Once the ship plunged into such a succession of gigantic seas that

Jane felt: "Everything will give way now." But somehow the *Annie Marlow* came through. Jane strained her eyes at the porthole again. A livid cascade of lightning illuminated the whole sea and sky in a mad gold suspense. Awful chasms, abysses, and parapets of black clouds, with jagged edges.... Whatever thunder followed may have added to the uproar, but was not distinguishable as thunder.

And then, all of a sudden, Jane wanted Davidson more than she had ever wanted anything in her life. She wanted his quiet smile, and his aloof strength. The need was an actual pain, a dull, unintelligent throbbing. She felt for the pain—oh, that cursed arm again.... At the same time she was conscious of a dim rectangle in one wall of the cabin, with a shadow bulking in it—some strange illusion. But after she had looked at it a while, she remembered the door; and then she knew that it was Davidson who stood there. She even believed she could hear his voice faintly calling to her across a measureless gulf.

"Yes, yes, I'm here," she almost shrieked, trying to make her way toward him. She felt for the edge of the door, found it at last, and got to her feet facing him. He was immensely tall in his wet black oilskins. She could not see his face.

"Are you all right, Jane?" came his voice close to her ear. She felt his breath for a second, a precious scrap of life and warmth.

"Yes, I'm all right," she shouted back.

"Just came down—to see if you needed me. Now I must go." Their hands met somehow, and held on for a second in a mute exchange of comradeship. Then he had melted into the obscurity outside, and the released door slammed viciously.

He had come—to see if she needed him! She stood in the dark treasuring this. And now he had gone back to the *Annie*, who did need him very much. Was he up in that awful fury now?... The ship leaped; Jane felt her rising on an endless flight, which changed to a quivering, painful struggle upwards. A tremendous crash came, and it was as though an entire range of mountains had been precipitated upon the ship. She was buried, lost, extinguished. There were smothered slammings and crashes, and the roaring of a thousand giant waterfalls, pouring, pouring.... Still buried in that sea. She reeled, shaking beneath the blow. She seemed to give up, only to begin struggling quietly again, stifled under the weight, a crushed ship. "She'll never get through this—never," Jane thought. And Davidson? Where was he?... Still the ship was trembling, as though alive, patiently trying to cast the thing off.

She came out of it at last. Jane could only guess how much the ship had suffered for that victory. She could not know that the mainmast had snapped off clean, carrying away with it a ruin of splitting timber, streaming rags of sail, and a whipping tangle of rigging. She had no way of knowing that Stevens, the mate, and two of her sailor friends had lost their lives.

Some time after that a curious release came, a comparative hush, with a low thrashing of seas and a snarling of wind. It was as though the treacherous purpose had been accomplished, and now the elements rested. Jane waited a while, listening; it might have been hours or only seconds. At last she ventured to look out the porthole again. Surely the seas were less now. Or was it only that they seemed less in contrast to that monster which had nearly extinguished them? The water beat less madly against the ship, and crests were not so high. But the ocean itself was closer than before, closer and blacker. There was no sky at all that she could see; nothing except sinister gleams of that black water.

The ship was sluggish now, not rising so promptly to meet the seas. She kept her head down, and let them slam over her with sickening thuds in a dreary rhythm, only shuddering now and then, as if hurt, tired....

The door burst open again, and Captain Maynard stood outside, haggard under his sou'-wester. "We're leaving her," he called hoarsely to Jane; and she knew intuitively that this was the supreme confession of his life.

She stared at him horror-struck. He seemed to be shaking with exhaustion and half-suppressed grief and anger.

"Pack your things and come on deck," he told her. And he was gone, swallowed in the grayness....

Leaving her! That meant she was going down beneath them —that she could bear it no longer and had surrendered. Her struggle was at an end. But—leave her? In the life-boat, of course; but how could any boat live in such a sea?... Pack up her things... in pitch dark with a ship going down under her!... Where was everything, anyway? She found the chest of drawers that was built in under her bunk. Her one small suit-case should be in the lowest drawer—yes, it was. She opened others, and her hands met vaguely recognizable objects—shoes, for instance, and a blouse. She was astonished to find them there, as though they must have gone through some terrible transformation in the course of the night—as though it were strange beyond belief that a shoe should still be a shoe. She put them into the suit-case deliberately, wondering at her ability to do this thing at all.

Then she realized that she was not yet dressed. "I can't go up into the storm in pyjamas," she reasoned deliberately. She slipped into the first clothes that her hand touched—the rebellious red skirt, an old green blouse, an overcoat. She grew calmer and calmer, even began to calculate as to what else she had better look for in the way of personal belongings. There should be a comb about somewhere, for instance. And then there were the books—three or four of them, old companions. Where were they? Lying about on the floor, of course. She would look for them, too, while the ship was going down. One of them had been sliding about in that far corner for some time, but she had not been able to make the effort of reaching it. Now she rescued it, felt it over, recognized it—*Lord Jim*....

She emerged into a world of black wreckage. The *Annie*

Marlow was a battered skeleton, swaying unevenly under the impact of seas that still poured across her decks, tireless in their determination to sweep everything away. Although she could not see the schooner's bow, the forward slant told her that it must be under water most of the time. The poop was comparatively high.

She found her way into the little knot of anxious men who stood with weariness depicted in every gesture and in the droop of their broad shoulders. Someone had a lantern. In their black sou'-westers they faintly resembled a band of monks. Oilskins gleamed occasionally. She tried to look at their faces when the lantern lighted them, and thought she had a glimpse of Davidson, busy with the life-boat, which had a dozen times narrowly missed being smashed or carried away. The ocean was a turbulent waste of black angry water. The *Annie* rolled ceaselessly, as if frantic with exhaustion, like a tormented soul, and at every swing her bow inclined still closer toward the sea that had caught her at last. The captain's face was that of a ghost suffering beyond all mortal words or help.

"Look out! Squall!" came someone's cry. A savage gust enveloped the ship, and a demoniac rush of water came. Jane, who had sought the standing rigging of the jigger mast for something to hold on to, clutched the shrouds with all her strength, and waited. There was a roaring, an almost gleeful howl of wind, a crash somewhere—and then she was falling, falling in the dark through a measureless chasm while the shouting of wind and sea became fainter and fainter, sounding far up above her somewhere, dying away into silence....

She awoke with a sense of peacefulness, and of swinging lightly through space. Of swinging on, poised like a seagull; rushing down rivers of wind, soaring up hills of it—winged and free. Half-seen rainbows, stars, meteors seemed to flit around her, to stream past her. She was one white soul, unencumbered by earthly trash, darting through a friendly sky.

So civilization was lost, was it? Surely there were no chains now—chains of the flesh, chains of the world. Well, it was time some of that perished....

As if the very thought was too rebellious, the air was suddenly full of hard thudding pains that held her with iron fingers. She could see their black wings beating over her, and hear the growling of their voices. She shrank from them; lifted a hand to fend them off. It struck wood—only a mortal hand after all; and her eyes opened straight into an immense sky, black and full of bright, scudding clouds. Nearby loomed a silent figure, rugged in the moonlight. Once, centuries ago perhaps, she knew she had seen that same shape, unstirring and somber—a symbol of the sea.

The sea! She felt and heard it all around her, heaving and whispering. At that feeble tap of her hand, the man, who had been silent as a carved figurehead, seemed to leap into life. Almost instantaneously he was bending over her, looking anxiously into her face. "Jane! Jane! Awake?"

The pains that had possession of her were still beating frenzied black wings together. "You're not one of them, are you?" she wanted to ask, but her voice had fallen into a hollow of the sea.

Davidson gave her a drink of water, out of the little cask in the bow of the boat. His hands trembled. She struggled a minute and sat up, while he steadied her. The illusion of freedom had vanished now. Pathetically mortal and clumsy she was, after all. The sea tore past, slantingly. Great waves toppled high and threatening, changed into abysses almost before they had come. Black and gray waves, gleaming with moonlight, crested with fragments of it. A wild sky, with those white clouds, and the moon racing like a frightened creature through them.

Jane was in the captain's sailing skiff, which had hung beneath the life-boat. It was chasing along like a porpoise. It soared up on to a pinnacle, poised there dancingly, then, with a chuckling of water under the keel, swung into the shifting hollow. This was merely playfulness. There was no danger in the marbled sky, and the wind was light. But there was an illusion of tremendous swiftness, like flying.

"How do you feel?" he asked her after a while. Words were like children's wooden toys that jiggle on an elastic, after the spring has worn out and half the paint has rubbed off, leaving an absurd and doleful expression on their small faces.

And when she answered, her own syllables sounded no less odd, as if English were some weird foreign tongue which they were attempting to speak for the first time. "All right," she quavered—then collapsed against him in a little heap. "Water," she pleaded. "More water."

Davidson was almost holding his breath, as if its motion and sound might send her slipping away from him again. And slowly the black wings ceased their thundering; but they left her bruised and aching from head to foot. "Where—is everyone?" she asked faintly.

"Jane—I don't know."

"Oh, I can't think!" she exclaimed, and put her hands over her eyes.

"Hurt, aren't you?"

"Yes, what did I… something hit me?"

"Great mass of stuff falling…. Wonder you're not—dead. Anything broken?"

"I don't know. Oh, why don't you tell me where we are? Did the ship go down?"

"Don't look so reproachful," was all he said.

"I don't understand," she repeated. "I don't understand anything."

"Neither do I," he told her.

She lay down again in the bottom of the boat, which was just long enough, and looked at the sky. When she stirred, everything crashed and pounded in her body. Davidson sat in the stern, and held under his arm the handle of an oar he was using for rudder. Steering somewhere that cockle-shell with its little white sail—shelterless, without even a compass. He looked old, a trifle grim; always he appeared to hold mystic kinship with the tall gaunt waves. He guided the skiff through them with a subtle, half-tender understanding. He knew them, and the treachery of their natures.

She lay motionless, and tried to think. As her strength came back slowly, she began to remember and to understand. After a while she looked across at Davidson again; and she saw that he was haggard with weariness. His eyes were changed; his teeth were clenched as though their tenseness was holding him up. She tried to move toward him, but could not wrestle with the entangling faintness that would not let her go. The world turned swiftly upside down, and she saw the speeding sea above and the sky below with the moon gliding through those fleece-clouds that looked like Arctic ice floes. When things had righted themselves, she got to the stern of the skiff. Her muscles were trembling; but even then she felt secret exultation because her bones were miraculously intact, and he would not have a cripple on his hands.

"Let me take her—David." She could not remember just what his name was.

"You'd better sleep, Jane."

"Let me take her—please."

He looked at her and smiled a very little, relinquishing the oar to her. "Keep her as she is," he said. "As near east as you can. You can pick out a star ahead—any star you like—your favorite star—only check it now and then by the North Star, because that's the only one that stays put. If the wind changes, call me. And some day we'll get to—God knows where. And—call me—when you're—too tired." He drew a deep breath, shuddering, and curled up his tall frame in the bottom of the boat.

His head leaned toward the forward seat, but he was asleep before he touched it.

Jane sat in the stern and steered with the oar. This *was* no dream, then. The feel of its handle was comforting. It was real. As real as anything ever was. Just now one could not be quite sure. "Keep her as she is." The little sail held steady; she watched it, alert. She would have to bear up. Stars were few and rather dim because of the moon. But old Polaris gave her confidence, when it wasn't in a cloud. For the first time she realized what an abstract thing a direction is. Ashore she took them for granted; usually knew where she was just by a feeling, or by familiar landmarks. At sea there was nothing. A mere star couldn't give you the feeling that a tree could, or a church steeple. Perhaps it did, though, to a sailor. How fortunate that whoever had invented stars had put one in the center of things where it could do nothing but chase its own tail, so to speak, in one spot. That was thoughtful. Otherwise the earth had not done a methodical job in casting off these stars.... What? That was nonsense, of course.... The stars rose up in multitudes and shouted at her all together, reproaching her for impertinence. The universe was a cosmic din. *Careful—Davidson's asleep!...*

It was pretty grim. Davidson looked sick, and she was half delirious. If anything should happen to him—well, then there would be nobody even to mention a star. But he would last. He was made to last a long time. He was dead tired, that was all. How long had he been at this job? For all she knew it might be days and days. How could she tell how long they had been adrift, or how far they had come? There was no record of it on the sea's face. And where were they going? Had he thought, as he set that easterly course, that some day they should land on some shore or other?

She could answer none of this, of course. She could only steer. She steered for hours, and still the night held on. She steered for centuries, and yet the dawn refused to come. She steered for aeons, and the moon hung high. The motion of the little boat was subtle and haunting. The white wing dipped gracefully now and then. And Davidson slept on. She wished he would wake up and be companionable, for it was pretty lonely, this steering a coracle at a bare horizon of sea with nothing but a few stars for friends—the sea under you and the sky over you and the whole world so empty and strange.... And then her thoughts edged back to New York. A phantasmagoric city of diabolical green and gold rose up swiftly and reached out the arms of a monstrous robot. She drew back, the thing faded, and she felt comforted by the simplicity and grandeur of the sea. There was meaning and a kind of beauty—this wistful human effort in a symphony of elements which were perhaps friendly—who could tell?—and certainly were beautiful, sky and peering stars, great restless sea, warm wind of the tropics, and now—a line of gray was beginning to grow over in the east—now the sunrise. She felt exalted, and opened her heart to all this.... And Davidson slept, tired out with his brutal fight against a sea which now had forgotten that brutality.

The exaltation was not without its icicle of fear. As the line of gray brightened, she wondered if she had strength, heart, staunchness, to cope with this and see it through. She steered on, waiting for the sun, longing for a rest, determined not to wake Davidson. Ahead the boat's wing beckoned pensively, ghostlike in the gray. She was more alone in that moment, while he was sleeping, and the sun had not yet quite decided whether it would rise that day, than she had ever been in her life.

Davidson woke with the first rays. He opened his eyes and saw Jane's face in the new white light. The sea looked young again. Jane's face was passive yet triumphant. He marveled, and adored her.

She smiled when she saw he was awake. This was how life could go on—if two people marooned in an open boat could still be cheerful to the sun and each other.... Half standing in the bow, he peered off ahead. There was nothing to be seen, of course. He expected nothing.

"My trick at the wheel, Jane."

He took the oar quietly from her grasp. She shifted cautiously to the bow seat—there was no middle one—and sat clasping her knees with her hands.

"Everything still hurt?" He wished he could replace her aching bones, which weren't good enough for her, with better ones of pure gold.

"Yes, but I'm all right. I can stand it. This soaring gets into one's fiber. I think I'll feel it all the rest of my life. Tell me, where are we bound for?"

"Jupiter, I guess. I'm trying for the coast, of course, but the currents are wrong. I may as well say it—there's so little hope that it would take a magician to see it—and then he'd have to have a microscope."

"So little as that?" she asked with a casual interest that astounded him. It was what she had expected.

He pointed to the tin of biscuits and the breaker of water that lay in the little boat's bow, telling her the whole story without the added harshness of words. She met his glance unwavering.

The sun was beginning to assert its cruelty, but the breeze held. The sea's floor, intense blue, rose and fell swiftly. You looked at its continual hovering and waving, and then turned for relief to the sky, pale and strangely still.

"What's all this about?" Jane asked abruptly.

"What do you think?" He did not move.

"I can't tell—I've never been shipwrecked before," she said. "Only I know I've never been so conscious of the—unreality."

"I'm afraid it's real, Jane—damn real."

"Is anything?"

"Hunger and thirst are, when they get you."

"Isn't there anything edible floating around?" she asked quaintly. "Jellyfish or something? Seems as if there ought to be."

His chuckle was small in that colossal solitude, yet it contained infinite warmth and comradeship. Jane looked at him a moment, and held out her hand. He grasped it as though across an abyss.

Unutterably tired as she was, after all; and bewildered—she wanted to be bewildered, but must hold up for his sake. She crouched in the bottom of the boat, at his feet, and leaned her head ever so little against his knees.

"We'll see it through, won't we, Jane? Together."

Davidson was greater than the sea, master of it. A cliff, rugged and furrowed by storm and tide, but dominating both. An oak-tree that no gale could break, though it made a mighty harp of the branches. Death was a nothingness, danger a wisp of thistledown upon the wind, and civilization had never existed at all. Nothing could hurt him. He was eternal.

"Sure, we'll see it through."

The material world had given way. It was weak and paltry, and it was unimportant. But Davidson was *there*. He was real, and could be counted on. The simplicity of his acceptance, and the strength of his passiveness, could never be shaken, by time or suffering or despair or death.

[8]

Long afterwards Davidson was to remember a certain moment on the *Annie Marlow*'s poop deck as the most dire moment of his life. In times of stress he would compare his trouble to that past horror, and sigh with relief. That was the ultimate. Nothing the world could do to him would ever approach the intensity of it. Thinking of it, he would feel impervious to discouragement, money, life. He never regretted having seen the bottom of the pit of despair, for it served as armor and shield. It was the moment when he realized that Jane was not there with the others.

They were lowering the life-boat in the thick of fiendish confusion. In the uproar of squall and rain that had suddenly descended as if released from long imprisonment, the sea was like the inside of a volcano in eruption.

The men had been pumping hard most of the night, and were exhausted and bleary-eyed. That was why he had forgotten to look for her, make sure that she was with them. And now it was too late. Now they were launching the life-boat, and the schooner was sinking.

It was the captain who bawled out anxiously: "Miss Jane there?"

Someone's voice answered faintly: "No, sir!"

Davidson shouted in anguish: "I'll get her!" and, snatching a lantern, he had dashed away from the others.

"There's no time! God, there's no time!" the men protested in a despairing chorus.

The schooner was rolling her decks full of water, and each shuddering heave seemed her last.

"Wait!" Captain Maynard quietly commanded.

But they rebelled. Hours on end they had fought for the ship and for their lives; were they to be denied at the last their one little chance of escape? And for what? One more life—a girl who had probably been swept overboard anyway? Maddened with terror, intensified by the loss of the first mate, they had forgotten all discipline. They forgot even their shipmate Davidson. During "flyin'-fish weather" they were passable sailors; it was in a crisis like this that it became obvious to what pitiful degree of inadequacy the seafaring profession had fallen.

By main force they carried their captain to the life-boat, and launched her. She wheeled dizzily on a great black pinnacle, and then fell into unthinkable depths. At the same instant the ship vanished from them, and they could see nothing but turbulent blackness....

Davidson knew none of this. He knew only that he was hunting for Jane, and that he would never leave that sinking ship unless he found her. His life was for her, with her; and he had not known it until now, when perhaps she was lost to him forever.

He flayed himself without mercy for not having been more careful of her. A stupid brute.... For all he knew, she had been lost overboard. But he would not believe that. He would believe that she was here somewhere, and he would find her. And he would never leave without her. That thought gave him a curious calmness, a sense of quietude.

"Jane! Oh, Jane!" He held up the lantern again. Nothing.

Could she have gone down below? Below decks it was up to his waist, almost, in water. He got to her cabin at last, calling her. Nothing. Only the mournful slamming of a door somewhere, the creaking of the ship, water sloshing, seas hammering, wind lamenting. He called again, agonized. The water mocked him.

Never leave the ship without her. That was something to hold to—a purpose, at least. He had nearly deserted her once. The horror of that! But it would be atoned now.... The ship was shuddering, giving way to the sea; but still she fought a little, numb with terror and weariness.

His mind became clear and steady. He climbed out on deck again in a leisurely manner, preferring to die in the open; and as he tramped up the companionway stairs he tried to picture Jane as he had seen her last. Where had she been? He made powerful, deliberate efforts to remember, and suddenly it seemed that in the light of a swinging lantern he caught a glimpse of her holding on to the rigging with both hands as a voice rang out: "Squall!" The jigger rigging... starboard side...

Nothing but a tangle of wreckage there. The topmast had snapped in that squall, and come hurtling down with whatever running gear had not been blown away before. Was she in that awful heap, then—mangled, crushed?... Never leave without her—never leave.... He shoved something aside, and wire rope spat at his bare hands viciously. He wrestled with it. There was—a piece of topsail, most likely—a faint suggestion of something white in under there. And then he saw that it was Jane's upturned throat.

He got her out of there at last. He had lifted her up in his arms, and her head fell back limply. There was no doubt in the world that she was dead. Her face was that of a little girl lost and lonely, wistful beyond words. He stroked aside the tangles of her hair, but she could not feel his gentleness, or know his sad triumph. He had come back for her, and found her....

During all this he had been too absorbed to notice the absence of the crew. Now he stood looking over the edge of the poop with Jane in his arms, wondering if he were possessed by some fiendish hallucination. The life-boat was not there, that was all. He stood like a man in a dream. The *Annie Marlow* herself awoke him. For she was trembling hard, lowering her bow steadily, and going down, down....

It was not until then that he remembered the captain's skiff, with the dismounted mast and boom that the old man had made himself, with which he used to amuse himself in the quiet harbors. He leaped at this one dim chance, working fast in the dark, always believing that in another second he would feel the rush and suck of the whirlpool. And it seemed that hardly more than one swift heart-beat after he had launched the skiff, with Jane lying in it, the ship gave a great sigh and slipped into the hollow that rose in tumult and came together over her. It was like the extinguishing of a light. She was there no more. There was only the sea.

Much to Davidson's surprise, the boat lived through that night. The mast and boom lay in the bottom of it, and to one side, projecting a couple of feet over the bow. Davidson unlashed the little sail from between them, and folded it over Jane, trying to protect her from the smashing clouds of spray. He steadied the boat with an oar. Between seas he bailed with his sou'-wester. He felt the waves diminishing, and saw the dawn come. The sea was an ancient cornfield of gray and battered stubble, rough and unkempt. The sunrise was a smear of ambiguous lighter color. That was east, then. It was the first he had known or even suspected of direction for many hours. Rain had stopped, and the skiff rode the waves without taking parts of them over her small bow. Daylight had brought relief.

He took the sail from Jane's body, and looked into her face. She was white and lost, and they were awesomely alone. The sea and the world had forgotten them long ago. Perhaps the sea and the world were right. There was no way of telling whether he himself was really alive. There was no one to ask, and nothing to believe in.... Was Jane breathing? No, the boat's motion... For all he knew, there might be no sharp demarcation between life and death. Maybe this was their passage through eternity. Desolate sort of eternity, though.

He set up the mast. It was a solemn rite. The boat would drift about aimlessly in the gray wash no longer. The little sail flapped pitifully as he released it, like a soft white creature suddenly put out in the open by itself, and frightened; then it steadied as though it had got over the worst of its trouble. The boat steadied a good deal, too. Feeling the tiller, she stepped out determinedly, with a purpose. She could go on now, for someone was steering.

All that day he sat there alone. In his terrible solitude he saw the setting of the sun and the stealthy falling of dark, all the while watching over the body of the woman he loved. Then at last she had awakened....

THEY GAVE all their strength to this fight, yet that strength was pitifully small, and it dwindled with the supply of biscuits and water. Those little crumbs lasted several days, but at last were gone—"weevils and all," Davidson declared. Hunger was not the most painful enemy. The worst of that was over. Nothing was left of it except increasing weakness and weariness. It seemed to Jane as though her body were held together by a few very taut elastic bands. But when the water was gone. ...

They lost all sense of time, of course. There was no time to count, in this long blue torture. They watched the sky in despair, longing for the blessed cool wetness of rain. Even the wind had despaired, exhausted. A few languid zephyrs rippled the sail now and then. All hope of progressing anywhere was shattered by this tropic calm. Sometimes they took down the sail and used it for shelter against the sun....

"Is there a chance we shall be picked up?" Jane asked.

"Yes—a very little one."

"What do you think about dying, Daveson. Better, maybe?"

"How?" he asked.

"We might jump overboard. Swim, and swim —and—swim..."

"I can't swim," he told her. "And anyway, I want to hold out for that little chance. I want to live."

"So do I."

She played her part determinedly, faithfully. When she complained it was in jest. Civilization? Well, a soda-fountain, perhaps. But there were no such compromises. It seemed that she had been swallowing red-hot embers. Another day or two crept by, and they still steered watch and watch, shipmates. Davidson's cheeks were hollow, and his eyes blazed. Soon she realized that her voice was useless. She could not speak above a painful, half-choked whisper. No, there were no compromises. She wished she could talk with him, if only a little. Their scraps of conversation had been precious.

"Daveson, do you believe in God?" she had asked once, as they exchanged the oar.

"I don't believe in anything on earth, still less anything off it."

They, and the oar, were floating in a blue void.

"God was hammered—and—hammered—into my head years ago," Jane pursued. "But I rebelled. I didn't like Him. Not their little God, anyhow."

"I believe in you," Davidson faltered.

That was the last coherent conversation. Every time he woke her, it was harder for her to move. It came like a rough intrusion. She had to struggle up against the weakness that held her crushed flat underfoot in the bottom of the boat—the burden that was each time harder to throw off. Sometimes she wondered whether it was worth the fight. Why not just lie there and die? The restfulness of death! But Davidson's face, tormented with weariness and starvation, would make her remember. Until the last, her small strength was promised.

She lost all sense of gravity. The world would not pause. It was a pulsing whirl of hot blue, with Davidson's face somewhere in its eddies. She could scarcely hold the oar, while the sea poured back and forth and the sky wheeled. The sail looked old and haggard, too, as frail as though the merest puff might make it melt away into air. It seemed to be made of no real solid material. She could see no recognizable world. But she held on to what there was. She steered a while, then found a shadow bending over her. Her hand did not know enough to let go of the oar of its own accord, until it was taken from her. She slept, then, until the relentless shadow came again to wake her. That was in the desolate hours some time after midnight. She steered again—a small, worn-out ghost.

The end of strength came with terrifying suddenness, as if all her muscles had agreed to surrender together from their feeble hold, and had left her unsustained. Dizzily the oar eluded her grasp. She kept it from sliding into the sea. It was her last effort. She felt a sense of victory, as if with that faint gesture she had saved the boat. The oar was safe. It was all she could do.

"David!" she said faintly, in an agonized whisper; and slipped forward, helpless. She could steer his course no longer. He roused himself from his half-sleep; and as he touched her she gave him a tiny wisp of a parched smile.

"Shipmate," he whispered, so faintly that she scarcely heard him. He took the oar, and bent over her. Her head was on his knees....

Then he felt a coolness about him, as though a wind had sprung up; and the air surrounding him was brighter. Struggling, he raised his head and looked. Yes, the dawn was coming. It was light. The east was like a ship with immense rose-colored sails. Dawn? What good was the dawn? Beauty. It could give them that while Jane's life faded—his own, too, soon enough.

With a sudden wildness, he stared ahead; and kept on gazing fixedly into the sunrise, incredulous and awed, wondering why his eyes were playing such tricks. Then, very gently, he roused Jane. With awful weariness she lifted her head, and he felt remorse at having disturbed her to share this insane delusion. He pointed; she looked out ahead, and he felt a quiver run through her.

Sometimes it happens that, just as you have reconciled yourself, after long struggle, to some harsh decision the world has made upon you, these seemingly unalterable circumstances may alter, as though a black curtain had been raised to reveal a gleaming stage.... Sometimes, after a Nantucket sea captain's wife has strained her eyes for days from the look-out on the roof for the sails of the schooner long overdue, just as she has abandoned herself to a grief so benumbing, a torture so exquisite, that the world has no room to hold it—sometimes he comes home.... And sometimes, when two people are dying together in an open boat, hundreds of miles from any known land, the sea and sky form a prodigious magic, and dawn clouds lift from an enchanted island.

It showed through rifts in the rose and gold clouds, almost as ethereal as they. In that mystic light, land and mist were jumbled in a glowing mountainous heap of colors, and over them was the tense sky thronged with still brightening feathers of cloud. The very water beneath the keel of the skiff was alive and magical; and the little boat herself seemed to be holding her breath. A marvellous iridescence came over the island, a gleam of pale gold and lavender, of green and soft blue, intermingled subtly, woven with the wings of crimson mist. The sea was silver-blue, and the island drifted between it and the sky, gleaming like a fire-opal.

Wild-eyed, Davidson stared at the fusion of those colors. It was ineffable loveliness given at a moment of despair and surrender. It was hope and happiness and beauty, coming together at a time when he was sure they were all completely lost. He had always held, deep down, an obscure faith in life—that you could live without being forever disillusioned, that sometimes you were given a piece of beauty unchallenged and untroubled—"a woodpile without a nigger," he said to himself—that there were some few remnants of a good old-fashioned fairy-tale magic left, to live for. This passage in the open boat had shaken that faith. He had deliberately accused it, face to face, of being a tinseled liar; he had chucked it overboard and watched it sink. And now, here was a living proof, a symbol, of that faith; it had been quietly drifting along with him all the time—or perhaps, perverse creature, was merely following him because he had abandoned it—and now a score of ardent voices clamored in his heart to say that he had not been wrong after all.

The mist-screen lifted and broke here and there, showing a green peninsula with a tuft of feathery palm trees; then a soft abyss of blue velvet between two gilded ridges; a sharp purple mountain with red clouds hovering about its peak. Clouds and island were still half-melted together, half-submerged in an ocean of colored light.

The sun cast gold spears radiating upward through the colors, making them paler, making clouds stand separate from the land, and the land look more real and substantial. In a few more moments the sea was its own clear blue once more, the clouds had drifted clear, and ahead of the exhausted pair in the open boat was a real earthly island, as though sea and sky and sun had created it at that very moment expressly for them, seeing and rescuing them in their direst need.

All this time Jane had never spoken or moved. Only now she looked up at him, smiling as much as her blackened and tortured lips would allow. The magic should not be tarnished with a few choking words. She leaned her head against his knees again, and that small gesture of companionship was an eloquent thanksgiving to the sea and to him....

They remembered little else of that day. They had crept from the skiff and fallen in warm pinkish sand. The beach rose at a rather steep slant to a forest fringed with palms. They staggered up into cool fragrant shade, and found a few coconuts, fallen before they were ripe. Davidson had one tool—his jackknife. It took all his strength to cut through the green husk.... Water, milky and cool, and the soft white jelly that lined the shell of the unripe coconut—this was their first food. They opened another, and moistened their faces with its water.... There were flickering shadows and shearing lights, fragrances, and an odd poise to the universe.

The island was kind. It seemed to understand their plight. Its long crescent of a beach had welcomed them like an enchanted threshold. At its south end it tapered into a low green peninsula, lacy with palms, and at its very tip two magnificent ones leaned out over the sea, heads together. Sometimes they were two plotting mischief-makers, sometimes two lovers. To the north, the beach gave place to rocks, and finally rose in cliffs that were like the crude castle of a giant.

Behind the circle of coconut palms that edged the beach, the forest was not dense, although it was luxuriant. It was a friendly forest, with few harsh brambles and thick creepers. Its floor was covered with mosses and small vines and flowers, broken by clumps of ferns, some nearly as tall as Davidson, yet delicately feathered as frost on a window-pane. Flowering trees threw brightness and fragrance among the more sober green of mangoes and breadfruit. Some of these flowering trees had immense clusters of flame-red flowers; some were white; some pink like apple-blossoms. And there was a modest white flower with the fragrance of a marvellous wine. But far more important to the shipwrecked pair were papaia trees, with their fantastic clusters of big, smooth-skinned yellow fruit, easily reached; and alligator pears, guavas, bananas, and pale wild oranges.

There was nothing to do but rest in silence, and nibble cautiously at the fruits, a few of which they collected by almost superhuman effort. They felt very sick. That weary writhing of the little boat haunted their muscles. In spite of being starved, it was hard to swallow anything. They lay on the beach all day and all the next day almost without speaking. The sea whispered at the edge of the sand, and the big palm fronds rustled.

Jane could do nothing but dream, and her thoughts edged back softly but not understandingly over her life. This was too different from anything she had known or conceived, for her to understand it. Not so long ago the perpetual dust of Professor Myers' office threatened to be her only atmosphere, perhaps forever. That dust! There was none here. Where was she now?... There had been Millie, gay and heartless, and other friends, apparently always in trouble, whom she had sistered. There had been disillusionments, mountain-high. Your voice could laugh, but sometimes your soul didn't. It stayed underneath and languished. She was hurt to find life made up of so many *little* things. At first she believed most faithfully that they had a deeper meaning and a coherent larger purpose; but after a while she saw to her dismay that the deeper and larger things were merely shadows cast by the small. So she buried the whole great treasure of winged dreams and iridescent shades under an oak-tree in the farthest corner of her heart, and planted a bush of wild roses over it. A small grave of dreams. Secretly and silently she buried them, a little ashamed, as a burglar might be who had long pursued some gleaming ruby necklace, and, having by infinite stealth and risk obtained it, found that it was red glass.

After that burial—now that the world had jolted her down to its own level—she had gone straight ahead with life, not liking it very well, but liking a few of the ways it had and some of the friends it had given her. She tried, serenely and patiently, to help them a little, to give them something of herself and of a curious wisdom she had evolved; yet she had a dim vision of herself always standing a bit aloof from them after all, half-smiling—a little gray goddess with dull brown hair. And that would have been her life.

But, because she wasn't gray enough, after all—she had missed it by a shade—there came the red skirt and the *Annie Marlow*. Where was that poor ship now? She thought of dark green sea-caverns, and the slow waving of great fishes' tails, deliberate and soft and half-seen in dimness, coming and going and interweaving.... And then that good-hearted crew, and old Captain Maynard. Where were they? Drifting around somewhere in the life-boat, starving and suffering and dying? A shudder... She herself had come so near the edge of a great granite cliff overhanging a valley of black and purple shadows....

And then, Davidson, who had saved her life, for whom she was beginning to feel something like earnest adoration. He was still a mystery. His sense of values and appreciation of the poetic side of life were sometimes a little hard to reconcile with the sea. Strange that he could come to her straight out of this sea, in all the grandeur of his simplicity, and understand her, when not one of the friends whose lives had been more like hers could come so near.

Thinking of him, all at once she wanted him. That, also, was new—the feeling that she needed companionship. He was stretched out beside her in the shade; and she spoke to him. "Daveson, have you got another orange over there? I honestly can't move, to speak of."

"I'm trembly, too."

"I like having you around," she said. "My thoughts wabble so. How's your state of mind?"

"Haven't any."

"I was thinking—about the others—wondering what happened."

"No one'll ever know, I guess. I'm afraid they never got anywhere, Jane. And I'm sure I don't understand why we did."

"I'm curious to know where we got to," she said.

"Well, as far as I know, no land has any business to be here."

"Could it be the coast?"

"We were hundreds of miles from the coast when we were wrecked," he told her, "and you know how much progress we made in the skiff."

"An island, then."

"Must be. Perhaps it's Atlantis. Some day we'll explore."

"Do you really have hopes that we'll ever be all right again?"

"Well, I don't feel any worse, do you?"

"I feel like a starfish," Jane said. "A sick starfish...."

"Maybe we're dead. I don't know."

"The other world doesn't seem to exist," she went on. "I've been thinking about it a long time, trying to figure out which of them is the dream."

"Don't you believe there's room for both of 'em?"

"I don't know. It doesn't seem likely. If we survive this, we may find out."

"Be a shame if we didn't survive, having stuck it out this long."

"Yes. I want to. I'm going to try to. What shall we do? Do you think we'll be rescued, or what?"

"Maybe there are people around," he said. "We'll explore, when we can. Maybe we'll have to make out here a while."

"There seems to be stuff to eat growing round."

"Yes; we won't starve. And another thing. I've got matches.

Waterproof container in the biscuit tin. Probably O.K. We can build fires, to keep warm, if it ever gets cold here, and to cook things."

"What things?"

"Well, breadfruit, for instance. Isn't one supposed to roast breadfruit? I'm not an expert in the field of tropical cooking, but I know we can't exist very healthily on just fruit."

"What is breadfruit, then?"

"Potato-y stuff, I think."

"I believe it will all be sort of natural to me," Jane suggested. I've camped out a lot."

"Without a tent? Without any blankets, cook-pots, or a single useful implement of any kind, except a knife? This isn't a summer vacation, Jane."

"S'pose there are wild beasts around?"

"Might be. Almost certain to be poisonous snakes. Furthermore, in the tropics there's always fever, and no quinine within a thousand miles."

But in spite of this dismal note, Jane could not seem to come to grips with reality. She was conscious only of a dreamy peace.

"I didn't mean to frighten you, Jane. Likely nothing that happens to us here can seem very bad after the boat. I just don't want you to get the idea that our troubles are over, or that this is a ready-made fairy-tale paradise, that's all."

As evening came, a thousand shrill-voiced crickets burst into chorus, and bat-wings swooped overhead. A new breath of subtle fragrance came from the island that had sheltered them—the fragrance of tangles of jasmine flowers. Stars came, and the great fans of palm trees stirred softly. Davidson slept near her. It was not a ready-made, fairy-tale paradise. But she knew of nowhere in the world she would rather be.

[9]

They might almost have spent their lives in that one corner of the long beach, exchanging low-voiced conversation, moving only in order to shake low-drooping branches of an orange tree, or pull down another banana. But on the afternoon of the fourth day, black clouds began to pile up over the sea. Leaves rustled and shivered, turning up their pale lower sides. Jane and Davidson had moved slowly along the beach, with the vague idea of finding shelter from the threatening rain somewhere in the woods or cliffs.

Davidson pointed. "Maybe we can crawl in under that big rock that leans outward. Up there near the top of the cliff."

"If we can get up to it," Jane said.

Getting up was not so hard as it looked. They had edged around tidal pools fringed with seaweed, climbed giant steps, crept along narrow ledges, peered into dim crevices. Almost straight below, the sea rose and fell with lazy, swaying rhythm. It seemed blue beyond anything that blue could be. Farther back, along by the beach, it changed abruptly to clear blue-green; and sea urchins could be distinctly seen, very black and bristly against the magic of flickering lights on the sand. Higher and higher they climbed, among sharp black pinnacles, up-thrust turrets of rock, easily three hundred feet above the sea; and, always exploring, searching for shelter, they had come on to a broad level shelf just below the forest. Here, almost entirely concealed by giant ferns and flowering vines which drooped down fringily from above and nearly met the ferns, they found the entrance to a cave.

They pushed flowers aside, and stepped in cautiously. Davidson himself could easily stand erect under the arched ceiling. The cave was cool and green and soft with moss. When their eyes were used to the gloominess, they could see, in the rock walls, gleams and sparkles of mica. A little lizard, of a non-committal color, with bright alert eyes and a long tail, ran up one wall, paused to look at his visitors, and ran on to the ceiling, where he clung and continued to eye them upside-down. With a keen cry, a white-winged bird flashed by outside, and carried away the last of the sunlight; for a moment later black clouds were upon the island, and the cliffs were lost in rain.

"I'm tired—tired beyond words," Jane said suddenly, in a faint voice.

"Well, no wonder; that was quite a climb for two ancient mariners."

"I thought I was all right again, and strong, almost."

"You're doing grand—just grand, Jane."

Some parts of the floor were damp, but for the most part it was fairly dry. They lay down in the moss; and quite simply he put his arms around her and held her close to him. She lay still, and thought about him, who had protected her so valiantly through storm and shipwreck, hunger and despair, fear and sickness. She was content. That she should be lying in his arms was too natural even to wonder about. In some far-away corner of her consciousness, the fleeting thought occurred to her that some day they would be lovers. But even that was nothing to wonder very much about. It, also, would be natural as the sunrise....

"Well," she said, "it's beginning to look as if we were marooned, Daveson. We've been here four days, and not a trace of anybody."

"We've got to depend on ourselves, I guess," he said.

"What would you think of making this cave permanent headquarters—home, sort of? Be nice to have a home, wouldn't it?" She chuckled. "We might lose this castaway feeling—this dreamy feeling of belonging nowhere and nothing being real."

"It's a good cave, as caves go," Davidson admitted. "Sure, I'd just as soon be a caveman. Time's going backwards: we'll be our own Neolithic ancestors."

"That's just what some scientific expedition will think, when it discovers your bones," Jane put in. "You'll get stuck in a museum, Daveson—Exhibit Y. Rather interesting thought, the vulgar mob gawping at your large bones—you who like to be the most inconspicuous person in the world!"

"How about you?" he retorted. "Remember, I'll have company in that glass case. You'll be right alongside. 'Caveman's Girl Friend'; or, maybe, 'Male and Female of Missing Link.'"

"Sure, I'll stick by you," she promised solemnly. "But in the mean time, I don't see how our Neolithic ancestors could ask for a better cave. Cool. High up with the wind and birds. A little damp in spots, I admit. We can lug the sail up from the boat, and sleep on that, and my overcoat. A little darksome and gloomy, of course...."

"We'll shove some of those vines back out of the way," he suggested. "Be a heap lighter, then."

Jane was awed into momentary silence at the almost dizzying realization of how this rock-bound "home" of theirs was suspended far above a rumbling sea, while the eternal forest grew on its very roof.

"It doesn't look as if life was going to be so difficult and dangerous," she said presently. "We've already found food and water and shelter, and we haven't been devoured by lions, that I know of.... I'm looking forward to exploring, when I'm strong enough."

"And I've a couple of ideas I want to chew over some more," Davidson said. "When I was a kid, I read *Candide*, and was specially tickled by the very end of it. 'Cultivate your garden.' It rang true. It still does. That philosophy covers just about everything. If we're really stuck here, we could do worse than have a try at a garden."

"Waste of time round here," Jane objected. "The whole island's one immense garden already."

"But we could collect things together a bit. Go hunting yams, for instance, and okra, and such truck—transplant 'em—get a lot of 'em together in one convenient place."

"Bet you wouldn't know a yam if you saw one."

"Well, that remains to be seen. Read up a bit about that sort of thing, once. And there's always the good old method of trial and error."

"You'll need a couple of tools," she reminded him. "A shovel, and a hoe, and..."

"I'll make 'em," he said. "What are my hands for, anyway? I kind of want to use my hands again. You see, being stranded here is—well, sort of a challenge. Hard to explain... a challenge to one's ingenuity and sense of humor, and everything else. And I want to see what I can make of it. I guess it's just an ordinary male reaction—I don't know."

"Why don't you turn hydraulic engineer?" she suggested. "Find out where the water drips in from—dry out the cave a bit."

"That's one thing," he agreed, "and another is fishing. Without any equipment. How to go about it kind of baffles me. It eggs me on. I keep wondering about it. Nets? How to make nets? Coconut fiber? Spears? Could I learn to spear fish the way the South Sea islanders do? You see, it's all pretty difficult and interesting to think about."

"You're dreadfully ambitious for a person so recently shipwrecked," Jane told him, with faint protest in her voice. "I admire you, but you make me feel tireder than ever."

He chuckled. "Oh, I'm not going to begin tomorrow," he assured her. "I'm just thinking ahead, that's all. Fun to lie here thinking of all the things you're *not* going to do tomorrow. We can afford to lazy round and think.... You know, I've a hunch we'll be here quite a long time."

"I don't mind confessing I'm glad," said Jane.

"Not frightened?"

"Not very. I don't believe I care a bit whether we're rescued or not."

He drew a sigh, as if of relief. "Neither do I," he agreed. "If it doesn't take too much effort to keep alive, I think there may be some peace here—and I've tried to find peace all my life. And she thought his arms tightened a little, just as she fell asleep.

In the morning, the cave was filled with shimmering, elusive light. It silvered the tips of tall ferns that stood sentinel at the opening; it was reflected in blue and green and gold sparkles from the scales of the little lizard, who had shifted his position until he clung at the very rim of daylight, half outside the cave. Jane and Davidson got up lazily from the moss, and went to the threshold of their front door. They were in a high world, from where they could look straight out into the wonder of a new morning. The towers and pinnacles of rock, yesterday so desolate in the impending rain, were touched with magic, and at their feet the sea glistened with a new and younger blue.

"Let's explore today—I think I really feel like it, at last," Jane said.

Davidson was leaning against the front of the cave, looking at her. The sun glinted on her long tangled brown hair, made it shine with little twists of gold; and her face was young and eager. The pale, pinched look was fading slowly away. She turned, and their eyes met. Both smiled.

"Yes," he said at last. "We'll explore. But first—breakfast."

They pushed between the ferns on one side of the cave mouth; and by climbing a steep ledge, clutching the thick vines that fell across it, digging their toes into small crannies, they were able to get up to the level of the forest, and stood triumphantly on the roof of their dwelling-place. Then they went into the woods in different directions, to hunt breakfast.

Leaves sprinkled wet pearls as Jane brushed through them. They were a great diverse population. There were soft lacy ones that drooped graciously, little lithe aspiring ones that grew tensely upward, long slender grayish ones, big triangular glossy ones—every shade of green and gray-green and yellow-green, blended together subtly in a chorus of colors. They were conversing, too, these leaves, in a language of almost imperceptible nods and stirrings and secret smiles, and slight flickerings where golden ethereal beads of light broke into green mercury over edges and tips and stems.

Jane found her heart hammering so hard that it shook her, and she did not feel the twigs and branches of undergrowth against her face. "What is it?" she asked tensely; and answered herself: "I guess I'm getting well; I'm in love!" And she began to run, back toward the deeper woods—running away from the intensity of her own feelings, running to find a quiet corner where she could rest and think, all alone. She leaned against a tree, to catch her breath. This quiet soothed her. A green smell came from the moss and ferns. Earth. Flowers starred the little glade here, and every petal of every flower was an entire world. A solitary cricket cheeped nearby—a small golden cry of life.

She felt wild and ethereal, part of the woods. She stretched out her hands, and leaves met them caressingly. They rustled a little as a fragrant breath of wind strayed through. The woods were singing now. There were a thousand small glimmering things stirring in her heart—and a deep, persistent calling, like waves.

Slowly, out of a mist of confused happiness, she became aware of another calling, of Davidson's voice: "Janie! Where are you?"

They perched on the edge of the cliff, and nibbled their fruit. It was gay, spitting an occasional orange-seed far out into blue mid-space.

"Davidson!"

"What, Janie?"

"Got your knife?"

"Sure."

"Well, cut off my hair, will you?"

"No, I like your hair."

"Well, cut off some of it, then. It's hot and heavy and tangled. I haven't anything to comb it with, and it gets in my eyes, and it's thoroughly messy and uncomfortable."

"I see your point, but I hate to."

"Go ahead! Courage! I want to swim today."

"Swim? Are you up to that?"

"Of course I'm up to it. In fact, I'm crazy for it. So be a good shipmate, and cut it off. I want to feel the wind on the back of my neck."

He opened the jackknife that had stood by him through the thick and thin of several years, and took hold of a bunch of Jane's long hair.

"Does this mean—" he stopped to ask—"that I'm going to have to try and shave, or anything like that?"

"Of course not. I think your tawny beard is getting exceedingly picturesque."

"It must be."

"What do we care how we look?" she demanded. "For the first time in our lives, it doesn't make any difference." She looked at him, and the sweeping realization came over her of the full import of this. "Do you realize how grand it is?" she questioned. Her eyes gleamed with eagerness. "There are no mirrors, Davidson! We're free of them. Oh, mirrors are one of the worst things about a hateful civilization. No *mirrors!* Do you realize the glory of that? Do you realize what it means?… It means I can be beautiful, for the first time in my life!" she burst out triumphantly.

Davidson smiled. "I've always thought you were beautiful," he said simply.

She laughed at him, secretly afire with inexpressible joy. Then she shook her head, serious again. "No," she said. "Always, before, I've been plain—plain old plain-Jane. I've had friends, and they liked me, but nobody ever thought I was anything but plain. I couldn't get away from that, and accepted it, all my life. I never cared or worried very much. But now, all of a sudden—I don't know why—I *want* to be beautiful. And I *am*—because—well, because I feel that way. That's enough—here, where there are no mirrors. I feel like the island itself—shining and iridescent.… Come on, get busy on my hair!"

Reluctantly he plunged into it, holding small bunches of it firmly in one hand, and slashing with the knife. It was a slow and difficult job, but before it was finished quite a lot of Jane's hair managed to get free and blow merrily out to sea. What was left looked pretty ragged, but he saw that she was right about it, and not only from the practical point of view. Short in front so that it could not get in her eyes, it allowed new lines of neck and forehead and cheeks to be revealed; it made her look younger, more carefree, like a gipsy princess behaving rather naughtily and happy about it. The last traces of the old Jane were gone.

She shook her head, feeling it, ruffling up her hair, letting the wind stir it. "Wonderful!" she exclaimed. "Thanks, shipmate. And now let's go."

The coral sand on the beach below was shiny and hard, in some places snow-white, in others shading to pink and purplish.

The sea was a thousand colors, changing and shifting subtly. Waves rushed at the beach, blue, shading to green, glinting with red, and—for a magic second at the break—pure gold.

"I'm going to strip," she said. "Don't know why I haven't before. Modesty in mixed company, I s'pose. But I don't want to be modest any more."

"Better be careful!" he warned. "I've never seen a naked woman. There's no telling what it may do to me."

"You're a sailor, and you tell me that!"

"It's the truth," he said.

"But it's amazing. How did it happen?"

"I don't know," he mumbled. "Always been shy, I guess. Sort of steered clear."

"No amorous escapades in your whole career?" she asked, still incredulous.

"Sure; when I was in grammar school I carried a little girl's books for her; and when I told her I was going to run away to sea, she cried."

"And afterwards? At sea?"

"Well, the other chaps had plenty of stories to tell, but they didn't sound like anything I wanted. They got their money stolen and acquired diseases."

"And so," Jane repeated slowly, "you've never seen a naked woman. S'pose you can stand the shock?"

"Well, I don't guarantee the results."

"I won't hold you responsible, then," she said. "But I'm a confirmed nudist and sun-worshipper."

"I think I'm going to be, too."

"That's another thing I missed in New York."

"There are roofs," he said.

"There are also airplanes," she reminded him. "Well, let's have a ceremony. Strip together, and bury the remnants in some special place, as an offering to the sun."

But the wiser Davidson objected. "It can be cold in the tropics," he warned her. "We'd better save 'em. Stick 'em back in the cave; out of sight, if you like."

Jane unlaced her shoes, and kicked them far and wide.

"Probably a good idea to retrieve them, too," he said. "Though I hate to spoil the fun."

"You know, you've made me almost self-conscious," she protested. "What if I don't come up to long-cherished expectations?"

"That's the least of my worries," he said; "and anyway, I won't hold you responsible."

"Well, then, off with them! Here's to the sun!"

She was lithe and well-muscled, with strong shoulders, deep chest, and a straight back like a young boy's. There were still a good many bruises on her body, and she was too thin from days of starvation: there were shadows between her ribs.

She flung up her arms, in the rapture of feeling wind and sun against her skin; and, tossing back her short hair with a new careless gesture, she ran down the beach a little way before dashing into the sea that waited for her—hungrily, Davidson thought, tense with desire.

Her swimming was easy and agile, with leisurely grace: face in the sea, hair floating loose like seaweed, elbows arched one after another, arms and shoulders gleaming silver for an instant at each stroke, body rolling a little from side to side—a finished "crawl." The water was warm silk.

But she was soon tired. She lay floating on her back, gazing at the domed roof of the blue world in which she was imprisoned. The sea's almost imperceptible long swells cradled her. Then, with a slower stroke, she swam out two or three hundred feet more. Looking straight down through the wavering blue crystal atmosphere, she could see a garden of ivory castles, purple fans, chiseled coral boulders, and companies of bright little fish, sometimes holding still as though preserved in blue glass, sometimes darting with a suddenness that was like a conjurer's trick: they were there, poising on their jeweled fins; and then there was space where they had been—that was all she saw.

She swam back slowly to shore. By now the sand was almost too hot to walk on. She walked on the edges of her tender bare feet, curling up her toes a little. But except for that, and a sense of unusual well-being, she was not in the least self-conscious, which only added to her happiness.... "Davidson! There are corals deep down—wonderful caves and towers and palaces; and little fish that make you think a rainbow somewhere has burst into millions of pieces, and the pieces have come alive."

"What a mermaid you are!" he observed.

"Why don't you come out and see?"

"Don't you know that sailors can't swim?" he asked. "It's one of the incongruities they all have in common."

"That's ridiculous," was her verdict.

"It may be ridiculous, but it's true."

"Well, then, I'll teach you. It's the grandest feeling I know."

"You rest a while first," he warned her. "And don't get too much sun at first. You'll turn into a red ember."

"Grandpa!" she mocked.

"Maybe so, but I'm going to watch out for you, shipmate. You aren't any ox yet, you know. I could play a tune on those ribs of yours."

"I s'pose you're right." She threw herself down, still glistening, on the sand beside him, and lay breathing deeply, arms above her head. "I've never in my life swum in water that was so —beautiful," she told him. "Beautiful—beautiful—I use that trite old word again and again. But it means something, here. You understand me when I say it, don't you, Daveson? We'll give back to that beaten and trampled-on poor old word all the meaning it ought to have, and more. More, Daveson, because beauty will be our religion, our new god—this island's god."

"Thought it was the sun we were worshipping."

"Oh, there are quantities of gods," Jane informed him. "The sun is one of the biggest and best. But to me they're all subordinates—essential fragments of the one supreme one, which is Beauty. It's beauty we live on, after all. Without it we'd starve and die a horrible death, spiritually. The hunger for it is the one thing all life has in common. It may not be recognized as that, and it may have very different forms. I think that's the answer to those indefinable yearnings we all have sometimes, that we can't quite understand or put into thoughts...."

He wanted to say that to him she symbolized all earthly and heavenly beauty. He wanted to fling a swift arm across her breast, and never let her go again. But already she had escaped fleet-footed down the beach, leaving him only her laugh, and the print of her gold-white body in the sand. She was collecting shells now, and exploring the tide pools at the foot of the cliffs—those warm pools that fairly seethed with quaint small life: crabs, anemones, starfish (one brilliant red one looked unreal, as though it had fallen in a pot of paint), and strange unidentifiable shelly or wormy creatures. Davidson joined her. They stepped cautiously, to avoid the barnacles with which some of the ledges were carpeted. Sometimes they held hands companionably, as they crouched down to peer into a pool and laugh together at some small oddity.

They climbed down closer to the sea, and stood on rocks that were covered with slippery wrack. Fringes of kelp lifted and fell, swirling.

"Look!" Jane said. "Those shellfish—musselly-looking things. Wonder if they're edible."

"Too bad they aren't oysters," Davidson said.

"We can't be choosy. Anyway, I'm going to try one. Where's your knife?" She had pried loose one of the bivalves from a cluster of its companions, and was trying to pull its shells apart.

"In my pants pocket, of course, halfway down the beach.

That's the trouble with your sun-worship; how does a chap carry his knife?... Here, let me open him."

"Pretty slimy," she observed. "But I'm no sissy. Here goes!" And she swallowed hard.

Davidson laughed at her expression. "Better stick to oranges," he advised. "If you don't enjoy these critters, what's the use of forcing yourself to eat 'em?"

"But they're quite good," she said. "A little peppery, as if they'd been seasoned."

"Somebody was mighty thoughtful," Davidson mocked. But then he tried one himself, and admitted that its sliminess was the worst thing about it, and that it really was a relief from a diet of little beside fruit.

Jane wanted to swim again. She lured Davidson into the water, and set him to thrashing his big arms and legs, while she rollicked around him. "There's hope for you," she told him, "even if you are a sailor." So, swimming and learning to swim, chasing up and down the beach, eating fruit and shellfish, they spent the whole day; and not until dark was beginning to fall could Davidson get Jane to leave the sea.

When at last she came ashore, she realized again with desperate suddenness how tired she really was. All at once she was clumsy and heavy as lead, missing the buoyant support of the water, feeling that gravity had mysteriously and ruthlessly doubled its power. She thought it odd that the water should seem a more natural element—fish out of water was no word for the way she felt now! "Damn! My strength goes, just like that," she protested, snapping her fingers. "I wish I'd get over it, Daveson."

"You silly child, you've been banged up, and shipwrecked, and starved, and sick, and nearly dead in a dozen ways," he reminded her. "What d'you expect so soon? I shouldn't have let you swim so much."

She sighed. The cave at the top of the cliff looked incredibly high and far away. She eyed it doubtfully. "Let's stay on the beach tonight," she suggested.

For answer, he picked her up gently, and carried her toward the cliff. Her wet hair brushed his shoulder. Up the giant steps and the winding ledges he walked cautiously, breathing hard from the weight of his burden, feeling at the same time stirred and triumphant, as on the night he had carried her half-dead body out of a tangle of wreckage on the *Annie Marlow*. Only now she was very much alive, and warm, and naked.

"I love you," he said. But—irritatingly if it had not been so absurd—she was sound asleep.

She did not wake up when he put her down in the moss. She did not wake at all till long after the big green-lighted fireflies in the vines at the cave mouth had folded themselves away under the leaves. She was dimly conscious first of the fragrance of those flowers outside, then of the softness of moss against her unaccustomed nakedness—soothing to sunburned shoulders—and then that Davidson's chest was against her own, his arms around her once more, and that she was happy to be so intimately close to him. She lifted her hand, and cautiously caressed one big solid shoulder. At her touch he started as though from an electric shock.

"Sorry! Didn't mean to wake you," she whispered. "Glad you're here, that's all."

And the next thing she knew he had hunted and found her lips in the enchanted dark, and was kissing them hungrily, though reverently, and caressing her with hardened hands that were surprisingly tender.

"Janie! My little Janie!"

"Yes," she said.

There was nothing in life, except to be his, part of him.

[10]

Davidson was whittling. He sat in the mouth of the cave, with the big green ferns around him, the rocky turrets and soft blue sea for background. He was naked and tawny-colored among green fronds. The thick soft hair on his chest and forearms was spun gold in the sun. The hair on his head was getting scraggly now, and it was oddly bleached on top; the beard was perhaps an inch long—light brown, with glints of gold, and here and there a suspicion of red. In fact, Davidson looked primitive and comfortable, and as if he belonged there. He sat tensely concentrated over a little block of ebony wood which he was shaping with his jackknife; and despite all Jane's teasing, he would not tell her about it.

"All sailors whittle," he informed her. "It's another of our common weaknesses, like not being able to swim, and liking to make love. We just can't help ourselves."

"And you won't tell me what it is?" she pleaded.

"Sure—it's ebony."

"Brute!"

"If I told you what it's *going* to be, it would turn out to be something else," he protested.

"Oh, I didn't know that. One of the subtle secrets of the art of whittling, no doubt."

"Sailors never confess what they're whittling," he went on. "Bad luck."

"Well, I'll try to be patient."

"After all, Janie, there's plenty of time."

"'Scuse me, will you? I'm going for a short swim."

"Sure—but don't turn into a mermaid. I shouldn't like you half so well with a fish-tail, or fins."

He felt more at peace with life and with himself than he had ever felt before. Every now and then he glanced up from the whittling, and looked out for a moment into the glowing sea. Every leaf in the fringe of bushes trembled; beneath, the waves were small voices. This world belonged to him. The real one was lost outside somewhere, and was of no consequence anyhow. He hoped it had been chucked over the edge into black grinning chaos.

Paradoxically, he was awed and even a little startled when he thought about the superb naturalness of their love the night before—a naturalness which would have been impossible in the mad rush and whirl, the gigantic conflict, of the city. This was the way it was meant to be, and mixing them up till they were hopelessly lost in a jungle labyrinth of complexes, conventions, inhibitions, and all the rest of the long words which merely meant unhappy struggle.

He thought fleetingly, with horror, of the morbid despair of his own boyhood, the blind groping for beauty and for freedom, the tragic squalor of the life his parents lived, in which he had been brought up, from which some inextinguishable silver flame of desire had prompted him to rebel, to run away, to take precarious refuge in the immense aloofness of the sea. And probably, he thought, that same story, with slight variations, was at some time, in some degree, the story of every human being.

What made his particular story different from others, was

that he had won. He had completely escaped morbidness and squalor—not only in heart, but in the flesh as well. He had left it all behind, apparently forever; and was surrounded by nothing but beauty—undreamed-of, unimaginable beauty; for so far, certainly, nothing had occurred to justify his first reasonable fears about the island. He was conscious of a surge of gratitude —not exactly to a God whom he doubted, but to whatever circumstances or fates had combined to create this magic. Perhaps it was Jane, after all, to whom gratitude was due. So he thanked her again, silently and worshipfully, and bent over his whittling.... And Jane, who was clambering down the cliff for an early dip in the sea, felt much as he was feeling—ecstatically at peace, with a knowledge that all was well with the world.

She stood on a shelf of rock three or four feet above the water. Seaweed, black and fringy, heaved in a blue, bottomless void. She looked up toward the top of the cliff, but Davidson and the cave were hidden behind tall jags of rock. Between these jags the sea surged and withdrew with a rumbling suck, and eerie swirlings of seaweed.

With sudden abandon, Jane flung her arms above her head, and in the same motion hurled her lithe body into the air, straightened it, and shot cleanly into the sea. It was a superb gesture: her way of shouting joy. Silver bubbles streamed up behind her. She sank, more and more softly, making no move to bring herself to the surface again, but waiting, prolonging the pleasure. Presently she was gliding up instead of down. She looked toward the surface—saw it like a silver film above her before she shattered it. Then, tossing back her hair, she swam vigorously.

For her, swimming was a means of expression that transcended all others that she knew. She had learned it in the cool lakes of Maine; she had taken to it at the age of five or so like a small fish. Swimming opened up an entire new world of possibilities. She had long known the joy of coasting around a small island, sometimes under low-dipping pine branches, sometimes past rocks where turtles sat sunning. She knew the beauty of an under-water world, mystically blurred for human eyes, with its shifting sun-rays, streams of bubbles, golden ripple reflections; a silver-green mermaid world where fish were at home; an alluring world because she could not stay down in it very long at a time, but had to be content with brief glimpses.

In fact, swimming was a way of getting about which did not involve sweat, dirt, or blisters on toes; it was a continuing fresh coolness, a perpetual caress; an escape from gravity, clothes, solidity. And the motions of a well-rounded crawl could certainly give as much creative ecstasy, as much joy in supple grace and power, as any dance.

In New York, swimming, like mountains and sun-worship, had been lost. Now she lived its delights all over again, and they were greater even than she had remembered, because of the clear brilliant buoyancy of this sea, and the glitter of sand, corals, and small fish.

She came ashore at last, feeling rather superior to mere fish—because, after all, fish couldn't enjoy her world, and probably weren't over-sensitive to the beauties of their own, whereas she could be keenly alive and appreciative in both of them.

"Davidson"—she repeated the thought aloud at the top of the cliff—"I'm better than a fish." And she explained about the two worlds.

"Shouldn't boast, Janie," he chided her. "You can't move as fast as a fish."

"Fast! Who wants to move fast? Too much speed in modern life anyway—everybody knows that."

"Even in fish life?" he queried.

Sleek and glistening, she flopped down beside him in the ferns. "Certainly," she insisted. "Modern fish are stream-lined, like modern cars, but they don't look so silly."

"And are their bodies by Fisher, too?"

"Certainly—who else?"

"That's where he got his name and reputation, I s'pose.... Well, as I said before, just as long as you don't grow fins..."

They went exploring. Back of the cave, the woods stretched for perhaps two or three miles, then rose into a meadowy hilltop, which projected like a bare shoulder from a loosely flung fur mantle. It was toward this hill that they made their way. The woods were for the most part easy enough to get through, although now and then they had to battle underbrush, climb over a mossy windfall, or back away and try another place.

The tree-trunks, dark brown and gnarled, grew up and lost themselves, as the trunks of tropic trees seem always to do. In northern countries, Jane thought, a tree had a more definite personality. Each was an individual. You could see where it came from, and where it was bound, even when many grew thickly together as in a pine grove. They would be growing in harmony, but each knew its own mind, nevertheless. She remembered a certain pine grove on the slope of a pastured hill; and even now she could feel the mighty lilt and sway of those trees before a northwest wind that polished the blue of the sky. She stood there in a tropic island jungle, and heard, for a fleeting minute or two, the long low rushing of that far-away wind.

Here, you saw a section of trunk which rose up and turned into a cloud of green and gray shadowings. Branches intertwined and seemed to grow together. Vines added to the confusion. It was beautiful, but mysterious. It was better not to try to untangle them by following one single column upward. They did not want you to understand them, these tropic woods.

After a while a pool of light began to show ahead, apple-green and translucent. It was the end of the woods. As they went on, this emerald pool became still brighter, and seemed to radiate a warm glow. Great flowering vines grew at the edge of it —purple blossoms in clusters, and white and yellow ones, hibiscus, honeysuckle, jasmine. When they could find no other hold, they grew in loops and arches over each other. A fragrance, tangled as their tentacles, arose from them. Some had sharp reddish thorns, others smooth green curving stems.

And butterflies—fragile flaming creatures; freedom and the quintessence of high ecstasy; beauty measured in wings. A universe of butterflies triumphant. A breath of azure silk with a sheen like a Persian vase; a lace of yellow and gold; a pair of wings made from the secret essence of orange-blossoms. There was hovering and swirling, stooping tenderly over favorite flowers; flirting, poised on a path of fragrance; swerving up into the breeze; coming to rest, wings spread out in sunlight. The keen joy of flight—wings and sunlight and petals... petals... sunlight... wings....

Jane had loved butterflies longer than she remembered. The swift movements of their wings spoke to her, and their colors had symbolized another and more fragrant world. That world was—this island! She had found it, then! She turned to Davidson, to tell him all that she was thinking, to share her exultation with him....

The hill streamed with rivers of green-gold warmth. Each tall grass blade radiated a quivering atmosphere, and the earth was hot underfoot. But Jane and Davidson were becoming used to this. If you wanted to shade your eyes, you plucked a banana leaf, and allowed sunlight to pour over your body in gold cataracts and waves that were almost visible.

They made their way to the top of the hill; and around them, brilliantly colored, was the enchanted circle of their kingdom. Northeast of the hill lay a valley, like a green trench, down which a little river ran, and across the valley the mountain rose almost vertically out of the sea. This was the same mountain, with its rugged green shoulders and tumultuous cone of reddish-purple rock, which had dominated the island as they stared at it from the sea at dawn. It had seemed unbelievably tall and remote. That was illusion, partly caused by their own exhaustion, partly by the confused splendor of the clouds. In reality it was not much higher than the hill they were on now, but it was wilder and grander. At its foot, just across the valley, the woods looked very dense and luxuriant. Down the mountain walls tumbled the same brook that drowsed along so peacefully when it reached the valley—a series of wild flying cascades that gleamed in the sunlight. And now, for the first time, they could look out at the sea on the opposite side of the island, glimpses of blue between a row of sand-dunes that stretched southward from the mountain. On the other side of the hill was the dark fringe of forest through which they had come, dipping to the achingly white crescent of their beach. It seemed far away; and the sea beyond it could hardly be the same sea in which Jane had swum that morning. It was an impalpable soft blue now, like the blue of spring flowers.

"And still no people," Davidson commented at last. "It becomes increasingly obvious, Janie, that we're marooned."

"No matter how feverishly hard I worked my imagination," she said, "I couldn't conceive of a more delightful place to be marooned in. I'm less and less afraid of it all, Daveson."

"I think we can make out of it a life that will be pretty grand," he said, "if we try hard enough. Interesting to see if we're equal to our opportunities—if we really can become part of the earth, and get along without a single civilized trapping—except a knife."

"What a defeat for civilization it will be, if we can!" Jane exclaimed. "Prove it's all superfluous, just as I suspected; prove that the only necessary thing it's ever invented is knives!"

They worked in a circle around the hill some distance below its top, and found a corner just under the fringe of vines that edged the woods. Here, in a bower of bright flowers and sunlight, they rested—Jane watching butterflies, Davidson earnestly whittling again at his mysterious block of ebony, covering it with his hand if she became too inquisitive, and laughing at her.

"I'll show it to you—maybe tonight," he promised.

She lay on a carpet of grass and petals, and looked up into a thousand miniature miracles of flowers and leaves and light. A tremulous scarlet hibiscus, balancing on no stem that she could see, stared her defiantly in the face. From a crowd of gentle white flowers floated an occasional reminiscent petal, drifting down on rays of light that shot through the upper leaves and played subtle havoc with colors and shapes. Each leaf was a single layer of green-gold light, imprisoned and materialized. Flowers were no longer flowers, but by-products of that light, so intense that it could not be contained in mere rays and flickerings, but had to burst into jets of many-colored fire. Butterflies were a still more extravagant expression of it—light gone wild with ecstasy, light broken free from all shackles, embodied light winging in and out of fragrant archways and palaces.

"And old Professor Myers—" Jane began in a low voice—"old Professor Myers sends men out with nets and bottles and pins to catch them and take the light out of them, and bring them home dead. And they call it collecting butterflies. More like—collecting dust."

"Don't they say it's 'in the interest of science,' and all that?"

"Yes—in the interest of science that isn't content until it's taken everything to pieces to see what it's made of."

Davidson pondered. "They forget something pretty important," he said after a while. "They forget that the most vital things get damaged and lost in the course of trying to analyze them. It's pretty ironical."

"You mean—the light, the life, get lost, Daveson?"

"Sure—like—like quicksilver. Can't put your finger on it. But what they lose is the real butterfly. All they have left is a bunch of dead nerves and a little colored dust—so they say that's what a butterfly's made of. I think any unpretentious heathen chap's more on the right track, when he maintains that even a stone has a soul."

"I'm a heathen," Jane said. "I've always wanted to be free to go heathen without any interference or criticism. I believe everything alive has a soul—flowers, animals, birds—trees, of course —and on this island even stones can have souls, if they like. I suppose that's why I've always loathed the so-called sport of hunting."

"Even for food?"

"No, that's different. It's reasonable and necessary to hunt for food. The Indian does, and the Eskimo. But he takes only what he needs. Nature's creatures were made to prey on each other. The bird I hate is the one who dresses up in some fashionable sport store, and goes off armed with all the fashionable and expensive gadgets, and then proceeds deliberately, stupidly, to slaughter deer. Just for the fun of it—the famous so-called love of the chase, and the lust to kill. That's pretty foul. As for collecting butterflies—some time," Jane went on dreamily, "I'm going to tell Professor Myers what you were saying. You hit the nail on the head again, Daveson. I'll have it out with him."

"When you get back?" he questioned.

She snapped her fingers in annoyance. "For months," she began again, "I tried to get certain thoughts formulated so I could discuss them. I wanted a few simple words—just the words you've given me. A dozen times I had it on the tip of my tongue. 'Professor Myers—you're wrong, somehow, somewhere.' But I couldn't tell why or get any further with the idea. And now that I understand, I'm marooned on an uninhabited island where I can't do anything about it."

"But, Janie, you couldn't anyway. Nobody would listen or care. If it's the old man's life to take butterflies apart, you can't stop him, you know."

"I can't help feeling," she insisted, "that if I could bring him here so that he could see what I'm seeing now, he'd understand, too.... Taking to pieces a breath of light and magic to see what it's made of, and calling that entomology...! And yet, Davidson, he's a dear old man with the kindest heart in the world, and he understands lots of things."

"Want to write him a note?" Davidson suggested. "Let's see —we could hang it round a gull's neck, or put it in a bottle— except we haven't got a bottle; or pin it to a porpoise."

"Sort of a nautical free delivery," Jane smiled.

"Sure; modern stream-lined mail coaches—bodies by Fisher..."

"Nobody back there would understand anyway, I guess," Jane said, serious again, "except the few who have always understood. We'll just have to keep it to ourselves, Daveson. This is our world, a brand-new one, and it can have its own independent laws and religion and philosophy of life. And we're king and queen," she added, "and can have everything as we want it."

"Here's another thing I sometimes believe," Davidson said. "What is all this taking apart of butterflies, vivisecting dogs, inventing always more and bigger telescopes, but the human passion to have everything *explained?* What is religion itself, but a way of accounting for why we're here, how we got here, how the earth began, and all the rest of it? Human nature apparently rebels at mystery. If a man doesn't understand a thing, and can't account for it—well, he'll account for it anyway, if only by some far-fetched fairy-tale like Genesis."

Jane nodded slowly. "Yes, but don't get science and religion too mixed up. Some of the time they're at cross purposes. A few of the more up-to-date and intelligent clergy accept science; but a good many of 'em mistrust and fear it."

"They think it's a sin against the Bible, I suppose," Davidson suggested.

"Sure. They feel that the evolution idea, for instance, in some profane way explains the origin of life; whereas God knows the poor old scientists are completely gumfoozled about the origin of life. They don't even pretend to understand that."

"I think it's rather grand as a mystery," Davidson put in.

"Oh, so do I. I love it as a mystery. But some people seem to fear being so utterly in the dark. They'd rather believe in Genesis, just as you said. Well, let them!... Ever thought much about evolution, Daveson? It's glorious. It means that every form of life came from a simpler form. It means there are no sharp demarcations between species—oh, how that problem bothered the poor old classifiers in Darwin's time and before! It means that all life is one immense varied river. That makes me feel on intimate and friendly terms with the earth and the other creatures on it. If you really believe in evolution, you can't conceive of man as so very distinct from other animals."

"It kind of takes the edge off his vaunted superiority, too, doesn't it?"

"Oh, sure it does! All life is one, plants and animals together."

Davidson was thoughtful. Then he said: "You've made fun of science often enough. Yet it was the most detailed and painstaking research that brought this evolution idea to light."

Jane conceded this. "Of course," she agreed. "And it has brought to light a great many interesting and useful facts. Medical research, for instance."

"Well," he pursued, "probably every known fact helps to complete the picture. Probably even your friend Professor Myers' butterflies' antennae fit in somewhere."

She smiled. "But you yourself just said they lose one thing they're after," she reminded him. "They can't analyze life. In a way you're right about the dead butterflies fitting into the picture. My objections are based less on reason than on the fact that I dislike cases full of crucified insects. I wish they could study evolution not in a closed office, or a stinking laboratory, shut away from fresh air and daylight, but first-hand, in the open. Maybe it would be more real that way, and maybe they'd get a better general perspective, even if it wasn't so scientific. It's life I'm interested in."

"And paradoxically," he said, "they have to study life through death."

"Yes—and it seems to me like a long way round."

"Well," he suggested, "you and I can study however we like, and the graybeards can stick to their microscopes in peace. There's plenty of room for various kinds of studying, and probably they supplement each other somehow. Anyway, why should we worry about it?"

He was watching the light play upon her brown and white body. Leaf shadows, frail, ephemeral, quivered and flickered across her shoulders and her breast. Once the elusive shadow of a big butterfly wandered erratically up the whole length of her, zigzag, from her ankles to her face and the ragged brown hair that was golden over her forehead where the sun bleached it, and curling a little in the joy of its freedom.

She herself was dreaming now, watching the thronging butterflies, her eyes following their radiant wings in and out of the flowers. She was half-hypnotized by warmth, and by those flickering, weaving, ceaseless movements. Davidson smiled, and went on with his whittling.

And evening came, with crickets in chorus—a long golden chain. Dew was in the air now, and fragrances like cordials in exquisite glasses. Then fireflies came—multitudes—myriads—a never-completed pattern of sudden soft lights, greenish-gold. Only crickets and fireflies and fragrances shared the world.

Jane and Davidson crept from their hide-away, and walked out on to the grassy hillside, under a tremulous sky pricked with stars. They passed through a fringe of woods. Their footsteps here were nearly soundless. The trees were asleep. There was nothing—only the two of them there together in a void of tropical dark.

The rhythm of their footfalls took possession of Jane like a primitive dance. Who were those people who danced over crops they had planted—danced to the gods of the harvest, treading down the earth, pounding it with their naked feet?... She herself felt very primitive. The swing of her own body was part of the forest. Just ahead of her, broad shoulders rose and fell a little, half-invisible, almost mesmerizing in their steady swing.

When they came out of the woods again on to the open hillside of grass, he dropped back beside her, and put his arm around her, to hold her tight against his side; and they walked on as one person, every step, every slight swing, made together in a unison of muscles that was almost music. The island, taking possession of their mood, seemed to have given in return part of its own rhythm and grace.

They rounded the crest of the hill, and a warm wind rushed at them. There was a sense of spaciousness. The sky was straight above—nothing came between. Where they had come from, the forest showed a black fringe of trees. For a few minutes there were only stars. Then, out of a gulf beyond the edge of the east the moon floated, casting an arch of pale rose color on to some wispy clouds just above, slowly transfiguring the entire island into a soft black etching on a background of pale light. The world was still now; but if you held your breath and listened hard, there were always the voices of little creatures in the grass, and the small sound that a leaf makes, and the low far-away murmur of the sea.

"Here's the top of the hill," Davidson said. He turned, and put his hands on Jane's shoulders, looking into her face. And that new moonlight had destroyed the work of the sun—for she looked very white against the soft dark of the island. To her, his tall frame was masterful and a little austere, in silhouette against the sky. The wind made the grass ripple against their knees.

"I want to talk to you," he said. "I've finished it," he added cryptically.

For a minute she could not think what he meant. Then she remembered, "Oh, the whittling! Let's see. Did it turn out what you expected?"

"Yes, but not so good, of course. Like a poem or a painting, or anything else, whittling never satisfies its creator."

"Well, that's all the more credit to the creator, Daveson. Horribly smug to be satisfied, especially with yourself."

"It was a labor of love, anyway," he said. And he opened his big hand to show it to her. It was a slender ring of smooth-polished ebony, precise and symmetrical, resembling those worn by African tribes. Only instead of lines and crosses scratched into the outside of it, Davidson had cut a row of tiny, fanciful figures that stood out in slight relief; two porpoises, bounding, backs arched; an anchor; a butterfly. These Jane could just make out in the moonlight.

It was a piece of workmanship such as he had never even approached before in idle hours of tinkering. Accomplished with nothing but a reasonably sharp jackknife, it would have done credit to the most ingenious wood-carver. It was the expression of one of those rare inspired impulses that seize artistic persons once or twice in a life-time, when, stirred by deep emotion, they are mysteriously capable of work such as they had only dreamed of, and are never able again to match.

In the lovely, unearthly light on the hilltop, in the warm wind, with the grasses rippling, the little ring lying in Davidson's big square hand had an air of mystery and magic. Neither he nor Jane spoke, as he slipped it on to her finger. This was a solemn rite.

"And so now we're married," he said at last.

"Is it legal?" she inquired archly.

"Of course it's legal. What do you mean—'legal,' anyhow? By what law?"

"I don't know." She glanced upward. "The law of the stars, maybe."

"Right," he agreed. "I don't know, and I certainly don't care, but I'm fairly sure that's a law no justice of the peace would dispute."

"He might dispute it," said Jane, "but he just wouldn't know any better. Anyway, I feel tremendously married."

"Well... After all, two thousand stars for witness that were shining long aeons before old Adam was heard of. *They* ought to have authority—and sacredness, too. They've got us on record."

"I'd like to see the book."

"Well, you'd find us written down in silver fire."

"Something like this," Jane said. "Shipwrecked pair: little island in corner of World No. 5,792,431...."

"Who would *dare* say it isn't legal?" he demanded.

"It's awesome to be so much married," Jane said. "It's frightening. D'you suppose the stars grant divorces, too?"

"Don't like the way your mind works," he protested. "What a rebel you are!"

"Yes, I am a rebel, I guess."

"Now *I'm* frightened," he told her.

"Don't be. What I rebel against is—is—well, giving in to ugliness—that puts it in a nutshell. And you're the most beautiful lover in the world."

"Forgive my curiosity, but do tell me how you know that!"

"The stars told me.... I love your ring, David. It's a work of art, and magic."

"Glad—it was the best I could do."

"That's why I love it. I love it ever so much more than any ring you could have bought for me, if we had met in the world of bought things. Because you made it—and it's you."

He sighed with gratitude. "That's what I hoped you'd feel," he said. "You've said what I didn't know how to say. You're wonderful. You understand everything.... You know, Jane, I liked something you said a minute ago—about ugliness—not giving in to it. That's what I've been trying not to do, all my life."

"It pays," Jane said. "You stay more alive to lovely things, if you're a little bit choosy."

"Let's promise together," he said, "never to give in to anything ugly."

"We don't need to. We don't have to worry about ugliness, here. We don't even have to go hunting for beauty, because it's all around us.... Daveson, let's not hide away in our cave tonight. Let's just sleep out here, under the moon."

[11]

There was no way of keeping track of the time. That was measured by the life-span of a leaf. Good to have done with it for once. Let the leaves go on measuring the infinite and whispering about it among themselves. The waves, too, kept up the cosmic rhythm, if one could entirely interpret and understand it. Jane never could. Sometimes it seemed that with just one more beat she would know what those waves were saying or singing. But it remained a mystery.

Every morning was the bursting of a giant pearl. Jane, sitting on the threshold of the cave, clasping her knees, would watch the confusion of clouds and lights in a sky that was like the iridescent lining of a shell. Light glinted warmly on the eastern edges of rocks, and on Jane's shoulders that were uniform brown now. The well-developed muscles of her arms caught the light, too, and stood out copper-colored from the brown. Her hair was bleached several shades lighter; and Davidson's beard was a good two inches long.

They would wait silently until the gold spears began to shoot out of the sea, making the colors grow pale—until the first great gold sparkle of the sun appeared, swelling fast, an enormous bud of light ready to burst into flower. They would raise their hands, then, in solemn salute to this visible god who ruled their island, their day and night, their warmth and light, their very food supply—the god of flowers and butterflies.

Then down swiftly to the sea. By now they both knew the winding ledges of the cliff so familiarly that they could take the trip almost at a run; and neither hot sand nor barnacles bothered their well-hardened feet, these days.

Then came the playful running along the shore, arms flung upward in joy. There was companionship with the young wind, and the thrill of bare feet pounding against coral sand edged with foam. The very air glowed with color. Blue and bright, the sea lifted and fell, tangled with the sun and a streaming soft wind like a golden brook. Flying hair, flashing feet—and all of a sudden the end of flight, the strong clasp of golden arms, a whirl of blue sea, and Jane's face against a tawny chest. Then the plunge into restless waves, the coppery sheen of wet shoulders, and a shower of spray from the heart of a rainbow.

"Jane, you're divine, all excited that way in the sunlight."

"Davidson, Davidson, Davidson! Oh, it's so beautiful to be alive!"

On top of the cave, but back a little way in a sheltered hollow, was a long flat rock which, along with some small stones strategically laid on top of it, served as stove and fireplace. For rainy weather, there was a fireplace in the cave as well, but for the most part they preferred the open sunlight, and the feeling that they were really out in the world.

The whole business of fire and firewood had involved a good many problems, a good deal of humorous head-scratching, and a little discouragement. At first neither of them had been able to make any headway with fire-building by approved primitive methods. They possessed a few dry matches, to be sure, but these couldn't be expected to last forever.

"We've got to dope this thing out before they're gone, in

fact," Davidson said. "Seems ridiculous, when it's so damned hot, not to be able to concentrate a little of the heat in one small spot. I could, if I had a burning-glass."

"I don't believe we'd need any fire at all to fry an egg or roast a breadfruit right now," Jane observed. "Say—here's an idea! How about kindling a fire tonight with one of those enormous fireflies. That ought to work."

He studied her face, which was solemn. "All right," he said. "We'll try that."

Eventually, of course, they decided that the simplest method was never to let the fire completely die out. It was easy enough, when they learned the tricks, to bank up hardwood coals so that they would last till morning. Then, a few dry twigs and a little blowing was all that was needed. If it started to rain during the night, Davidson would inevitably get up and rescue some of the coals.

Fire opened up infinite possibilities as far as the prosaic matter of diet was concerned. Roast breadfruit, for instance, was an overwhelming success. It took a long time to cook it, but it was worth waiting for. Roasted bananas were another success. And then there were eggs. First they had tasted those of the gulls, which nested all over the cliffs. But these had such an unpleasant taste that they gave up the idea in disgust. However, one day they noticed that an entirely different sort of bird shared part of the cliff, farther around on the northeast side. They were smaller, and looked like some sort of pigeon. Their eggs, though small, were much more edible than those of the gulls.

Lack of any sort of utensil in which things could be cooked made it necessary to bake everything, even eggs, in hot ashes. One day Jane tried the experiment of cutting a cooked and steaming hot breadfruit in half, hollowing one half out a little, and breaking eggs into the hollow. Stirring them gently for a few minutes scrambled them. A little milk from a ripe coconut worked well for sauce.

"We've got no kick coming," they agreed.

Furthermore, pigeons' eggs were not the only ones available. Sometimes, at the far end of the long beach, Jane and Davidson would find clumsy tracks leading to mounds of sand full of round turtles' eggs, left to hatch in the heat of the sun. Although they never happened to catch sight of the huge sea-turtles that laid these, they gathered them up whenever they found them, like treasure-trove.

The inside of the cave itself was a good deal more comfortable now. Davidson had hunted out the tiny stream that dribbled through it—tracked it persistently to its lair in the forest, and changed its course by building a dam of mud and stones at a strategic point. He declared that he hadn't had such a good time since he was a kid playing in muddy alleyways. Not only was it fun, but it worked. After a few days water ceased dripping in the cave, and some of the moss dried up. Using the sail of the skiff for a basket, they carried bundles of dry pink sand up the cliff, and with this filled the hollows in the floor, until it was even and smooth. This also made the cave seem brighter. When they built an occasional fire inside, at night, the leaping reflections of its flames danced on that smooth hearth of sand, catching specks of gleaming mica. The roof and walls approached and retreated eerily; shadows leaned like lithe witches out of obscure corners.

The vines at the cave mouth had been skillfully looped back, so that, without being torn or damaged, they were out of the way, although they could be pulled down at any time to hide the opening as before. In the day time, it was now comfortably bright inside. Furthermore—luxury of luxuries!—there was a bed. Jane and Davidson had carried in armfuls of fragrant ferns from the woods, and piled them up high and soft. They did not seem to Jane quite as satisfactory as the fir boughs of the north woods, and after they were dry and crisp they rustled at every movement. However, they were comfortable enough, especially with Jane's ragged old overcoat spread over them to keep the stems from sticking into bare skin.

Various arts which were new to both of them had to be mastered. For instance, fat pink shrimps, excellent food, abounded along the fresh-water streams of jungle and mountain. Davidson cut sharp-pointed sticks, and practiced shrimp-spearing, as he had once seen South Sea natives do; but at first he had a complete lack of success. Jane laughed heartily at his attempts, and was no better herself.

"Can't be done," was her verdict. "Besides, do shrimps really make such wonderful eating?"

He persevered; and one day, as much to his own surprise as to hers, he withdrew his dart with a small pink body impaled upon its point. From then on, having learned that it was possible, they both grew gradually adept. There was plenty of time for practicing....

Breakfast was always a gay affair. Jane, still dripping, just out of an iridescent sea, would be sitting back on her heels by the fireplace, blowing on the embers, strategically arranging small dry sticks, looking up triumphantly when they broke into flame.

"What's for breakfast, Jane?"

"Eggs. Does Your Highness prefer turtles' or pigeons'?"

"Kingfish steak, please. We haven't done much about solving the fishing problem, have we? Don't you know some kind of magic you could sit in the sea and sing, enticing fat kingfish from all around? You look as if you ought to know magic."

"I feel as if I ought. Some time I'll try.... Turtles' or pigeons'?"

"Oh, both."

"You aren't ever satisfied, are you, David? At least two kinds of shellfish, shrimps, eggs, and endless fruit and vegetables—and me—and you have to have fish, too."

"You see, it's still sort of a challenge," he explained.

"You have to have something to hunt, is that it?"

"Yes, males are like that. And now that I don't hunt you any more—don't have to—"

"You'll take fish for a substitute," she put in. "Well, that's flattering. I've always liked fish."

She would often spend an hour or two crouching close to the sea, where the cliff dropped abruptly into a great green hollow, so deep that even the sun rays got discouraged. Probably a paradise for sharks, scientists, octopi, great ancient oysters nursing fabulous pearls, and writers of adventure stories. At another place the bottom could be seen, crystal-clear, thirty or forty feet below. The wall of the cliff was spangled with myriad bright forms of sea life. Extravagant fish lived here, some softly iridescent as a rainbow, others garishly striped, some like blue metal, or fragments of exotic china. Some had streamers and some spines, and their bodies were of all imaginable shapes; long and thin, eel-like; flat and round, like a pancake; tiny as a needle; or so thin that they seemed to have only two dimensions instead of three.

Jane would watch and study their movements, trying to figure out just where it was that even the most agile of human beings failed so utterly by comparison in the matter of swimming. Maybe, she thought, if she watched them long enough, her own muscles would somehow absorb those subtle, simple techniques—those lithe bendings of brilliant bodies; strong swift flicks of tail and fins, poising in water like a hummingbird on air; dashes that her eye could not hope to follow.

Educated persons usually had a firm belief that they knew more than simple folk. Did they, really? And was their particular kind of knowledge worth while? Scientists, for instance, seemed to understand all about these fish. They gave them Latin names, observed their habits, looked at their brains under microscopes. Pretty low form of brain, too. There wasn't much, presumably, that you could teach a fish. Their scholastic ability was not high.

But did that prove anything about them? If so, what? Here, you might quite comfortably believe that they were a higher form of life than man. This was a far cry from the laboratory. Never mind their I. Q.'s. Beauty had been built into them—fiber by fiber, muscle by muscle, scale by scale.

Davidson was mostly interested in catching them. They presented, as he said so often, a challenge to his virility. He, too, studied their movements, but thought of them as prey rather than as teachers. And, bit by bit, a little clumsily at first, but improving immensely as it went on, he began to fashion a net of coconut fiber with a small mesh. This was a long, tedious job—the sort of thing that would have become drudgery if taken too seriously. Little by little they added to it. Often they worked on it for a couple of hours at midday, when it was too hot to be active—she at one end, he at the other, at first clumsily experimenting, later more dexterously twisting and weaving and knotting.

At first they had planned to make a garden, bring down from the hill such rooty vegetables as yams and taro, and planting them in a cleared space above the cave. Then they had abandoned that idea; it seemed like unnecessary labor.

"It savors of regimentation," Jane protested. "Yams don't want to grow in rows, any more than you and I do; besides, it's more fun to go scrambling round for 'em all over the countryside."

So, instead of making a spade and a hoe, Davidson concentrated his energy on an axe....

"No, not an axe," he would explain to her. "You couldn't call it that." It was a hard, sharp-edged stone wedged into a handle of wood, and held there by a piece of wire which had been part of the skiff's rigging. He contemplated this effort with a good deal of misgiving. "It isn't a patch on the ones you see in museums made by the Neanderthal Man," he asserted, shaking his head comically.

"Yet they say evolution is going on."

"Nonsense! Here's a case where it's going straight backwards. What would Darwin make of this, for instance?"

"He couldn't do as well himself, I bet," Jane affirmed.

"That's right. Stick up for your cavemen.... Funny, isn't it, to think that some time some snooping scientist will find this axe, and take it home convinced he's discovered relics of the Missing Link? He'll be knighted and receive medals for outstanding scientific achievement!"

He swung his tool heavily at a dead branch. It came clattering down, and the axe stayed together. He looked at it, surprised. "You know," he said, "this thing may really be of use when it comes to collecting firewood."

"You'll never have half the fun getting firewood with it as you did making it," said Jane. "Better start on something else."

"Oh, you're beginning to know me, are you?"

Every now and then they would have a sort of wood-gathering fiesta. They dragged in dead branches that lay on the ground; they cut more, stacking them in a dry place at the back of the cave. They would work perhaps half a day at this, happy to be doing anything, no matter what, so long as they were naked and in the sun. Then, streaming with sweat, their backs glistening with it, their eyes stinging a little, they would dive from the rocks at the foot of the cliff, into the sea that was neither cold nor warm.

A fresh-water shower was also at their service, but for this they had to walk. First, through the woods, skirting the slope of the hill; across the meadow valley on the far side; then up the stream and into the forest again—wilder forest now, more like traditional tropic jungle. They crept under vine arches, and brushed aside great lacy fronds of tree-ferns. The moss all through here was deep and soft. It overhung shaggily even the edges of the brook, and spread out over boulders like a rich Persian carpet. The brook was the only pathway through this forest. They waded up its bed in silence. Every once in a while, when it slid over the face of a rock or was blocked by fallen branches, they had to leave it and make their way into the woods for a short distance. The ground was buried in centuries of dark uneventful leaf-fall.

There was an air of mystery about this jungle. You might expect to see owls with large yellow eyes and soundless wings staring from branches, feathered sphinxes without color, almost without tangible form. If you held out your hand, it seemed ghostly white. Great black columns of trunk loomed.... But Jane and Davidson had followed the brook before and knew the soft-footed way of this forest.

At last they broke out on to an open ledge between upper and lower reaches of woods. There was a pool of sky, and the woods parted in a glade, like a fairy circle. You could edge around toward the south, and the mountain wall dropped precipitously. There was nothing below but tops of giant mango trees with their leaves quivering in unison when the breeze marched through them, and gleaming with touches of sunlight. A cascade plunged hilariously from a height far above, landed breathless in a swirling pool, and spilled more gently on to the ledge where Jane and Davidson were standing—a sparkling curtain of water. Fine spray splashed out from where it struck the ledge, and made small rainbows. Jane would stand underneath the shower. Her hot skin thrilled as that fragrant water went rippling down between her shoulder-blades. She held up her arms to it, and her face; it slid between her fingers, and streamed off her ragged hair. She twisted and turned in it, and Davidson, waiting for his turn, would smile with deep approval, in which there was often a touch of awe.

"You're the loveliest thing I've ever seen," he would tell her quietly; and, knowing that he meant it, she loved to hear him say it.

That dash of water would reawaken her energy. She would

glance at him dangerously. "So—you want something to hunt!" she would exclaim with a mocking smile. And she would be off down the brook again in a series of agile leaps, with him in hot pursuit only a couple of deadfalls behind.

In the woods it was a question of agility in dodging among trees, climbing over tangled barricades, hiding behind dense enormous ferns. Jane took pleasure in learning to do all this without damaging her feet or getting more than superficially scratched. She never wearied of the joy of being naked out-of-doors—naked near the earth, like a wild animal; and she had become, at least in the woods, more than a match for the tall Davidson, who tended to get involved in creepers. "I'd make a good spy," she would boast happily.

But in the open—it was another matter. Up the hill through the long grass they would strain, he gaining at every stride; for, although her wind was just as good as his, or even a little better on account of so much swimming, his long legs more than made up that difference. Sometimes she would be far enough ahead so that she had a chance to hide; she would lie panting and perspiring in the grass, feeling it tickle her skin, her heart pounding hard; wondering if she had hidden herself too well. He would come chasing up; she would spring to her feet and be off again, zigzagging like a butterfly, until, almost completely worn out, with laughing as much as with running, she would feel a pair of long heavy arms thrown around her shoulders, and down they would tumble together.

He would turn her over gently, and caress her. "Silly! What's the use of taking showers, anyway?"

"So we can run, and get dirty, and then take another one. That's life, and a good sort of life, too."

"Well! Am I acknowledged to be a good hunter now?"

"Am I good game?"

"You don't know half," he would tell her. "Aren't you glad to be caught?"

"You're a very conceited hunter."

"Well, aren't you?"

"That would be telling."

"Most beautiful princess, do you surrender?"

She would, gladly.

Love to them was so simple and whole-heartedly natural that she often wondered what was the matter with it when civilization got hold of it. She remembered, dimly through her happiness, that she had heard only wild hysterical outcries, wails of despair over love. People thought of nothing much else, and yet thinking about it made them unhappy. There was alarm and panic; people lost their heads. There was insanity, and there were strange suicides....

In the main, life on the island was serene. It would even have been unexciting, except that it was always so beautiful. The adventures were little things, such as finding a new batch of turtles' eggs in the sand, hunting fruit in warm misty rain when the woods were dripping, running in the early morning along the edge of foam in the wind. Leaves fell, but trees were never left naked and cold-looking. The process of budding, growing, falling never ceased. It was odd to have no seasonal changes. This took away their last opportunity to keep even a vague hold upon sense of time. There was the moon, of course. They had tried to keep track of how many cycles it passed through, but they soon forgot.

"Soon now," he observed whimsically one day, "we'll be watching each other for the first white hairs."

As usual in the tropics, it rained more during one part of the year than during the other, and it was colder then. There were some days when Jane would throw her overcoat around her shoulders, and Davidson was glad he had saved his old flannel shirt. But for the most part it was luxuriously hot—tending to be too hot. In spite of this, Jane and Davidson remained fairly active a good deal of the time. They were determined not to let tropical climate destroy the zest of living, the pleasure of active exercise. For two or three hours in the middle of the day, however, they had to surrender, and rest in the coolness of the cave or the woods.

Primitive existence could not be entirely without misfortune. The worst hour Jane had ever spent in her life anywhere was when Davidson, with the only tool he had, his jackknife, one by one pried half a score of sea-urchin spines out of the bottom of her foot. She had lain flat on her back in the shade at the top of the beach, and concentrated every ounce of will that she possessed into the single act of holding still.

Minor scrapes and scratches were inevitable. The only disinfectant they had was sea water. These many minor wounds had to be left to nature and the sun. In general, the excellent state of their health prevented trouble. Once both of them had a bad time with bramble scratches that festered. After that, they were more careful of brambles.

There were plenty of insects, especially in the wet season; but after the first few months these did not seem especially bothersome. "The mosquitoes can't hold a candle to the Maine ones," Jane would cheerfully insist. However, she developed chills and fever, whether from insect bites, diet, or dampness, she had no idea. For a few days, while she lay helpless and miserable, Davidson was frantic with anxiety. He had no idea how to fight the thing, thousands of miles from quinine or a doctor. He kept her warm, and that was all he could do. For days she was weak and could eat very little. It was more than a month before she was her normal energetic self.... But aside from these episodes, their good luck was little short of miraculous.

Jane tried to make friends with the gulls and pigeons. The gulls, especially, were majestic creatures, with a wing-spread of three or four feet. She liked to lie and watch them circling about the cliffs, lighting on the rocks or in the sea, taking off, sailing, using the wind expertly. Let man try as he would, mechanically he had never approached the primitive perfection of a bird's flight. Perhaps, she thought, airplane engineers ought to do as she was doing. She giggled at the ridiculous vision of long lines of engineers prone on their backs on tropic beaches, studying the way a gull used his wings. ("Make the poor gull self-conscious as hell," Davidson said.) After she had watched a long time, she began to get the feel of it, to live those motions although lying quite still—at last she could almost predict each move the bird would make. In another day or so, if she could only absorb just a little more of this perfect philosophy of flying, she would be soaring up there with them.

But better even than to watch them flying, was to have one of them feed out of her hand. So far she had not had much luck with the gulls; but the pigeons were almost as at home with her as those in Central Park. This was the final touch needed to make her feel absolutely that she belonged here, sharing the existence of wild free things—one of them herself....

The fish-net was finished. That was another great achievement. They went out from the cave at dawn to try it in a little cove which Davidson had used more or less as a measure in making it. The floor was sandy, dotted with black sea-urchins; the sides were two rocky promontories. Gulls seemed to favor the place, and Davidson had often seen fish there. Stretching the net between them in a loose roll, they walked out toward the sea, Jane on one promontory, Davidson on the other. The whole island, each individual rock and wavelet, and their own bodies, were touched with an early goldenness that was like no other color on earth. But Jane hardly stopped to think of the picturesque side of this expedition. She was busy keeping opposite Davidson, keeping the net from dragging. She hardly even glanced at his splendid back and shoulders touched with bronze, as both of them stooped to drop the net in the water. One side of it, weighted with a row of stones carefully wound up in the mesh and tied there, sank quickly to the sandy floor; the other side, floated on a row of wooden blocks, stretched between them across the cove. Then, slowly, with a steady pull, they dragged it back toward the beach.

"And I don't expect there'll be a single fish in it," Davidson called across to her; but his voice told her that he was as excited as a little kid.

"There might be a pot of gold," she called back softly.

When they were nearly in they could see that more than a dozen frightened fish were darting about in an ever decreasing semicircle on the shore side. Of these, a couple slid through the mesh, and another dodged around one end. They seemed to be all of one kind, about a foot long and marked with brilliant lengthwise stripes of blue and red and green, these colors merging into one another in a display of iridescence that would make a rainbow feel ashamed. Their eyes were black and gold; their beautifully shaped fins were thin leaves of silver.

Davidson's face was eager with concentration as he maneuvered the big net the last few feet, and drew the fish ashore. "I think these are what Spanish sailors call 'damsels,'" he said; and added impetuously: "Who said I couldn't make a fish-net?"

"They're too beautiful to eat," Jane said.

"What'll we do with 'em, then? Let 'em go? The first catch in my fish-net, and all that trouble?"

"Well, David, we can't eat nine large fish in one day. Your net works almost too well.... Are you satisfied at last? Feel like big, virile he-man, and all that?"

He ignored her teasing, and just looked thoughtfully at the bejeweled creatures, flapping hysterically in the sand.

Jane spoke up again. "I suggest we keep a couple of 'em, and let the others go, as a tribute to various gods. We owe tribute to sea-gods, coconut-fiber gods, sun-gods, and gods of luck—also whatever gods arranged that color-scheme!"

"You pagan!"

"Of course! I'm getting religious in my old age. I've always wanted to be religious, only my gods have to be picturesque."

[12]

"Jane—come here and look."

She had just awakened. Early morning light filled the cave, shimmered faintly golden on the sand floor. She stretched lazily, then got up and came to where Davidson stood, on the threshold, pointing out to sea. She followed his finger, but saw only the long blueness.

"I don't see anything," she told him.

He dropped his arm, but still stood staring.

"What is it?"

"I'm not quite sure," he said. "Look again, Janie—just under that little cloud."

"In the sky?"

"No—the sea."

"Davidson—not a ship!"

"I'm not sure," he repeated. "But there's something."

The possibility of a ship anchoring in their harbor had not occurred to Jane for a long time. She had come to feel that they would live here all their lives and eventually die here. She looked on the island as indisputably, irrevocably theirs, their home, their kingdom. She had even thought that some day, in spite of all the obvious difficulties, she would like to have children here. What would the landing of this ship, if it was a ship, mean to their world? Instinctively she drew back from the idea. It was an unknown quantity, and to be feared. It was the intrusion of something alien.

Yet mingled with these feelings was intense curiosity—and of course the instinct of gregariousness common to everyone except perhaps a few carefully self-hardened cynics—an instinct enormously intensified by long isolation....

"Yes," Davidson finally said. "It's a ship."

She could barely make it out now, herself—a microscopic speck—oh, less than a speck—on the rim of the world.

"Davidson, what—?" But she stopped short. A thousand unspoken questions were in her mind, but how could he answer them?

It would probably be noon before the ship could get in, for the wind was light. Jane and Davidson went about their usual daily life, trying to be unconcerned, but succeeding very poorly. A scrap of civilization was coming—white sails were pressing in upon them; how could they turn their backs upon such an invasion? Davidson, like Jane, was uncertain as to whether he should welcome or fear it. Only, when the ship came near enough so that he could tell she was a schooner, his eyes seemed to light up. Jane noticed it, and was more frightened than ever.

"Pretty," he said, very low. The sun was blazing on her tall sails. Did she look to him much as the *Annie Marlow* had looked to her years ago?

"What shall we do, Daveson? Go down and meet these people?"

"Sure—they may be in trouble—need water or something."

"Or maybe they're pirates," she suggested. "What'll we use for clothes?"

He looked at her and smiled. "I forgot how naked we are," he said. "Let's ransack the oddments and see what we can find."

The dreary little pile of clothes was in the back of the cave. They hauled them out into the sunlight—tenderly, for fear they would fall to pieces. Jane put on her old red skirt. But the faded green blouse split down the front as she struggled with it, and she looked at Davidson in dismay.

"Put it on backwards," he advised her. "And now let's see what's left of my pants."

Fortified by these threads of civilization, they sat on the rocks in front of their cave, watching what was going on below. They heard the purring squeak of gaffs coming down, and the rumble of the anchor chain. The schooner was still pretty far out —of course the captain would not risk her in the shoals of a strange harbor. A boat was lowered. It looked as if there were three in it, apparently dressed, or half-dressed, in traditional tropic fashion, with white pants and wide-brimmed hats.

"They don't look very piratical," Davidson said. "Let's go down and see what it's all about." But for a minute or two she could not help holding back. "Come on," he urged. "It's probably one of those wandering scientific expeditions, out after bugs and corals and compass variations."

There were three in the boat: a big, dark, bearded fellow; a tight-set young man in a helmet; and a thin tall man with distant blue eyes and gray hair showing beneath his hat. He carried a large butterfly net. That was the first thing to catch Jane's eye, and she resented it.... Butterfly-hunting on her island?

"You're right," she whispered to Davidson. "Scientists."

The men were too absorbed in their landing to notice the islanders. But presently the big man looked up and caught sight of them, standing quietly at the edge of the woods. "Hello! *Hello* there!" he shouted impulsively. Then he added: "D'you speak English?"

Jane laughed frankly, and Davidson found his voice. "Castaways," he explained huskily. "*Annie Marlow*."

The big man hung fire a minute, and then fumed with jerky energy. "*Annie Marlow!* By jings!" he exclaimed. "I remember. Lost with all hands. I remember. Well, for Christ's sake!"

They shook hands all around, and introduced themselves. The big man was captain; the young, tight-lipped one was Thomas, geologist of the expedition; the one with the net was Richardson, an entomologist of whom Jane dimly remembered having heard through old Professor Myers years ago.

"Off on a holiday?" she asked, trying to be casual.

"*Holiday!*" the skipper exclaimed. And he looked quizzically at the others. "No, you couldn't call it that."

"How'd you happen to land up here?" Davidson asked. "And where are we, anyhow?"

"You got us, brother," said the captain. "I can tell you the latitude and longitude, but that doesn't help much."

"You mean, the island isn't known about at all?" Jane asked.

The geologist shook his head, and the captain went on explaining. "We knew this part of the ocean hadn't been explored, and we wanted to chart currents and such stuff. And Mr. Thomas here had a theory that if there did happen to be any islands round hereabouts, they'd be—interesting—from a geological standpoint.... Say, is there any water on the God-damned place? We've got mighty low. Had me worried."

"Sure there's water," Davidson said. "And plenty of fruit and stuff. I bet you could stand some fresh stuff, couldn't you?"

"Sure could!... My God! So you two've been living here all this time!"

"How long is it, anyway?" Jane asked.

The captain considered. "*Annie Marlow*," he repeated slowly. "Well, must be nigh on to three years ago we heard about her being lost.... Three years!" he exclaimed, as the thought struck him forcibly. "Say, I'll bet you're a'mighty glad to see somebody.

Musta been hell-fired lonesome. It's a damn wonder you found enough to live on.... Well, we're going home to New York. How does that sound, eh?"

"New York!" Jane exclaimed sharply.

"Impatient?" the skipper queried. "Well, it won't be long. A few days ought to finish up our looking round here, hadn't it, Ned?" he asked the young geologist.

"She's a darn pretty schooner you've got there," Davidson remarked.

The rather coarse-looking captain changed countenance, and for a second he looked out to sea with the same affectionate pride that Jane had seen many a time on old Captain Maynard's weatherbeaten face.... "Sailors!" she exclaimed softly to herself, half-exasperated, half-admiring.

Besides these three men, they learned that there was a crew of mate, cook, and three seamen, and an indefinite number of other scientists, all working day and night over collections and records, all engulfed in back-breaking work. Their method was to land anywhere that looked scientifically promising; there they would camp for a few days and collect feverishly almost everything they came across. During the next interval at sea they would compile their records and slave intensely over tabulations, analyses, charts, graphs, amid batteries of delicate instruments. They had been under way for two years now, and were ready to run home to their laboratories and see what they had actually accomplished.

The islanders showed Captain Porter where to fill his water-cask, a few hundred yards back of the beach in the woods; and Jane helped him fill with wild oranges a basket he had brought along. The skipper was mightily concerned for the well-being of these castaways.

"Say, wouldn't you folks like to come out to the schooner? Guess we could scare up a couple o' bunks for you. Bet a decent feed would taste a'mighty good."

Jane thanked him cordially enough, but said they were doing fine—in fact, they had worked it out to a point where they were eating regally.... The captain looked at her in unconcealed amazement, doubtless thinking that the long ordeal had made this poor child daft. He scratched his head, while she continued to pick oranges, oblivious. Presently he asked her if there wasn't anything they'd like to have brought in to them in the morning: blankets, a water-pail, matches...? Wasn't there anything in the way of grub she had a yen for? Not that they had anything very fancy....

"Why, yes," she told him frankly, from a branch half-way up the orange tree. "I've sometimes thought I'd love a slice of bread and butter and sugar."

At this the burly fellow burst into a long roar of laughter. It struck him as incongruous beyond anything he had ever heard that this girl, marooned so long in terrible solitude without any of the things that made life worth living, should voice this naive and child-like desire for bread and butter and sugar. He, in her shoes, would have had torturing dreams of beef-steak, tender, running with red juice... or a fat turkey... chestnut stuffing....

After they were gone, Jane and Davidson climbed very quietly back to their cave. They sat down on the rocks, and watched the boat reach the schooner's side, and the three men climb up the rope ladder.

"I don't like that Thomas chap," Jane said suddenly. "He looks hard and selfish. I wonder what he's up to with his geology."

"Well, it isn't any of our business."

"Davidson, are we going with them?"

"I don't know," he said.

Her resentment surged up. "But why should we?" she demanded bitterly. "The world hasn't anything for you and me. What would we do in—New York—of all places! Aren't we happy here?"

"They'll think we're crazy if we stay here," Davidson mumbled.

"Well, isn't that our business? We'll go off and hide on the mountain till they've gone."

But Davidson did not answer. He only stared at the little schooner as if he could not take his eyes off her. "How I'd like to have one of my own," he sighed, "and sail in her all over the world!"

A silent panic seized Jane. She knew that the sailor in him was awake and rampant, that he was hearing waves slap against a courageous prow, and the song of wind in the sails—cold northern wind—a virile wind, instead of these tropic zephyrs. Was this, after all, any kind of life for a red-blooded man: flowers, butterflies, fishes? Was she going to lose him, then—lose him to the sea? Was every white-winged ship to be her rival?... Twice during the night he got up restlessly; she saw him stand silhouetted in the mouth of the cave. She knew he was staring down into the harbor where he could see the pin-pricks of the schooner's riding lights. Then he would return, with a curious sigh.... Jane lay perfectly still, with her hands clenched by her sides, looking straight up into the cave's black roof, as though lying awake and tense, without relaxing, was somehow a way of fighting the sea. Davidson slept fitfully enough. Once, as he turned over, his arm fell heavily across her chest, like a gesture of reassurance.... I against a ship, thought Jane—I against a ship....

The scientists came ashore in the morning, six of them, and some of the seamen as well. They brought a tremendous pile of dunnage: tent, mosquito nettings, shovels and pickaxes, water buckets, cameras, bottles, scientific instruments. It made Jane laugh a little to see them laboriously carting all that stuff ashore. Such extensive preparation was incongruous and amusing, when she had managed life so very well with no earthly possessions whatever. Civilization certainly did burden one with luggage, she reflected—oh, Lord, masses of mental and material luggage to be carried....

They did not go down to meet the party this morning. Jane stood on the ledge in front of the cliff, watching the little group of men on the beach.... All at once an explosion, a terrific ghastly scream from scores of birds' throats, Jane's scream mingled with them, a thunderous clatter of wings from the cliff, and the unbearable sight of a crumpled bird reeling in his flight and falling, stricken—falling....

Jane stood glaring savagely. She could see the detestable Mr. Thomas, his shotgun smoking, walk up the beach to recover the bird he had killed. And suddenly she felt that she could not tolerate these meddling scientists—coming to her island to catch butterflies and murder birds, and bringing their cursed little schooner under Davidson's sailor eyes, tantalizing him, maybe luring him off to sea. She could no longer control her rage, and, half-crying hysterically, she went running back into the woods, tearing through the brush, jumping over the tangled deadfalls until, completely broken in wind, she could not run any longer. And even this violence of hers could not make her forget the horror of seeing that free, living creature struck down before her very eyes in the midst of its flying....

This running away into the woods had always been her favorite escape, from other people or from herself, beginning with her childhood in Maine. The woods of Maine were very different, though. There, she had looked up into a wavering lattice of pine branches, sparking silver in the sun. She remembered that one day, alone and half-afraid, she had put her arms around a young white pine, leaned her slender body upon it, and felt at once as though she had a friend. That tree had seemed solid and permanent. As permanent as anything on earth could be. Not even the earth itself was really permanent. Some day maybe the machinery of the universe would go wrong—the balance would be upset—and the earth would go catapulting into its sun like a very small moth into a gigantic flame.

She remembered, too, liking the way a tree lived—drawing its own sustenance direct from the earth, dispensing sustenance generously to the world around it; roots solid in the earth, growing and gripping; branches free to wave in the wind and to sparkle in the sun; trunk flexible, swaying with the weather. You could learn something from that. If you understood it properly, you could read from it the equivalent of many dusty bookshelves of philosophy. Once people had worshipped trees. A sensible worship, too, since without them the human race could not live.... She had decided then that, in her own humble way, she would try to live as a tree did.

She wandered restlessly among tropic creepers, and tried to forget the murdered seagull—tried to dispel her fears about the island. She could not get away from the haunting idea that the visit of these scientists somehow spelled disaster—disaster on a larger scale than the sacrifice of a few specimens. She was overwhelmed by a new realization of the transitory nature of everything in life. Nothing could be counted on, anywhere. All was shifting and mirage-like. That was pretty difficult to accept. Human nature had an unfortunate clinging tendency, a tragic desire to make life settle, a pitiful expectation that it would stay settled. Human nature could never get used to the idea of life as a relentless river, eventually carrying everything away with it, bringing new things, carrying them away in turn.

Beauty changed. You yourself changed, perhaps more than anything. Perhaps this was good, if you could only learn to accept it. Perhaps it could keep you happy and interested, if you only knew how to use it. It might enable you to revolve in the same direction as the world, instead of bucking it, trying to make it revolve as you wanted.

Jane laughed, then. Once she had complained at absence of change. Now she was bitterly fighting this menace of change.

She had often called herself a rebel, hater of civilization; now she was wondering if it was not wiser to try and go with the world. And the paradox was that all these conflicting thoughts had some measure of sense and truth. She felt herself temporarily posted at a vantage point, a mountain outlook from which she could survey the landscape. She saw the whole intricate mesh spread out below, a spider-web of feelings, motives, opinions, dreams, complaints in conflict with one another. They were all true, they were all false; and, looked at from far away, they were all a little bit absurd.

Even this peaceful island was the scene of confusion now. The scientists had their motives, doubtless as real as her resentment of them. She had her dreams. Davidson was torn by two desires. And the ogre that was civilization, that had so considerately left them alone for nearly three years, was now brooding again over the scene with a cynical eye, laughing, doubtless, as the bird fell, a white crumpled thing in the sunlight.... She almost wished she were devoid of emotion, for apparently it was futile, or absurd, or both, to want anything too much, to believe anything too strongly, to get mad, or to be unhappy. Yet how unlikeable a person would be, who did none of these things!...

The scientific party camped on the west side of the hill. For Jane, there was not the slightest possibility of any friendly relations with them. Davidson strolled over to the tent once in a while to chin with them, and he brought back amusing tales of their doings. Once he brought back a small package wrapped in a napkin. For Jane, he said, with Captain Porter's compliments.... There was one sailor in the party, a young chap named Wilson, whom he liked. This Wilson had for years been saving money, a few pennies at a time, so that some day he could buy a little boat of his own. Talking together, the two men found that they shared a dream—and their friendship was cemented.

Fragments of their conversation were repeated to Jane, and she could guess the rest. For the most part, Davidson did not talk much about the sea. But there was a new touch of restlessness in the atmosphere. Often she would find him brooding. He would struggle with these moods, and throw them off, and be unusually kind and tender to her for a while; and she knew that he was doing this consciously, logically—and that it never quite worked. It was pathetic, and hateful because it divided them. She surmised that he was trying to fight it intellectually—rationalize it out of existence. She racked her brains for some way to help him accomplish this—some way to steel him against the whisperings of the sea. There were moments when she was frantic with fear and exasperation. She would have enjoyed burning the schooner that drew Davidson's eyes so irresistibly, except that that would have stranded this unwelcome company indefinitely on the island!

One evening Davidson came back to the cave gloomier than ever. Jane asked no questions. She supposed it was another attack of the sea. But presently of his own accord he spoke to her. "Bad news," he said very softly. "We're through here, Jane."

And although she had been fearing this for days, half expecting it, she felt all the breath go out of her body, leaving her limp.

"What's happened?" she asked faintly.

"They've found what they were after," he said. He was holding his head in his hands, not daring to look at her.

"But I don't understand," she protested. "What were they after, David?"

He answered in one word. "Gold," he said.

[13]

New York was exactly as Jane had known it would be. As the schooner came close and swung into the harbor, using her auxiliary engine, the water was gray with hard usage. Skyscrapers rose up, domineering, in a gesture of ugly triumph. Undefeatable, inevitable, that city. There was no more permanent escape from it than from death. Some of the buildings were blackened with waterfront soot. Terribly high and frowning, huddled together in a grim crowd. It occurred to Jane that perhaps even they were tired of standing with their feet in filth, looking inevitable.

Jane rested both elbows on the bulwarks, and then her face on her arms. Going to her doom without looking at it. No use to look. Couldn't avert it by looking any more than by hiding one's eyes. A subtle hideous cloud of odors—typical welcoming gesture. It suggested—what? Stale fish, garbage, sewage.... A tug passed them, like a squat black goblin. A radio aboard it poured forth jazz interspersed with a long eulogy concerning tobacco.

Jane did not want to see the troop of big gulls that trailed the schooner. Their wings were dingy, and their calls greedy and hollow. Not at all the same breed of gull that had followed the *Annie Marlow* to sea!...

She had forgotten how much noise there was. The city had a continuous savage roar, pierced by jagged shrieks of automobile horns, now and then shaken into shrapnel by an elevated train or a heavy truck. There was no escape from that din, an enormous pressure on ears used to the sea and the leaves. No escape until eventually, having defeated an unwilling desk clerk, they found themselves in a mousy green-carpeted room in a cheap hotel. Even then the roar could be heard—muffled to a dull growl outside.

They sat down on the bed. Davidson put his arm around her, and felt that she was trembling. For a while she said nothing at all, then laughed a little, hollowly.

"Hurrah!" said Davidson. "Do that again. What were you thinking of?"

"I was thinking that now we're *really* marooned," she said.

She got up and walked nervously around the room. As she passed one corner, she was startled by a quick flash of movement beside her. A mirror, of course. The first she had seen. She looked at her own brown face, crowned with its ragged mop of hair that stuck up and out in all directions like a Fijian's—and at sight of herself, looking so ludicrous and forlorn, she could not help laughing again. It was more nearly genuine this time.

"Number two," said Davidson. "We're getting on fine."

"Good God, Daveson! No wonder those customs people looked at us so queerly. It surprises me they let us land at all."

"Wilson told 'em about us," Davidson said. "He's a decent chap, Wilson. Loaned me some money, by the way."

"That's lucky. I wouldn't have thought of it."

"A rather essential commodity," he said glumly.

"Yes—and one of the chief things wrong with the world. Being a slave to that trash—ghastly to think of it. Money! And now it's ruined our island, too."

"What would you think of getting in on the gold-hunting down there?" he asked.

"I'd hate it," she said vehemently.

"I was talking it over with Wilson. He seems to know a bit about such things. He said you couldn't possibly get in on it without capital. Not a chance. The worst kind of closed-corporation gyp-game affair. I could go as laborer and pan for the blasted stuff, and get about two bucks a day at best."

"I wouldn't even want to live there," Jane said indignantly. "Not with that going on. It seems criminal, that that island, so far away from anything to do with money, should be torn up for it now. It makes me want to kill somebody. Watching them blast and drill would be like seeing a thousand seagulls killed every minute. It would be like eating into my own flesh with their cursed steam-shovels. It would be—giving in to ugliness, Daveson—and we promised we'd never do that!"

"Jane," he said softly, "don't rave. Save your strength. And remember one nice thing: that when we last saw it, it was still untouched and peaceful and lovely. We can keep it forever."

"You're right," she said. "We've got to think about the present, and about New York. What are we going to do?"

"I'm going to a barber," he said.

"Me to—and then?"

"Well, we have to live somewhere—somewhere cheaper than a hotel. Any ideas on that?"

"Oh, sure, I've worked that problem once or twice before. We'll chase up a one-room-and-kitcheonette affair, and keep house. But I've got to have a few rags to cover me, even to see landladies in. I'd never get anywhere, looking this way."

"What will you use for money?"

"I don't know. How much did Wilson lend you?"

"Ten bucks," he said.

"That'll just about pay the hotel, and the barber, and a few meals," she said.

"Couldn't you borrow some somewhere? Haven't you friends in town?"

She thought of Professor Myers, and wondered if she could ever muster courage to go traipsing into that office looking like a lost gipsy, to ask for a loan.

Then suddenly her eyes lit up. "Idea!" she exclaimed. "David, I've got some money myself. In a bank—somewhere in a bank—let's see—Greenwich Savings—that's it! Hooray! We're saved!"

"How much?"

"About two hundred. That'll tide us over beautifully, till we get going."

"'Get going,'" he repeated sadly. "Where, Jane?"

"Yes, let's talk about that."

"I'm afraid there's nothing very cheerful to say about it."

She looked at him intently, and it seemed to her that now was perhaps as good a time as any to talk to him about the sea.

"Why did you want to leave the island?" she queried. "Was it really the gold, or was it—the sea?"

"The gold," he said unhappily. "I'm a sailor, and I can't help getting restless, Jane, but I've sense enough to know that going to sea hasn't much for me any more. It's a futile life. I want it, but I know better, that's the story."

"But you did want to have a little boat," she said softly.

"Of course—who hasn't dreamed pleasant dreams of little boats and far places? Why think about dreams now?"

"Well," she said, "if we worked hard for a few years, and saved our money, why shouldn't we have one, and sail it everywhere, and maybe discover new islands?"

And they both smiled, at the incongruity of saying these things at this time, in this place.

"Have you any plans at all?" she asked him. "For tomorrow, I mean. After the barber."

"Yes. After the barber, I'm going to traipse down to the waterfront, and see what's doing?"

"But—Davidson, you won't have to go to sea, will you?"

"Let's not think about it. I'm going to try everything else, first. There might be a job on a tug-boat, or a fish-barge."

"It would be hell to be a sailor's wife," she said.

"I know it—but I'm afraid you are."

"It would be nice, on the other hand, to be a schooner-captain's wife. I'd love that."

He smiled, but not happily. "You incurable little romanticist!" he mocked.

"Is that so far-fetched, then? Aren't there any other *Annie Marlows?*"

"Oh, a handful—sure. But every storm that comes along leaves fewer. And the crews are men that have been in those particular companies for years. Besides, I haven't got captain's papers, only mate's. Most of the captains are graybeards. If I wanted to do that, I'd have to stick at sea, and stick at sea, and do nothing else for years—and when I was an old man I might get a schooner, if there were any left."

"You make it sound grim, all right."

"It *is* grim."

"Davidson, as soon as we find a place to live, and get settled, I'm going to wander into my old office. If there isn't a job there, there might be a lead. You'd feel less—less crushed, wouldn't you, if I had a job, too?"

"No!" he exclaimed vehemently. "I'd hate it. It would make me feel like a worm—a third-rate worm."

"But why? I'd *want* to help."

"Well, you'll probably have to. But how do you think it makes a man feel, that his wife has to work for her bread?"

"But if it makes a dream come true sooner?"

"Dreams, dreams—always dreams," he muttered.

"But they *are* important, Daveson, even in New York. Perhaps especially in New York. And by the way, New York's no place in which to be a lady of leisure."

"Sorry to go up in the air," he said. "But about this idea of you having a job—well, I'm old-fashioned, I guess. I just want you to be my wife."

"Which reminds me that I'm not," she said. "It's rather an amusing thought. We're carrying on an affair, Daveson. I'm your mistress. Isn't that sort of funny?"

"What are you talking about? Don't you think the stars have any authority here? Haven't you got on your finger a ring I made?"

In the morning they determined that, however severe the struggle might be, however hard it was to get going again, they would sail into it with no procrastination. "Because," Jane said, "if we hang around and rest up, what courage we've got will start petering out, and we'll be left like leaky balloons."

"What's first, Jane?"

"Well, I thought I'd collect my money. Then shop. Then hunt up a place to live. And then meet you here tonight. We'd probably better stay another night here."

"And meanwhile I'll explore fish barges, etc."

She climbed into the absurdly ripped green blouse, which she had mended after a fashion aboard the schooner; and the red skirt, which she still loved. She had no stockings, and her shoes were tattered. Then she tried in vain to smooth out her hair by running her fingers through it. "I'm off," she said.

"Good luck. Don't get run over."

Breakfast: coffee and two stale doughnuts at a corner drugstore. After that Jane wandered off uptown to look for her bank. Reason told her she was in the city, but spiritually she could not accept it. Too vast a change, and too swift and cruel. Immensely tall buildings shot up around her, buildings that made her feel dwarfed and frightened. Streams, floods of people swept past her, jostled against her. They were like an ugly wind. Mostly they did not notice her at all; but every now and then someone did, which was much worse. An occasional face turned over a shoulder to stare, and then to laugh. A girl with garish red lips pointed Jane out to her companion. A man yelled: "Hi there, Cinderella!" People—she had forgotten people were like that. She stood on the curb, ridiculous in her short skirt, her frowsled hair. Traffic poured by. The city roared. She was really frightened, all of a sudden—cruelly frightened. She did not know how to get across the street, through that ceaseless mad flood of traffic. Her heart was pounding. The circle of great towers moved unsteadily and rocked in upon her, throwing ghastly shadows, and then wheeled back to leave cosmic spaces.... Cowering, she sat down on the curbstone, and waited, as calmly as she could, for her senses to clear.

"What's up?" said a voice overhead. "Hi there, miss! What's up, I said?"

Jane looked into the grinning face of a burly policeman. "What's up?" she repeated slowly. "Oh, nothing. I..."

"Are you sick?"

"No; I'm looking for the Greenwich Savings Bank."

"Right across the street," he said, grinning more than ever, and pointing. "Here! Let me take you over."

Traffic lights changed, the currents of people mingled, conflicted, altered. The policeman grabbed her arm firmly, and escorted her with mock solemnity to the opposite sidewalk. She thanked him timidly. "Thick, isn't it?" she said, by way of conversation.

He looked at her curiously. "Don't forget the one-horse shay next time you come to the big city," he advised.

She summoned all her courage, and swung into the bank. A somber and awesome palace of marble that made her feel smaller than ever. She filled out a withdrawal slip, and handed it in at one of the long row of gilded windows.

"Well, where's your bank-book?" the young clerk demanded.

For a second she was nonplussed. "Oh, that!" she began. "I haven't got it; it's..."

"Sorry, miss, but we can't do anything without it. Next, please!"

"But listen!" Jane exclaimed. "I've been shipwrecked—the book... I..."

"Whaddya trying to pull on me? *Next*, please!"

Jane turned away. She could not cope with this. Not in these clothes, anyway. On the other hand, to buy clothes she must have money. She moved slowly toward the door. "Now what?" she mumbled aloud.

Somebody touched her shoulder gently. A girl with piercing brown eyes under the low brim of a jaunty black hat was looking at her and smiling. "Do excuse me," she said, "but I heard what you said, and wondered if I could help. Have you really been shipwrecked?"

"Of course—why should I make it up?"

"Jiminy crickets, how I envy you!" the girl exclaimed. "Was it exciting? Look here, can't we be friends? I've never known anyone who has had adventures."

Jane smiled, a little puzzled. "Of course," she said. "My name's Jane—Jane Carey."

"Mine's Margaret Kingsley," said the other. "And I'm tickled to death to know you." They shook hands. "But this isn't the time to chew the rag, is it, Jane Carey? You're sort of up against it, aren't you? Can't I help? Now, please don't be stubborn and independent."

Jane was a friendly person, and succumbed easily to friendliness. "Sure, you can help, if you want," she said. "The immediate problem is, I can't fight for my money till I have some decent-looking clothes, and I can't get any clothes till I have my money."

"You look swell just as you are," the other said. "It's a darn shame to spoil it. But I can see that we've got to, if you're going to live round here. Now, look here. It's easy as pie. I've got charge accounts round various places. You just buy whatever your heart desires and your body requires, and pay me when you can. By the way, I've got nothing to do today, and I'd adore to come with you, if you'd like moral support; on the other hand, if you'd rather go alone, I can understand that, too."

"But wouldn't you be ashamed to be seen with me?"

"Don't be ridic! I'm proud of naming one exciting person among my friends."

"Whatever do you do that makes life so uninteresting?" Jane queried.

"Fashion model. Mannequin. Advertising model, etc., etc. Pose in corsets. Parade like a peacock in evening dresses, with a doll-like smile. I'm always either strapped or flush. Right now I'm flush, so you needn't feel bad."

"You'll be a good one to dress me, anyhow," Jane said. "You'd better come along."

"Well, let's go, then," said the other. "Where do we start?"

"Underwear," Jane said. "Haven't a stitch on under this rag."

Margaret giggled delightedly, and the two set off, a ludicrous contrast, arm in arm.

With each purchase Jane's confidence grew. She slipped into new underwear in the women's rest room of a large department store. That made it possible to try on dresses. Jane picked out two of them. Next came shoes and stockings. She watched her own gradual transformation with interest.

"Say, I'm beginning to look almost civilized," she commented to Margaret.

"Yes, drat it, you are. But only from the shoulders down. We've got to do something about that sublime mop of hair, I'm sorry to say. We've got to make you look like everybody else. How long since it's been combed, Jane?"

"I don't know. Years."

Margaret sighed. "Gosh, what wouldn't I give never to comb mine again!... Well, let's go chase a hair-dresser."

Jane emerged from the hair-dresser's clutches with her

brown hair washed and sleeked, trimmed into a conventional short bob, and finger-waved. She looked at herself in the mirror. "'O dearie me, this is never I,'" she quoted, laughing.

"You know, Jane, you're really pretty—but not half so pretty as you were," Margaret said.

"However, now I'll get by," Jane said. "And I'm going straight back to that bank and talk to the manager."

"Atta girl! But I'm not quite through with you yet."

"What more?"

"Well, a hat, for instance. And some gloves. Pocket-book, handkerchieves, comb, powder, and lipstick."

Jane sighed.

"Sick of it?"

"Well—isn't it lunch-time yet?"

Margaret looked at her watch. "I should say it is! In fact, it's two-thirty. I was so enraptured watching you struggle with civilization, Jane, that I never thought about time. Haven't had so much fun in years. Well, 'let's have another cup of coffee, and let's have another piece of pie.'"

The rest of the afternoon was taken up with odds and ends of shopping; and, when it was finished, it was too late, and Jane too tired, even to think about apartment-hunting. She said goodbye to her friend, and walked slowly back to the mousy little hotel, and Davidson.

Davidson looked at her incredulously. "My God!" he said after a while. "You've painted your face."

"Is it awful?"

"It isn't you. It's a very handsome young lady, but not Jane."

"That's just what I think," she said. "It's New York. You'll get used to it."

"No. What have you done to your hair?... You make me feel as if I had a mistress."

"Well, haven't you?"

"No. I had a wife once, but I guess she's lost—same as the

island. Jane, somehow I thought you'd stay the same through anything."

"I couldn't," she said. "You'll have to learn to see through the superficial. You wouldn't object so much if you could have seen how they laughed at me before I got some clothes."

He gritted his teeth in impotent resentment.

"What sort of luck did you have?" she asked him.

He looked pale and dusty, and she guessed from his voice that he was tired almost beyond endurance. All day he had been about the waterfront. He had hoped to land some sort of job with a towing company, or a ship-chandler—anything to keep him in New York—probably in the harbor or along the waterfront, because it was the only life he knew. He had looked over the shipping, talked with sailors and stevedores and tug-captains, hearing only how desperate conditions were, being discouraged everywhere.

"Never mind, Jane—tomorrow..."

There was no rest. In the morning they separated again. Jane, a little heart-sick and fearful, walked uptown. She was steadied by the fact that now no one took any notice of her at all. In fact, she looked like any other reasonably well-dressed young woman with a good figure and an intelligent face. She was New York, as she had said to Davidson last night.

As she walked, she thought over the bank-book question. Had she taken it to sea with her? Today it seemed that she had left it with Millie; but she could not remember for sure. Millie?... She wandered into a drug-store, found a telephone book, and stood absently thumbing its pages. No results there. Then she had an idea, and called the switchboard of the apartment house where they had lived.

"Does Miss Carson still live here? Miss Rogers, then? Both left a year ago?... Any address?... No?..."

Frustrated in that quarter. Nothing left for it but to go to the bank and try to make somebody believe her.

She selected another of the long row of gilded cages. "Have you still an account in the name of Jane Carey?" she asked.

The clerk referred to large books, and finally shook his head. "Naw," he said. "She took it out of here a year ago."

"But—" Jane began. Then she turned away. So that was it! Millie had her bank-book; Millie had been desperate for money; Millie had moved from the apartment a year ago, and taken Jane's money with her!

That meant—well, if Davidson didn't land something right away, it meant that she would either have to borrow indefinitely from Margaret Kingsley, or else find herself some sort of job without allowing herself even the brief reprieve she had hoped for. She wondered what had happened to Millie; what trouble she had got into desperate enough to make her rob her best friend. Rob? No, it couldn't be called that until it was understood. On second thought, it would be like Millie simply to assume that Jane had been devoured by lions....

What next, then? Professor Myers' office? Perhaps Mary Rogers would still be there. Perhaps through her Millie could be found.... She hardly dared believe that the office would still be in existence. If it was, maybe she would have the heart to ask for her old job back again.

The building stood where it had always stood, overshadowed on all sides by newer creations which deprived it of even the little sunlight that might ingeniously have filtered down to its windows. Some time this building would give way before the onslaughts of efficiency, and another lithe shining tower would stand over the shadow of these ancient dark foundations.

She walked steadily into the hall, then drew a deep breath and pushed the office door. Her eyes, accustomed to the brightness outside, could hardly pierce the duskiness. Then a cry came from the other side of the room: "Janie!"

It was more like a confused dream than a real experience. Here came Mary, rushing over to her, grabbing both her hands.

There sat Miss Perry, behind her ledgers, with an almost warm smile of welcome. And then the door of the inner office opened, and Professor Myers himself came out, bowed, white-haired, looking much older than she had remembered. He stopped short, and ran his hand over his hair.

"Why—why, Miss Carey! Well, well! Back again from your travels!"

Jane went to greet him, a little shakily. "Yes, I've come back."

"Did you have a pleasant vacation?" he inquired, as though she had been away in the country for a couple of weeks.

"Oh, yes; I certainly did," she assured him. Vacation! As if the three years—four years—what was it, anyway?—as if all that time had been just a sort of leave of absence from Professor Myers' dingy little office! Her heart sank.

"And, Miss Carey," he was saying now, "I really must show you our latest treasure." He held open the inner door invitingly. On his desk, in a small glass-topped box, an enormous butterfly... breath of azure silk... metallic gleam... rare old Persian vase... the island!

"South America," he was saying. "Remember that old fellow —what was his name?—Ottocruntz, or something? Well, every entomologist in this country and every other was laughing in their sleeves at him, but he's brought back the goods. Marvellous creature, isn't it? I'm keeping it here until it goes to an honorary throne in the Museum. Ought to go into the Metropolitan, instead of the Natural History, as a matter of fact."

In her terror, Jane clung to the butterfly. Those dead wings, once tremulous and vibrating with life and ecstasy... beauty captured... butterfly triumphant?... other worlds?...

The old man was now beginning to cast about uneasily among the disordered piles of papers on his desk. "Have you—" he began.

Jane stirred sharply into life. "Yes!" she cried. She picked up his glasses from beside the butterfly box and handed them to him with a small, cynical bow.

"Thank you," he said patiently. "You know, Miss Carey, I always say that it isn't so much whether you lose your glasses—"

A tremor ran through her. "No," she chimed in quietly, "it's the finding that matters."

He nodded with a distant smile. They stood, philosophizing in echoes, a recaptured naiad and a kindly ghost, one on each side of the butterfly which separated them like a symbol of all that had come rushing in between the two since they had stood this same way years ago.

"Well," he resumed, "you're coming back to us?"

Jane forced herself to smile. "But would you want me, with Miss Rogers here?"

"Oh, didn't she tell you? She's leaving us next month.... Yes, I rather suspect it's a young man who's the villain in this piece." And he smiled the fatherly smile that she remembered. "Of course we want you," he added.

"Let me think about it," she said. "I really just dropped in for a visit, this time."

"Of course, of course. You know, Miss Carey, I was thinking about you just the other day—wishing you could be on hand to help me write my new book."

"Another!" she exclaimed. "What's it to be about this time?"

"Butterflies," he said.

What was it she and Davidson had talked about long ago—something she thought Professor Myers ought to be told and made to understand, about butterflies? But the words eluded her now. She could not even remember what it was that had once seemed so obvious. It was blurred in distant haze.

"But," she said, smiling, "I don't know anything at all about butterflies."

"You don't have to. I want you to type the manuscript for

me, and maybe help me reword some parts of it. There'll be an enormous index to make, letters to write, and eventually proofs to read. And besides all that, the regular office work. I could pay you pretty well, Miss Carey; in fact, I think I could just about double your old salary."

"I'll call you up," she promised. "I think I'd like to come. Thank you for asking me." She gazed another moment at the butterfly under the glass. Blue wings hovered in the foreground of her thoughts....

In the outer office, Mary pounced at her again. Miss Perry had gone out. "Jane, where did you go? What did you do? I do so want to hear all about it!"

Jane waved her hand airily. "What's this I hear about you?" she asked. "That's much more important. Anybody I know?"

"A classmate of my brother's. You'll meet him soon. We're getting married next month."

"I'm terribly glad.... Know anything about Millie?"

"Yes, but it isn't a pretty story," Mary said.

Jane's face fell. "She got into trouble?"

"Yes—with a man. She was going to have a baby, and she didn't have any money. I don't know what happened to her. She just went off one day, and didn't come back. I couldn't keep the place alone, on my pay, and so I moved, too."

"Mary! And you haven't any idea where she went?"

The other girl shook her head.

"I wish I knew how to find her," Jane said.

"I wish you did, too. You could cheer her up as nobody else ever could. It was pretty awful, Jane. She didn't let on a bit—you know how she is; but I just know she was all broken up. She would cry at night, and try not to let me hear. And you see, she couldn't dance any more, and lost her job, of course. She was simply stranded, high and dry."

"Who was the man, anyway?"

Mary shrugged. "She never would tell me anything," she said.

Jane was silent.

"Where are you living?" Mary asked.

"Nowhere yet," Jane said. "I've got to find a place. Down in the village, I expect."

"Coming back to work?"

"He's asked me. I'm to let him know in a few days. He's going to write a book about butterflies."

"He's been swell to me," Mary said. "I've been here ever since you left."

"He's the kindest person in the world," Jane said quietly. "But I wonder how much he knows about butterflies."

"What do you mean, Janie? He's studied 'em all his life."

"Yes, of course," she agreed quickly. "Well, kid, I'm off to hunt houses. I'll drop in again—let you know where I live, and all."

"And tell me your adventures, Jane."

"Sure, if they're interesting enough. It's been swell to see you. Give my love to the lucky devil, and I hope you'll be all-fired happy.... By the way, what day is it?"

Mary laughed. "Thursday, you crazy nut," she said. "June 21st, to be exact."

"Thanks. Time to be thinking about vacations, honeymoons, and all that sort of thing—what?... Well, so long!"

Jane looked for a subway station. There it was—blue light on the corner. It was disgusting still to be able to find your way around New York! Nobody could lose that demon of a subway. Might as well try to push over a granite wall.

She was a little bit particular, as to this matter of a place to live. If her salary was to be twice the old one, she could afford to be particular. Friends were important to her happiness, and she wanted a place where they would be glad to come. She had never quite made up her mind whether your house enticed friends, or friends made your house enticing. However, she would give the house the benefit of the doubt, and choose it carefully.

At last, after long weary walking round about Greenwich Village, and discouraging interviews with grimy proprietors, she stumbled on what she wanted. It was a quietly furnished apartment, with fresh-looking blue curtains, blue dishes in the tiny kitchen, a window-box of geraniums, and enormous windows with big square panes.

"Used to be a studio," the landlady explained, "one o' these here artists, you know. Plenty of light, you see—sun, too, mornings."

The place was pretty and picturesque, in a simple way. There was a small bedroom, leading off the living-room; and in the living-room itself a blue-covered couch that could be unfolded in case of company. The more Jane looked at the big windows, framed in the long curtains, the more she liked the place. Plenty of light! That was certainly a selling point, in New York!...

Davidson's shoulders were drooping, no doubt about that. He looked more silent and grim than ever. Jane suffered for him. She did not dare ask what sort of day he had had. She knew, all too well.

"I've got a place to live in," she told him. "I think you'll like it. It's got windows."

He stared gloomily. "Who's going to pay for it?" he mumbled.

She sat down on the floor at his feet, and rested her head on his knees. "I went to see the old professor, too," she said.

"Well?"

"Well, I can have my job back, if I want it, at twice the old pay."

"You're lucky," he said.

Jane was suffering for him. She had an inkling of how it all must be hurting him, that she could walk into an office and be offered a well-paid job, while he, who wanted so badly to protect and take care of her, could find no work at all. He was tight-lipped and bitter. "I'm glad you're so clever," he said. "But if you think I'm going to hang round and be—well, your gigolo—you're mistaken, that's all."

She bit her lips and said nothing. But presently he began to stroke her hair, in the old familiar way; and then he bent down to whisper in her ear: "Sorry! Better luck tomorrow."

They moved into the new apartment. Davidson came out of his gloom long enough to admire it a little, and help her carry home some groceries from the corner store. That just about exhausted the money he had borrowed from the sailor Wilson. After that he went off downtown again; and then, because sometimes two can laugh more easily than one, Jane telephoned Margaret Kingsley to come and have lunch with her.

"Some time," Margaret said, "I do wish you'd tell me the story. How it began, the shipwreck, the whole thing. And I'm curious about that ring." She pointed to the plain dark circlet of ebony, with its tiny carved figures, that Jane always wore—that was, to her, sacred.

"Would you believe it, Marg?"

"I mightn't believe all of it. It would probably sound too good to be true. But I want to hear it, anyway. It'll make a marvellous tale."

"What worries me," Jane said, "is that I'm afraid it's coming to an end, and not a particularly happy one."

"Stories don't end happily in life," Margaret asserted. "The better the beginning, the worse the end."

"Don't be morbid!" Jane warned. "I'm depressed enough already. You see, I'm afraid I'm losing my lover."

Margaret sat very still, almost without breathing. Then, in a queer small voice: "I lost one once," she said. "Hurts, doesn't it?"

Davidson came in late that afternoon. The droop to his

shoulders was more pronounced, and his mouth was grim. "God, Jane, this is a racket," he said after a while. "There just isn't a job in New York."

She left the peas on the small stove to take care of themselves. Davidson needed her more than they did.

"You know what I've got to do?" he went on. "Well, there's no use hanging round here any longer—I've got to go to sea again."

She flinched, but said nothing. She had a pretty fair conception of what he was up against. No matter where he turned he faced brutal conflict. He would have been willing to sacrifice his own feelings, overcome his repugnance, and accept any job, however hateful, that would keep him near Jane; but such a job was not to be found. Going to sea meant even a greater sacrifice, involving both of them. And yet Jane was sure that, in spite of her need for him and his longing to keep and protect her, the deep subtle call of his old profession was strong, almost like the instinct of life itself. She could offer him nothing to offset it except herself and the dismal prospect of prolonged emasculating idleness.

She understood how hopeless it was to argue with the question. A dull pain dragged slowly through her, associated with a burning greenish odor from the stove. She slipped away to rescue the peas. The floor underfoot was a blur, and her hands were ice-cold.

But after supper there was another shock in store for her. "You see, I met an old shipmate of mine this morning," he told her. "Mate of a freighter—Nelson Line. He put in a word for me aboard and—well, I'd never have got the job without him, and I didn't dare miss the chance. We sail tomorrow night, Jane."

She smiled forlornly. "I thought you hated steamers," she said.

"I do," he admitted gloomily. "But what am I to do? There's nothing else; and obviously I can't get a job ashore. That's the mean thing about the sea, Jane. A chap who's gone to sea is branded. Can't do anything else, ever, even if he wants to—nobody'll take him. I'd have been better off if I'd learned shoe-making," he said bitterly.

"Where's this freighter going to?" Jane wanted to know.

"I'll get paid off in Seattle."

"And then?"

"I know that country, and have a few friends there. There's a schooner—she runs to Hawaii with lumber. I know a chap who makes his living with a little motor-boat, salmon-fishing summers off Alaska. I want to see if there's anything in that. And there's a trading-schooner—I sailed in her once—she goes up into the Arctic Circle summers, to trade with the Eskimos."

"But—" Jane began fearfully.

"Janie, if I work anything out there, you shall come out to me. If I don't, I'll come back."

"I rather like that salmon-fishing idea," she said. "Don't you?"

"I don't know anything about it."

"If you had a boat," she persisted, "could I come with you?"

"Oh, Janie, you're always looking so far ahead!"

"I have to. If I looked just at the immediate future, I wouldn't want to live."

He whipped his big arms around her so fiercely that he hurt her. "You've got to live," he told her almost angrily. "And you've got to be happy. Don't you see? Otherwise, you make all my failures worse. Life would be unbearable. I need you. You've got to help me!"

She had never seen him violent and tortured; she loved him in this pain more than she had ever loved him. She was glad that his embrace was hurting her; physical pain was a relief. Somewhere in her mind was the consciousness that his unhappiness was in a way her fault; without her, his life would still have been a problem, but it would not have approached this present insidious complexity. Till now, their relation had meant only happiness to both of them. The world had changed that. They were now forced to serve unwillingly as each other's torturers.... Through all this was the undercurrent of her irrelevant feminine pride in him: she was glad his shoulders were so wide, his arms so strong.

"Of course I'm going to help you," she told him. "I shall work, and save my money, and you do the same, and it'll be no time before we'll have enough to buy a fishing-boat, or carry out any other scheme you think up."

He kissed her, and her mouth was twisted with the pleasure of it. She longed unspeakably for his love.

"You aren't afraid, are you?" he asked.

"Well, I don't feel any too brave," she confessed.

"I don't believe I'd want you to. I suspect that awfully brave people are heartless. You're better: acting brave when you aren't —sweet coward!... You aren't afraid I won't come back?"

She shook her head.

"I couldn't leave you," he said. "You're mine, part of me. I'll never leave you," he repeated roughly. "My old shell, yes; but my heart and soul, the most of me and the best of me—no, no."

"I love your shell, too."

"It isn't worth much," he said. "I can't even earn a living."

"You could live with me, you know," she muttered.

"And let you support me? That would be fine, wouldn't it?... No, Janie, we're going to do better, only it'll take time."

"And strength," she added.

He sighed. "We're not going to talk about this any more. Our shells have to forget it, because this is the last time they can be together—for a while. You're beautiful when you're sad, Jane. But then, you're always more beautiful than anything on earth."

"Except the island," she said.

"To me you *are* the island. You make it real."

She lay in his arms, and at each breath their bodies were pressed together.

"The island," he repeated. "We have that always, whatever happens to us now. Nobody can hurt that, or take it away from us."

"No."

"Let's think about it. The hill—"

"The butterflies—" she said.

"Fireflies... stars..."

"*Our* stars!"

He was right. It was all alive, more vivid than ever—a vision, a dream, but strangely more real even than reality.

"Janie, there's a star outside the window."

"Not an electric light?"

"A star," he repeated. "One of the ones that married us."

"And there was the waterfall," Jane pursued.

"You standing in it," he added.

"You chasing me in the wind and the flowers," she said.

"And catching you—kissing you—"

She was a wild white wave, combing in long ecstasy higher and higher to shatter in iridescent surf; then ebbing back, ebbing, merging at last into the sea.

[14]

He was gone. There were some facts you could deny, or argue with, or ignore, but there was nothing to do about this one, except coldly look it between the eyes and say: "I'm not afraid of you."

But Jane was afraid. When you were one with another human being, and suddenly were made to drift about and act as an independent unit, what happened? Where and who were you then?

The first few days of his absence had taken an amusing, almost entertaining aspect. For she was constantly turning to him in all the varied, multitudinous details of life. She would forget he was away; she could not keep the fact in mind. Sometimes she laughed aloud at this—and as she laughed, turned to share its grim humor with him.

Then these incidents became painful and exasperating. Instead of sudden stabs of loneliness which had come at intervals in the beginning, she was haunted by an almost unceasing ache, alternating with deadly weariness. Without him, the city was more alarming than ever. Alone in her apartment, she had moments of real terror. On the island she had never minded darkness and isolation, the rumbling of the sea, rustling of leaves, odd sounds made by forest creatures. But here the huge grumble of traffic kept her awake; she flinched when the windows shook with it. And no Millie to keep her company. She considered finding some other congenial room-mate, but rejected the idea: some time Davidson would come back, and he must be able to come freely to stay with her. So she went on by herself, fighting the city, wrestling with her loneliness, and by a miracle of perseverance holding her own.

Davidson wrote to her sometimes—short, curiously worded letters—mere skeletons of thoughts, with their fabric left to her understanding. He wrote in little phrases separated by curved dashes. From anyone else she would have thought it a barbaric manner of writing, but from him she adored it. Mostly these were dashed off hastily at sea, sometimes to be posted within a few minutes. "Just coming into San So-and-So—funny little place—in fact it can't really be called a place—just a pier with a light on the end—to keep one from walking off I suppose—I love you."

Every once in a while a much longer letter would come. She soon learned that these were his 'longshore letters, written when he had perhaps an entire evening at his disposal. Even they did not tell her anything very concrete about what he was doing, and the chronological order of events in his life. He simply assumed that it would not be interesting to her, since to him it was commonplace enough. He would recount scattered pieces of what had happened since he had written last, and then dive into philosophical meditations and humorous descriptions.

She was glad when old friends began showing up, one by one. Some of them had never heard that she had gone away, and others supposed that she was dead or had forgotten them. Before the *Annie Marlow* adventure, her friends had been the one part of New York life that had made her happy. They were a diverse crowd. There were young married people, lonely girls struggling with their first jobs, boys trying to work their way through Columbia, girls who had gone to business school with Jane when she first came to New York. Most of them were hard up or making bad weather of it in some way: she had made few contacts with the idle rich.

People confided in Jane. Before she had been back in the city very long she had heard a good many sorrowful tales, and several little tangled situations had been put tenderly into her hands. People's difficulties had always secretly astounded her, because she was simple at heart, and believed in simplicity. Now they seemed even more absurd and out of place. Perhaps that explained her success in handling these matters: she never took them quite seriously, but always with a touch of secret humor, while no one suspected that she was not solemn as a judge. In a way that was what they made of her, she reflected: a friendly and unofficial judge. She felt that she could fill the post more ably now, because of Davidson and the stars, and the sea that had stamped its rhythm upon her heart.

The office was the same as always. Miss Perry sat eternally at her desk, wiry and grayish, with impersonal eyes. Like Professor Myers, she seemed to have aged. The whole office and everyone in it appeared dustier than ever. And the horrible part of it all was that these small changes were merely superficial, and by their nature served only to intensify the dismal sameness that went on underneath. Every now and then she would be overwhelmed by an odd sensation, as though, like the light princess in the fairy tale, she had lost her gravity. Perhaps the most surprising fact was that she had been able to readapt herself to this old life, even painfully and with difficulty. It was wrong. She and the office should both have undergone such a transformation that their reunion would have been impossible. Instead of which, here she was with nothing but an ebony ring and a few rainbow streamers around her shoulders to prove that Lost Island and Davidson had ever existed. The ring was part of her flesh. As for the rainbows—well, they were pretty ragged, pretty battered, and in any event not suitable to wear to a respectable job. Every now and then she would put a few pieces into the trash basket.... She was almost sure that never again would she discuss dreams with Miss Perry.

New York had all the same old things wrong with it. The same gods, Money and Speed. If you refused to bow before those altars, it was too bad for you, that was all. You lived in the murk, with never a really fresh piece of wind or a first-hand ray of sunlight. It was no wonder people sometimes lost their heads, and drank and dissipated.

Jane was living in two worlds: a shadowy, dim one superposed on a background of brightness and gleam. Sometimes these made war. Her hardest job was to keep them reconciled, to make each one of them give her something of value. The one thing that never failed to amuse her and keep her busy, was this interest she took in people. She could even get a kick out of the old game of watching faces in the subway, although that tended to be a depressing rather than a stimulating game. Rows of fat business men behind newspapers, all devastatingly alike. The women were possibly a shade better, though it was a scant shade. Subway men certainly put the species to shame. There were pale effeminate creatures, whom you had to look at twice to be sure they weren't girls; short pudgy Jews in striped shirts; strange droopy men with mustaches. Only once a week, or twice in rare weeks, you caught a glimpse of a brave upstanding creature with an honest gleam in his eyes. Another interesting fact about subways was that people headed for different destinations differed hugely. You could make quite a sociological study of that, if you could stand the diverse smells.

She would gladly have traded all her friends, old and new, to be with Davidson. She was more aware of him now than when he had been constantly with her. Overshadowing everything she did, following her wherever she went, was her longing for him.

At first this ghost was very definitely Davidson, with his moody eyes and his characteristic walk, that looked so leisurely, and a little awkward, and was really so fast. And then, as time wore on, she could no longer say for sure that it was he, that it was anyone at all; it was just a longing. She had always tried to be honest with herself, and she was not too old-fashioned to question whether this longing might not be simply for companionship, and love, rather than for some one person whom she could not have. After all, nearly a year had gone by....

Her friends took it for granted that she was just about the happiest creature on earth. She had established herself with them in that capacity, and nothing she did could change their conception of her. When she was quiet and serious, they never suspected her. That was just Janie's way. She was, as far as they were concerned, a known quantity. This was humorous to her and a little painful at times, for although she liked to keep within the protection of her secret, she sometimes felt a human pang because they did not understand. Her heart was cold around the edges, and no one knew; sometimes it froze into a small sharp icicle, like a waterfall in winter time.

Margaret Kingsley came nearer than anyone else to understanding. Sometimes the two girls had lunch together; but lunch was crowded and unsatisfactory. More often Margaret would meet Jane outside the office after work, and they would cook supper in Jane's kitchenette; afterwards go to a show, or just sit talking.

"I have more fun with you, Jane, than with any of my boy friends—not that that's saying much."

"They must be pretty awful."

"Indescribable," Margaret said. "What are the prospects of your having one some time?"

"Well, I'm just getting round to the idea that it might be fun."

"Atta girl! Don't stay married to a ghost. Not healthy."

"Sounds pretty cold," Jane admitted. "Sounds almost like pneumonia. But you know, I think you're married to one, yourself."

"Maybe. But it doesn't pay. I know that's true, even if I don't practice what I preach. Jane, I haven't really enjoyed anything since—except you—and it was nearly three years ago.... What's the matter with love, that it always goes so wrong? Either they are cruel to each other, or else get bored to extinction."

"I don't think there's anything the matter with love," Jane said. "Only civilization has kind of dressed it up in plate-glass armor, and invested it with some sort of mystery that has no particular business to be there. We're hampered and fettered with the good old iron shackles of tradition, inhibition, et al., and then we're surprised when we trip and fall down and hurt ourselves. And then, I think people get so mixed up with a kind of dreamy-eyed mock romance of their own invention that they can't tell that from the real article. They play a game, thinking it's sincere. A girl thinks any man is her rightful, one-and-only mate if he's a bit convincing and a bit mock-romantic. And any poor wretch can be that. They learn it from the movies, and get it down pretty pat."

"You had an island," Margaret said.

"Yes—that was my luck."

"Even if I should ever get shipwrecked," the other girl went on, "it wouldn't be with the right man. It would be the fat old steward, I'm sure. Or else the island would turn out to be a barren coral reef."

"You're too romantic," Jane said.

"Romantic! What do you mean?"

"Well, when people find life unexciting, as you seem to, it's sometimes because they themselves are way off in gold clouds, looking down snootily upon this little ash-heap of an earth, and thumbing their noses at it, not even trying to get properly acquainted with it. Of course it looks like an ash-heap, at that distance."

"It's sort of hard not to turn up your nose at life," Margaret said. "Especially when it's hurt you. Sort of a defense."

"Maybe it's a defense," Jane said, "but I don't believe it's a good one.... You don't mind my saying this, do you?"

"Shoot, kid!"

"You don't have to take me seriously, anyhow. But that kind of defense—shutting yourself up in a castle, and thumbing your nose between the bars—doesn't hurt the world a bit, after all. The world doesn't even know about it. You want revenge, but you're just wasting your energy; you're just hurting and limiting yourself."

"I know that, sort of subconsciously," Margaret admitted. "What's the secret of your own resilience, Jane?"

"Oh, I don't know. Whatever it is, it's no secret. My friends help. You help, for one. I'm interested in people. And I have a tendency to laugh. I know I'd get a kick out of posing in corsets, or selling sausages. I like to think I can get some sort of a kick out of most anything. I think I'm better at that than I used to be. Takes practice, and you have to try a little. If you don't care about people, there are other surprising phenomena, such as tadpoles growing up to be frogs, or the fact that light comes in waves, or the question of space being infinite, or the birth control movement. And little things—that you can't possibly see from your castle. You've known me long enough to know what I mean. Today I saw a dirty kitten playing with a broom in a grocery store. It made me laugh out loud. The other day I walked out to the Washington bridge, and there was a perfectly passable sunset. There are lots of things: a glass of wine, maybe, or a good tune on a neighbor's radio, a new bud on my geraniums, an evening with you."

"You seem to have doped it out pretty well. You make me feel a bit ashamed."

"Oh, it only seems to run smoothly because I've trained it to, Marg. Hard work, of course. If I were in your shoes, looking out of that castle window, I'd buy a telescope. You'd see some pretty amusing things, if you'd only set yourself a different scale."

"What would you do, Jane, if you had my dumb pack of boy friends?"

"Oh, come now! Everybody has a spark or two somewhere. Something he's interested in, or can do well, or likes to talk about. Just hunt around till you find the spark. Then blow on it.... Oh heck, let's not talk philosophy any more."

"But you're so good at it."

"Do I really help any?"

"Of course you do! You're the sanest, most practical creature I ever ran into."

"Well, you help me, too," Jane said. "You've an uncanny feeling for clothes—line and color. I'm dressing a hundred per cent better since I knew you."

"That's pretty superficial help," Margaret said.

"Nothing is superficial that makes you a well-balanced person," Jane asserted. "Besides, people ought to supplement each other, exactly as you and I are doing. I can get a kick out of that in itself. Just come down off your beloved Olympus, and you will, too."

A FEW DAYS LATER, at five o'clock, Jane was standing outside the door of the building her office was in. The city was just lighting up. A murmur, forever growing to a roar and then subsiding, like a gigantic pulse: countless fragments of humanity, the chorus of millions of voices, the tired beating of millions of heels against the pavements, the great varied streams of traffic....

"Jane!"

This voice came from a group of people on the steps, some of whom were coming out in a hurry, and others trying to force their way in. She saw a young man pushing toward her, with light brown curling hair and eyes of rare shining blue.

"Jane! Gosh all hemlocks, is it you?"

"Wait a minute! Take it easy!" she commanded. "I can't think..."

He grabbed her arm. "Jane!" he exclaimed again.

"Wait... oh, I know...! Heather!... Johnny!"

And right there, on the steps of the building, in the crowd, he flung his arms around her and kissed her, laughing, as if he hadn't kissed anyone for a hundred years.

"You old parachute! Wherever did you drop from?"

"Where did *you* drop from, you'd better say, Jane. I've been hunting you for years. Did you get lost in a cloud, or what? I had an address once. I kept writing there, and all my letters came back." He was talking so fast and eagerly that his words fell over one another.

"I don't know where to begin, John. But let's go home and talk—"

"All right!" he put in.

"And I'll tell you the tale of my life, and you'll tell me yours. How's your father, and Heather?"

"Well, I'm afraid Father's not so young as he used to be—can't do so much; but Heather's alive and kicking," he added with a sudden burst of enthusiasm.

"You look as young as ever, John—in fact, younger."

"I am. Why wouldn't I be. I've found you!"

"Life's been treating you well, what?"

"Except for not being able to find you."

"Oh, forget me, you liar! What have you been doing with yourself? Married?"

"Ye Gods, of course not! Do I look like it? Do I sound like it?"

"Well, not exactly."

"Are you?"

"Well, no."

"Surprising!"

"So what!" said Jane.

"So I think I'll kiss you again," he said.... "By the way, I've got a car some place. Which way is west, Janie?"

"A whole car of your own, you plutocrat?"

"Well, a whole Ford.... Here! Maybe this is it."

They worked their way slowly uptown. Whenever they came to a red traffic-light, John kissed her. "Damn!" he would say, "it's going green!" or "Hurrah! We'll never make this one!"

Jane was much too weak with laughter to protest, even if she had wanted to. Between traffic-lights she wangled out of him bits of his own history.

"...It isn't very interesting, but you see old Aunt Angeline kicked the bucket and left me quite a nest-egg."

"Atta girl!" said Jane. "Who'd have thunk it of her?"

"You disrespectful wench! You might at least thank her for my having a Ford."

"So now you're a gentleman of leisure, is that it?"

"Well, not exactly. I've got an income that I can't quite live on, so I piece it out by—well, I've been doing a bit of writing, to tell the truth. Not very good, though. Published a few articles and a story, and I've got a book in my head."

"Sounds good to me!"

"Think so? Well, you know what I do? I have a rather swell sort of life. Bum around—mountains, mostly—you know how I always loved mountains, Janie. And you—you loved them, too."

She turned to him, radiant. "Why, you remember a lot about me, don't you? You remember that mountains were my God."

"I should say I do! Remember the time—we were just little kids then—and we climbed Whitney Hill to pick blueberries, and we looked off at the White Mountains, and you said: 'Gee,

Johnny, I don't know about God, and I don't think I believe in Him, but I sure believe in mountains.'"

Jane laughed joyously. "Oh, Lord, what times we had! All those quaint ideas that we were so solemn about. They were secrets, too, weren't they? We never dared tell anyone else. But you and I always understood."

"Well, I'm faithful. I stick to mountains most of the time, now. I hike all over the country, and climb everything in sight. Pack on my back, a string of Knorr's pea soup sticks round my belt, and off I go, for weeks and months at a stretch."

"Regular gipsy, what?"

"Yes, and you know what? I've got the grandest little log cabin in Maine, near Katahdin. Enormous fireplace, books. Sometimes I spend a whole winter there, writing, reading, tramping. How I've longed to show you that place, Janie! Fetch my wood in from the forest—trees all snowy—tracks of little animals. You'd love it. Tramp fifteen miles for provisions. I couldn't ever live long out of the wilds. It's in my bones.... Then every once in a while I put on a collar and come to town, see a show, talk to a publisher or two, see you."

He was like a little boy in his vigor and enthusiasm. "Tell you how it is," he ran on. "I couldn't go on living an ordinary sort of life, you see. I was scared I'd get caught in the machine—you know—The Machine, and all that. Had a job in Portland once. Nearly finished me.... There's been only one thing wrong, as a matter of fact. I missed you so, Janie. I wanted the kid I used to pick blueberries with. I kept thinking of you with your hair flying in the wind, and the way you laughed, and the way you loved butterflies, and how you were the grandest pal on earth, and what a grand runner you were. I didn't know—until you went away after that Charlie business...."

"I thought of you, too, Johnny."

"Did you? he asked eagerly. "You did!"

"Yes, I thought of you saying: 'Why doon't ye pin a note on the duck, Janie? If Heather's aroond, Andra's no far awa'."

"Oh, Jane, I'm glad you thought of me, even if it was just something ridiculous. Tell me some of yours now. I just bet you've a yarn to spin!" His eyes were shining.

"I bought a red skirt," she said solemnly. "That sums it up."

"Hope you didn't pay too much for it. Where is it now?"

"Well, I left most of it on an island. You see, I got shipwrecked. That's why I didn't get your letters."

"What an imagination!"

"No, honest!"

"Well, hadn't we better get you another?"

"Another island?"

"Sure, if you like. I really meant another red skirt. Become you very well."

"You seem to understand," said Jane.

"Oh, sure, in my scatter-brained way. I know you meant it as a symbol of fun and freedom, and that something happened to it. Well, I'm glad you had it. It was time. Let's have some more!"

"You bet!"

"Like to dance?"

For a minute she held her breath. Then suddenly: "John—that's *it!*" she exclaimed.

"What's what?... Let's go slow, Ford—miss this light."

"I knew there was something. Ever since I got back from that island—"

"Loon Island!" he chuckled.

"I've known there was something I wanted, and in the city. I couldn't think... Dancing—that was it! Rhythm and jazz."

"Everybody needs that, if they're any sort of creature at all," said John. "It's in the bones. Maybe you've been in love. Realize it more then. Of course you've been in love! Anybody so alive—"

"And so beautiful—" she put in.

"Of course! You were in love with me, really, all the time; only it probably had another name."

"It certainly did," Jane agreed dryly.

"Of course," John said, with every appearance of solemnity. "Well, a-dancing we will go."

"You seem to know a lot about me," Jane said.

"Does that annoy you?"

"No, amuses me."

"Of course I know a lot about you. Didn't we climb Whitney Hill together and pick blueberries?"

"What's far more important, we talked about God," said Jane.

"One thing I know about you is that you adore to be kissed. Don't you?"

"How am I supposed to answer that?"

"It doesn't matter how you answer. It's true, anyway. When you were standing out there on the office steps, you were simply dying to be kissed, weren't you?"

"Not necessarily by you."

"Oh, I know that; but even I was better than nobody, wasn't I?"

"Is that why you promptly did?"

"Sure; I'm a gentleman."

"So what!"

"Don't you know? A gentleman is one who always pleases the lady.... Oh, don't bother to say it. I know you aren't a lady."

All of a sudden a few tears of fierce relief welled up into Jane's eyes, in the midst of her laughter.

With dancing came even greater relief. Either she had forgotten, or else, as John suggested, had never known its fascination. She had not realized the intricate splendor of jazz, with its thousands of scintillating tricks that made the senses stand on tiptoe with pleasure. They whirled, dipped, swung their feet back and forth, until Jane practically lost all sense of the polished floor beneath them; for all she knew, they might be dancing in space, unbound by any gravitational laws. If ever she had been unhappy, or had any trouble or worry of any kind, it was utterly erased now—drowned in primitive rivers of music.

"You haven't had enough fun lately," John said.

"Is that so obvious?"

"Yes. You dance desperately, as if it were the last dance on earth. You're hungry. You've been taking life too dismally hard."

"Maybe."

"You've been thinking," he said accusingly.

"Is that so bad?"

"Janie, if you value your happiness, don't ever think!"

"How does one stop?"

"I'll see that you don't have time for it any more," he said.

"Just do this once in a while, and I won't take life hard."

"And buy a new dress," he said.

"Money, John!"

"Buy one anyway. Let me give it to you. I'd love to, as a sort of welcome-home present.... Don't say no, because think what a kick it would give me."

"Do you really think clothes make a difference?"

"Didn't you hear me say you take life too hard? I want you to be light-headed and frivolous, for a change. I want you to get a kick out of superficial things. I'd adore you in something new and sparkly, showing off your backbone. I bet you've got a swell back, with muscles."

"Muscles aren't in style," said Jane.

"That's because they're rare articles."

"John, I never knew how much I loved to dance."

"That's easy to explain. You never danced with me."

"You're pretty good, I have to admit."

"You're in love with me, you see."

"Oh, am I?"

"Certainly!"

They tried a hundred old steps, devised new combinations of them, changed abruptly from slow and sedate to hilarious and abandoned. They danced patterns around the glass pillars of the ballroom; they slid and skipped and skidded, experimented with new positions; sometimes they danced with the music, and sometimes in utter defiance of it; every now and then they broke into spontaneous, uncontrollable laughter, like schoolchildren.

Once Jane thought of Davidson, and it occurred to her that he was a living violation of everything John was dinning into her ears. He, too, might be happier if he would dance now and then. The thought of the tall sailor dancing was so incongruous that she chuckled aloud; and at the same time another part of her life, Davidson's, was shocked by that chuckle. The Jane dancing so ecstatically in John's arms, glad to let him kiss her lips in the corners of the room, brimming over with delight at the pleasure of flirting with him, was another Jane, certainly, who had little, if anything, to do with Davidson's Jane. He would hate and despise everything she was doing tonight. She knew this, and yet curiously she had no sense that she was in any way disloyal to him. When you were two or three kinds of person at once, capable of enjoying two or three unrelated kinds of life, there was no reason why you should not live two or three separate lives—just as long as you carefully kept them separate!

At midnight they strolled over to the bar and drank a good many little sparkling glasses of Amontillado. It warmed them even more than the dancing had done; it lit Jane's cheeks a little, made her eyes sparkle, and wrapped the room in golden mist. When they waltzed, it seemed that she was coming close to the motions of a swallow, soaring and skimming, touching the tops of waves. But now it was dancing with John, and not the dancing itself, that was exciting. The pressure of his hand on her back made her tingle; her fingers were suddenly aware that they liked to curl around his hand.

"If you tell me once more that I love you, I might believe it," she warned him. "You'd better look out."

"That would be hell, wouldn't it?"

Their dancing became more and more a unison of movement; they pressed closer together, forgetting the separate steps, forgetting the music itself, in the pleasure of that embrace. And when the music stopped, they went on dancing. Somebody, seeing their rapt faces, laughed coarsely.

John put her into her coat, and walked her outside. Cold night wind made her hot face sting, ruffled her hair, made her feel wider awake than she had ever felt in her life. It was three o'clock, and the streets were almost deserted. Only an occasional light shone out from the enormous sides of buildings that flared up into the dark.

"New York at its best," said John.

In her apartment, he took her in his arms again—not playfully. "I've loved you all my life," he said.

"What sweeping statements you make!"

"Well, how about you?"

"It had another name," she said mockingly.

"Yes, but now?"

"Right now—I love you," she told him.

"I think you'd better let me stay tonight."

"There's not much of it left," she retorted.

"You'd better let me stay. It's what all our dancing has been leading to."

"Of course, but—"

"You'd be miserable if I didn't, you know."

"As a matter of fact, I'd probably fall asleep in two minutes," she told him.

"I don't believe it. And anyway, I'd be miserable. And after all, I've loved you all my life."

"You'd better let me think about it."

"Wrong, Janie! You shouldn't ever think. And anyway, loving

isn't something to be thought about. It's a need of the heart and the body. It's a beautiful need, and ought to be fulfilled. It only gets ugly when it isn't fulfilled."

She looked squarely into his blue eyes, and laughed a little.

"Nothing that's beautiful is ever wrong," he said.

"You glorious pagan! I quite agree with you."

"You're a pagan, too," he said. "I knew you would be, after you got away from Maine and Charlie, and had a chance. That's why I've hunted you so madly."

"I'm awfully glad you've found me," she confessed simply. "You've made me happy. And if you really want to love me—here I am."

[15]

John apparently hadn't the slightest intentions of ever leaving New York. He lived in a cheap hotel room which he rented by the week; and he attended to his business with publishers day after day. He would refer, in a confidential, mysterious tone, to his "Business with Publishers." As to its exact nature, Jane was quite in the dark. But in any event, that was the least of her worries.

In fact, John was pretty complicating, even if he was a Godsend. Nothing in all her varied philosophies was quite adequate to rationalize him. After several glasses of sherry, the two-lives theory sounded good; in the cold gray dawn, however, it looked more like plain selfishness. The whole thing had been pretty sudden, anyhow; she could not adjust herself to it. One day she was Davidson's—Davidson possessed her, heart and soul and body. The next day—she was still Davidson's, and also John's. Which was not reasonable. She agreed entirely with John, that nothing beautiful could be wrong. But that sword cut two ways: nothing wrong could be beautiful. If it was wrong to hurt people, then this was wrong, for it would hurt Davidson.

Better to starve herself? Starved, she wouldn't be of so much use to Davidson.... And so on, round and round.

In the mean time, she was impelled deeper and deeper into this conflict, which was at least an exciting and vital conflict, and therefore fun. She saw a great deal of John, and he never failed to amuse and delight her. They lunched together, perching on stools and giggling over their ice cream sodas; they wined and dined, saw shows, kissed at the red lights. And danced. At least twice a week, often three times, they danced.

One Saturday afternoon, he insisted on going shopping with her while she bought a dress. This was to make sure that he would approve of it. Of course he did nothing but hamper progress. He delighted at the same time that he infuriated the shop girls. He would stand off a little, as Jane appeared in some sparkling creation, and tilt his head critically from side to side, wrinkling his nose in perplexity. Jane would burst out laughing uncontrollably. "Nope! Nope!" he would say finally. "Won't do. Off with it!"

"Your husband seems to have his own ideas," one saleslady acidly remarked.

In about the fourth shop, Jane walked out of the dressing room in a glittering sheath of gold mesh that fell to the floor in an intricate graceful cascade. A deep swirling cape reached almost to the waist, and was held together on one shoulder by a blazing blue clip shaped like a butterfly.

The expression of approval on John's face was now almost as ludicrous as his disapproval had been before. Jane turned slowly around for him, and his approval increased. "But," he said at last, in awed tones, "I wanted you to show off your backbone."

Jane unclasped the butterfly, and the gleaming cape fell with a faint rustle. The front of the dress was held up by a slender gold loop around her neck. Her back and shoulders were bare.

John's eyes were very big. "'S wonderful!" he exclaimed

softly. Then he beckoned to the salesgirl, and whispered: "How much does it cost?"

This dress was the first that had ever meant anything to Jane; and she loved it because it symbolized new discoveries in life: it symbolized the glamour of music, of rhythm, of dancing; it symbolized patterns of colored lights, and glass pillars reflecting them iridescently—John's part of her life, which was magical and exciting, even if it was a conflict. She knew intuitively that Davidson would hate that dress. He would think she looked like a prostitute in it, and he would say so. She felt sorry, all at once, that he couldn't share these things that were beginning to mean so much to her. The contrast between the two men, her lovers, was amusing. In reality John was only three or four years younger, yet the difference might easily have been three times as great. He was so boyish and enthusiastic, spontaneously ready to be amused by anything at all, happy-go-lucky; while Davidson was quiet and brooding, moody, sensitive and stern, and intensely emotional in an altogether different way.... Give up John? Whatever happened, she couldn't do that. And they went on dancing....

Margaret Kingsley met him, and approved whole-heartedly. "If I didn't love you, Janie, I'd go out to vamp him myself."

"Go ahead!" Jane suggested. "Don't mind me, Marg."

"But aren't you nuts about him?"

"Sure—in a way."

Margaret shook her finger in reproof. "Mrs. Ghost!" she mocked softly. "*He's* holding you down."

"You'd be surprised how little *he's* holding me down," Jane assured her.

"Well! That sounds interesting."

"Of course I love Johnny," Jane told her. "In a different way, that's all. I can't take him too seriously. He wouldn't want me to. It isn't like that."

Sometimes Margaret dug up one of the boy friends who

seemed to her so unexciting, and the four went dancing together. On one of these occasions, Jane coralled Margaret between dances.

"Marg, remember what I said about everybody having a spark somewhere?" she asked.

"Good Lord, Jane, don't tell me Freddy has one!"

"Of course he has. I found it in just one dance. It's photography."

Margaret made a weary gesture. "Oh, I knew that!" she exclaimed. "And of all the dumb—"

"Now listen here, Madam Olympus! He's amusing as hell about it. He was telling me how he made himself a darkroom in the attic; how he tried to pipe running water into it, and nearly flooded the house, thereby getting himself in so bad with the family that he's had to conduct his experiments in secret ever since. And did you know that on a package of a certain kind of film it says: 'Open in total darkness. Instructions inside'? How's that?... You ought to go to his place some evening and watch him work. He's already invited me, by the way. That kid's an artist. Why don't you come down off the mountains? Does the air in the high altitudes agree with you, or something?"

Margaret sighed. "You're right, Janie; gosh, how I envy the way you get on!"

But there was a great deal in Jane's daily existence that was pretty far removed from fun.

One evening trouble came over the telephone. "Hello, Jane Carey," said a voice that was only half familiar. "You don't know?... Gawd, is it that bad? Why, I'd recconize your vocalizin' any place."

"Millie!"

"Uh-huh. The same, sweetheart."

"Where are you? I want to see you."

"Nerts to you. You can't see me, kid. I just want to tell you something."

"But Millie, I must see you!"

"Didncha hear me say nerts? Listen! It was me took your dough, and I'm gonna pay it back. Started an account in your holy name the other day."

"Millie, I don't give a hang about the money. I just want to see you. What are you doing?"

"Never you mind about that, honey. What are *you* doing, by the way? And how did the jolly ol' lions treat you?"

"If you knew where I am, why didn't you phone long ago, Millie?"

"Well, I just happened to see you in the book tonight."

"Won't you come to see me?" Jane pleaded.

"Can't we be quits, Janie? Can't you lemme alone? You'd just preach at me, or something. Well, I don't wanna be preached at, see? Maybe I'm happy just like I am. Maybe I wanna go alone."

Jane changed her tone. "Go plumb to hell for all I care," she said. "I loathe preaching, and wouldn't waste my voice on you if I got paid. I'd just like to see you. Can't you get that through your dense cranium?"

Millie chuckled a little. "Now you're beginning to sound like you," she said. "Oh, I dunno. I'll think it over."

Jane felt that she was on the right track. "Well, never mind; don't come if you don't want to," she said.

"I'll come," Millie said, and hung up abruptly.

It was a good many days later that she came, late at night, and furtively. "Anybody here?" were the first words she said, as she thrust her tangle of black curls inside the door.

Jane fairly hauled her inside and hugged her in a bear-like embrace. "My ribs!" Millie protested. "Hear that crack? Ouch!"

Jane thrust her off a little and looked at her familiar face. Only—it wasn't quite familiar. The plucked eye-brows were the same, and the war-paint—a little more war-paint, if anything; but her cheeks were thinner, and her eyes troubled. She was wearing a tight black satin dress, with silver trimming, and one of her arms jingled with assorted bracelets. She positively reeked of cheap perfumery. Her black pumps had silver heels.

"Thought you wouldn't like it," Millie said, half-defiantly, as she stared back. "But it's your own fault, you know."

"You nut, I'm tickled silly!"

"Cut out the sentiment, and give an account of yourself," Millie insisted. "Couldn't you even send an old pal a post-card?"

"I got shipwrecked," Jane began.

"Shipwrecked, your grandmother! Did you get your backbone broke, too?"

"Damn near."

"Shipwrecked!" Millie mocked. "That's a hell of a note, when you have to tell fancy stories even to me. Kee-rist! Kitten, I'm disappointed."

Jane grinned. "I won't believe yours, either."

"I got shipwrecked, too," Millie said.

Jane waved her hand. "Not interested," she said solemnly.

"Well, I s'pose I gotta explain, on account of your dough. It was thisaway. I fell in a big way for a yegg. Mary was shocked, the little darling, but anyway I went and spent a few nights with him, sociable-like."

"Oho, a bed-time story!"

"Yeah—and why I ever fell for his line—" She stopped and scrutinized her old friend. "He said he'd get me a job in a real show!" Millie exclaimed. Jane was careful not to show the slightest spark of interest. "Well, tha's all, except I almost had a brat, and I swiped your dough, and the yegg vanished in thin air, and I couldn't get a job, and I started taking in men for a consideration—for quite a consideration—and they like me, and here I am—kind of fell in the woild, you see, when all the time I wanted to be a Pavlova."

Said Jane: "You little idiot!"

"Aw, quit the preachin'."

"Well, I don't give a damn," said Jane.

Millie smiled again. "What would you do, kitten?"

"What do you care what I'd do?"

"Well, I don't, much. I can't imagine you in my shoes, anyhow. What d'you know about it? Bet you never even had a lover—you old-fashioned, sensible-shoes Jane."

"Only a couple of 'em," Jane said.

"Don't brag. 'Tisn't nice, and I don't believe it."

"You don't have to."

"Two of 'em, honest? Then you're on to what I'm talkin' about? You know how it is when you want to sleep with a guy?"

"Sure, I'm on," Jane said softly.

"Hell, ain't it?"

"Sure."

Jane was thinking fast and furiously. She thought that possibly at this point some sort of constructive idea might register. The horror of it was, she had none to offer. She did not have at her finger-tips small jobs on the stage, or in restaurant floor-shows. She could lend money; but that at best would be mere temporary help. Besides, she was quite sure Millie would have none of it.

"Well," Millie said, "I'll be moseyin' along. Customer," she explained, with a faint leer. "Don't worry about your dough, beloved lioness."

"Oh, hell! That's the least of my worries," Jane said impatiently.

Millie kissed her briefly, and went out, slamming the door. But the taste of lipstick stayed, and the smell of the cheap perfume. Jane went to one of the big windows, and thrust her head outside. It was a hot spring night, faintly damp; easy to think about lurid passions. A street light burned pale blue below. Somewhere a cat squalled. A far-off radio hurled out faint jazz, of which only the rhythm, and very little tune, could be heard. Jane felt restless and helpless. Again she was up against something she didn't know how to fight. Not give way to ugliness?... She was determined to do something about Millie. If she couldn't, then she would have failed; as a friend, as a human being. None of her other triumphs over friends' troubles would mean a thing to her if she couldn't help Millie. As she brooded, sick at heart, she wondered if it might not be a good idea to call Margaret into consultation. She tried to picture Millie in fine clothes; but she could not picture her without garish make-up and livid nail-paint.... Besides, it was dancing the girl wanted, in a show or restaurant. She could be good at that. Jane wondered if she knew anybody connected with shows or restaurants; and decided that, since she didn't, she would make a point of becoming acquainted with one or two as soon as possible. Persons who had that mysterious thing called Drag....

Leaning on the wide window-sill, over the musky fragrance of her geraniums, she put her head down on her arms. As she leaned there in perplexity, half-crying, she thought of Davidson, and knew for sure that it was he, and not John, whom she desired most. John stood for all that was fun in life—but Davidson was life itself....

Jane's doorbell was a romantic one—sometimes, it seemed, even sympathetic, for only a few days later Davidson himself rang it. She fell blindly into his arms, laughing and crying at once. His heart, beneath her cheek, was shaking both of them.

The long winter had suddenly ended. A warm wind had sent every branch and twig flicking off melted snow; the voiceless white brooks, whose cascades had so long been transformed to icicles, were awake and alive again. It was spring.

She drew away a little, but only enough to put her own arms around him, and look up into his face. "I don't dare kiss you," he murmured. "You might fade away and be a dream."

"I won't," she whispered back. Before her rose the vision of the lost island in the dawn: the bright sea, the island gleaming like an opal, and gold spears striking through the clouds. The sails of the little boat that had been their prison through those days and nights, were radiant and magical. They were at the gateway of a fairy world, where mortal husks were to stay behind with all mortal chains and fears, leaving only a great brightness and enchantment to be their own forever. All this, during the moment that he kissed her, as if somehow he was laying it, like a precious offering, upon her lips.

After a long time he held her off at arm's length, his hands on her shoulders, looking down into her face as though to make quite sure.

"Been happy?"

"I wanted to cry on your shoulder, Daveson, about how I missed you."

"Well, now you have two serviceable shoulders."

"But I don't want to cry."

"Well, is that all they're good for? You mustn't ever cry about me," he said gently. "I hate to think of it."

"Don't you like to be missed?"

"Yes.... I mean—oh, now you've got me all mixed up."

"Any answer you make is sort of wrong, isn't it?"

"Don't talk to my shirt, talk to me."

"You're rather high up, and anyway I like your shirt."

"You'd think we'd been apart a thousand years, instead of one."

"Davidson, it's been thousands of millions of years.... I wish you never had to stop kissing me."

"I can kiss you all night every night for a week."

"Only a week!"

"How many times do you suppose we can kiss in a week?"

"Not enough," she said. "Not enough to make up for this year. We'll never catch up, Davidson. We'll owe each other tremendous debts all our lives.... How's everything?"

"Oh, I'm working—that's the best I can say. In a steamer, chipping rust. Sea's getting to be more of a washout all the time.

Don't let's talk about anything so unpleasant. Let's talk about you. You've let your hair grow, haven't you?"

"Like it?"

"Very much," he said. "It's more like you. You weren't meant to be fixed up by hair-dressers, anyway.... May I take it down?"

"You're losing your grip, Daveson. Why ask?"

One by one he plucked out the pins, and presently her hair fell like a soft brown wing over his calloused knuckles. He played with it gently, running his fingers through it, winding it around his big wrists, burying his face in it, loving the warm smell of it.

"You're beautiful," he said.

And the telephone rang. "It would," she said.

"Don't answer it."

"Oh, I have to. It may be a girl I know who's in trouble."

But it was John's gay voice. "Hi, pal! Are you getting set for the big date tonight?"

"Oh, had we a date tonight?"

"What! You've forgotten?"

"Sorry, John. No can do."

"Hey! Whaddya trying to pull on me?"

"You sound like a bank clerk," Jane said. "Next, please!"

"But listen here, you can't—say, what's the matter, anyhow?"

"Something has occurred which renders it impossible for me to accompany you," Jane said primly.

"Oh, talk English. Are you sick?"

"When did you ever know me to be sick.... No, thanks, ridiculous boy, I don't need any of Lydia Pinkham's pills."

John sighed windily, and it reverberated in the receiver. "What is this thing called love?" he wailed at last.

"What, indeed? That's the question."

"Well, lunch tomorrow, then?"

"O. K."

"Well, goodbye, and I hope you won't sleep tonight."

"I probably shan't," said Jane, and hung up.

Davidson was looking at her wistfully. "An admirer!" he exclaimed.

Jane nodded and laughed. "Didn't you like the way I passed him off?"

But he was grim. "I'd like to knock his block off; that would teach him not to come prowling around my wife!"

Jane wrinkled up her forehead. "But Daveson, you didn't expect me to live in a convent, did you? You mustn't be jealous of Johnny. We knew each other when we were kids in Maine."

"I'm jealous as hell. I don't care if it is unreasonable. I never claimed to be reasonable—about you. Where was he going to take you tonight?"

"Sometimes we go dancing," Jane said.

"Dancing!" he repeated stonily.

"What's wrong with that?"

He shook his head. "Nothing, I guess," he said glumly. "Only —somehow I never thought of you—that chap's in love with you, isn't he?"

"What makes you think that?"

"How could he help it? I bet he looks at you with his eyes all shining."

Jane smiled. "Oh, Daveson, let's not spoil this evening talking about him."

"One more question," he said.

"Don't!" she pleaded.

"Then it's true, and he's your lover," Davidson said.

"Davidson, what if he is? Can't you see that it doesn't matter?"

"Doesn't matter!"

She tried to tell him about her two selves. She was not conscious now of any rationalization. At this moment it seemed to her absolutely true. She could even feel the two personalities inside her, who, instead of fighting each other till one of them was dead, were moving on side by side, as sensibly and peacefully as they could manage.

Davidson smiled ruefully. Then he sighed a little, and said in an entirely changed voice: "Jane, you wouldn't believe how the world keeps shouting at me to take my hands off you—let you go free, and go free myself, because I'm useless and worthless, and can't make any money, or look out for you as I should. And now that this chap… well, it's another reason, that's all. You wouldn't be lonely…. Oh, I love you, and want you to be happy, Jane. I can't make you happy—not in this civilization. You'll want to—be married and have children—and I'd be a selfish brute to—"

"Davidson, aren't you going to marry me some day?" She was frightened at his calmness, after the passion that had swept him only a moment before.

"I want to confess something. It's time I was honest with you."

"Aren't you always?"

"Well, not with myself, then. Yes, I've been fooling myself, living on pretty dreams, but dreams don't wash with the world, Jane. No good."

"Dreams are half your life," said Jane in an echo. "And—the best half. The only half that counts."

"Not with the world," said Davidson.

"Just what do you mean when you say 'the world'?"

"The beast you get your living off, whatever you want to call it. Just let me tell you what I'm up against!…. You don't want to hear it, though. Only—I doubt very much, Jane, to put it honestly and… I doubt if we'll ever be married."

She drew his hand away from his eyes and made him look at her. "We *are* married," she said.

"Jane, I can't earn a living. Not even for myself. I'm an utter tramp. Don't you see? I've no way of getting on. My profession —trade—whatever it is—it's *gone*."

The world would receive him like a granite wall—and it would hurt. That had been Jane's thought years ago in the *Annie Marlow*. Davidson was a man whose livelihood had dropped from beneath him. And there was nothing to take its place. To one who had known the tall white glory of sails, the sea's bitter strength, the great harmony of the wind, nothing ever could take its place. The insidious nature of the tragedy he was facing began to dawn on her afresh. He was without a calling, a drifter on the face of the sea. He was in the last analysis cut off from his shipmates because of spiritual barricades; and from the rest of mankind he was isolated because of shyness and his own cynicism.

To clinch the situation, he was not in the least interested in the world or what it could offer him. He was a seafarer, hopelessly unfitted for any other existence. And he was ambitionless. To go into the rush and whirl of the thing, to learn a trade, for instance, and take the ladder patiently rung by rung, changing all his habits and ideas, to concentrate slavishly on something which did not appeal to him anyway—that was as much out of the question as to create, stone for stone and tree for tree, a new island with his own bare hands.

Before Jane had come, life had been fairly simple. You drifted about from one ship to another, with little spells of intensely enjoyable leisure between. Sailing ships were declining, of course, but you could still pick up a schooner here and there. There were even a few wandering barks and barkentines. Between voyages you read and meditated about life. There was nothing very much to worry about. You laughed with your comrades, and went off on a bat with them occasionally. That was all.

Then Jane arrived in the middle of his tranquil wandering life. She was aloof and alien and beautiful beyond mortal words —a goddess, and yet miraculously his own. All of which was simple and natural enough, so long as there had been an uninhabited island to shelter them. After that the horror began, an interminable nightmare. The waves she caused agitated his quiet pool into frenzied rapids. He was in a state of chaotic frustration, about which nothing could be done. The old former life could not serve his needs any more. The sea could not serve him. Any kind of life at sea meant separation from her, not just for part of the time, but for most of it. Not the sort of existence to offer to the woman you loved.

The sea was false, and yet for him there could be nothing but the sea. There were steamships, with ridiculously low wages and short voyages, after which you were usually paid off. Then there still lingered a schooner or two here and there, but such jobs were mere casual oddities; you couldn't support a wife, maybe a family, on oddities. And even if you could, what would be the use, when you would be away almost all the time? Like being single, yet without the same freedom from responsibility. And anyway, right now chances were a thousand to one against your getting any sort of a job at all.

With this problem staring him in the eye, he did not think it would be cowardly to go away from Jane and never see her any more. Rather, he was afraid that he was not brave or strong enough to do so.

"I can make just enough on one job to tide me over till I get another. As for that fishing-boat scheme, right now I wouldn't dare buy one, even if I had the means. The state of things—depression, they call it, but I think it's an excavation. Sailors are willing to work for nothing but their keep, and a thousand after every job. What can you do?"

"Things won't go on like this forever, you know," she said.

"They may. They're going down and down and down. Jane, I don't want to hurt you, I don't want to leave you; I'm just confessing, that's all. I'm frustrated. I can't do as I want, and I don't know how to cope with it."

"Kiss me," said Jane.

"You silly! That won't help the material side of the question."

"The material side isn't the most important side."

"I'm not a romanticist, Jane; I've taken too many hard knocks."

"Neither am I a romanticist; but please kiss me."

He did, and she shivered. "Cold?"

"No, a rabbit ran over my grave. Didn't that help the material side of the question just a little?"

"Yes."

"Then, you see, it really is true that the material side is only part of the whole thing. Even an excavation can't break love."

"No," said Davidson.

"We're going to conquer this thing, you know. We're going to stick together and pull each other through."

"Jane, you could make a better life without me pulling you down."

"I don't want anything but you."

"Why?"

"I don't know."

"And this other fellow—"

"Doesn't mean a thing," Jane said.

"Will you wait?"

"Of course."

"Years, maybe?"

"As long as I live," she told him—and she believed it, too.

[16]

At the end of the week, when his steamer sailed, Davidson was considerably cheered up. But Jane, although glad of her victory, was left exhausted. Every ounce of the spirit and determination she had given him during that week had correspondingly drained her own resources. She could not even keep up a pretense of courage. She was haunted by grotesque visions of the monstrous ogre with which Davidson was fighting a losing fight, almost single-handed. And there was nothing she could do to fend off the iron fist. Even in the wilds of an unknown island, there had been no ultimate escape from that fist.

Civilization—and among its other sins, it had abolished the ships that were Davidson's life, and the life of many other men as well. More speed wanted, greater dependability, room for more cargo; everything must be keyed up to the highest possible pitch of speed and efficiency. Why? That was the irony of the thing. Where was it all bound? Only to more speed and efficiency, a continuing hectic circle, while hearts were crushed in it. And they called it Progress, and worshipped it....

But there had been Lost Island. Again and again she came

back to that, and her eyes would shine. If you had a Lost Island in the past, and a sense of humor with which to fight the present, you could get along. If the world sometimes got to be too much for your sense of humor, you could cry a little, instead of laughing; then laugh at yourself.

Davidson wrote from San Francisco: “Putting out tonight—weather hopeless—fumbling in the dark Janie, but hoping—expect to be in New York again in a month—I have read *Chance* —I love you.”

“Fumbling in the dark” with his awkward, willing hands, and getting hurt—it was an excruciating thought that tormented her through long nights, mingling incoherently with her wondering in vain what she could do for Millie, who had not even called her up again.

There was always John, indispensable John. He was a little restless now, for he had been a long time away from Maine and the mountains; but he was always on hand with a warming bottle of wine, or a compliment that made life temporarily easier; always ready and eager to dance, at any hour of the day or night, and eternally amusing. Jane could not help thinking that here in the lap of civilization at least, he was ever so much more—well, comfortable—than Davidson, who was so ready to be hurt by a misinterpreted word, or thrown into a dismal mood that would last for hours and wear her out.

John never lost his buoyant spontaneity. One morning, at about two o’clock, he jangled her doorbell, rudely waking her out of a sound sleep. She started up, wondering if she was dreaming, and it rang again. No doubt this time. She scrambled up and put on a light, scuffled into her slippers and threw a dressing gown around her.

John was tense, excited, his blue eyes gleaming. “Sorry to get you out of bed, Jane. But I had an idea—I do sometimes—and I’m that crazy I just had to come and spring it on you, or die of it. Let me in?”

"Of course," she stammered, with a laugh.

"I'm like you; I do absurd things once in a while, such as calling on a young lady at two in the morning."

"How often have you done that?" she inquired.

"Oh, my craziness usually works differently. Mountains, for instance. One day I was industriously shingling the roof, at home, and all of a sudden I hurled my hammer into the air and went and climbed Pike's Peak."

"But Pike's Peak's in Colorado."

"Well, that's where I went."

"What are you up to now?" she inquired.

"Janie, I think you'd better come to Maine with me."

She looked at him wide-eyed for a minute. "What a thing to bring up at this hour!" she exclaimed.

"On the contrary, I make all my important decisions at this hour. I'm at my best early in the morning; haven't you caught on to that yet? But let's get back to the point. You're getting thin."

"Is that the point?"

"You bet! I don't like women to be too thin. Slender, of course, but not pencilly."

"I don't see why your views on the female form need concern me."

"Who should they concern, if not me? Don't I take you dancing three nights a week at least, flaunting you in public places? Besides, you aren't happy. You may be able to fool anyone else in this world, but you can't fool me, because I know."

"How, may I ask?"

"I've been wondering. It isn't by any outward sign. You're a pretty good actress, all right. But I guess when you love a person, you know those things. You're happiest when you're dancing."

"Well, nobody can be ecstatically joyous all the time," she said. "Life isn't built for that."

"You work too hard," he said.

"And you keep me up too late."

"You think too much. You worry. You're too sympathetic, and suffer too much over other people's woes."

"That may be true," she admitted. "But as for working, I have to earn a living."

"You put too much stress on that. Earning a living is all very well, but what's the good of it if you don't enjoy the living you sweat so hard to earn?"

"Well, that particular vicious circle has got everybody," she said.

"Yes, but listen here! I've got the solution, so why not at least listen?"

"Well, shoot!"

"You're getting pale," he said.

"No personal remarks!"

"You've lived in Maine," he went on. "You know that it's the answer to all the ills of the body, and most other ills as well. Why don't you come for a lengthy visit to my cabin by Katahdin?… Now wait! Let me exercise my salesmanship uninterrupted."

"You don't have to sell Maine to me. I remember."

"Good! But let me sell myself. I'm capable of all sorts of things you wouldn't suspect me of."

"Oh, Johnnie, I'd suspect you of anything."

"In this Maine project I want to be quite the under-dog—your humble servant, in fact."

"Get along with you!"

"Now, you hold on! I'll marry you, or not, whichever you like. I don't give a damn about that. But—here's the real proposition. If this idea of loving—or loving *me*, anyway—is worrying you, then the hell with loving, say I! We'll be comrades, brother and sister, holy and pure and chaste; or, you can call my cabin a health resort, and me your solicitous doctor, if you like that better."

She looked at him quizzically, her head a little on one side. "John," she began at last, "is all this nobleness founded on supreme love, or just natural human kindness, or what?"

"You needn't make fun of me," he protested. "I'm in dead earnest."

"Supreme love, then," she said.

"Of course! Why do you doubt it? Now, isn't it all reasonable enough? You can't refuse, can you? Janie, that cabin in Maine is going to be a hell of a lot better with you in it—and it was pretty good anyway. And listen: you know there are lakes in Maine, and little green islands in the lakes..."

"Islands!"

"Wouldn't you like to camp on one—just the two of us, with my tent for a house?"

"What a subtle irony it is," she exclaimed, "that you should offer me islands, John!"

"Isn't it a rather swell irony, though?"

"There are other people in the world," she said after a little.

"Janie, you'll never make me believe that your troubled friends are worth getting thin for."

"It isn't only them."

"Where *is* this mysterious lover of yours, Jane? He stands between us, yet I never see him. Is he a wandering sailor, or what?"

"Your humor is grim," she said. "That's exactly what he is."

John drew in his breath sharply. "But he's making you unhappy," he protested. "Can it be worth while?"

"Yes; it's my life."

"You mean, one of them."

"It's one I couldn't get along without. John, now it's my turn to talk. I'm going to start playing fair with you, right this minute. I've been trying, but I've been too confounded selfish."

"Don't bother about it," he said.

"I must. John, you've been weeks and weeks in New York..."

"Business," he mumbled, without looking at her.

"Business, shucks! You're hanging around to give me a good time. And you *are* giving me a good time. I've adored the dancing, and the wine, and—the loving, too. But it isn't fair to you. Now you know; why don't you go to Maine yourself?"

"Business," he mumbled again, and smiled. "Don't you think you're making me happy, too? Nobody on earth can dance like you."

"I know," she said. "You want to stick around and watch me, in case life gets too much for me and I collapse. Then you'll tenderly pick up the pieces. Noble of you, pal, and I appreciate it. But don't worry. I'm not going to collapse."

"Oh, you've made up your mind about that?"

"Definitely. Years ago."

He looked at her wistfully. "Wouldn't you miss me a bit?" he asked.

"Oh, that's no secret," she said.

"Well, then!"

"But I'm not playing fair," she said. "Not to anybody."

"You're too big for one life. So you needed me, too."

"Pretty gross, isn't it?"

"No, it's grand, and honest. I've never struck anyone as honest as you, Jane. Don't mind if I say things crudely sometimes."

"And you aren't even jealous," she said. "I think that's rather remarkable."

"Is he?"

She smiled a little, and nodded.

"The simpleton!"

"No—he likes to possess, that's all."

"I bet he's dark and sort of grim, and has a moustache."

"Your humor is remarkably perspicacious. John, don't carry it too far. Hurts."

"Sorry." He put his arm around her. "Maybe—well, maybe I *am* a little jealous."

She smiled again. "That's all right. Nice of you to admit it."

"I wish I could carry you away out of this," he said. "We could go to the mountains—anywhere out of New York. You don't belong here, except for dancing. It's horrible for you to be here day after day. We could be kids again, and I could watch your hair go flying, as I used to. Haven't you the courage to break away from sordid things?"

She shook her head without speaking. "John, be a reasonable boy, and go away and let me sleep, will you? I'll think about it —honest."

"Thinking again!"

"Sorry it upsets you so, but I guess that's the way I'm built."

"Well, go ahead and think, if you have to, but think it out my way. Come to Maine with me, just for while, Jane—for a vacation."

"A vacation—from life?"

"From *one* of them," he answered. "And watch your weight, young lady. If I catch you losing as much as another pound, I'll kidnap you!"

He was tempting her more than he knew. The very mention of the cool green woods of Maine.... And a kind of peace to be found there—an echo, almost, of the Lost Island peace. Davidson thousands of miles away, tired and discouraged and bitter, and—yes, inadequate. In the world you had to take good things when they were offered. It was not much use to stick to vague shadowy ideals and dreams that might never again be allowed to come true. You might have the best intentions in the world of being true to ideals, and fighting and suffering and sacrificing for them most nobly; but the world was hard-boiled and indifferent; the reaction was inevitable. You became selfish, too, grabbing good things where you saw them, forgetting other people, forgetting dreams. She felt torn, and miserable. Was it really worth while to deny oneself for the sake of a dream that was, perhaps, ended? But—could you deny a dream, when it was interwoven with the vital fibers of your heart?

New York—anything to get away from New York. But Davidson—anything for him. On Lost Island such conflicts—unreasonable, brutal—never arose to confront you. Here they sprang up like the mythical warriors from dragons' teeth. On Lost Island one man, one dream, one cave, one world. Here all these were insanely multiplied and distorted. Lost Island… and John offering islands, too!…

A few weeks later Davidson came again. He came very quietly through the door, without saying a word, and took her in his arms. A little shudder went through her.

He stood with his back against the door, bending over her—unnaturally quiet, even for him.

"Daveson, what's happened? Why so solemn?" she asked finally.

"I just want to tell you something," he said, "and then I'm going away again. I've got to leave you—forever."

She stared at his tense face. "You're taking it all in one plunge, aren't you?" she said.

"Isn't that best?"

"Yes, but I can't move so fast. Doesn't register, Daveson. Won't you even come in and sit down, and tell me slowly and simply what's the matter?"

He sighed, and relaxed a little. "Oh, sure," he conceded. "Sorry to be so blunt."

"Well, it seems sudden to me," she said, "but of course you've been brooding over it for ages."

"Yes, I have. Ever since we got back."

"I know," she said.

"Jane, I'm no use." He made a despairing gesture. "It's all so futile. I can't do anything. I can't even tell you…"

"Do you love me?" she asked simply.

"That isn't the point," he said almost gruffly.

"Of course it is!" she cried.

"Blithe about it, aren't you?" he protested bitterly. "Women are queer. Can't imagine any reality but love. If there are other realities—unpleasant ones—they evade them."

"You're annoyed with me," she said.

"A little," he admitted. "I'm trying so hard to think this through; and you *won't* see it with your head, but only with your sweet, stupid heart. How can I ever make you understand? Won't you try? You make me feel worse than ever," he complained.

Instantly she changed, enfolding him in a real and serious attempt to understand this trouble. She found his hand, and held on to it as though it were the only reed that kept her from falling into endless depths; and a dim reminiscence came over her, of floating, without gravity or support, in a blue haze, with one solid concrete object to hold—an oar, that had been.

"First I want to tell you a story," Davidson said. "Once there was a man. Not much of a man, though. He was a sailor, and a very stupid one. Well, at first that didn't matter. It was all right until he met a girl he wanted to marry. And then he needed some money. But he was too stupid, I expect. This chap was walking around one day, and he saw a bunch of people in front of the post office, and so he went up to see what was going on. And they were auctioning off a little sloop. This man had an eye for two things in the world—his wife, and little boats."

"You just said he wasn't married," Jane put in.

"This man looked at the boat, and she was sound as a bell, and had sweet lines and a brave way about her. Well, he had a little money in the bank—just enough—and he bought her."

"Good for him!" she said.

"He bought her," Davidson went on severely. "He played round with her in the Sound, and liked her. And then one day he thought to himself: 'I could sell this sloop, if I trimmed her up a bit, at about twice what I paid for her, and that would help get me to the point where I can—marry my wife.' Well, this man really was very stupid. He painted her, and rove in new running gear, and made her happier than she'd been for a long time. One day a rich chap offered him nearly three times the cost of that sloop. But the sailor had been getting fonder and fonder of her all this time he'd been at work on her. 'What'll you do with her?' he asked. 'Oh,' said the rich chap, 'I'll stick a good high-power auxiliary in her—make her into a little pleasure-boat.' And that stupid sailor said he guessed he'd keep her a while longer.... A little later came another sailor, an old shipmate of his, and looked at the sloop; and there was something in his eye, though he didn't talk much, that said he liked her—that said he wouldn't tear her to pieces and load her up with machinery. Well, the stupid man sold her for only a few dollars less than he'd paid for her, but the sailor couldn't pay right away. He took her out into the Sound, and got into a gale and lost her and drowned himself into the bargain. And the stupid man never got paid at all."

"His wife would understand," Jane said quickly. "She would have wanted him to do just that."

"Dearest," he pleaded, "don't you see now?"

"I see you," she answered, smiling.

"I've been back a year, and not a cent to show for it. I've picked up an odd job here and there, taken a voyage, got paid off, looked around for ships and found nothing but steamers, lost what few dollars I did have. It's too ridiculous, and—I can't marry you, Jane. I couldn't profane it by asking you to come to me in poverty and rags and dirt."

"I'm not afraid."

"I'd hardly ever even be with you. I'd have to be out trying to pick up a crust here and there, like a damned seagull. I'd be with you when I was out of work—that's about all."

"I can work," Jane said. "I've some money saved up already."

"Do you think it makes a man very happy to feel that he can't even support his wife?"

"When it isn't his fault?"

"You couldn't be happy with someone who wasn't good enough."

"You're the best in the world."

"Not by the world's standards," he retorted, with some irony.

"But who cares about the world's idiotic standards?"

"We're living in the world, and you have to," he answered bitterly. "That's what I'm finding out."

"I don't believe I could live without you," Jane said gravely after a while.

"I had sort of a happy thought," he said unhappily. "We could get along on what we've *had*—feed on the past all the rest of our futures. There was enough, and it was good enough, to hold us forever."

"Like camels," she said bitterly, "living for days on what they put in their wretched bellies at one meal. Ye Gods!... I can't even *conceive* of a life without you," she went on distantly. "It's like trying to imagine infinite space. Imagination gives up."

"Luckily, perhaps," he mumbled.

"Don't be cruel. All the time I've known you, you've never been cruel to me."

"Dearest, it's life that's cruel—the world—civilization—to me, too."

"Men are notoriously fond of passing the buck."

"Jane, you're fighting me. Can't you help at all? Don't you see what I'm up against?"

"I love you," she said.

"Women are notorious for their lack of logic."

"I used to believe that," she said vehemently. "But now I don't know—I don't know, Davidson."

"Well, I love you, but that doesn't get us anywhere."

"Where do you want to go?"

"The island," he murmured.

"Oh, well, if you're thinking in terms of the island—"

"Aren't you? Don't answer all at once. Think. When you think about love, isn't it a green hill in the starlight? Don't you think of the sea, and the fragrance, and the magic? And haven't those become part of us and so part of our love?"

"You mean you don't believe our love could stand without those things?" she questioned, incredulous.

"I don't believe it would be so good. I think it would be a disillusion—in the midst of poverty, and unrest. And I won't have that, Jane. It's been the only completely beautiful thing in my life, and I'll never let it become less, even if I have to give it up. I think it's too good for the world, and I won't have the world touch it. Jane, don't you remember what we said back on the island, the night we were married?"

"You mean, about not giving in to ugliness?"

"Yes."

"But that's just what we *would* be doing," she exclaimed, "if we let the world win out."

"No," he said, "the only way not to let the ugliness win is—to keep the lovely thing away from it."

"It all sounds very grand and idealistic," she said. "But, you see, I just want—to live." And at the same time, she could not help wondering, for a fleeting second, if he was right.

"You don't understand, then," he mumbled, as if to himself. "I didn't know. I thought you might, when I told you how much I was feeling it all. Jane, I hate to leave you without your understanding."

"But you're not going to leave me!" she cried.

"I have to."

She looked at him, wild and breathless. "Oh, it's like that, is it?" she questioned faintly.

"Yes, it's like that."

She got up heavily. And all her feelings went suddenly numb, as though she had been wrestling with something far beyond her strength. That, she thought, was what happened in the worst crises of life. You were simply deprived of feeling. It was nature's way of helping you survive. Survival seemed the only thing important to nature; how, or why, was none of her business.

"Let's take a vacation," she said softly, "and have some supper."

Davidson, temporarily alone with his half-won victory, would have been very glad to exchange it for defeat. He had known that he was about to hurt her almost inhumanly, but this silent, dazed reaction was frightening him now. A consciousness was growing upon him that, with all his understanding of her, he had never entirely taken into consideration the full intenseness of her need for him; and somewhere, nearly extinguished by troubles that crowded and clamored around him, was a single small sparkle of happiness and pride. Did he have, really, the slightest right or reason to lay open both their hearts on this mysterious imaginary altar to Beauty? Was Jane, perhaps, right that love was the only beauty that mattered?

He only knew that his feelings and resolves were seething about him in a frenzied chaos—a storm of black and white snowflakes, with Jane, terrified, in the midst of it, buffeted and shaken. Cold perspiration broke out on his forehead.

She said nothing at all. Mechanically she went through the motions of getting some supper ready. She did not know how to think of the future; but for a fleeting second it crossed her mind that next week she would go dancing with John, and that his cheeriness, her dress with the gold cape, the warmth of music, the delight of dancing, his easy goodnight kiss, would be an infinite relief. It seemed that you suffered only up to a certain point, and then the animal was forced to protect itself; as though through the opening of some automatic safety valve, you could not suffer any more.

It became more plain every second that Davidson was right. You could not bring into this world a perfection briefly attained in another, and expect it to endure. And it was obvious that to marry him would mean throwing them both into relentless circles of strain and worry, over each other as well as over materialistic things. He would be constantly in fear of failing her, wondering whether she was conscious of being failed, always aware of his worldly shortcomings, wondering whether he was imposing beyond reason on her love; and, most important of all, continually torn between her and her eternal rival, the sea.

As for Jane, she would be too much on the alert, too much under strain to foresee and intercept these fears of his, trying too hard to keep him reassured; and, even supposing she could succeed at all in this, it could only be when she was feeling on top of the world; and how could anyone be on top of the world all the time? The sea had won, that was all. She could not contend with the sea.... And dimly, fleetingly, in the back of her mind came again, like a tiny pricking, the secret knowledge that she would be wanting now and then to dance.

Some time, being Jane, she would stage another rebellion. It would not be the same kind of rebellion, though. Real adventures could never be repeated. It was a mistake to try to go back, hunting again for the places where there had been high ecstasies. If only a person could have the courage to push forward, over deserts and swamps and glaciers, he would certainly make new discoveries, perhaps as bright as the others. One way to begin an adventure was to buy a red skirt....

This life was over. Davidson was right—to end it quietly and honestly was all that mattered now.

All this, while she fussed at supper. She came back from the tiny kitchen to set the table, and he saw that her expression of terror and tenseness had gone. She nodded to him almost gaily.

She brought a big salad in a blue bowl; crackers, cheese; Hamburg and fried potatoes; and, last of all, with an air of mystery, a dark bottle and two small glasses.

"Red wine," she said, "for our un-wedding night." The drama of that made her smile.

"You understand, then."

"Yes." And she felt, rather than heard, that he sighed tremendously, as a condemned prisoner might sigh, relieved beyond words to have suspense ended, and nothing now to face except death.

He looked at her across the small table. She was just a little flushed with the wine. Her straight brown hair had fallen out of place across her forehead, and her eyes sparkled. She was happy in a kind of desperate way—a little bit artificial, histrionic. Her wispy blue blouse had fallen half off one pale brown shoulder. It was a strong and solid shoulder rather than a graceful one, but at the sight of it a tempest surged through Davidson, toying with his resolves as the wind of open sea shakes the great white sails, trying to tear at them, lift them free of the lines that hold them, hurl them out into space to a fierce destruction.

Once she looked at him piercingly, and said: "Anyway, I'll never again know what it means to be afraid."

"I haven't known, Jane, since the night I fished you out of the wreck. That was when the dream began. You were so helpless and white, and you had nobody but me. I wanted to take you away somewhere, so you couldn't be hurt any more."

"And you did!" she said, smiling.

"Yes, that part of the dream came true. I loved you, but I wanted you all to myself. I've always been jealous, Jane. I could almost have been jealous of the butterflies. That's why I was so hurt when I heard about—him. I didn't want to believe it. I knew then that I'd lost you."

"But you hadn't!" she cried.

"Yes, in a way I had, because I couldn't satisfy all of you, and

I couldn't share you. Jealousy is pretty ugly. I didn't want there to be anything between you and me that wasn't beautiful."

"There can't be, now," she told him. "Nobody can ever share what you and I have had. That's a different part of life, closed and locked and sealed. You were right, David. I wanted you so much I lost track of other things—the most important thing."

"Lost Island."

"I was thinking of Beauty."

"It's all the same," he said.

"Well, we've given up both our hearts to that goddess now," said Jane. "She can't complain. Nobody could give her more than that."

He took her in his arms for the last time, and sat stroking her hair. She belonged to him still. She would belong to him always, only soon she would stand, a precious goddess, fragrant as wild roses, on some high pinnacle, inaccessible and remote, his own and yet lost to him, given to his ideal.

She herself was back again on the starlit hill in flower-scented grass; and a pang of hope made her wonder why this could not happen always; even in a shack in the slums, or anywhere else, why could not being together make the island come true, all the rest of their lives? But then she knew that would be asking too much of any magic. It would rebel under such a burden; it would resent being called on, year after year, to be dragged through the dirt so that they might go on dreaming.

"David! Kiss me, and go quickly."

She was trembling a little, and he felt like a traitor. "I'd be even more of a traitor if I stayed," he said.

"Good luck to you, sailor."

He kissed her on the lips again, softly. "Maybe," he said, "it's lucky I'm a sailor. We're forever getting shipwrecked, or buying little boats with our last pennies, and bumming round. And somewhere there might even be… The old sea has secrets still."

[17]

"John, you're an old kidnapper, that's what you are!"

"Glad?"

"Sure I'm glad, but I think you're a menace to the country, all the same."

"What do you propose to do about it, Janie?"

"That's just what I'm trying to figure out. Dangerous business, you know, to transplant a person several hundred miles without even giving them a chance to breathe. New York—presto!—the Maine woods."

"But you *are* glad?"

"Yes, that's the one flaw in my arguments. I am glad."

"I want to be—oh, awfully good to you, Jane. After all, I took you away, almost by main force, to spend your nasty little two-weeks' vacation at my sister's house in Portland, and now I've got to be good."

"You're incredible, Johnnie. I always knew that—ever since you said: 'Why doon't ye pin a note on the duck?' Remember?"

John threw back his head and laughed happily. His eyes met the rare blue of the sky over Maine on a clear day. She looked up too—not at tenements or skyscrapers, but into a wavering lattice of pine branches. A green and gold dragonfly whisked overhead. A song sparrow was chattering about summer time and the sun. This was Maine again. It had not been an illusion. There was really sunlight here.

Now that she was sure, she dared to remember a time, not long ago, when there had been a creeping darkness around her, over her—stifling, thunderous. She beat her wings in anguish against iron—and no release, no hope, no beauty, seemed even remotely true any more. The world was a glum black smudge. No prospect of its ever changing. You marched on, round and round, until you fell gasping from exhaustion. And she had too much strength to fall from exhaustion. Life was apparently hardest on strong people, then. The weaklings could simply die.

She remembered how she had cursed the world, hated the world, screamed at the world for driving Davidson off from her—for driving him off into the clean wide seas on an endless quest. In a way the victory was his, for he had not compromised with love. He had taken the iridescent essence of it in the palm of his hand, sorted out of it every grain of earthly dust, locked it up and thrown the key into his ocean. His victory and hers—but at the price of all the happiness in life. The sun had gone out—civilization had extinguished it as though it were a frail candle.

She had been deathly tired and sick—more so, it seemed, than during her days in the open boat. She remembered standing at Times Square one afternoon, waiting to cross to the subway entrance, and the ring of buildings had moved unsteadily and rocked in upon her, throwing ghastly shadows, and then wheeled back to leave cosmic spaces. Throngs and floods of people had swept by like an ugly wind; and over their roaring and droning a babel of sharper voices had hovered, each one clamoring for instant attention. "Jane, won't you marry me?" "Aw, shucks, kid, cut out the lion-fever stuff. Don't be a weepin' willer." "Have you seen my glasses, by any chance?" "Somewhere—there may be another island."... The traffic lights changed—the currents of people mingled, conflicted, altered. She went on with them blindly, and fell down the subway entrance into complete darkness....

"You're right, Johnnie, I ought to be much more gracious about the way you yanked me out and set me down in my woods again. Tell me—I'm a little browner and sunnier today, aren't I?"

"Yes, now you're—you're almost Jane, instead of that little wispy ghost with hollow cheeks and immense tragic eyes."

"It's the woods," she told him, laughing. "I belong here, you know."

Always the woods had calmed her. They were home. She could bend her body lithely among close brush and low branches. She could make her way with amazing soft-footedness—almost as quietly as the rustling squirrels and rabbits themselves. She loved the fragrance of wintergreen and sassafras leaves, and balsam needles. Years ago, when life had seemed very complex considering its futility, she would go out alone among leaves and moss, hills and streams, and they would sweep away the world's tangles much as she brushed aside dewy cobwebs in the undergrowth. Now, in this bitterest experience of her life, had the woods lost their magic?

At first it seemed as though they had. Every creature, every leaf-shadow, every spore-laden fern, was in tune, while she was an outsider, grieving, unfulfilled. She felt white and conspicuous in a world where all colors blended as though they had grown there. And she could remember only the Lost Island forest, where she and Davidson had walked together, as part of each other and part of their world.

But after all there was sunlight here. Pastures ripe with steeplebush and gold-green hayscented ferns, luscious with blueberries. Pine groves and wild flowers and small animals. Walking alone for miles along narrow roads. Sometimes a deer dashed across in front of her, wide-eyed and alert, white tail in the air. Or a partridge would start up with a thunderous whir of wings. She would push into the woods after awhile, and wander quietly among shadows of leaf and light, quick to see a scattering of yellow lady-slippers or a cluster of white and lavender orchids. Sometimes a lizard—small curl of reddish color—would move against a wet brown leaf; or a chipmunk scurry by, his cheek pockets well stuffed. Veeries sang in golden spirals. And in the evening, hermit-thrushes answered each other from tree to tree.

There were countless things to be discovered when you roamed about outdoors, alone and in sunlight. She knew now the answer to a question she had asked long ago—when people were in love, were they still alone? Yes, always alone. Everyone on earth who thought about it at all was isolated, starkly, completely. Love gave a divine illusion. It gave companionship developed to the most subtle pitch—but beyond that it was an illusion. You were alone.

The Maine forest had taken her now, and it was pounding her against its earth, stripping away her half-shattered ragged rainbow. She was alone. And there was nothing to be counted on, anywhere. There were these woods, of course, but someday men from cities would come breaking in, and find here deposits of iron or of coal, or strip the place of its trees to build their own super-civilized dwelling places. Not even the woods, then, could really be counted on. Life was transitory, shifting, mirage-like.

Still, these forests would probably last her lifetime, after all. And then the candle goes out. She threw her arms impulsively around the trunk of a splendid young white pine, and laid her head against its rough bark. It reminded her of the day when she had first climbed the main rigging of the *Annie Marlow*, when she had clung to the sturdy topmast for strength and support. This was a very sympathetic white pine. Perhaps, in days gone by, it had been personally acquainted with that topmast. She almost felt that it was on communicative terms with her. A gust of wind shook its upper boughs—the masses of needles went sparking silver in the sun, and a vibration ran through the staunch old trunk. Its roots were in the earth, and its branches in the sun, and that was a good way to live.

Nothing could be counted on, all was transitory, and you were alone. Those facts were rather difficult foundations for a house of life, but perhaps you could build upon them, if you knew how. Or perhaps it was better to forget all houses and be like this tree, roots in the earth, boughs in the sun. A world of philosophy there—whole dusty bookshelves of it in two phrases!

This tree seemed permanent enough. For the time being, and for her, it could serve. Not even the earth was really permanent. Perhaps someday something would go wrong with the machinery of the universe—the balance would be upset—and the earth would go catapulting into its sun like a very small moth into a gigantic flame. But for the time being, this tree would serve well.

She looked straight up at the sky through surges of silver-green. Big bright clouds rolled by smoothly. She stared at them a long time, and then felt the swift sensation that she, her pine tree, and all the woods, all the world, were falling slantingly. She held on and watched, and drifted more and more into the swinging illusion of the thing. She and the pine tree were falling through space together. It was a long fall, and an oddly companionable one. She laughed a little at that. Life was relentless, but there was nothing more it could take away from her. She clung to her tree, ruthlessly divested by life of an entire world—a complete paradise—but the magic had been, and it was hers—as much hers and as real as anything could be in a transitory earth where no one could entirely possess anything.

The first thing to do was to dispose of this abysmal sorrow. Intellectually, logically, she had banished it long ago—in fact, on the day they had parted, and she had opened her arms to release him. "My mind's right with you," she told his shadow afterwards, "but oh, beloved, my heart's making bad weather of it."

He was right, of course. To take a love that had been divine, and force it to continue on a worldly plane, might have been cruel and heartless, and led to a towering disillusion. Better to sorrow, then—better to sorrow your heart out. This way, the essence of the rainbow could be forever treasured, preserved in its crystal. Uncared for, it might have waned until at last the crystal was only an empty shell.

Nothing in life was permanent. That was a terrible fact to take and be on friendly terms with. You were content to let most things shift and change, but there were a few you craved to hold with might and main. That was where bitterness came in—when you saw that this changing was a relentless river, eventually carrying everything away with it, bringing new things, carrying them away.

Even beauty changed. You changed. You were caught in the midst of complex currents of continual change. Perhaps it was good, if only you could accept it completely—if only your heartstrings would accept it. Perhaps it could keep you alive and happy and excited, if you knew how to use it. That was how you revolved in harmony with the world, instead of trying to buck it, to alter its direction according to yours.

Jane laughed, then. To complain, as she sometimes did, at the absence of change, then to struggle with the fact of continual change; to call herself a rebel, a hater of civilization, and then to philosophize about revolving along with the world.... It was impossible to solve anything there. You went round and round in circles. And all those conflicting thoughts had some measure of truth. She felt that at last she had come to a point of vantage—a mountain outlook where she could rest awhile and study the landscape. She saw it all below—a confusion of feelings and opinions and complaints spread out in complex circular patterns. All had a touch of absurdity. They were all true, they were all false, they all conflicted. Life was a complex circular pattern. It was absurd to believe anything too strongly—absurd to want anything too much—certainly absurd to be unhappy. She should be happier than most. She could survey the thing from a mountain outlook, and see it in totality, whereas if you lost yourself down there you took it all very seriously and followed some strand on and on without even realizing that it *was* circular and that there was no use in it. And she thought of the man pursuing the horizon in Stephen Crane's poem....

Some of her feelings and thoughts she could confide to John. He would understand pieces of them, and they would discuss life animatedly as though it were an intellectual adventure. He would carefully follow all her winding passageways, but only with his mind. When it came to living, there were no winding passageways and no corners that were for him especially dark. When life was difficult, he went away and climbed a mountain, and came back with his heart washed in star-dust and his hope and faith high. If only she could go back from the Maine woods to New York feeling like that!

Till now she had hardly dared to think about New York, even for a minute. Now she would set to work systematically to map out and build up for herself a possible life there. Millie had gone on the road, so there was the question of a new roommate, for instance. And a job. Maybe there was another job in the world beside that grubby little one in Professor Myers' office. She would ask John that evening. He had various surprising contacts with editors, printers, publishers. How about a bookstore? It might actually be fun to sell books. She would become adept at looking at a customer and knowing what was wanted. She would learn how to advise solicitous aunts what to buy for their infant nieces, or what a strapping father should present to his daughter on her birthday....

A qualm of despair rushed over her, a little shudder of rebellion. Why did people have to go on this way, fighting the world to wring a meager living out of it through devious channels? Channels? Gutters, rather! Why weren't the trees enough? Why couldn't one dance in fairy circles and thrive on frosty red wintergreen berries? Well, there was John. She distinctly saw that thought, overhead and a little to one side, hovering elusively. It must keep on hovering for some time before she could use it. Perhaps it would never come any nearer or be any brighter....

Now to stop rambling and get back to that city. She would miss this tree. She and it had lived through some vivid moments together.... There was the roommate question to attend to. She would need someone who was very happy. A happy person in New York? Doubtless there were a few, but they would be harder to find than fairies. One by one, she thought about the girls she knew, beginning, as nearly as she could judge, at the top of the happiness list. It was amusing to speculate about them this way. They ranged themselves in her mind like a row of marigolds, the brightest at one end, shading by degrees to duller, more wilted ones. After awhile she came to the very end of the line....

It was a long time since she had found courage to call on Margaret Kingsley, in her miserable corner down town, with not even a window-box of pansies for company. But now that the Maine woods had stiffened up her back a little, perhaps she could use this new strength—hold on to it by using it—by playing tree to somebody else. She had long been used as a tree by her friends. It was odd, and significant, that in her need she could turn only to the original tree itself—roots truly in the earth, branches waving in the sun!

Suddenly, from overhead, came a rush of song—notes that

were clear and cool as moonstones, trailing up to a cascade of opals. Into the song of that hermit-thrush had crept all the joy mingled with all the sadness of her thoughts since she had come out by herself into the woods. As if the bird understood. Sunlight glanced through the leaves. The woods were alive and breathing gently. She was a pagan. She was in tune with them.... Clinging in silence to the white pine tree, she closed her eyes, but the cloud motion went on. She fell softly through infinite space, while a hermit-thrush sang. A far cry from New York!...

"MARGIE, you look grand this morning in that green dress."

"Really like it, Jane? I think it's not so bad." Margaret Kingsley was brushing her hair thoughtfully in front of the little mirror.

"Howard tonight?"

"Yes, he's meeting me at the store, after I finish selling corsets to my ugly old ladies."

"Oh, well, I'll be at my books all day, too—selling sex books to timid little women, books on woodcraft and fishing to pudgy business men, and the mediocrest novels you ever saw to everybody."

"Don't forget you found Howard Castle in that bookstore of yours."

"You don't let me forget it, do you?"

"Honest, Jane, I can't so much as think about him without being practically electrocuted.... It's a good life, you know."

"Sure, I know. Nasty weather today, though." Jane drew aside a rather dingy curtain and looked out into gray sheets of rain.

"Oh, by the way, Jane, I was thinking—whatever has become of John these days? Haven't seen him in ages."

"He went to Canada to nurse his battered emotions. Didn't I tell you?"

Margaret turned around. "Why don't you marry the poor guy and put him out of his misery?" she inquired.

"I may sometime."

"I think he's gorgeous," said the other; then turned to her brushing again.

"Well, marry him yourself, and save me the trouble," Jane suggested.

"Janie, you aren't still—married to a ghost, are you?" A visible tremor went through the girl as she spoke. "Oh, Jane, it sounds so cold and shivery—married to a ghost."

"Don't talk about ghosts in weather like this. I've got to go to work, you know—smile all day at the dear customers —if any."

It seemed to Jane that during the last year she and Margaret had pulled each other up pretty well, braced back to back. They had taken all the best odds and ends of life that they could find, and mingled them into a mosaic sort of pattern which was life. "Not much like the dreams, Marg, but it isn't so bad, either, if we stick together."

Still, Margaret was right. There was no sense at all in being married to a ghost. You could love the past and hold it sacred, but it was futile to try to live by it in the present—to mingle the two and build the present upon the dream that had been. Millie would doubtless have called her "Mrs. Ghost." The thought made her chuckle, and she wished Millie were on hand to share it. She missed Millie a good deal, especially these last few weeks, for it seemed that Margaret's standing was precarious—that any day now would see her carried off, body and soul, by her young poet. But then, any day now Millie would come home.

She would come in late some evening, with a great scuffling of heels and a gorgeous painted mouth, wearing a skin-tight black satin dress and a fluffy black fur-piece thrown casually over one shoulder. "Hello, lioness!" she would shout gaily. And Jane would never mention Mrs. Ghost at all....

And then it would be just as it was five years ago. Margaret would marry her poet, but Millie's fifteenth—or was it sixteenth?—fiancé would be sent packing. Millie was now further along in the world of vaudeville and choruses, and Jane worked in a bookstore instead of an entomological research bureau, at a wage of five dollars a week more, but otherwise... it was fearful to think of civilization going on and on like this, trying to kid itself into believing it was eternal and immortal.

She had an odd sensation, then, as though, like the light princess in MacDonald's enchanting fairy tale, she had lost her gravity. It was incredible that she should come back from her kingdom outside the world—come back and be able, even painfully, to adapt herself to life on earth again. It was incredible that the earth should still exist. She and it both should have undergone some supreme transformation. Instead of which—here she was. She was conscious that a few floating ragged streamers of rainbow still clung about her. She must carefully strip them off now, and put them into the trash-basket. In a few minutes it would be time to sally out to work. And you couldn't go to a respectable job in a bookstore with rainbow rags drifting about your shoulders, or star-dust in your hair....

Jane laughed again, but there was a gleam of danger in her eye. Sometime, not too far off, she would stage another rebellion. It would not be the same kind of rebellion, though. One could never repeat the real adventures. That was why so many people were unhappy, she reflected. They tried to go back and repeat the things that had made them happy before. They tried to retrace the trail and visit again the places where they had known their highest ecstasies; whereas, if only they had the courage to push on, forward, over deserts and swamps and glaciers, they would sometime make new discoveries as bright as the others, or even brighter, perhaps.... One good way to start a rebellion was to buy a red, red skirt....

The rain surged down with a steady drone. Well, it was time to go to work. Couldn't hang about the window all day. She peered out once more into the gray. As far as she could see, not even a cat was out.

AFTERWORD

In the early summer of 1929, Barbara Follett met Edward Anderson aboard the *Vigilant*, a five-masted, 242-foot schooner that shipped lumber from Hoquiam, Washington to Honolulu, Hawaii. Barbara—fifteen, brown-eyed and slender, long auburn hair tied in pigtails—was a whip-smart habituée of masts' crosstrees; Anderson—twenty-five, six-feet-two, reserved and somewhat stoic, the sea in his blood—was the ship's second mate.

Barbara and her mother Helen were sailing back to the United States after ten months at sea. Armed with a typewriter each, they had explored islands in the Caribbean and the South Pacific—a journey inspired by Barbara's father (Wilson Follett, who was my grandfather) having deserted his family in New Haven, Connecticut, for a woman twenty-years-to-the-day his junior (Margaret Whipple, my grandmother). The voyage from Honolulu to Hoquiam took a month—ample time for Barbara and Anderson to become good friends. *Lost Island* is dedicated "to E. A."—Edward Anderson—and the story's two main characters are very much based on the real Barbara and Anderson.

Barbara Follett on the *Vigilant*, June 1929

To put it mildly, Barbara's emotional state was at a low ebb in the summer of 1929. After ten months in too-close quarters, tension between she and her mother was high. Of more serious concern was a recent incident too scandalous for Helen to describe when writing to her best friend, Anne Meservey, that April. (In her letter "Dr. Tyler" is Margaret Tyler, who was caring for Sabra, Helen's younger daughter. For complete transcriptions of Follett correspondence during the period covered here, please see *Barbara Newhall Follett: A Life in Letters,* Farksolia, 2015.)

> Sudden was our departure for this island [Samoa]. Between us and Dr. Tyler, Bar has had a smash—emotional and nervous. It was bound to come sometime when the condition was right for it. And it came to a climax in Tahiti. Follett's attempt to smash his family for his own individual freedom has worked one hundred percent. Bar is now the victim. I can't tell details.

Helen wrote to Anne again in May, shortly before sailing from Samoa to Honolulu.

> Barbara has gone to pieces. Her writing job is not anywhere near finished. She has lost interest in things, in living, in writing. She says, herself, she is "homesick." [...] She is in a critical condition, and likely to do anything from running away to suicide. And my advice is not what she wants. She must have a man to help her.

Helen was correct in thinking Barbara wanted to run away. While sailing to Honolulu on the *S. S. Sonoma,* Barbara secretly wrote to friends asking them to lend her money. She was planning to escape to Montreal, the home of a ship's engineer about her father's age (Wilson was 42) whom she'd met in the Caribbean. Barbara was keen to find a man to fill the emptiness left by her father, to whom she'd been devoted. Anderson's presence on the *Vigilant* will have comforted her a great deal.

On arrival at Hoquiam, Barbara and Helen stayed on board with Anderson for a week. The three held "cherry- and ice-cream parties" and explored the town's old growth forest of pine, fir, spruce, hemlock, and cedar. A year later Barbara would write:

> I suppose that I spent about the happiest month of my life during that sea-trip in her. And it lasted even during that week in port, when I took over the cabin-boy's job.... Life was beautiful then.

After that week in port Barbara and Helen took a bus to Pasadena in southern California. They were almost completely broke, having waited in vain all year for Wilson to send them money. My grandfather had none to speak of either, having been fired from his editing job by Alfred Knopf due to his affair with Margaret, who was also working for Knopf. (*Lost Island*'s Miss Perry might be based on my grandmother—106 Perry Street in Greenwich Village being their home after Wilson left his family for good in March 1928.)

Barbara, who had not attended a day of school in her life (she was home-schooled), was enrolled at Pasadena Junior College, while Helen sailed back to Honolulu for a job at the Bishop Museum and to begin writing *Magic Portholes*, the first of her two books recounting their months at sea (the second was *Stars to Steer By*). Barbara was to live under the guardianship of Mildred Kennedy and her colleague, Florence Brown. Miss Kennedy, a wealthy and deaf friend from Boston (and founder of the Boston Guild for the Hard of Hearing), had come to the Folletts' rescue.

Barbara was also to begin seeing a "psychiatrist," Ture Wilhelm Schoultz. Schoultz was in fact not a psychiatrist, only a pretend one; his income came from massaging Hollywood stars. A handsome thirty-six-year-old émigré from Stockholm, Schoultz claimed to be a Swedish count—a deceit discovered in 1931 by the third of his four wives, Katrina Van Wyck. A more disturbing fact about him occurred several years before he met Barbara. He was working as a masseur in Memphis, Tennessee, and was engaged to Mamie Cox—the daughter of the pastor of Memphis's Central Baptist Church. In 1919 Schoultz was tried in court and convicted "of attempt to violate the age of consent and by offering indecent exposures and proposals to high school girls" and given a one- to five-year prison sentence. He appealed his case up to the state's Supreme Court, claiming he was the victim of mistaken identity. His fiancée and future father-in-law stood by him, and it appears that he avoided jail by marrying Mamie and fleeing the state.

Barbara's experiment with formal education and "psychiatry" lasted mere days. In mid September she ran away to San Francisco, where she rented a room in a boarding house on O'Farrell Street in the Tenderloin neighborhood under an assumed name, K. Andrews. (Whether or not Schoultz had made any unwanted advances toward Barbara I don't know, but it wouldn't surprise me if he was at least part of the reason she wanted to escape.)

Barbara wrote a note to her mother before skipping town.

> Dear Helen:
>
> Promise you won't be flabbergasted? Brace yourself!
>
> This is my last hour in the town of Pasadena. I'm leaving for the far east, via Vancouver, where I'll be met. Then I plunge whole-heartedly into a very large job which consists of being private secretary for a whole class of marine engineers who have gathered together for the purpose of working out miracles and life-old dreams in a prospering engineering shop. And I'll live, by myself, very quietly and respectably, in a tiny apartment, and work like the very old Nick.
>
> I'm not going to tell you, for the time being, where I'll be; and names, jobs, and headquarters have all been completely changed, you see. So we're unfindable. Besides, I want to be alone with my Disillusion or my Fairytale—as the case may be.
>
> And I expect I'll be seeing you again in this incarnation.
>
> Love, B. F.

Mildred and Florence suspected that San Francisco was Barbara's destination, and contacted the police there. Three days later Detective Sergeant Clarence Hurlitz found Barbara in her room. She tried to escape through a window or—depending on which newspaper headline one chooses to believe—she tried to leap to her death. Either way, she was restrained and detained in the Juvenile Detention Home until the Los Angeles probation officer could figure out what to do with her. Barbara refused to live with her guardians any longer, so a new home was needed while her mother made the long journey back to California. Fortunately, old friends of the Folletts who were now living in Pasadena—Alice Dyar Russell and her family—offered to look after the teenager. After Barbara left California six months later, Alice would become one of her two most important correspondents (the other was Anderson).

That the girl who'd famously written *The House Without Windows* when she was twelve had now been arrested was too juicy a story for the press to pass up. Dozens of articles quickly appeared in newspapers nationwide. With Helen still at sea, Wilson and Margaret drove across country from their rented farmhouse on the Maine coast, where my grandfather had been trying to write a novel (*No More Sea*, published by Henry Holt & Company in 1934, was voted third in that year's Pulitzer Prize for fiction). But before they left Maine, none other than Ture Schoultz came to visit! I suspect he was trying to ingratiate himself with this new couple who, given the chaotic whirlwind Barbara had been living in since her father's desertion, might soon become her legal guardians.

My grandmother wrote to Anne Meservey on September 24, 1929:

> I believe Wilson is going to write to you about what we have learned about Barbara and her mother. Helen herself never wrote to him, but a Dr. Schoultz from Pasadena came to see us

yesterday, and told us all about them. It is possible that we are going out there to try to make a home for Barbara. I hope so. I think that I could help to make her happy again. I shall be grateful for even the chance to try. And I believe that at last we are going to have a divorce and the chance to marry.

Truant Child Genius Says She Ran Away Because She Craved Literary Freedom

Barbara Newhall Follett Appalled by Plans for Education

A child genius beating the wings of her young aspirations against the bars hedging in the freedom of youth. This is Barbara Newhall Follett, famed in the literary world as an example of precocious literary talent and author at 14 of two successful books.

At the Juvenile Detention Home, where she is being held pending the arrival of an official from Los Angeles to take her back to the friends from whom she ran away, she told of the experiences that led to her latest adventure. She wanted to live her own life and carry out her own plans for developing her literary skill, she said, but most of all she did not want to be forced to enter college nor to trim her sails to the standardized pattern. So she left a note of explanation, took an assumed name and came alone to San Francisco September 16.

LONGED FOR FREEDOM

"I came away because I felt I had to have my freedom," she said. "I was utterly suppressed, almost frantic under the plans that had been made for me. I did not want to enter college nor live the standardized existence. I have never been to school in my life. Perhaps I might like it, I do not know. But this I know, I do not want to like it. And so I came away and I suppose I will have to go back."

According to the girl's story, she had been on a long ocean voyage with her mother, Mrs. H. T. Follett. They reached Los Angeles July 29 financially almost stranded and beset with "difficulties." Wealthy friends of Mrs. Follett's, two elderly women engaged in scientific research, came to the rescue. They advanced money for Mrs. Follett to return to Honolulu, where she was to continue some literary work she had begun, and took charge of Barbara, who was to be placed under the guardianship of Dr. Ture Schultz of Pasadena and entered as a student in the Junior College at Pasadena.

APPALLED BY CONDITIONS

The thought of school and a strange guardian was too much for the young girl, whose education had been gained through books, travel, adventure and the association of the famous people who gathered about the home of her father, Wilson Follett, author and associate in the Knopf Publishing Company.

"All the plans were made. I had picked out my course of study—botany, Spanish, English and algebra. I was to play my fiddle in the school orchestra. But I couldn't stand it," she explained with a gesture of repulsion. "The whole atmosphere of Southern California seemed poisonous to me. I had some money my mother gave me before she went away. It was enough to last me quite a while. So I came to San Francisco by stage. I left a note behind and took an assumed name.

ADORES SAN FRANCISCO

"I had been to San Francisco before and it has been the dream of my life to come back. If ever I have a real home anywhere I want it to be here in this adorable city. I want to live here and work here and dream out my dreams here. Yesterday I went to Golden Gate Park. It is the most beautiful spot in the world. I have been everywhere and I know. They can take me back to Los Angeles but they can't take that beautiful memory away from me.

"This has been a sordid humiliating experience, but perhaps some day it will be literary material. Four little girls in their blue uniforms were in their cages next to mine. Looking through the bars. One of them even tried to wink at me. Why are older people crushing us this way? It seems to me I cannot wait six whole years until I am 21 in order just to be free."

LOVES THE SEA

Barbara professed a great love for the sea and a keen interest in marine engineering. She and her mother made a cruise of nearly a year to the West Indies, Martinique, through the Panama Canal to Tahiti, the South Sea islands and the Hawaiian islands. They returned to the coast from Hawaii on a lumber schooner, the Vigilant, as stewardess and stewardess' assistant.

Barbara had been at sea before and her second book, "The Voyage of the Norman D.," published when she was 14 years old, was based on her sea experiences. A letter of commendation and encouragement from William McFee is one of her cherished possessions.

In San Francisco, she said, she had planned to find work as a typist while continuing to write under careful and expert criticism. Her father, Wilson Follett, she has not seen for more than a year.

"My parents aren't permanently separated," she said with a wan smile. "Like many writers, they are both a little crazy. That's all."

Barbara Newhall Follett

Girl Writer, 15, Tries Suicide To Cheat Law

Attempts to Leap from Window as Officer Serves Warrant

Los Angeles, Cal., Sept. 20.—(UP)—Barbara Newhall Follett, 15, held in San Francisco for Los Angeles authorities, was sought merely because she was listed as a missing person, the district attorney's office said today.

Two Pasadena social workers reported that she disappeared from her home three days ago. The telegraphic request sent to San Francisco asked police there to aid in locating her, it was said.

San Francisco, Sept. 20.—(UP)—Barbara Bewhall Follett, 15-year-old authoress whose novel "The House Without Windows" written at 11 was enthusiastically received in the literary world, was surrounded by a protecting wall of silence today after her arrest for Los Angeles authorities, and her attempted suicide.

Registered at a small hotel as "K. Andrews," the girl was arrested by Detective Sergeant Clarence Hurlitz, who grabbed her in time to prevent her from leaping out of the window of her room.

Hurlitz had orders to arrest the girl for Los Angeles authorities, but did not know why, and Warren H. Prescott, Los Angeles probation officer, maintained silence.

According to Hurlitz, the girl asked permission to write "two last letters" before trying to leap through the window.

Two of the dozens of articles covering Barbara's arrest in San Francisco. Left: *San Francisco Chronicle*, September 21, 1929. Right: *Daily Register Gazette* (Rockford, Illinois), September 20, 1929.

After a court hearing behind closed doors to keep the press out, and with Helen still away, Barbara moved in with the

Russells. She wrote to Anderson, who came to Pasadena to support his young friend as soon as he was able.

In late October Helen arrived at last, and the two parents and their lawyers fought each other for custody. The court left the decision up to Barbara. For a short time Helen also lived with the Russells, but with Wilson and Margaret visiting often and ratcheting up the tension, she moved to a hotel and didn't see her daughter for a month. Wilson and Margaret continued to visit but it was all for naught. In November, Barbara chose Helen over her father, whose disdain for Anderson was a contributing factor. Meanwhile, the stock market continued its crash.

Alice Dyar Russell & Barbara in Pasadena on March 4, 1930—Barbara's sixteenth birthday

After wintering in California, Barbara and her mother began their journey back east by sea, while Wilson and Margaret moved to Hollywood to work for Metro-Goldwyn-Meyer as script readers (fellow readers included Dorothy Parker and Lillian Hellman; Bernard F. Dick's book *Hellman in Hollywood* recounts the dramatist's unhappy time there). Barbara and Helen boarded the *S. S. Marsodak* on March 4, 1930—Barbara's sixteenth birthday—and steamed through the Panama Canal and up the coast to Washington, D.C. There they stopped for two months to work on *Magic Portholes* and to decide where to go next. The fatherless house on Armory Street in New Haven was too painful to contemplate. They were still broke, and Anderson put his meager fortune at Barbara's disposal while offering advice regarding work. (Barbara quoted this brief excerpt in her April 28 letter to Alice; unfortunately Anderson's letter hasn't survived.)

> I only pray it doesn't cast you into the day-laboring class. I've been in it long enough to know what it amounts to, and what its probable end is. The sort of existence that leaves a woman a slattern at forty, and a man a dolt. Or if they have some perception, leaves them with a sort of misanthropic cynicism, bereft of ideals and appreciation of life.... This must all seem very serious and dull, coming from me.

Barbara and Helen decided to try New York City for their new home. Less expensive than Washington, New York offered more job opportunities during these early months of the Great Depression and was home to many publishers. They arrived in June 1930. Helen stayed in Midtown while Barbara moved in with her friends George and Alice Bryan in Pelham, a few miles to the north. Three years earlier George Bryan had been Barbara's chaperone on the *Frederick H.*, on which Barbara served as cabin-boy during her trip from New Haven to Bridgewater, Nova Scotia; she renamed the ship in her second book, *The Voyage of the Norman D.* And Bryan had been first dedicatee in *The House Without Windows*: "J. H." stands for James Hook, Barbara's nickname for him during their pirate-playing days on Little Lake

Sunapee in New Hampshire, where in happier times the Folletts and Bryans had summered.

Barbara quickly found work writing synopses of "putrid novels" for Fox Film Corporation. She was also making a little money by editing and retyping the manuscript for her friend Dr. J. Harland Paul's book, *The Last Cruise of the Carnegie* (Williams & Wilkins Company, 1932). When Barbara and Helen left New Haven in September 1928, their plan was to try to follow the course of the *Carnegie*, whose crew they had befriended earlier in the year. It was to be the schooner's last cruise because, while anchored in Apia, Samoa on November 29, 1929, a barrel of gasoline exploded, igniting other barrels and destroying the ship. The disaster took the lives of Captain James P. Ault and Tony Kolar, the cabin-boy.

Barbara also enrolled herself in the Packard Commercial School to learn shorthand and other business skills. While attending classes she landed a part-time job as a secretary at the Personnel Research Federation on West 39th Street; after graduation this job switched to full-time. By now she was reunited with Helen and sister Sabra in a tiny apartment on West 122nd Street, near Grant's Tomb. She had a little more time than usual during this busy summer since her frequent letters to Anderson were on hiatus. He had signed on with the *C. S. Holmes*, a trading schooner that sailed from Seattle to Barrow (now called Utqiagvik) on Alaska's North Slope, a four-month return trip. In May she wrote to Alice about the most recent letter she'd received from her wandering sailor:

> Anderson sailed on the 16th [of May 1930], as per schedule, sailed right out into space. Look up Point Barrow on a map of the Arctic regions—that's the end of the route—then they turn around again and circle Alaska toward home—if they don't encounter a nor'-easter, or an iceberg, or the pack-ice. Before they sailed he sent off one dashing letter, of quite a different

> tone from what you'd expect of a person embarking on such a mean voyage. He described his own particular position aboard, half-way between sailor and engineer (there are four gasoline engines for sails and cargo, you see); and then he wrote several pages in mocking echo of the "tourist literature" on Seattle, concerning statistics and what-not. And then he seemed to run out of material, and said "Well, goodbye!" or words to that effect. A person like that sort of takes one's breath away, seems to me. Very startling and over-powering.

At first Barbara found New York acceptable, but also missed the mostly solitary, outdoors-filled life she'd had in New Haven and New Hampshire. She wrote to Alice in July:

> Yes, I have bearded New York in its lair. I find it not so appalling, in fact I rather like it, as one likes some colossal piece of machinery; and struggling into the sardine-packed express "L" at quarter to nine in the morning is almost exhilarating. It thrills me to see all those millions of faces, all going to their respective puny jobs, and all so tense and rushed. I don't know, but New York has so far done me much more good than harm. I feel more of a sympathy and understanding for People In General than ever in my life before, because I am One Of Them, which I never was in my life before. I find myself buying my chewing-gum from a cripple in the street, rather than in a drug-store.
>
> Yes, I long and long and *long* for the sea, and woods, and quiet, and more sunshine, and the wind, and a little more room, please, and not so many people on my feet, if you don't mind. And there are times when I feel my heart beginning to curl up just a little at the edges—the first step, the warning symptom, to its sickening and dwindling. I keep holding out my arms—I mean my spiritual arms—like an amoeba or sumthin. A ceaseless need. Sometimes I think it's the sea, and sometimes I

think it's Anderson's correspondence, and sometimes I think it's just space I need, and the wild. And I can't have 'em!

She missed hearing from Anderson dreadfully. In August she wrote to Alice:

> Then, too, it won't be so very long before Anderson is home, and I believe I could go through *anything* with an occasional letter from him to keep me going. I never realized before how he and I had gotten to depend on each other's support. We each have had such ghastly times! It's quite beautiful, I think—two hungry souls beating their wings desperately and finding such joy and strength in one another.

And in October:

> I have set aside a few days around the middle of this month—marked them off mentally with red ink—for the days during which I may hear from my wandering sailor. Of course one can't tell—I might hear tomorrow, or I might never at all. Rather uncomfortable suspense. I don't know quite what would happen to me in that case, and I don't care to speculate. If I don't hear before November, I shall be worried. I haven't many bulwarks. My family isn't a bulwark at all. You are, and he is. He is so simple at heart that he would be laughed at by some of this world, and distrusted by most of the rest—my farents, for example—my fermenting farents. He is the soul and essence of the sea. He can sit on a schooner's taffrail at night and become so utterly a part of the ship and the sea and the night that it makes you cease your breathing for awe. He is rugged and uncut, and, though so far above the standard of most sea-farers, he still falls far short, in some ways, of the shore-world's standards. He is ignorant—of the little things that don't matter. But he is so real that he puts to shame

> thousands of people who probably would consider themselves far "above" him.
>
> And he answered a need of mine that nothing and no one else could answer, by knowing how to laugh, and by being serene and tranquil and deep as the trade-wind Pacific. Bulwark, oasis, anchor—what-you-will. Mysterious, too, in his comings and goings, as the sea with its tide. A romantic soul.

At last she received a note from Anderson saying he was back in Seattle. She wrote to Alice on October 13:

> Of course I can't believe it yet. It's been a terrible gulf. It will be a long time before things can be as they were. I had half expected that the threads would just pick up again where they broke, but threads don't do that. There have been too many vital changes. [...]
>
> When he gets more or less organized again—not before—I shall gently hint that we would both like to see him this winter. I have a good idea that he'll take the hint. It's very easy to ship coastwise, especially in the winter, and it's rather hard to ship anywhere else except offshore. I feel somehow as though we should have to talk and laugh before balance can be recaptured. I am all up in the air now. I have concentrated all my faculties on trying to believe that that little letter is genuine, and not some ghostly aberration come to haunt me. I felt as though I were writing to a ghost, Saturday afternoon.

Correspondence with Anderson having resumed, Barbara did her best to accommodate New York and the increasing drudgery of office work, while Helen tried to find a publisher for *Magic Portholes*. Barbara wrote to Alice in December:

> Anderson and I commune continually; we nibble delicately at the earth as though it were a piece of cheese, and we fool with

> stars as though they were a handful of beads. He (wise man!—) is hanging on to his job for dear life, while I stand by and approve. On the other hand, I hang desperately to my job, while he stands by and approves. Thus we get along, though it's very unsatisfactory not to be together. I think he writes better and better all the time. His comments are really immortal.

In May 1931 Anderson returned to Alaska on the *Holmes* and Barbara began to write *Lost Island.* She wrote to Alice in June:

> I'm writing a book. A good book. The one about wings. The first chapter is done, and the second is well under way. The plot is mapped out rather clearly—in my head. It begins rather dismally, but soon acquires some sun. There will be sea (naturally), and a romance (?), and a satisfactory amount of misery. The plot is exceedingly old and trite, but it's going to be handled in a new way. It's about a shipwreck, an island, and so on. But it doesn't turn out very well. It leaves you a little poised in mid-air. [...]
>
> This style of writing of mine sounds rather curt in a letter, doesn't it? It's a new development. I think I rather like it. The novel is more or less written in that style. Some sentences which aren't really sentences, you know; and no long, involved ones. W. F. [Wilson Follett] wouldn't approve of that, I suppose, he being the champeen sentence-twister and wordsmith of the generation!

And on July 4:

> There are three chapters of my book in existence now—pretty fairly good I think. Its title so far has been "Lost Island." Does that sound intriguing? The few persons whom I have so far confided in have liked it—also have been enthusiastic over the

> outline of the story. I am having a good deal of fun wrestling with it. [...]
>
> Alaska is a Hell of a long way off! No mail until October. But that's something to anticipate. He is such a faithful soul. Two letters a week, and sometimes three, from the time he landed last fall till the schooner sailed this spring. He'll come back. I have an idea that he's unbreakable and eternal. [...]
>
> But oh, oh, in N. Y. the moths feed on the wings of your soul. This is probably an unhealthy attitude, I know. But I *do* think the world is rather horrid. Most of my dearest friends seem to be in deep trouble, and I can't do anything about it.
>
> Perhaps that's why I cling for dear life to A. He, with no tools and no material, has nevertheless made something most beautiful and real out of life. I don't know just how. But he is a rock and a shelter. I'll never forget or forgive WF's attitude toward him. That was mainly what caused the sharp and sudden break between him and me. It was unwarranted and ridiculous and *mean*. My respect for WF did its loudest blowing-up over that.... A. is a treasure.

Eager for a break from the city, Helen and her daughters rented a log cabin in the Vermont countryside for July and August. The cabin was on a hillside overlooking woods sheltering Barbara's beloved hermit thrushes—across the Connecticut River from Hanover, New Hampshire, where she'd been born seventeen years earlier. She wrote to Alice on July 14:

> I certainly don't think there is much to be said for this so-called civilization. It's barbarous, that's what it is. The primitivest of the primitive were never capable of such outrages as this Jinx civilization. That's one of the things "Lost Island" is about—sort of a fling, a kick, a dig at the world. Not a nasty one, just a grieved one. I wish we were back to the cave days. Even nowadays there are some tribes that are happy. Look at the

> Polynesians, for instance. Naturally we can't be happy in their surroundings, but that's not the fault of the surroundings. It's our fault—and civilization's. Damn, damn!
>
> But lest you think I'm becoming very despondent myself of late, let me assure you that this is my normal state of mind, when I allow it to come to the surface. That is, I *always* am grieved at the world. But I usually don't allow it to come to the surface. I sink it. And I do love listening to those hermit-thrushes. They are divine. And there are a few beings whom I love a great deal, and who make most of what there is of Good in life. But I don't believe in God. God got discouraged and gave up long ago, and I don't blame him, I'm sure!

Many of the themes in *Lost Island* mirror Barbara's real world—her disdain for New York; civilization—in particular its worship of money; unfulfilling work in dusty offices; her troubled friends; her love for and reliance on Anderson; her devotion to beauty and nature instead of a biblical God. Further themes will become apparent soon.

By the end of her Vermont vacation, Barbara had almost finished Chapter 6 and had made three new friends, one of whom had just graduated Dartmouth College: Nickerson Rogers. Just as Davidson is based on Anderson and Jane on Barbara, there's a lot of Nickerson in John, Jane's childhood friend from Maine. One day that August these four new friends drove 350 miles northeast to Katahdin, the tallest mountain in Maine. Katahdin (or, as Barbara liked to spell it, Ktaadn) was a mountain she'd longed to climb with her father before his desertion. The party camped a few nights on Chimney Pond and explored the great mountain and its trails. In 1933 Barbara would write about her Ktaadn adventures in a thrilling short story, *Rocks* (see Appendix 1).

Back in New York, Barbara's job kept her increasingly busy. There was good news on the book front, however: *Magic Port-*

holes had finally found a publisher in the Macmillan Company. There was even talk of serializing it for the radio. And to Barbara's profound relief, Anderson was back in Seattle. She wrote to Alice in November:

> In words, then, know that he has returned, and all's well. He has been writing to me in his usual clear, faithful way, and between us we've just had the Airmail-envelope presses going to their full capacity. He is one of the world's best, I think—and if other people don't think so, they needn't, and you can tell that to the farents, and be damned to them!

And on December 22:

> The book crawls along—crawls is just the word to describe its progress the last month or so. It's about two people who found out the rhyme and reason for a little while, but had it snatched away again. It's *supposed* to tear one's heart, you know. If it doesn't, a little, here and there, then it's no good. Promise you'll be torn, A.D.R? I may send you a copy of it before I show it to Messrs. Harper etc. I want to try to get a copy to E. A., you see, and perhaps I'll ask him to send it to you, or you to him, or something like that.
>
> He remains the best thing that I can see in life. (See???) It's his steadiness and strength and complete trustworthiness that makes him stand out so, in a complicated and discouraged world. I won't do any quotationing now, because I haven't time, but sometime I will. In the meantime, oh, thank God I've got him!

As 1931 drew to a close Barbara was becoming more and more restless, and increasingly mysterious in her letters to Alice. In the same letter as above, she wrote:

> I want to see you, very much. Who knows? The world is fairly small, when all's said and done, and I've an odd presentiment that I shan't be sitting at this desk for more than a certain amount of time—another year, say. I don't know what's going to happen after that, but I just have a small, dim suspicion, that's all. If the world has any justice (I never believed it had much), or a shred of happiness in it, or even the most erratic tendency to keep its promises—well, I shan't, that's all. And if that sounds vague and mysterious and so forth, it's just because I don't *dare* to do more than vaguely, dimly hint that things could take a sudden turn. (Sudden???) And if the world so much as suspected that I was in danger of telling you anything about its secret mechanisms, it would swoop down on me at once and cut off my head.

So far she hadn't mentioned Nickerson and the two others she'd met in Vermont (we know from *Rocks* that their names were Dinny and John). Over the winter these four met several times in New York to discuss a grand adventure they had in mind—a walk along the 2200-mile-long Appalachian Trail. Benton Mackaye (co-founder of the Wilderness Society) had come up with the idea of a continuous hiking trail from Maine to Georgia through the Appalachian Mountains; his proposed A.T. would connect several existing trails with new ones cut to link them up. The full length of the A.T., from Katahdin to Mount Oglethorpe, wouldn't be finished until 1937. Barbara wrote to Alice in March 1932:

> You are right when you surmise that I have been rushed and busy—more so than ever, since the beginning of 1932. My life is getting almost crowded, in fact. The job, of course, takes eight hours a day straight out, and everything else has to be jammed into the fringes. Since I can't satisfy mind, soul, or body with

> the job, I have to jam into the fringes almost as much as another person would put into an entire day. [...]
>
> The more important thing I have to contribute is that *Lost Island* creepeth onward, in spite of God and the Devil (represented by various personages, of course!). In fact, I've gotten to that delectable point where there remains only about a chapter and a half—or possibly two chapters and a half—to be written. That will complete the first draft. Then to sail into a good thorough revision, editing, chopping, piecing, cross-hatching, weaving, repairing, tearing, rending, boiling, steaming, and general subjection to energy. I think I can have it in Mr. Saxton's hands—willing or unwilling hands—by June 1 at the latest. That's what I'm aiming for, anyhow. And I still have faith in the old thing, which is quite a point, you know.

Eugene F. Saxton was editor-in-chief at Harper & Brothers. In 1928 Harper had advanced Barbara $500 before her sea trip with Helen; they planned to publish her observations while she was away. But Barbara was too distraught during the voyage to write to Saxton's satisfaction, and Helen was forced to spend the advance; and what little remained was stolen on a steamship in the South Pacific. To make amends, Barbara wanted to give Saxton first refusal on *Lost Island*. Her letter to Alice continues:

> When all this energy is accomplished, I'm going to bat out about three copies, of which two will be passed around among a few individuals. You are going to be one of the fortunate (?) recipients. I shall want your criticism—I mean, if you *are* willing, and want to give it—rigorous and stern and unsparing. There will be four or five other people, who will probably all contradict each other. Then it will fall to my lot to Think It Over, and do some more pounding. Among these selected critics, I'm going to pick out at least two entirely impersonal

ones. For instance, a Professor of English at Dartmouth whom I encountered last summer.

After that job is all completely finished, and the black spring binder reposes under Mr. Saxton's nose, I'm going to sail into another job I have in mind—not such a lovely job, but an even more important one, because my entire existence rests upon it. It will be the introductory material for another book—a book about an adventure I think I shall have this summer. Woods and mountains. A. D. R., I'm going to tell you about it, and you must rise to the occasion, because I'm terrifically excited over the whole thing.

I've gotten together a party of four congenial brave souls—of which I am one (I hope)—and we may add two more members. Then, starting about the middle of July, we're going to Maine—Ktaadn—Thoreau's country—and from there we're going down the Appalachian Trail, two thousand miles, Maine to Georgia, camping out, and carrying upon our sturdy backs the necessities of life. It will take between three and four months, and be the greatest release imaginable.

Well, I've even higher ambitions than that. I'm not just going to take money out of the bank, leaving a hole, to indulge my pleasure. I'm going to struggle to make the thing pay for itself, and the only way I know how to do that is to write about it. And as I said I've some ideas for the introductory materials which can be put into words before ever the adventure takes place. And that's what I'm going to do after *Lost Island* is carefully finished. All four of us are very much together on this. We're going to cooperate to the nth degree, and I think that among us all we'll succeed. You couldn't imagine a more congenial party. We are getting together this spring for house-parties at intervals, during which we paw over hundreds of maps, draw up provision lists, talk, laugh, anticipate, and in general have a grand time.

The party consists of an amiable lad with occasional

unsuspected depths whom I met last summer when H. and I were living in the Vermont cabin; a pal of his, who has a remarkably good head on young shoulders; and a girl who is really a grand scout, with whom I get along quite beautifully. In fact, we all get along with each other beautifully. No friction anywhere, as far as we have been able to discover. There may be two others added to the Grand Expedition, as I said; and we would like of course to have an elderly leader, than whom no finer could be imagined than Meservey of Hanover [Arthur Bond Meservey, Anne's husband, was Professor of Physics at Dartmouth College]—only I'm afraid Meservey of Hanover is tied up.

Well, that's the general idea. It may crash completely. Nothing is certain about it. But we're all hoping, and pulling together. We're all slightly rebels against civilization, and we want to go out into the woods and sweat honestly and shiver honestly and satisfy our souls by looking at mountains, smelling pine trees, and feeling the sky and the earth.

We went up to Bear Mountain this last week-end, for the Appalachian Trail strikes through there, and we explored ten or fifteen miles of that section of it. It gave us a tremendous thrill. I can't tell you what it meant to our world-weary souls to have our feet on that narrow, bumpy, winding footpath that goes clear from Maine to Georgia, marked out by little silver monograms on the trees, which change to yellow-painted arrows over rocks and ledges. Over Easter we're all gathering the clan again, for another expedition somewhere. These short trips help us to get personally adjusted and strengthen the congeniality still more. It also helps to give us an idea of what we need by way of food and clothes, and also puts us in training, more or less.

It will be a terrific trip, of course. There will be times when we'll probably be cold and wet and uncomfortable and grumpy. But we're ready for that—almost covet it in fact. Pitting one's

> strength and personality against the wilds—the greatest sort of opportunity on earth.... Well, there it is. My room is plastered with trail maps even now!
>
> All this time I haven't so much as mentioned A., have I? Well, I've had him in the back of my mind—in reserve, so to speak. Luckily, the *C. S. Holmes* job holds. I guess he'll be going north again next summer—the third time. There really isn't anything else to do, with conditions as they are all over the world, especially along the waterfront. His life is odd and stern—verging on tragic, at times. He feels that now and then, and has down-spells, during which I am hard put to it to be cheerful and cheering. I am pretty sure, though, that next fall we shall actually be together, and discuss everything from moths to meteors, including money and mice and merriment and misery and—but that almost exhausts the m's I can think of at this Moment. That discussion will doubtless decide a good many points about this universe and the nature thereof. Right now he is a little sad, and alternates between letters about the futility of life with humorous epistles about politics in Seattle and other things.

How different Barbara's life would have been had she married Anderson, a possibility she hinted at in her list of m's! Barbara's long March letter continues:

> I have a philosophy of life—one which has been evolving for many years, but which has suffered interruptions and repressions and smashes. Now it has taken root again—or, rather, I realize that its roots are not dead, but just beginning to be powerful. If it grows and thrives and survives the vile climate of trouble and difficulty and set-back, it may take me to almost any part of the old earth where I want to go. What is this philosophy, you ask? Well, I'm testing it warily, leaning on it cautiously, exploring it tenderly, thinking about it profoundly;

and if I come to the conclusion that it's any good, I'll tell you sometime. Not until it has proved itself a little, though. I've lost faith in a number of things—or, rather, I've withdrawn from them the crushing weight of my faith. My philosophy aims now to stand upright. Tree-like....

I expect the next year to decide a number of important points. Beginning this summer. I think this summer will tell me a good deal. Being in the woods, standing on mountain-peaks—time to meditate and dream and get a perspective on life. There is nothing more soul-cleansing than to stand on a mountain, when you are inclined to feel hopelessly sure that the world is 99 100ths mankind, and see that vast tracts of it are blankets of forest and trees, after all! Mountains affect inward matters in the same way—reassure one about inward things in the same way as they do the visible things. So I expect to find out several things during the Appalachian Trail expedition—assuming and praying that it works.

Then, coming back from that to this—the complete contrast, the need for instantaneous adaption, and the fresh perspective on this—these things are also going to tell me a good deal. I mean, I shall be ready then to make certain decisions, about philosophy and about life.

Then I'll remedy the inner workings of the universe!

Barbara elaborated her philosophy to Alice in May:

I have decided that there are a good many big and fundamental things wrong with the world, and that nothing can be done about it; furthermore, that one *must* revolve quietly along with the world instead of trying vainly to buck it. If you compromise enough—to outward appearances, at least—and if you fully realize what a messy world it is, and are reconciled to certain facts, such as continual change and permanence in nothing—why, then you can have a surprisingly good time. That's what

> I've discovered anyway. I'm having a better time of it these days than I've had for ages—almost approaching gaiety sometimes, in fact.

Barbara's evolving philosophy is what the last part of *Lost Island* is about: Jane-Barbara's struggle to survive in a meaningless, indifferent world while experiencing, once in a while, joy. As for love—is one's best course to sacrifice personal happiness for someone one loves more than anyone, while possessing the knowledge that such sacrifice will inevitably make both parties miserable? These are heavy themes for a girl of eighteen.

By the spring of 1932 Barbara's internal conflict was clear to her, I think: faithfulness and devotion to Anderson or fun and adventure with Nickerson, who had been visiting New York often and, almost certainly, taking her out dancing. (Or could she, like Jane, try to live two lives—have her cake and eat it too?) Two lessons of *Lost Island* are to embrace the moment; and that adventure is a vital ingredient in a full life. Therefore, what better time to escape the dusty office and desperate city and take a long cruise on the *Annie Marlow* to parts unknown, or to begin a long walk through the woods and mountains of New England?

By late May Barbara had almost finished *Lost Island* and continued to prepare for the Trail. Adventure's call was increasing in volume. She wrote to Alice:

> Yes, Anderson went north again. He is now first mate of the schooner, and rather happy about that, of course. He is doing awfully well, considering everything. I MAY see him next fall—but don't you breathe a syllable about that, even to yourself! I'm keeping it a very strict secret from myself. If you know what I mean. I mean there are some things in this world that don't happen if you so much as admit that they're possible. Perhaps they sometimes happen if you keep your eyes tight shut and don't think at all.

> Oh, I *was* in the woods yesterday. I'm sure of it, because I've a sunburn. It was beautiful. Light green leaves with gold light breaking through them; wild geraniums, birds singing, a lake to swim in, grand companionship—the wild open spaces—but principally sunlight. I know from that taste of it that I couldn't by any hook or crook stay here very much longer.

As far as the Rare Book & Manuscript Library at Columbia University is concerned (that's where Helen deposited her and Barbara's papers in 1970), the above letter was the last Barbara wrote before heading north with Nickerson (Dinny and John didn't join them after all). With *Lost Island* complete and under Saxton's nose, she left New York at the beginning of July, then camped with Nick on an unnamed island in Squam Lake, New Hampshire for two weeks, where she swam and paddled and strengthened her city muscles. The pair then hitchhiked to Katahdin. A year later Barbara would write *Travels Without a Donkey* (see Appendix 2), a delightful account of their month-long journey by foot and canoe from Katahdin to Lake Umbagog on the Maine-New Hampshire border. She hoped to publish it and so portrayed Nick as her husband; to do otherwise would have been too scandalous for the 1930s. (Sadly, *Travels* wasn't published until I transcribed and posted it on my Farksolia website in 2012.)

Barbara had letters waiting when she and Nick passed through Oquossoc in the Rangeley Lakes region of Maine sometime in August. She learned that Saxton had passed on *Lost Island*. While in Oquossoc, Barbara replied to her mother's letter.

> I had a letter from Saxton. Oh, hell! Does anything ever satisfy him? Well, here's the letter. I don't see what I can do about it now, except suggest that if you feel like it you might trundle the MS to Alfred K [Knopf]. Also, old man [Frederick Taber]

> Cooper had a lead or two. He could be looked up via Ethel [Kelley]. But don't go to wearing yourself out over it, because I doubt if it's worth it.

Barbara at camp in 1932; photo by Nickerson Rogers

Barbara also invited her mother to accompany them over the Presidential Range in New Hampshire's White Mountains, but Helen declined. The couple continued their walk, pausing for a night at the hut on top of Mount Moosilauke in early October. This was the same hut Barbara and her father had stayed in for several days in October 1925—where she encountered hoarfrost for the first time, calling it "frost feathers." She wrote again to her mother:

> N. wears well. I don't know anybody else in the world (at least, of the male sex) whom I would want to be thrown together with so closely for so long through so many variegated adventures. We haven't even scrapped at all, which is rather remarkable, considering how constantly and intimately we've

> been together since July. I've never had such an enjoyable and satisfactory relation with anyone. We're going to chuck it, clean, when we feel like it, but now it promises to hold out ad infinitum, and it's grand.

In the same letter she again asked her mother to join them—this time for a section of the Long Trail through the Green Mountains of Vermont. Again her mother declined. She also wrote to Alice:

> I've jumped the whole structure of what life was before: I've jumped the job, jumped my love, jumped parental dependence, jumped civilization—made a pretty clean break—and am happier than for years and years. I've a new, and I think a better, structure of life, though time alone can tell that!

And she wrote to Anderson, informing him about her summer and Nickerson. As is the case with all of Barbara's letters to the sailor, it doesn't survive, but we do have his reply, which I think was waiting for her in Williamstown, Massachusetts—their next mail stop.

The couple descended Moosilauke, crossed the border into Vermont, and walked down the Long Trail to Massachusetts, where their journey ended in Williamstown, about five hundred miles from Katahdin. Here's Anderson's letter—he was delighted to hear about Barbara's rebellion against civilization and domesticity, and now wanted her for himself more than ever. Poor Anderson!

> Oct 21 1932
>
> Bar, you wonderful woman, you can't imagine how I feel today. You think I am pained, or unhappy, then know that I feel quite the opposite. Now I know that everything is real that you are not after all, an ordinary person. Now I know that, had I but

dared tell it to you, you would not have laughed at my own ambition, a 'madder' one than yours.

I *must* tell you now. I hate domesticity. I'm afraid of domestic people. I hate daily routine, and dollars and cents calculations; I wanted, *more than I want you,* to escape all that; the idea was breeding when I met you first. Perhaps you can guess what form my escape would take. I am going to have my own ship and go in my own way to do the things I choose. That is why I am working, for that, and not for the grubby comforts of domestic security. Before I met you, the idea was in a singular tense, then I had wild fancies that you might be a kindred spirit, and understand, but yet I was afraid to put words to it, and when you became efficient and psychological and, as I feared, ordinary, it was still harder to bring it to light. I then hoped that I could convert you to my faith after we came together. Yet it seems that you are as strong an advocate as myself, so therefore I feel as happy as if you had really known, and understood. We shall never grow old now Bar. This talk of love, that word love, what do *we* mean by it, not what you thought I meant. Poor abused word, with the weight of the whole world bearing down upon it. Happiness, contentment, security, bah, give me freedom. Why do you think I wanted to be definite and frank; because I wanted to feel free, and feel I was myself. Now I do, and I am happier than I've ever been before. You terrified me with talk of clothes, and dinners, and responsibilities, that is why I failed to make you love me. We two should have been more careful with that word love. It meant more than either of us realized. Now I know why I loved you, and why I still do, and even if you never see me again, I shall not cease to love you. I do not feel *jealous* towards your new companion, though I don't deny that my greatest wish is to have you myself. He can probably take better care of you than I. Yet you are my woman even if you try to deny it. You are life, and adventure itself, and you're completely wasted on anything else. Perhaps I shall meet you someday, maybe you'll come for a cruise.

There'll be no need for talking it over. (In fact what has talk done so far.) Would you come, or would [you] *discuss* it. Eepersip tired of the forest, and went to the sea, you know. So you must write to me, so that I may find you. Now you really are worthwhile, and to think I grieved over your *changing*.

Listen Bar, this is terrifically important to me. I want you. A year ago I was doubtful. Do you dare or care to take a real chance, on a real adventure. Think Bar, roll the words on your tongue. Marquesas, San Lucia, or what sounds best. Dolphins under the bow, flying fish, and the changing sky and water. Better than a cave perhaps. There'll be books to read too, when the mood takes you. Dungarees, and bare-feet, or shoes and skirts, whatever the mood asks. High latitudes or low, wooded shores or coral reefs, nature smiling warm, or nature riant, fearful. This has been my dream, this is why I have wanted you. This is why my woman was so treasured. I do not say 'please,' or 'do.' If you're the one, you'll know, if not, then solitude has no fears for me. The best years of life together. The end painless. No 'thou shalls.' Away from the pale ledger-minds; only the task of living to face.

You see. Auna, I'm myself now, you've lifted a tremendous load from my mind, now we need not be self-conscious or fearful of painfulness. You think a lot of 'Dartmouth' don't you? Are you sure? Come Bar, tell me, is he everything. Does he deserve all of such a one as you, can I not lay a fair claim to you. Do you think I'm working for its own sake, and saving for its own sake. Open your eyes. Life is not as transparent as you think, nor perhaps as obscure as you may have fancied. Let me rescue you now, from that *cave*. Step back a few steps, and let's start afresh, the way we should have started. Let not the dream be too easy of accomplishment, let it be not only today's but also tomorrow's. I do not say you may tire, but what of him, may he not. With me it might be harder, but more lasting, I know. Dungarees or skirts. You're the woman. You're my woman, but woman-like you're wondering about happiness, and so you deny me, thinking of the 'best happiness.' Put on your cap and coat and come West. Have a talk with me. If D's real, he'll understand, if he won't have it, then be a rebel and come on general principles, and if you don't like our prospects I'll see you safely returned, even to him. Surely you can take a month off.

I'll wire you the fare; the cave won't disappear in the meantime, nor will he. Try it. Try him, try me. Don't you think it would be a good adventure. Just to see, and know.

I want you,

A.

But as she'd told Alice, Barbara had "jumped her love"—Dartmouth was her man. The easiest path regarding Anderson's letter was to not answer it, and I think that was the path she chose.

By now—early or mid November—it was becoming too cold to continue living outside comfortably. They thought about wintering in Florida, but decided on something more exotic: Spain. Barbara's letter to Alice shortly before sailing across the Atlantic explained her plan.

Dearest ADR:

You wanted to hear from me promptly—right away, return air mail and all that. But, you see, in the rather odd kind of life I'm living right now, such things can't be done. When your letter was forwarded to me, I was—well, where was I, anyway? Williamstown Mass., I guess—just in from a week's stretch of Green Mountains. The next day we pulled out, hitch-hiking. I'm in New York now, at the apartment, but only till about tomorrow. Then I light out again.

Now I'm in Brookline, Mass., clearing up a few earthly details before sailing for a little island off the coast of Spain—if you can believe that! No wonder you are puzzled. The reason I didn't try to go into any sort of detail in my first letter [the one written on Moosilauke] was that I wanted—well, to sort of feel around first, if you see what I mean. [...]

I don't enjoy going into terrific detail about myself, by mail. It seems so rather brazen and cold-blooded. And I've been writing fewer letters than ever. But to put it briefly, New York irked me past endurance, and I had an opportunity to quit it all. I thought about it pretty hard for a while, and then decided that in spite of certain complications, "obligations," and whatnot, I would chase them to the four winds and *take* my chance. So I did. I and a comrade escaped to the Maine woods (Katahdin, in fact) and then started off tramping south down the footpath that runs intermittently all the way from Maine to Georgia—the Appalachian Trail. It was a tremendous summer. There were mountains and forests, rivers and fields, sunlight and starlight, fir boughs and birds singing. But it was not only a summer. It will go on.

Those are the brief facts—which, of course, are not a satisfactory offering. You see how hopeless it is to give you a good idea of what it's all about, and why. Besides, it's all based on such subtle intangible things—except the boat to Spain, which is fairly tangible. I've tossed a lot of things to the winds, of course. I mean, I'm gradually getting to be a fairly "shady" character, but it's worth it. When it isn't worth it any more, I'll change it some how. There's always a way out, if you have courage—there was even a way out of New York!

Sometime my devious paths will lead me to you. I know that. Then there can be a real discussion, and real understanding. Right now I'm living in kind of a golden ethereal mist, and I haven't typewritten for a long time, either! So I'm handicapped, more or less. Besides, the things I want to say are too new. They are still seething and surging around in my heart, but they haven't been able yet to take their shape and wings and fly into the sun. It's all pretty experimental, anyway. This I know—life is better than I thought. It can continue being good, if one only knows how. I'm trying to learn. I am learning, a little.

Helen has both backed me up and condemned me. Of course, it's hard on her. A very subtle and complex question of ethics is involved—whether 'twere better etc. I've found this out—you can't arrange your life so that everyone is satisfied, including yourself—unless you are a very uninteresting person. And the break had to come. I'm not claiming I'm right (how foolish it is for anyone ever to claim that he's right about anything!), and God knows I may end up in an awful mess. Still, all I can do is follow the best I know—take the greenest and most verdurous trail that I can see. If it ends in a desert or a swamp, maybe I can go back and try another one. And that makes a cosmic adventure of it all.

We sail within a couple of weeks, probably. This was quite unexpected and out of the blue—we meant to go to Florida for the winter! I think you would like this person who has been constantly with me since the first of July, and intermittently for about a year before that.

Anyway, maybe I'll drop you a few lines from Majorca or Minorca or somewhere!

With much love, and the best of luck to you.

Yours,

Barbara

In limbo and desperate, Anderson wrote again, on November 23. Barbara might have received his letter before sailing, or Helen might have forwarded it to her in Majorca. In a poem accompanying his letter, Anderson prays to Virodine, goddess of Farksolia—the world Barbara had invented when she was nine.

(She described Virodine in 1924 to Mildred Kennedy: the goddess "had charge of all Nature. In fact she *was* Nature.")

Dearest Barbara,

I could not help, a prayer. I love you. I love you. Write, please write to me. The long storm has hurt too much.

Forgive the way I wrote it, it was much earlier; want can exist on hope, for me awhile; if you'll but say a little "That it doesn't make you unhappy because I want you" "That it doesn't spoil a new something" If I would but really know, I would rest, no matter what. But this dreadful thought that we hurt for no reason other than lack of understanding is unbearable. Don't you see, Dear. I love you, therefore you may trust me.

A word of hope, please, or a word of reason why there's none; you didn't go from me, you drifted away. If no one took you, drift back; if someone did. Tell me. You've been so vague. You hurt. There's something of you within me that you left behind. A true word would remove it, and leave me in peace, content that you were happier. If there's a ray of your affection left, don't try to kill it, for I love you.

A.

A Prayer to Virodine

Oh Virodine from you I pray a miracle
Teach her please a want expressed in me
Send back Auna of the darksome moody eyes
She was not flame, but spread, cool and warm, a russet charm
To match her autumn tinted hair
It seems not fair that I should lose her now
For I have learned of much to give
Sympathy, and knowing wisdom besides just love
Dear Virodine if I may humbly bow before Auna's shrine
Will you not bid her stir and murmur,

"I only left and had strange dreams awhile."
She needs so little, yet so much.
We should have a rare exchange
A sort which does not take to keep a captive to oneself
But roams in freedom, seeing, feeling, understanding, understood.
If I'm a spirit, twas her creation, she must not push her
work aside.
The cry is need; To recognize, that here as
well an earthly glamour has been too long denied,
and threats to turn on spirit and devour.
The counter-point of detail all around, dins in my ears.
Drowns out a grander symphony that yet too softly murmurs.
She must return; Don't let her say a "coward" plea
There's nothing now we could not face, no nothing
She must come to me.
If she was sad, so was I.
If she lost something, so did I.
If something died, twas in us both.
Twas only sorry tact kept us apart.
She says she does not want a nest on ground: And nor do I.
All cluttered round with routine.
Perhaps it was your wish that we should learn thus so
That when together we'd evade more lacerating hurt
The petty gods now strewn away, in absurd posture, facing
bolstered up.
From which I turn to gaze at One
I turn to you and ask Auna back.
It is not time for her to go to poppy isle.
Till I am ready too
Oh! place a word of hope, and promise on her reluctant lips.
Some little thing to live upon, or I shall starve.
Bring her to life for me, by sacrificing 'all' the wrong in 'past.'

Did Barbara reply this time? I think not, but letters would be exchanged when Barbara returned to the United States. For now, however, she and Nick had more adventure in mind. Their steamship, the *S. S. Rex*, arrived in Gibraltar in December 1932; from there they visited Morocco for a few days, then sailed to Spain. They visited Malaga looking for walking opportunities and, finding nothing suitable, sailed to Palma in Mallorca where, pretending to be married, they spent the rest of the winter meeting locals and fellow travelers, practicing Spanish, working in a pension for room and board, reading and writing in cafés, and the like. In spring they shouldered their packs and walked for ten days around the coast from Palma to Port de Sóller. Barbara kept shorthand notes during the walk, and typed them up for Helen when they got back to Palma, via train from Sóller. These notes comprise Appendix 3.

Mallorca proved enough of Spain for the travelers. After their long walk they spent another week in Palma, transcribing notes and stories on a borrowed typewriter. The stories included the aforementioned *Rocks* and another New England mountain tale, *Mothballs in the Moon*. Then they sailed to Barcelona where they caught a train bound for Grenoble, the French town nestled below the Alps. While waiting for the train Barbara wrote to Alice, who was no doubt left bemused by Barbara's previous letter from Brookline. Who was this mysterious Dartmouth graduate whom Barbara had spent almost a year with, day and night? And where did his existence leave Anderson? Here's the middle part of Barbara's letter of May 4, 1933:

> You are absolutely right, my dear, in resenting my not having taken you more into confidence. Try to believe that it wasn't so much that I didn't want to tell you all about it, as that I was all up in the air myself, not sure just what was happening and not knowing where to start or what to say in any event. It is bewildering to completely change one's life all in a minute. Do forgive me.

In brief, here is the story: I met this "mysterious figure N. Rogers" summer before last, when H. and I were living in that little cabin in Vermont. Then he showed up again that winter in New York, and we became good friends. He helped me through some trying times. We liked mountains—laid plans for getting away together the following summer. It was with him that I took that trip down the Appalachian Trail through Maine, New Hampshire, and Vermont. It was all so good that I decided to stick to it. In August I wrote [Walter V.] Bingham, giving up my job. This—all this—is a continuation of that adventure.

That is very brief. It doesn't tell you anything about the delicious little island in the middle of a New Hampshire lake that we camped out on for two weeks in a tiny brown tent. It doesn't say anything about the things we have been doing in Mallorca (which we just left last night), such as living in a cave out on the coast and swimming in magic blue-green water. And it doesn't say a word about the mysterious figure himself. Well, that's difficult. A picture may help a little. I just know that I have never "hit it off" so well with anyone or known a more congenial comrade. We've been together day and night for upwards of a year now, and no prospects of splitting up. Sometime we're going out to explore the great North-West; and we'll come to see you, if you'll have us.

It all happened like a shot, you see. I was sorry to do this to E. A., but when crises arise things change. Besides, I think that was drawing to a close; and this was obviously right because it was so damn *natural*. I believe in nature. We have to follow the best thing we know—the thing that is at the time best.

Helen writes that she expects to come over, with Sabra, in June. We shall join up with her somewhere, and I shall help her with another book [*Stars to Steer By*]. As for my book, *Lost Island*, I haven't ditched it at all. I finished it about a year ago, and I suppose it is now wearily going the rounds of publishers' desks

> under Helen's guidance. I still think it's a pretty good book. I haven't written much since—a little short stuff.

The couple spent a week in Grenoble, then crossed the Alps by foot through Switzerland and into Germany's Black Forest, reaching Freiburg in early June—a walk of about 260 miles. There they met up with Helen and Sabra. The party found accommodation on a farm in nearby Hinterzarten where they worked in the fields in exchange for room and board. With Barbara's help, Helen worked on *Stars to Steer By*. (In 1938 Helen would publish her third book, *Third Class Ticket to Heaven,* about her summer in the Black Forest. A reader of that volume would have no idea that Barbara, Nick, and Sabra were with her since none is mentioned. Nor would a reader of *Magic Portholes* or *Stars to Steer By* know how much Barbara helped write them.)

Helen and Sabra returned to the United States in September 1933, while Barbara and Nick continued to explore Germany before sailing back to New York from Hamburg, arriving on November 18. Instead of staying there with her family, however, Barbara moved to Boston to be with Nick. She rented a room in a boarding house in the city while he lived with his parents at 3 Perrin Road in nearby Brookline. I don't know where Barbara's first room was located, but by February 1934 she had moved to a "still cheaper" room ($3.25 per week) at 26 Cumberland Street, near Symphony Hall. She wrote to Helen on February 1:

> I have finished the story of the summer in Maine. It is my pride and joy. I adore it, and think it's by all odds the best thing I've ever done. But you won't like it. And I don't know what to do with it anyway, because it's too long for an article—sixty pages. Would divide nicely in the middle. I could get it out anonymous. I haven't any other title for it than *Travels Without a Donkey,* which suits it perfectly, once you've read it.

> Have rehashed about half of the novel. The other half is harder, though.

It's unclear how much rehashing Barbara did to *Lost Island* in 1934, which is its final incarnation. There's an earlier attempt at the novel in the Columbia archive, which I don't think is complete (it's only ten chapters, whereas in an October 1931 letter to Alice, Barbara mentioned she'd finished nine long chapters, which was "considerably more than half.") The first half of it reads like a rougher, sparer version of 1934's; however, after Jane and Davidson are "rescued" and return to New York, things are much different. That's because when she wrote it, Anderson was Barbara's only love—she hadn't spent an intimate year with Nick. When she moved to Boston late in 1933, she had many more arrows in her quiver to elaborate her ever-evolving philosophy. She wanted to sort out her conflicting emotions regarding love, relationships, how to survive in a world off balance while finding a little joy once in a while, and the like. No wonder the second half was harder to rehash!

To give you an idea of what the early *Lost Island* is like, here's how Chapter 10 ends. Jane is pregnant but hasn't told Davidson yet. After being married by Captain Porter on his ship, the *Sea Bride*, Jane and Davidson arrive in New York to discover that war has engulfed Europe. Young men from America are enlisting to fight. Captain Porter, who's getting on in years and has no heir, thinks highly of Davidson and wants to give him the *Sea Bride*. Davidson refuses—he hasn't earned her; moreover, he can't tolerate the thought that his peers are fighting and dying while he stays at home.

> "You mean, David," interrupted the captain, "you're going over there to save dreams! My boy, don't you know that's not what war's about—"
>
> "For a lot of those boys, it is," said Davidson. "What are

> they dying for? So their dreams can come true for their children —so their children can live to be free to dream! Free to dream— understand?" His eyes flashed as he spoke.
>
> "But listen to reason, David," continued the captain. "Suppose you were—well, a family man, with children—"
>
> "I'd go just the same. Wouldn't I, Janie?"
>
> "You would, darling." Jane threw her arms about his neck. "We wouldn't want you to do anything else!"
>
> "*We!*" Davidson raised her head, looked into her eyes.
>
> She returned his glance steadily. "Your son, David—or perhaps your daughter—and I!"

The chapter ends a couple of paragraphs later.

> Smiling now, Jane sat down again. He raised his head and looked sadly at her. "My son, Janie," he said slowly, "I may never know him. He may never know his father—"
>
> "He will know his father—whatever happens," said Jane, putting her arms around him. "Don't ever forget, David, your child's life began on an enchanted island where there was perfect happiness and love and peace—the very peace the world is crying for—"
>
> "You're wonderful, Janie," Davidson said, holding her to his heart.... "The day I found you in the wreckage of the *Annie Marlow*—and we nearly died together—"
>
> "And we were saved to live out a dream," said Jane. "Then the *Sea Bride* rescued us again just to prove, maybe, that dreams are worth living for—"
>
> "—and dying for, Janie."
>
> "Yes, and dying for, David."
>
> Captain Porter looked at them in their happiness and smiled. "Lost island?" he said quietly, as if talking to himself. "Not lost at all, as I see it—never will be...." He filled his pipe and lighted it, and made himself comfortable. "Tain't a lost world, either,

when young folks treasure it enough to want to die for it," he said tenderly. "It's safe in their hands... they'll see to it that it's a place where a man can dream... is free to dream..."

Letters in the Columbia archive are scarce following Barbara's move to Boston. There are only a few short ones to her mother before the next concrete date in the timeline: Barbara's marriage to Nickerson Rogers, on July 7, 1934, in Brookline. The bride moved into the Rogers' large house on Perrin Road, a quiet cul-de-sac near the Brookline Reservoir. In the months following the marriage there aren't any letters to or from Barbara apart from Frederic Taber Cooper's, whose praise for *Travels without a Donkey* glows from the page.

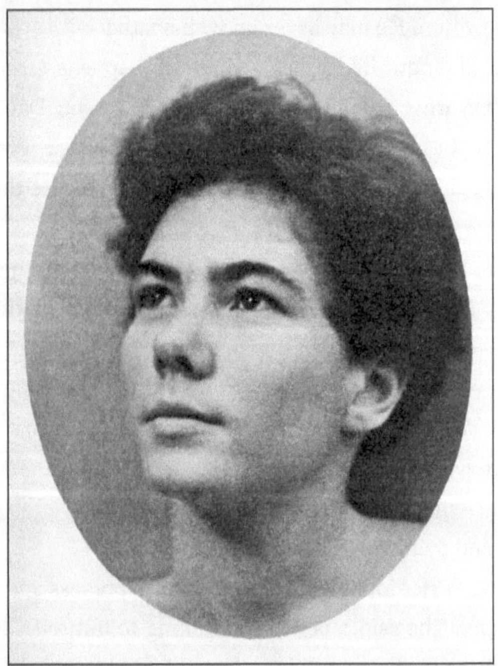

Barbara the newlywed in 1934

Around the time of Barbara's twenty-first birthday on March 4, 1935, she wrote to Anderson and enclosed a photograph. His undated reply follows:

Dear Bar:

I've just had a very strange dream, I dreamed I received a letter from you; Of course it can't be really so, and yet; Oh Bar! I'm afraid I've forgotten how to write letters. There just seems to be nothing quite appropriate to say.

You say nothing of yourself, and I want to ask a thousand questions about you. You don't even tell me your name; I've always thought of you as Barbara Hardy these last two years. A girl by that name wrote to a magazine about a sea-sick remedy some time ago, I read it, and as I recall, there was something hauntingly familiar about the way it was written. It may just have been a fancy of mine, yet it was real enough to prevent my trying to correspond with B. F.

Now that I look back, I can hardly understand how little I have changed. I still work on the *C. S. Holmes*. Times are tough as ever, I'm still a pessimist, and an independent ass. But you, how are you; about the only thing I can consider with surety is that you're about 21. If apologies are in order, let me extend mine. I think I'm the biggest fool in creation. Whatever it was went wrong, I know I was almost entirely to blame; No amount of verbal heroics could ever be worth the misery they put me in. Nothing that could happen, could have been worse than what did happen.

Bar! I cannot write coherently about myself just now, so I won't answer your queries about me, except that I have been getting by pretty much the same as ever. I'm not a captain, and I've no prospects of being one. I'm not married, and I've no money. As for escape, I've learned a lot about that too. There is no escape for those who think they need it:—More of this later if you wish.

(Hours later)

I've been reading your letter over and over, and I've been wondering. I'm really afraid of you, the reason is not far to search for, I'm still in love with you. Perhaps I shouldn't say this, yet why not; you may then understand me if I say that I don't think I'd accept just being friends the way you might expect or want us to be. I'd just be pretending and I don't think I could put up a very convincing pretense. I think you understand enough about me to accept this in the spirit it is meant, however funny it sounds.

However, I'm eternally grateful to you for writing, I wondered an awful lot about you; It's good to know you're alive and think enough of me to write; Although you say nothing of yourself, your picture conveys eloquent testimony of health and spirit. It would perhaps amuse you, could you but know the chaotic disarray of my thoughts when I read your letter; I may have said much too much in this letter Bar. If I have it's because of that one little word with which you concluded your letter. "Yours Bar" is how it reads; No doubt I'm a presumptuous reader.

Please write again Shipmate, even if you think you ought not to at least you once loved me, I think, and you can trust me enough to know I'll understand.

As ever

E. A.

(I suppose B. N. Follett will do as an address.)

As with all of Barbara's letters to Anderson, her reply is lost. But we do have his next letter. Reading between its lines, I find myself wondering if Barbara already regretted getting married. She'd been harshly critical of the concept in the past; readers of *A Life in Letters* might recall her withering letter to Leo Meyette, in which she berated her good friend at length for even considering the notion. Jane Carey herself ran away from the altar. Nor could Wilson's desertion have helped her embrace the idea of wedded bliss. Did Nick convince his girlfriend to marry him so they could live together without fear of scandal, which would've been unavoidable in puritanical Boston? Did she now want Anderson to save her from this new, until recently abhorred domesticity? It wouldn't surprise me at all.

Dear Bar:

I almost feel as if I shouldn't reply to this last letter; that is because it tells me so much, and yet leaves so much untold; Much that you said, I already know; You see Bar, I knew ever so long ago that you wanted more than just one life; The "restlessly sampling" you speak of was too obvious, even for a man in love, to avoid seeing.

Being a selfish person, I didn't care about being just "sampled." I know, also that part of you belongs to me, or at least is with me; and even had we made love, I doubt if that part would seem better to me. The part I have of you is so different from that which one can so easily obtain from so many women, that its very rarity makes it precious. That is probably the reason I say to myself, "I still love Bar." It sounds so funny at times, because we've never made love, and I don't think we ever will, nor do I feel so very sad at the thought now any more.

All of us wish more than one life, and the great art of it is in blending the many lives into one; Some I think, do it better than others, but no one, I think, has it perfect. I would be so happy to have you Shipmate, and yet strangely, it would not grieve me if you refused; That time which I had so eagerly awaited, working, saving & hoping for with such sublime idiocy, never materialized. One such experience is all the tempering our human metal needs, to render it resilient and crack-proof henceforth.

I have worked on the *Holmes* every year so far, not steadily but on and off, at other times I work on my own boat, a little cutter, of 40 ft, just the thing for me to play with on week-ends, on the Sound. When I get some money together, I'm going on a longer trip.

You mention a part-time job in a research laboratory, doesn't sound very prosperous. One thing, Shipmate if you should ever need to, please don't hesitate a moment if I can help you in the way of a little money. I am not extending a favour, rather, I would consider it a privilege to be able to help you if I could.

You have used the expression, "when we meet"; and I wonder if you mean that or are just saying it to make me say things. If you'd like to come West, I'll cable you the money, but it will have to be soon. I think I am able to take care of you. Needn't worry about a job, anyway.

I wouldn't say this if I didn't think that perhaps you might like to come. I don't want to presume on our past friendship, by asking anything like that.

I also think it better to say this now, rather than pen thousands of words describing ourselves to each other. I don't like writing to people I don't know; If you feel you are different or I am different, to the extent that only friendship is possible, why then, let us be gracious enough to say it, and then our two dead selves can rest in peace. If you have someone back there, recall that I also am someone Bar, and that it would be unkind of you, and undeserved of me to again commence a complicated cycle of garbled words and jangled feelings to end in another horridiferous misunderstanding.

It's all so simple, Bar, I want you, Besides I need help on my boat, with suggestions. Will you, or won't you, Yes, or No. Telegraph is quick, and if "yes" I'll cable car-fare. If it's no, a post-card will do, and we'll forget we ever wrote these two letters.

Yours

A.

Barbara wrote back, but just *what* she wrote is a mystery. Again, reading between the lines of Anderson's next reply it seems to me she was ambivalent about her new life; that she was torn between marriage to Nick, whom I'm sure she loved very much, and the unequivocal freedom she'd craved her entire life.

You'll recall her description of Anderson in a letter to Alice: "His life is odd and stern—verging on tragic, at times." But just as Barbara had done before marriage, Anderson lived by his own rules, a rebel to civilization and domesticity. Anderson represented freedom; Barbara feared she was losing hers. Anderson's reply—his last as far as the Columbia archive is concerned—is a little harsh and might have put her off continuing the correspondence. And she might have thought that writing intimate letters to a former love was not appropriate behavior for a wife, even if her relationship with the sailor had been platonic, as confirmed by Anderson's previous letter. (I regret to say that I misplaced this last letter from Anderson in *A Life in Letters*. It belongs here in the spring of 1935, not 1932, when Anderson hadn't yet bought his cutter, *Laila*.)

Dearest:

When I suggested that visit, I should have added that it be entirely on your own terms. It did not occur to me that it was necessary to say so. Evidently I am something of a stranger to you after all. The reason I asked a definite answer was because I knew it would be either extremely hard or else quite easy and simple to answer it. Under the circumstances I think one can be forgiven a little curiosity. How else could I learn if this reacquaintance of ours is prompted by sincerity or just a whimsical moodiness; a sort of nostalgic doldrum that sends the mind foraging amongst the old curios up in the attic. Those outmoded articles that are set aside when new interests, and new friends cause them to appear old and boresome by contrast.

Your reply to my direct request has strengthened a vague uneasy feeling that your letters are perhaps urged by some exigency of the moment. I have a feeling that all is not quite as it should be. What it is, I haven't an idea, but this is the impression your words give me. When you say that "the inconvenience and little pain" that would be caused by your leaving now, is also to be considered. I have uneasy forebodings of another problem. Pain and problems; what absurd things to waste one's life over; I've long ago cast such matters adrift, and am much happier for having done so. Thus you find me. If coming to visit me is to cause pain + inconvenience, and fill you with apprehensive thoughts of a 'stranger,' why then perish the whole idea. Things don't seem the same; when you were in Pasadena and I in Honolulu I did not pause a moment, but came without the least thought for inconvenience. I wouldn't do it now, and so can perhaps sympathize with your unwillingness to do so.

The reason I suggested it be soon, was due to the fact that I have not any definite plans for the summer. I can go North on the *Holmes*, or I can get a job ashore (at least I was offered one). I rather fancy taking a trip in the cutter this summer, but I'm a little bit afraid to play truant too much, gets to be a habit, and besides I'll have all next fall and winter even if I do go North. Anyway it's time for me to decide, and in all probability I'll go North. I can use the money. Were I able to talk to you I know it would all seem very simple, but writing letters hasn't ever gotten us anywhere. Of patience, I've a very small store; in fact it's a virtue entirely lost when practiced with women, as you once convinced me. Patience seems to spell insincerity in a woman's eyes. In fact I think women may even spell it as impotence.

So you see how I feel Bar. I wonder if you'll understand. Friendship and love are not mere words, yet that is about all we've been to each other; just words and ideas, and I'm a bit tired of just that. That is the reason I am not going to commence a long protracted correspondence with you. Nothing has yet been 'clarified' that way. All it ever did was to impose restrictions on me, I was so in love with you, that I forgot there were other women. How very quaint and old-fashioned Bar.

So let's be friends if that's what you think best, and if you want to come out here, then please come, and if you don't want to, don't, but for heaven's sake don't use me for psychic experimentation, and try studying my reactions to one impulse rather than another.

About my "ridiculous prejudice, about women wearing pants." That's the trouble with a lot of women, confound it. They want to wear the pants. But really! my prejudice is purely aesthetic. Most women are a bit knock-kneed, which is quite as it should be I suppose. Most women also have broad hips, and that's perfectly alright too. Now let's pause and reflect, what an incongruous sight, an otherwise perfect woman broad-hipped, a narrow head, etc., garbed in a pair of trousers designed for men; with the cunningest little pair of high-heeled shoes pecking timidly from the bottoms of the self-conscious pants. I cannot repress a groan. When women wear pants the hands are embarrassed, they never find their way into the pockets, as hands should do when idle. Pants on women usually fit too tight for that anyway; I've seen women in trousers carrying a purse; that would seem to solve the matter of the hands, but what good are the pockets in that case. Perhaps a pair of pants without the pockets and buttoned down the sides would seem more appropriate. A Mrs. K. wife of the captain of the Commodore came aboard once, resplendent in starchy, well pressed ill-fitting white ducks. Captain B. was away, so I invited her to wait in the cabin. She glanced at the proffered chair with suspicion. My sympathetic glance must have reassured her. She managed to be seated without any mortifying sound of fabric parting. Even the most genial of hosts could hardly have suggested removing the offending strides for the sake of the visitor's comfort.

Soon, it will be spring. I must then start to work in earnest. I've had a shockingly idle, lazy, pleasant winter. Now I'm sort of rubbing the sleep from my eyes. It seems hardly true that I'm awake and writing to you. This letter is rather long, isn't it? I think Bar that we are making a mistake in writing these letters. I know I can't help feeling a little helpless before you, even in a letter. How you really feel, I am not sure. I think I'll steer my own course, and if you think the future may hold something for you & I together, then please don't hesitate. I'd do anything for you, yet I'm not going to press the point in the face of any reluctance, at least not by letter.

One little word of your last letter offends me dreadfully: "Experimental"!! It has a vivisectional sound and a grubby researchy odor. Makes me think of guinea-pigs and pathologists. Shocking of you to use it. I know what you meant, and I say come or do as you wish; let it be a visit, a reunion, an adventure, or whatever you please, but please don't call it an experiment. I'm very far from perfect and if you seek faults, they're mighty easy to find. If you haven't found the perfect or at least ideal mate these past years, don't be deluded that I may be that nonexistent specimen. I'm not. So here we are, right where we started, and until you make up your mind, I shall bid you a cordial adieu.

E. A.

Anderson did indeed go north on the *Holmes* that summer of 1935. There are no letters to or from Barbara in the archive from 1936, but happily correspondence with Alice resumed in April 1937. By then Barbara and Nick had moved to a small apartment at 125 Charles Street in Boston's Beacon Hill neighborhood, around the corner from her secretarial job at the American Board of Commissioners for Foreign Missions at 14 Beacon

Street. (Anderson had mentioned an earlier job in a research laboratory, of which there were a great many in Boston, but I don't know which was Barbara's.) As for Nick, he and his younger brother Howard were working for Edwin Land at his brand new company, Polaroid. In a few years Howard would become a key figure in the invention of instant photography.

Barbara had also reunited with her father, who married Margaret in 1933. Helen had at last granted him a divorce in exchange for the house in New Haven, which she quickly sold. The Folletts were living with their two-year-old daughter Jane (my mother) on a farm in Bradford, Vermont. Barbara even began corresponding with my grandmother, but regrettably those letters are lost.

L-R: Wilson & Margaret Follett, Jane Follett, Grace Parker Follett (Grace was Wilson's oldest child from his first marriage, to Grace Huntington Parker, who died a week after giving birth), Barbara Follett. The occasion was my mother's second birthday, on February 9, 1937. Photo by Nickerson Rogers

In 1937 it's clear that marriage wasn't as thrilling as Barbara would've liked. She wrote to Alice in April:

> I've had one or two fairly high adventures, and am convinced that they are worth all kinds of sweat and pain and other troubles: in fact, they are the only things really worth suffering for. My greatest worry now, when I have time to stop and think about it, is that I am in a rather difficult position as far as Adventure is concerned, where that evasive spirit may have trouble locating me! Life right now is a very quiet adventure, though pleasant, at that.

In the same letter Barbara mentioned her new interest in interpretive dancing. She had begun taking classes with Mary Starks and her Dance Workshop Group of Boston. Starks, three years older than Barbara, had trained with Martha Graham and Mary Wigman and would soon open a studio in West Roxbury. Meanwhile, Nick's job at Polaroid was keeping him increasingly busy and traveling. When the couple managed to get away together, their destination was often the Squam Lake region of New Hampshire, 120 miles to the north, where they had launched their Appalachian Trail adventure in 1932.

While visiting Squam Lake in October 1937, the couple happened upon a vacant farmhouse on a hill. They found its owner and immediately rented it on "the incredible and absurd basis of $2.50 a month—the altogether delightful basis, I should add!" as a basecamp for their adventures. In particular they wanted a headquarters for skiing, a sport Barbara was keen to learn. The farmhouse wasn't too far of a drive from Bradford, and Wilson "crashed through" with his house-warming gift—an old kitchen range. It's quite likely that Barbara and Nick were outfitting their farmhouse over the Columbus Day weekend in 1937. If that's the case, Barbara wasn't in town when Anderson arrived.

Edward Anderson's life had taken quite a turn. On May 25, 1937, he married Willma Crayne, twenty-one, in Seattle. That same week he sailed, for the final time, on the *C. S. Holmes* to

Barrow, returning in late September. On October 5 the couple took a taxicab to Willma's mother's home in Toppenish, 160 miles southeast of Seattle. On their way to Toppenish, however, Anderson appeared to change his mind. They stopped in Yakima and booked a hotel room. Anderson told the taxi driver to wait outside. Then, instead of Willma continuing her journey to her mother's, Anderson got back in the taxi and instructed the driver to return to Seattle. Willma later reported that her husband had taken his straight razor with him, but not the rest of his shaving kit. She also said that he'd been acting strangely when he returned from Alaska, spending large amounts of money and hinting at suicide. "He seemed to have something on his mind, but would not tell me what it was," she told the Seattle police. "I asked him what was the matter several times, and he just said, 'You wouldn't understand.' If I questioned him further, he became angry."

Eighty miles from Seattle, at Naches Pass near Mount Rainier, Anderson told the taxi driver to let him out. According to the *Morning Olympian* newspaper of October 10, that happened at one o'clock in the morning; according to the driver, Bert Kichinko, Anderson had been drinking heavily. Anderson said he wanted to walk the rest of the way home. The driver argued but had no choice in the matter: the sailor persisted. But he didn't walk back to Seattle. When Willma returned four days later to find no one there, she called the police who, with the taxi driver's help, organized a party with bloodhounds to search Naches Pass. They found no trace of Anderson. On October 10, however, he telegraphed Willma from Chicago, telling her she would never see him again.

At seven in the morning on Hallowe'en, Warren F. Bowman, a truck driver, found a man's waterlogged body washed up on Chapoquoit Beach (then called Chappaquoit Island; the spelling varies) in West Falmouth on Cape Cod, Massachusetts. According to the *Falmouth Enterprise* of November 5, several items were recovered with the body. These included an Ingersoll watch stopped at 8:33 and a note written on the back of a stock certificate from Methow Mines, Inc., a gold mine in Okanogan County, Washington. The note was addressed to Willma.

> I can't resist writing a few words hoping that by some chance they may come to you. Perhaps the greatest fault of evil persons is that they never consider themselves as bad as they are. All my life I've been a fraud and always excused myself on the grounds of expediency. I married you for selfish reasons, thinking that a new inspiration might come. I do love you, whoever you are, and I have that inspiration now that it is too late. Loneliness is misery: dear girl, these will drive a person to do anything to seek release. It drove me to you and I was bad enough to try to deceive you.
>
> For several years the [a word is missing here due to water damage, according to the *Enterprise*] asked me to go to work and I never did because I distrusted their motive and in spite of a strong wish to work there I made various excuses. It was a cheap trick to allay my suspicions by letting us get married. One word of disapproval would have been sufficient. I'd have waited until returning from the north before making a proposal. Perhaps it would not have made any difference, but I like to imagine that you would have gone through with our 'bargain', anywhere.
>
> I'm out in the woods now, this is my second afternoon here. Awful hungry and out of cigarettes. Shoes the worse for wear and my Hugo Seren [Seren was a Seattle tailor from whom Anderson had recently bought a gray suit] a baggy mess. It's peaceful though and as long as it doesn't rain, quite pleasant. Thought I was west of Yakima but suspect that I must be east due to sun's bearings. Haven't met a bear yet. I am suffering the torments of the damned. I see you at times and want to talk with you. Starting to go crazy, I guess.

Poor Anderson! Did he intend to slit his throat in the wilderness, or was the razor for protection against bears? I suspect the former, but if so, again he changed his mind. Instead he made his way to Boston, and the only possible explanation for that, surely, was to see Barbara again. He hadn't seen her in eight years.

Anderson checked into the Hotel Paramount at 17 Boylston Street on Tuesday, October 12: Columbus Day. He stayed one night, then the next day paid for his room for a further week. But according to the *Falmouth Enterprise* of November 5, "he was not seen there again." His next known step was in the early evening of October 16, when he boarded the *S. S. Boston* bound for New York. At 8:30 he was served a drink in his stateroom, and his watch stopped three minutes later when he slipped into the dark water near Buzzards Bay.

When Anderson arrived in Boston, did he know where to look for Barbara? Did he know her latest address was 125 Charles Street in Beacon Hill, a walk of fifteen minutes across the Common from his hotel? I don't think he did, but it's not inconceivable that Barbara had written to him since moving there. (City records are unclear as to exactly when Barbara and Nick moved to Charles Street from Perrin Road, but they do show the newlyweds living with the Rogers family in 1935. And it's possible they lived somewhere else before moving to Beacon Hill.) Did Anderson even know Barbara's married name? He didn't when he wrote to her around her twenty-first birthday, but she might have told him what it was in her reply.

One thing he certainly knew was the Rogers' address in Brookline. Did he show up at 3 Perrin Road, a haggard and perhaps delirious sailor, demanding to know where Barbara was? Would the Rogers have told him—or did they refuse? If he didn't know it before, he will have learned Barbara's married name from that potential encounter, at least. Or did he also learn about 125 Charles Street? Did he knock on that door only to find no one home? Were Barbara and Nick even around? Were they decorating their new farmhouse and enjoying the trees, whose leaves were turning magnificently?

It seems likely to me that Anderson searched for Barbara as best he could given his fraught state of mind. He might have spent those four days and nights searching, increasingly desperate. Or did he hole up in a bar near the harbor and drink the days and nights away, planning his final exit? We'll probably never know.

The discovery of Anderson's body on Chappaquoit Island was big news on Cape Cod. "Certainly the tragedy, with its mystery, drama, and possible explanations is one of the strangest Falmouth has known," declared the *Enterprise* on November 5. The newspaper reported that Anderson was born in Aroostook County, Maine, on December 14, 1903 and described him as "six feet, two inches tall, weight 200 pounds, brown hair, small brown moustache, unusually long arms and large hands, scar left side of neck below ear. Also left leg below knee badly discolored from a wound." In addition, the *S. S. Boston*'s steward said Anderson had blue eyes. The *Enterprise* went into detail in describing the things found with the badly decomposed body, and tried to recount his recent years. There was no mention of Barbara.

> *. . . and doubly dying shall go down*
> *to the vile dust from which he sprung,*
> *unwept, unhonored, unsung.*

> Did Edward Anderson so intend to die? Perhaps. For when the sea gave up its victim Saturday morning on the lonely windswept beach of Chappaquoit island these mournful lines from

Sir Walter Scott's "Lay of the Last Minstrel" were found in his wallet—scrawled on the back of cheap hotel stationery. [...]

Both poetry and note indicate a mind unsettled, unhappy. What troubled Edward Anderson may never be known. He didn't stop at copying the last part of Scott's famous first stanza

Breathes there a man with soul so dead,
who never to himself hath said,
this is my own my native land.

More poetry, headed "Apology" seems to bear out the assumption that Anderson took his own life. As far as can be determined it is a paraphrase of part of Scott's poem which forms the theme of Edward Everett Hale's "Man Without a Country." It may be a combination of two poems, written in Scott's style.

This is the truth, so mark it well,
for tho' the minstrel raptures swell,
'tis I who tell.
Conscience will not be long relieved
with a nimble exigency is defense conceived,
it cannot accept unjust command,
without eventual reprimand,
the spirit bowed, fairly convicted,
reluctantly leaves, justly evicted.

Lillian Anderson of Cary Plantation in Aroostook County wrote to the Falmouth police about the body, thinking it possible that Edward was her long-lost brother who'd left home many years earlier. It's unknown whether Lillian's suspicion proved correct, and birth records show no Edward Andersons born in Aroostook County on December 14, 1903. However, a baby named Edouard was born in Fort Kent (also in Aroostook

County) on that date. His father, a blacksmith, was Docite Madore and his mother Laura (Lizotte) Madore. There seems to be no record of Edouard Madore after the 1910 census, but might he have been adopted by the Anderson family in Cary Plantation? (Did Anderson tell Barbara where he was raised, and did she give her *Lost Island* heroine the name "Carey" in his honor?) Lending credence to the theory that Anderson might have been adopted was the birth of another boy to the Madores, in 1915, whom they named Eddy. Giving the second son practically the same name as the first makes me think Edouard Madore was no longer living with his parents in Fort Kent. Sadly, Eddy died before his first birthday.

The discovery of Anderson's body was big news on the Cape, but was it big enough for Barbara to hear about it? There's no indication that she ever knew Anderson had died. If she had, surely she would have mentioned it to Alice, with whom she corresponded in 1937 through 1939. Barbara was not always a faithful reader of newspapers, and I very much doubt she saw the *Boston Globe's* short story on November 3 about the body, near the bottom of the second page. And from Helen's letters to Alice in the 1950s it's clear neither knew Anderson had died. Here's that *Boston Globe* article:

> *BODY FOUND AT FALMOUTH IDENTIFIED AS SEATTLE MAN*
>
> *FALMOUTH, Nov 2 — The body of a man washed up on Chappaquoit Island last Friday has been definitely identified as that of Edward Anderson of Seattle, Wash. Falmouth police have been notified by Seattle police that Mrs. Anderson would come on to claim the body. Anderson is believed to have drowned after falling or jumping from the Boston-New York boat Oct 16 as it passed through Buzzards Bay.*

Willma Anderson ("who is only 21 and a striking brunette" said the *Enterprise*) and her landlady, Mrs. W. A. Baker, in whose home Anderson had lived for the past five years, arrived for the funeral at Falmouth's Oak Grove Chapel on November 8. Reverend Ralph H. Long conducted the service and Anderson was buried a few yards away from the chapel, in Section N of Oak Grove Cemetery. His is an unmarked, grass-covered grave between Albert E. Nye and John Rogers.

Cracks in the Rogers' marriage widen in Barbara's letters to Alice in 1938. Nick's job at Polaroid was keeping him increasingly busy as "a sort of special salesman" and Barbara took her summer vacation without him, to his consternation. She wrote to Alice in early October:

> I am at the same job, doing much the same things as before, and liking it just well enough to hang on; or, rather, not disliking it quite enough to leave. If I had any bright ideas about what to leave it *for* I might actually leave. Nick, on the other hand, is coming up in the world a little. They have made him a sort of special salesman for Polaroid. That isn't really what it sounds. His job is to go about to various companies who are already interested or have inquired by mail, and give little informal lectures and demonstrations; or suggestions to people who are already using it and want to know more about it. It means he will skip around a good deal over the country—often by airplane, which he loves—will meet lots of people and sort of see the country a bit. I think it's fine, and so far he hasn't been away from home enough to make me object—much! By the way, did you see his comely mug in Life, Sept. 12, in connection with an article on Polaroid? And did you recognize him? (The young man whose rear view shows in the picture above is Nick's brother Howard.)
>
> I had a pretty good summer, the only hitch being that N. and I had no vacation time which coincided at all. I had a

month off, part of which I used in a very exciting and wonderful canoe trip with two friends in the wilds of Canada—when I say "wilds," I mean it, too; there was one stretch of four days when we didn't see or hear another human being, though we were on the move all the time. We fished, swam, sunned, and paddled and paddled and PADDLED from one lake to another, one river to the next, each one being lovelier and wilder than the one before. We camped on idyllic little islands and beaches.

Part of my vacation—almost a week, in fact—I spent with Follett and Margaret at Bradford. I had one heavenly day there, during which I helped F. get caught up on his gardening. We worked together till we dropped, and it was lovely. After that things kind of petered out. They were having a financial crisis at the time (just for a change!) and that was weighing them down. There was a bad spell when they thought they were going to be thrown out of the house for non-payment of rent; but that passed, and there seem to be articles coming in the Atlantic now. [Over the course of his career, Wilson wrote over one hundred articles for the Atlantic Monthly.] Margaret goes through occasional very bitter spells, and then recovers. The children seem to thrive. I hear that their house survived the storm all right, although the yard and garden are a tangled mess of fallen trees so that they don't know how to begin to clean it up. When M. wrote a few days ago, they had no light or water. [One of the most destructive hurricanes in recorded history struck Long Island and New England on September 21, 1938. Fortunately the farmhouse near Squam Lake suffered only minor damage: the roof lost a few shingles and one windowpane was broken.]

In 1939, Barbara's participation in the Dance Workshop Group gathered steam with concerts performed in Boston and beyond. It's likely she was one of the dancers performing with the Group in Burlington, Vermont, on March 25. Two days later the *Burlington Free Press* covered the recital:

> Miss Mary Starks and her group of six girls from Boston presented their demonstration of modern dancing before an appreciative audience at the University of Vermont's Southwick Memorial building Saturday evening.
>
> Miss Starks opened the program with four of the elementary dance studies in which she demonstrated the correct "walking" movements used in the modern dance. The five solo dances which she presented included several light compositions and her two most popular dances, "Working Gals' Blues" and "Alien City" which were more dramatic and portrayed a deeper sentiment. The costumes were very unusual.
>
> Miss Marjorie Houser, pianist, collaborates with Miss Starks in composing and arranging the various dances. The girls taking part in the demonstration are all professional women, and they dance together voluntarily after their working hours, purely for the love of dancing. By presenting these recitals, they earn extra money.

In late June, Alice received an unexpected letter from Linwood, Utah. Barbara was driving across country with Marjorie Houser and Marjorie's younger brother, Lee. Barbara was to attend the summer session of the Bennington School of the Dance, held that year at Mills College in Oakland, California, from July 1 through August 11. Meanwhile the Housers were planning to go camping in Lake Tahoe and Yosemite. Barbara told Alice to expect to see them all soon after the dance session ended.

> Marjorie is a wonderful girl, whom I adore, and who plays the piano for all Mary's dance classes, and writes the music for the dances. She is a marvelously talented kid, and a delightful

> personality as well. You will love her, and she you. I won't try to describe her any more, as I am hoping you will see her yourself. Enough to say that she is a real genius, with music in every bone and every nerve.

Alice wrote to Barbara at Mills saying she looked forward to their visit, and Barbara replied on July 9 describing her first week in Oakland.

> I am loving Mills College. The campus is perfectly beautiful, more like a rich man's estate than like any institution I ever saw. And we, being summer students—and pretty special at that!—are subject to no rules or regulations that even I could object to. The work is thrilling, as we have courses with several of the "big shots" of the modern dance. My "major" is with Hanya Holm, whom I have long admired.

Other big shots included Martha Graham (who hired one of Barbara's classmates, Merce Cunningham, for her company), Doris Humphrey, and Charles Weidman. An evening at Lisser Hall saw John Cage and his percussion ensemble perform while students danced. Near the end of the session a fifteen-person film crew directed by Ralph Jester shot footage for a short film, *Young America Dances*. The film was supposed to be distributed by Paramount Pictures but Bennington College refused to allow its name to be used, and the film was shelved. By the time the crew arrived, however, Barbara had injured her leg and was unable to dance. Instead she left Oakland a few days early; she and the Housers arrived at Alice's house about August 9. Barbara was planning to stay for several days, but a letter from Nick turned her world upside down. He wanted a divorce. He mentioned no third party in the letter, but Barbara suspected another woman was involved.

Shocked and bewildered, Barbara quickly made her way back

to Boston by bus, arriving at the Rogers' latest apartment at 574 Huntington Avenue on August 15. She found the place empty and some of Nick's belongings missing. She started telephoning anyone who might know where he was, and tracked down a Polaroid employee who told her he was in New York, giving her the name of a hotel. The hotel had no one there under Nick's name. The coworker thought Nick would be back in Boston the next day, but he didn't come home then, either. She wrote to Alice on August 17:

> I got home on schedule Tuesday night, after a trip which was of course pretty strenuous, and even horrible at times, but not as bad as I had expected, really. I managed to get some sleep, though not much; and I kept pretty well relaxed and calm and controlled, and busied myself with imaginary conversations which wouldn't have worked out, etc., etc. The last day was the tensest of all; I think that one day was longer than all the other four days and nights. It was so terrifically tense that I thought I would simply fly apart. But I'm pretty well put together, and I remained in one palpitating piece! When I got home I was shaking like a leaf, of course.

That Tuesday night Barbara also called a doctor friend, Charlie Dunlap, who lived nearby on Longwood Avenue.

> He came right over to me, bringing (a) three large, juicy and delectable hamburgers; (b) a bottle of whiskey; and (c) some sleeping dope. Well, the combination of those things, plus a good talk with him, just fixed me up. I slept well, and woke up yesterday quite relaxed and almost confident and hopeful. I spent the day very slowly and quietly doing domestic things, and time passed fairly quickly. I read and listened to the radio, and got to sleep last night under my own power without benefit of dope.

Nick returned on Friday morning. The following section of Barbara's August 22 letter to Alice shows just how uncomfortable the marriage had become. It also confirms her suspicion that there was another woman.

> The first thing we did was go away for the week-end in Vermont, where Nick had had a previous invitation. Well, Alice, all I can say is that what we conjectured was truer than true—I mean, that about the hell only beginning when I got home—not ending. I am glad I had thought it over so hard. I am glad I realized the importance of self-control. You see, the thing is really worse than I had thought possible. There IS somebody else. Just how serious I don't know, and I'm not asking any questions. That's part of the self-control. I haven't uttered one single reproach, or anything that could be construed as one. I've just dug my nails into my palms and held on, and held on, till now I think I'm getting to be quite a woman of iron and steel.
>
> Well, I think there is hope for my side—some hope. I know it will be a long, patient process that will take all my strength and all my intelligence for a great many months. I think it is worth it, and I am going to make the fight. I don't blame him in the least. He really thought I didn't care; only, instead of saying anything about it so that I could have done something about it before, he just kept quiet and everything slid and slid. But it's really my fault; I had it coming to me, I know.
>
> I think I've persuaded him to give me my chance. He is a very kind person, really, and hates to hurt people. He hated to write that letter; that's why it sounded so awful. I think that, if I can really prove that I'm different, why maybe things will work out. He still doesn't quite believe, as he says, that a leopard can change its spots! He thinks that in a month things will be all wrong again. So I say, at least let me have that month! I think I'll get it, and I think I can win if I've got the strength. I think he is a steady enough person, and a kind enough person, and also

> enough of an easy-going person, so that he won't go making drastic plunges if he doesn't have to; and if I can make a pleasant sort of life for him, I think he'll hang on. That's what I'm banking on, and I'm putting heart and soul into all the little things.

Barbara's self-reproach for her part in the marriage's unhappy slide is palpable, and sadly, quite familiar to me. My mother displayed the same sort of self-recrimination for her "failures"—not being a dutiful enough daughter; not cleaning the house well enough; not supporting her first and second husbands during their temper tantrums; not being able to quit smoking; not being able to enjoy life enough... the list of her self-identified faults was long and persistent. And my mother displayed the same kind of martyr complex as Barbara, who refused to confront Nick about the letter he mailed to Pasadena or about his affair. Just as my mother would have, Barbara blamed herself, not her husband. My mother inherited this self-persecution from my acid-tongued grandmother, whose ability to find fault in others and particularly in herself was astonishing.

Faced with a skeptical husband who was having an affair, Barbara tried to save her marriage. Was I too quick to think she was ambivalent about it when she wrote those letters to Anderson in 1935? Or had she since come to appreciate what comfortable domesticity offered after all? Had Eepersip finally been caught and trapped in a house with windows? Something fundamental in Barbara had changed since her wedding day. Now she depended on Nick; whereas before meeting him she'd depended on Anderson to a degree, but ultimately only on herself.

It's clear to me from my many readings of her letters and *Lost Island* that Barbara had periods of despair and might even have suffered from what psychologists today call clinical depression (a common trait in the Folletts; more on this soon). A depressed wife would *not* want lose whatever support a loving husband might provide. Her best course toward survival would be to try to win back her husband's love.

At first, Barbara's attempt to save her marriage looked promising. She conveyed her "progress report" to Alice on August 28:

> I will hastily make a progress report on my situation—or, rather, my Situation. Right now I'm on an up-beat, so to speak, so I shall quickly write and mail this letter before the next down! We are just back this morning from a week-end that really was very pleasant, considering. We sailed, swam, had a party with some friends, and explored quite a lot of Cape Cod, alone together, *looking for some nice country in which some time to have a summer place*. Of course, whether I am included in that pleasant picture, or somebody else, is an unknown quantity; but I was at least there for the exploration!
>
> We talked a good deal about things, and at one point the conversation got to a point where it was logical for me to ask right out whether he wanted to make a go of things. I had had the feeling up till then that he definitely did not want to. So imagine my amazement, my almost hysterical delight, when he said yes, he wanted to make a go of it. Right away he qualified it, of course. He said: "Don't get too excited about that; I'm not sure that I *can*." I said if he *wanted* to that was more than half the battle; with both of us wanting it so much, and pulling as hard as possible, I don't see how there can be any failure, really. Well, Alice, what he said gave me enough heart to keep up the struggle. I had hit a very low point just before that—a point at which it just seemed impossible to keep it up any longer. Now I feel that I can; and I feel that if I handle it right for the next difficult few weeks, or maybe months, I can still win this game.
>
> Things are far from fixed, you understand, but they are

> improving a little. This morning, when he left to go to work, he gave me a sort of rough pat, which is absolutely the first gesture of affection of any kind that has come my way! I still don't know how much of a situation I have to cope with in regard to this other person. I still have no idea who it is, how much he has seen of her, how far the affair has really gone, whether he is still seeing her at all, or how it stands. I know absolutely nothing, and I still refuse to ask any questions. Marjorie (she is now home, after a terrific trip, and has talked with Nick once about the thing) has an idea that the other person may be trumped up —that he might have simply set his heart on our separating, and thought that telling me that might send me hurtling off in disgust or rage. He apparently talked to her a little about this situation, and she claims he didn't sound a bit convincing when it came to this mysterious person. It would be lovely to believe something like that; it is a great temptation. But I have resolutely made up my mind that I have something pretty desperate to face in that respect; I am sort of disciplining myself to believe just about the worst possible, so that if ever I find out it *wasn't* that bad, the discovery will just be a relief. Well, I just don't know, and I have no way of knowing. Nick is the kind of person who may very well never tell me just what it was all about; and if he will only come back to me I don't much care anyway. That again is absolutely proof—to me at least—that I am a radically changed person. I used to be full to overflowing with silly little petty jealousies. Now that the real thing has come up, while of course I feel terribly hurt, nevertheless any feeling of jealousy I might have seems to be completely lost in the bigger thing—which is simply that I want him back!

The letter continues, and there's no wonder that Barbara was confused about what Nick wanted from her. Did he want her happy and independent, or at home and wifely?

> We have talked quite a lot about *my* future. This can be interpreted either favorably or unfavorably. Nick is very anxious for me to drop the Board job and get myself something in its place that I really like and that is interesting. In other words, he wants me to do the job with Mary, and another part-time one as well, if I can find one I like. Whether that is just his way of easing me gradually on to my own feet, I don't really know. It might be, but it sounds more like genuine concern for my own interests and happiness. He wants to see me live about as fully as possible. I say: "But how about meals, house-keeping, etc." Well, he says he'd rather see me doing an interesting job, in which we could afford to have somebody in to do house-work. It apparently doesn't mean as much to him as I thought it did, to have me personally doing it. I had thought that it was in that, among other things, that I had gone wrong, but apparently not. This leaves me with mixed feelings. I would be perfectly happy to do as he suggests on that; on the other hand, that makes it a little less clear to me where I went wrong before; I'm a little less sure of my ground. I feel that maybe the holes into which I fell are still uncharted after all!
>
> All this remains to be seen. I'm spreading out the whole confused picture before you as it unrolls. It doubtless will go through many fluctuations and perhaps complete changes. This is just how it stands as of today!

In late August, Nick gave Barbara the task of finding a new apartment—a task she had completed by October, when they moved from 574 Huntington Avenue in Boston to 48 Kent Street in Brookline Village, about two miles away. We have no way of knowing how she was faring in September and October since all writing from that period has been lost, including a letter to Alice dated September 11, which Barbara mentioned in her November 4 letter. We do have a small piece of evidence that *might* stem from this time, however—Nick's unsuccessful petition for a divorce in December 1941. His case was covered in the *Boston Daily Globe* on December 13:

> Dominating a party, making a husband uneasy and uncomfortable, and failing to cooperate in the home does not constitute cruelty on a wife's part, Judge John C. Leggat ruled in Middlesex Probate Court yesterday as he dismissed a divorce action brought by Nickerson Rogers of Cambridge against Barbara N. Rogers.
>
> Rogers testified that at a party at which his wife tried to be the dominating influence, she vetoed his suggestions for entertainment of their guests and made him uneasy and uncomfortable. She failed to cooperate in the home and went on Summer vacation without him, he said.
>
> Judge Leggat intervened during the husband's testimony, commenting that no evidence of cruelty had been introduced.
>
> "Did she ever strike you? Are you afraid of her?" queried the court.
>
> Rogers answered in the negative.
>
> Counsel inquired whether Mrs. Rogers had taken care of the home.
>
> Rogers answered again in the negative, and commented that he had put up curtains in the home.
>
> "That is no cause for divorce," said Judge Leggat as he dismissed the action.

It surprises me that Nick didn't mention his wife had been missing for two years in his grounds for divorce—or perhaps he did but that part didn't make it into the *Globe* (which seems unlikely), or perhaps his lawyer advised against it.

The next letter in the archive is dated November 4, 1939. "E" stands for Elizabeth—she and Phoebe were Alice's daughters. It's the last letter Barbara wrote to Alice, and might be the last letter she wrote to anyone.

Dear ADR:

I'm sorry you should have been caused to worry by me, when heaven knows you've had enough to worry about right at home! I'm glad E is coming along all right—but what a shocking experience—just as shocking as Phoebe's automobile crash. I *do* agree with you that the Russell family seem prone to accidents. I guess it's because they live so fully and have no fear and no caution! And I think they are right. And they take the consequences gallantly.

As for me. Have I really not written to you since September 11? That is shocking. Well, the above is the new address. It's a very big, old-fashioned apartment, with two fireplaces and a full-sized kitchen. Nick's brother is rooming with us now, until he gets married, in January some time. Yes, I'm working, sometimes half-time, sometimes full-time; and I'm dancing too; the dancing will go on until Christmas. After that I don't know what I'm going to do in a dancing line. I must get some additional training somewhere, and so far I don't know where.

But that isn't what you really want to know, of course. In my last letter I told you things were going well, and I thought they were. They continued to go well for a time—at least I thought so, and I was happy, and decided that the worst part of the ordeal was over. But that was too easy. No such luck! I don't know what to say now. On the surface things are terribly, terribly calm, and wrong—just as wrong as they can be. I am trying—we are both trying. I still think there is a chance that the outcome will be a happy one; but I would have to think that anyway, in order to live; so you can draw any conclusions you like from that!

Marjorie said the other day that she was thinking of you and had owed you a letter for a long time and would be writing one of these days. I don't see much of her these days. She is very busy, and having a lot more dates, etc., than last winter. She dashes in town to play for the dance group, and then dashes away again, usually before I am even dressed! She is having a fine fling for herself, and I'm very glad. I'd like one too, but don't quite know how to go at it, under the circumstances!

Best love to you. The reason I haven't written so long is that I hate to write when things are just up in the air—loose, kind of. I keep thinking Something will happen—must! But anyway, I'll try to do better from now on.

As ever,

Bar

On the evening of December 7, 1939, after an argument with Nick, Barbara left the apartment on Kent Street with about thirty dollars and a notebook, and no one knows for sure where she went.

The last known photograph of Barbara, ca. 1939

Nick waited for his wife to return. After two weeks he reported her missing to the Brookline Police Department. It doesn't surprise me that he waited that long; Barbara was a strong, independent woman—or at least had been until recent months. Here's the entry in the desk sergeant's logbook with an addendum added in 1940.

Thursday Dec. 21, 1939

Nickerson Rogers 48 Kent St. came to the station at 10 P.M. and reported his wife Barbara N. Follett Rogers same address missing from home since December 7th. She is 25, 5'7", 125.

[addendum] Reported on March 12 1940 he moved to 4 Hurlbut St Cambridge

The only clue we have about the argument on December 7 (and a vague clue it is) comes from Ruth Seabury, one of Barbara's supervisors at the American Board of Commissioners for Foreign Missions, who wrote to the Brookline police soon after Nick's visit.

> He and Barbara are to the best of my knowledge and belief very happily married, but for some time had had a very sharp difference of opinion on a matter which both regarded as of fundamental importance. Barbara had seemed very unhappy about it especially in her last day at home. She evidently decided to go her own way but her husband, hopeful of her return, has hesitated to do anything to distress her, especially if publicity were involved, for fear she might not return at all. He did, however, on December 22, report her absence to the Brookline police and at their request, I believe went to the Morgue on Charles Street in Boston. No clues were raised there, however.

I don't know what the police did to find Barbara. Apart from the logbook and a few letters from 1952 between Helen and the authorities, it appears that all records concerning the search have been lost or destroyed. Initially, Nick declined the police's offer to publicize the case, which isn't surprising given Barbara's history with the press, particularly when she ran away in 1929. Apart from visiting the morgue, I don't know what Nick could've done to find her, although I'd like to know if he checked the farmhouse near Squam Lake, assuming it was a place they were still renting. If Barbara wanted to disappear, it's hard to imagine another woman who'd do a better job of it.

In fact Nick *did* do something more—at least according to one of his daughters who spoke to Laura Smith on the telephone (Laura wrote *The Art of Vanishing*, published in 2018 by Viking—I recommend it highly). At some point, perhaps after receiving a threatening letter from his former mother-in-law in

1953—*All this silence on your part almost looks as if you had something to hide concerning Barbara's disappearance. I hope not since I have always trusted you to the point of believing you were doing all you could to solve the mystery*—he hired a private investigator to conduct a search, but nothing came of it.

There's very little in the archives at Columbia from the time immediately following Barbara's vanishing—no notices from the police, no letters to or from Nick nor from Barbara's family or friends. The next thing we know for sure is Nick's return to the Brookline Police Department on April 18, 1940. This time he requested publicity, and four days later a bulletin was sent by Officer McCracken to eight states.

> Brookline. 139 4-22-40 3:38PM McCracken Missing from Brookline since Dec. 7, 1939, Barbara Rogers, married, Age 26, 5-7, 125, fair complexion, black eyebrows, brown eyes, dark auburn hair worn in a long bob, left shoulder slightly higher than right. Occasionally wears horn rimmed glasses.

Nothing came from this bulletin. Using "Barbara Rogers" can't have helped; no one will have known that the missing person was the girl who'd made a splash with *The House Without Windows* thirteen years earlier. (I don't think the name "Barbara Newhall Follett" would appear again in the press until 1966, when Helen and Harold G. McCurdy published *Barbara: The Unconscious Autobiography of a Child Genius*.

When I wrote the final chapter of *A Life in Letters* in 2015, I didn't know about Anderson's death. I thought it quite possible that Barbara had gone to him. He had helped her a great deal in 1929 and by writing to her in New York. He had saved her life and then married her in *Lost Island*. Before Nickerson he was her bulwark, her oasis. Nor did I know about the remains of a body found in the woods near Squam Lake in 1948.

Daniel Mills, a Vermont-based writer of gothic fiction and podcaster of *These Dark Mountains*, was intrigued by Barbara's disappearance (see his essay *A Place of Vanishing: Barbara Newhall Follett and the Woman in the Woods, Los Angeles Review of Books*, April 5, 2019). He thought it possible that Barbara had committed suicide and might have gone to her sanctuary, Squam Lake, to do so. Even if the Rogers were no longer renting their farmhouse (and I think it likely that they were, given its tiny rent), Squam Lake and its surroundings were hugely important to Barbara. What better place to end one's life—to commingle with the pine trees and hermit thrushes and forest critters she loved so much? Daniel consulted local newspapers for reports of mysterious deaths in the area circa December 1939 and later. It didn't take long to find such a report.

In 1936, Elsie Lufkin Whittemore, twenty-five and pregnant, disappeared from her home in Plymouth, New Hampshire. Plymouth is a small town on the Pemigewasset River about seven miles west of Squam Lake. Local police and volunteers conducted an extensive search but couldn't find any trace of Elsie. The case grew cold until, on November 25, 1948, a deer hunter named Harold Huckins came across human remains entangled in tree roots beside Durgin Brook in the woods of Pulsifer Hill near Mount Prospect, about five miles east of Elsie's house. The remains were between a quarter- and a half-mile from Mt. Prospect Road, near the Holderness-Campton town line. Most of the skeleton, including the skull, had been scavenged by animals and washed away by the brook during snowmelt, but there were sufficient bones left to determine that they belonged to a woman of about twenty-five and that they had been there for several years—at least since 1939, said Dr. Alan Moritz, the pathologist who'd arrived from Harvard Medical School to supervise the examination. Dr. Moritz took the remains back to Boston and conducted a thorough review. He typed up a report with many photographs and, despite a few discrepancies, the New Hampshire authorities concluded that the remains belonged to Elsie.

What were the discrepancies? Horn-rimmed glasses were found with the remains, whereas Elsie didn't wear glasses; a retrieved shoe was size 7 while Elsie wore a 5 or 5½; none the belongings, including the purse, could be identified by Elsie's family. At no time did the Whittemores accept the finding that the bones were their daughter's; nor would the family receive the remains for burial; nor was a death certificate released.

One detail that would appear to discount the possibility that the bones were Barbara's was Dr. Moritz's conclusion that the deceased's height was 62 or 63 inches, while Barbara was 67 inches. He arrived at that height by measuring the length of a tibia and using a regression formula called Krogman's Table. However, Krogman's Table has since been improved upon, and modern regression formulae indicate the Pulsifer Hill body was 66 or 67 inches. On the other hand, the lone tooth recovered showed malocclusion, which Elsie was known to have had. There's no evidence that Barbara had such malocclusion, but there's nothing to rule it out either, and it's a common condition.

Daniel consulted maps and town records for the time period, trying to find the farmhouse Barbara and Nick might have rented and whom it belonged to. He found a likely candidate in the White House on Pulsifer Hill, less than a mile from where the remains were found in the woods. In the 1930s the White House belonged to the Pulsifers themselves; they were a farming family who owned much of the land in the area. The 1930 census shows the Pulsifers renting the White House to a Milford Morgan for $5 a month; and the 1940 census indicates that by then Mr. Morgan had bought property nearby and moved out. Therefore the White House would likely have been left, in

Barbara's words, "in quite reputable condition" when she and Nick drove by it in October 1937, and not abandoned and dilapidated like other farm buildings in the area. Furthermore, Barbara and Nick were asked not to disclose the small rent they were paying, possibly because it was only half of Morgan's rent and the Pulsifers didn't want him to hear about it.

The White House, which is still standing and is now a lovely property indeed, was about five miles uphill from the Plymouth railway station—an easy distance for a strong walker like Barbara. The Boston & Maine railroad provided a direct link with Boston's North Station, itself easily reached by tram from Brookline Village. So I think it possible that on December 7, 1939, Barbara took the train to Plymouth, arriving late at night. She either walked the five miles to the White House (if that is in fact our farmhouse) and spent the night there, thinking things over, or she walked the five miles to her final resting place beside Durgin Brook, where she hugged a favorite pine tree for the last time, swallowed barbiturates from her medicine bottle with water from her flask (both such items were recovered from the scene and Dr. Moritz concluded that suicide was the cause of death), and listened to the singing of the brook while the cold night carried her away.

You may be wondering why I don't compare my DNA with DNA extracted from the remains. That's because—like Eepersip, Elsie, and Barbara—they have vanished. Daniel Mills, Laura Smith, and I contacted every agency in New Hampshire that might have records of what happened to them, as well as Harvard Medical School, without success. Any trace of the remains' final resting place has disappeared.

Durgin Brook at the foot of Mount Prospect, New Hampshire, October 2019. Photo by Stefan Cooke

In the last chapter of *A Life in Letters,* I tried to convince myself that Barbara had once again escaped an intolerable situation and had started a new life. To reunite with Anderson (whom I thought still living in 1939) or to strike out on her own with a new name would be a grand adventure—perhaps the grandest of them all. Eepersip had escaped her family and the visible world itself in *The House Without Windows.* Barbara had escaped in 1928 when she persuaded her mother to leave her home and five-year-old daughter and go to sea. She escaped in 1929 by running away to San Francisco, and again in 1932 when she quit her job and her love and took to the mountains and woods of New England and Europe with Nick.

In 1939 Barbara tried to save her marriage but couldn't. Her husband was almost certainly continuing his affair with Anne Bradley, whom he would marry in 1944 (they stayed together until Nickerson's death in 2000). A journalist interviewed Anne shortly before she died in 2008 and relayed to Laura Smith the fact that Anne and Barbara had met each other in the 1930s, and that Anne had found Barbara "charming," so we know she was in the picture when Barbara was living in Brookline Village.

Surely, I thought, the likeliest explanation for Barbara's disappearance was leaving an unfaithful husband and starting over. Surely a young woman as vibrant as Barbara wouldn't commit suicide. A common theory among Barbara's followers online is that Nick murdered her, but there's nothing in her writing or anything I've read about him that lends any credence to that idea. It's true that Helen semi-accused him in that letter I mentioned earlier. However, I think it very unlikely that Nick killed Barbara or covered up her accidental overdose, which was jkel's theory in his *Astral Aviary* blog. (*Astral Aviary* makes for fascinating reading, but there are a great many factual errors and flights of fancy.) Rather, I think that Helen, who was having heart trouble in 1953, desperately wanted the mystery solved before she died (happily, she pulled through and lived until 1970).

Speaking of Helen, I wonder why she didn't do more to find her daughter. She left the search entirely in Nick's hands. When she wrote to the Brookline police in 1952, she didn't seem to know for sure that Nick had reported Barbara's disappearance to them at all! For that matter, what—if anything—did my grandfather do, aside from lecturing her on how to be a good partner in marriage (the irony!) in *To a Daughter, One Year Lost*, his anonymous letter in the *Atlantic Monthly?*

If Barbara had once again escaped an intolerable situation in

December 1939, however, the question of why she left no clue for her family and friends that she was alive *always* lurked in my mind. How could she be so devastatingly cruel? Did she want to punish Nick so badly that she kept him and everyone who knew her in the dark about where she went and how she was faring? That question never left me, and when I read the results of Daniel's research, my heart fell into my stomach. Writing this eighty years after her disappearance, I think it very likely that the remains found near Mount Prospect were Barbara's, and that she chose to die there on her own terms. But I'll probably never know for sure.

As I mentioned in *A Life in Letters*, many of the Folletts I've known have suffered from depression. Without question both my grandfather and my mother had it. I have it, too. In my thirties and particularly my forties, anxiety and insomnia were destroying my life. I felt panicky; and there were awful times when the act of stringing words together and speaking seemed insurmountable. One 2011 morning was so bleak that I asked my wife Resa to take me to the hospital. I hadn't slept in days and wished everything would end. We sat in a dreary psychiatric ward for hours, surrounded by misery. Eventually a doctor prescribed a few pills to help me sleep, and we went home. I reconnected with my therapist and this time followed her advice about medication. Taking an antidepressant is something I hate to have to do, but it, combined with exercise and meditation, has alleviated my suffering quite a lot, and my sleep has improved. Today life is manageable, although the familiar despair resurfaces from its depths five or six times a year and makes for a few grim days.

Of course Barbara didn't have the option I've chosen to alleviate my suffering, and as far as I know only had access to Charlie Dunlap's dangerous and addictive "sleeping stuff"—possibly barbiturate powder prescribed under the name Veronal. If the black cloud of depression engulfed her in 1939 and refused to lift, suicide will have been a great temptation. And if she had become addicted to the sleeping stuff, that will have been a contributing factor. She wrote the following to Alice on August 22, 1939; it's the last reference we have to her sedative use and I don't know if she kept taking it.

> I don't know whether I told you he [Dunlap] gave me some sleeping stuff. Ever since Nick got back I've had to take it every night. The days I can stand, because they are sort of full of little things; but the nights I could never stand without some kind of help in achieving oblivion!

Before I started taking my antidepressant, the only thing that stopped me from seriously contemplating suicide was Resa. We have no children, our parents are dead, and I'm an only child. I simply wouldn't let myself consider the notion of leaving my wife to pick up the pieces. If I didn't have Resa, who knows what I might've done? So I can easily imagine suicide being a tempting step for a depressed person whose marriage had failed, whose parents were no bulwark, whose sense of humor was AWOL, who was as aggrieved at the world as Barbara was. Having immersed myself in Barbara's world for the past eight years (not coincidentally the same length of time I've been taking the antidepressant—without it I couldn't have immersed myself in *any* world except the miserable one inside), it's Barbara's grieving that I identify with most strongly, along with our love of nature. You'll recall Barbara's words to Alice in 1931:

> Anyway, A.D.R., don't you lose your sense of humor, whatever happens. If you have that, you can keep your head above water —*just*. Sometimes it's by a hair's-breadth, but still it's above water. Without it one may as well lay down and die. [...]
>
> I certainly don't think there is much to be said for this so-called civilization. It's barbarous, that's what it is. The

> primitivest of the primitive were never capable of such outrages as this Jinx civilization. That's one of the things "Lost Island" is about—sort of a fling, a kick, a dig at the world. Not a nasty one, just a grieved one. I wish we were back to the cave days. [...]
>
> But lest you think I'm becoming very despondent myself of late, let me assure you that this is my normal state of mind, when I allow it to come to the surface. That is, I *always* am grieved at the world. But I usually don't allow it to come to the surface. I sink it. And I do love listening to those hermit-thrushes. They are divine. And there are a few beings whom I love a great deal, and who make most of what there is of Good in life. But I don't believe in God. God got discouraged and gave up long ago, and I don't blame him, I'm sure!

What would Barbara make of today? I think about that a lot. The 1930s were no picnic, and the worst war in history was knocking at the door, but at least its occupants were spared climate catastrophe hanging over their heads like Damocles' sword. 1939's citizens didn't live with the threat of nuclear annihilation; nor did 63 million of them vote a corrupt and vengeful nationalist into the Oval Office. Since Barbara disappeared our overconsuming society has destroyed the environment to whet its appetite for greed, control, and convenience. The oceans are dying, ice caps melting, wildfires raging. Plastic in the fish and the rain, old growth forests a distant memory, species going extinct at an increasing rate. Barbara would be appalled, but probably not surprised. I *wish* I could talk to her about it all, preferably with our senses of humor intact!

Another thing I mentioned in *A Life in Letters* was my mother's belief that her sister went to the mountains to die. Barbara was a subject too painful for her to talk about. In 2008 I gave her a printout of *Astral Aviary*, but it was too distressing for her to read. She died two years later. I wish I could talk to my mother about Barbara now, about the treasure chest of letters and stories she left behind, about our love of nature, about our grieving for the world. About the remains found beside a tranquil brook near Mount Prospect, thirty-five miles east Hanover, where both she and Barbara were born. About how the bones were discovered with pine tree roots entwined within them, buried deep in needles turned to humus, all flesh and tissue long since consumed by creatures great and small. About how a young woman's body became part of the New England landscape that Barbara loved so much. How the young woman ended her life on her own terms, answering to no one. And, as Richard Powers writes in *The Overstory*—a book I think my mother and Barbara would've liked—about how the dead keep the living alive.

> The Maine forest had taken her now, and it was pounding her against its earth, stripping away her half-shattered ragged rainbow. She was alone. And there was nothing to be counted on, anywhere. There were these woods, of course, but someday men from cities would come breaking in, and find here deposits of iron or of coal, or strip the place of its trees to build their own super-civilized dwelling places. Not even the woods, then, could really be counted on. Life was transitory, shifting, mirage-like.
>
> Still, these forests would probably last her lifetime, after all. And then the candle goes out. She threw her arms impulsively around the trunk of a splendid young white pine, and laid her head against its rough bark. It reminded her of the day when she had first climbed the main rigging of the *Annie Marlow*, when she had clung to the sturdy topmast for strength and support. This was a very sympathetic white pine. Perhaps, in days gone by, it had been personally acquainted with that topmast. She almost felt that it was on communicative terms with her. A gust of wind shook its upper boughs—the masses of

needles went sparking silver in the sun, and a vibration ran through the staunch old trunk. Its roots were in the earth, and its branches in the sun, and that was a good way to live.

Nothing could be counted on, all was transitory, and you were alone. Those facts were rather difficult foundations for a house of life, but perhaps you could build upon them, if you knew how. Or perhaps it was better to forget all houses and be like this tree, roots in the earth, boughs in the sun. A world of philosophy there—whole dusty bookshelves of it in two phrases!

This tree seemed permanent enough. For the time being, and for her, it could serve. Not even the earth was really permanent. Perhaps someday something would go wrong with the machinery of the universe—the balance would be upset—and the earth would go catapulting into its sun like a very small moth into a gigantic flame. But for the time being, this tree would serve well.

She looked straight up at the sky through surges of silver-green. Big bright clouds rolled by smoothly. She stared at them a long time, and then felt the swift sensation that she, her pine tree, and all the woods, all the world, were falling slantingly. She held on and watched, and drifted more and more into the swinging illusion of the thing. She and the pine tree were falling through space together. It was a long fall, and an oddly companionable one. She laughed a little at that. Life was relentless, but there was nothing more it could take away from her. She clung to her tree, ruthlessly divested by life of an entire world—a complete paradise—but the magic had been, and it was hers—as much hers and as real as anything could be in a transitory earth where no one could entirely possess anything.

From *Lost Island*, final chapter.

APPENDIX 1: ROCKS

This was the “Knife-Edge” of Mount Katahdin. It was a ragged edge of rock suspended in a space of clouds.

I was trying to climb backwards down a bristling hump, and the foothold I had got up by seemed to have vanished. I felt for it helplessly with one foot. I couldn’t see below, because the rocks were in the way. There seemed nothing to do. I clung, trembling a little. All around, great swift drops into space that swirled with mist. Everything was wet—grasses and hardy vines were pearled with small drops; so were my hair and eyelashes.

I took a chance, and jumped, backwards, for a narrow ledge below. Then the mountain and I came together in a clash. I bounced over a grassy shelf, and whirled through the air. “Nothing matters now,” I thought. A fleeting, heroic second.... I up-ended ridiculously on hands and knees, clinging to a thick tuft of grass. Well! It wasn’t a sheer drop, after all. Vaguely disappointing—life would have to go on, then. My face was cut and my nose bleeding. I got up slowly and laughed, because it had been drilled into me that it was good sportsmanship to laugh when such things happened. The faces of my three comrades were horror-struck and rather absurd.

The mountain changed after that. I was afraid of it. Afraid to step over a fissure from one rock to another—to worm around on narrow ledges, or walk cautiously down smooth steep inclines. All the way down Pamola Peak back to camp, I was frightened. Mist swirled. Rocks, rocks—peaked, rounded, rough, smooth, edgy—gray rocks and mist and a malevolent mountain....

The next day it rained. The gaunt, sheer walls that towered over Chimney Pond and surrounded it on three sides, were covered with a network of silver waterfalls. The pond rose and rose. Everybody's butter and bacon, placed carefully in the brook to keep cool, were swept away. The shelter roof leaked. I glanced up at those rock walls that went up sheer and were lost in clouds, and knew that I should always be afraid of them, unless somehow I could contrive to slip away from everyone and go exploring, quietly and alone....

There was a hunk of chocolate in my pocket, and that was all the equipment I needed. We had bailed out the shelter, and hung our sleeping-bags in the sun.

"I think I'll run down to Basin Pond and pick a pail of blueberries," I said.

But what I really did was double back through the woods behind the shelter, and join the trail toward Saddle Slide, feeling half-gleeful, half-afraid.

The upper end of that trail, the slide itself, is grueling. It is very steep, and the footing is a specially pernicious kind of loose sandy stuff. It rolls out from under you. You slide back. It buries you to the ankles. The whole mountain is a running river of gravel. You stand in it and wonder when it will stop. You bend your back and struggle on, sometimes on hands and feet. It is heart-breaking, but short. You gain the brim quickly, and step over on to level solid plateau that forms almost a right angle with the slide. There you are, panting, glad to see that the mountain is still there.

I stood in sunlight on the brim, with the wind blowing through my hair. Katahdin was spread out before me and around me. Below was the great North Basin, scooped out of the mountain; Chimney Pond and the camp lay in the bottom of it. Across this gulf loomed the gray shoulder of Pamola, eastern pillar of the semicircular wall. The jagged line of the Knife-Edge, really more of a saw-edge, joined Pamola to the rocky and wild Monument, highest peak of all. On this western side where I was standing, the mountain spread out monstrously—an ocean of gray-green plateaus, undulating, rising to an occasional dome or rocky point, dipping off into gulfs and ravines, or unexplored basins with ponds shining in their depths. Grassy stuff in springy tufts grew on these plateaus; also small shrubs and vines, such as mountain cranberries, so hardy that the berries survive the first snows; black crow-berries; curiously flavored mountain blueberries. Small bright flowers in sheltered places. Acres of knee-high and waist-high scrub fir, almost impossible to make way through. It spreads its branches flat, growing horizontally—in places you can walk on it as on a springy carpet.

Vast, lonely old mountain, it reared up, 5200 feet high, over low smooth hills, shallow valleys, soft furry forests of blue and green—a country riddled silver with twisted lakes and ponds and rivers. I stood on the rim of it, and looked over it, and it was mine.

Slowly I followed the faint trail toward the North Peak. At Caribou Spring, I kneeled on damp sphagnum moss to drink. And I thought of Dinny, back in the shelter at Chimney Pond. We had drunk together out of this spring, she kneeling on one side of it and I on the other, red head and brown head in the center; John had come frisking up and dropped down between us, impishly grinning. “Room for another caribou?” he asked. Red head, brown head, gold head.... But this time I was alone; and half expected, looking up, to see a caribou’s brown ghost staring at me with soft eyes....

Again the space of mountain prairie with its green swoops into ravines. The trails on this northern part of the mountain were faint and hard to follow—no more than lines of small and infrequent cairns strung out over long slopes. Sometimes you could see one squatting on top of a big rock against the skyline, hundreds of feet ahead. If mist should come up thick, you could lose yourself on these great wide plateaus as easily as if you were far at sea. I had a vision of wandering listlessly through miles of quivering grass and flat fir, finding only a wet sky and this gray-green waste, coming now and then to the crumbly edge of a prodigious unknown ravine choked with mist, on the wrong side of the mountain. I would lie on the edge of it and gaze down. Somewhere below, through the swirling masses of cloud, I would hear the voice of a great waterfall....

Above the expansive vagueness of these plateaus, the grim old Monument loomed, built of the jagged gray rocks I was afraid of.... Always I had known mountains, not always in friendly mood. I had been lost in a sleet storm after dark with a failing flashlight on the peak of Liberty, wind howling like a mad wolf; I had been bound for a week by snow and fog in the old house on Moosilauke. A long succession of mountain adventures, one mountain following another down the skyline like great blue billows. I had cast about in vain to find the meaning of their beauty and strange power: the storm of feeling with which they could shake me; the longing for them which sometimes fevered me; the completeness of the satisfaction they gave.

But this one—this isolated, untamed old mountain—why was it so disquieting? Was it because of tales I had heard—of guides coming back to camp insane with fear, of people lost, caught on exposed places in savage weather—of people hurt, killed, on sheer headwalls? Or was it because of the wilderness of forest and swamp in which the mountain stands, where wildcats prowl?

I would come to terms with this mountain. Those rocks must be explored—tranquilly, easily. They were grim and formidable, but maybe one could make friends with them.

Past the top of the Saddle Slide trail again, up the well-marked trail to the Monument. I felt secret exultation, because, in spite of awe and fear, here I was, a very, very small thing, quite alone, scrambling toward the peak of this old Jinx of a mountain.

Quiet gray rocks.... Why should anyone be afraid of quiet gray rocks?

Three men were coming down the peak, far above. Presently we met. They looked surprised. One of them had a coil of rope over his shoulder. They had crawled up the "Chimney" that morning. We discussed the weather; passed on; were lost from sight among—rocks.

"I went up the Chimney, too," I said aloud....

I had been frightened almost cruelly. It was the first time I had been hitched up in a rope party, or done anything that could be called "rock-climbing." The Chimney is a steep and narrow channel, a cleft that goes straight up, starting a little above Chimney Pond, and ends in a gulch between Pamola Peak and the Knife-Edge. This cleft has been blocked in places by enormous "chokestones," which have to be got over, or under, or through, or around.

The four of us had roped up, for the "fun" of it and for practice, near the bottom, before there was any danger. We scrambled over big rocks and up ledges, trying to keep out of waterfalls. Sometimes we looked up at the chimerical steepness and narrowness of the passageway filled with mist—a crude rock passageway that had no summit—that merely was lost in clouds. And after some time we could see the dark shape of the first chokestone, looming and menacing, pinioned treacherously between the two walls of the gorge.

John was the most capable one of us: later on it appeared that he was the *only* capable one of us. He knew about rocks; was at home with a rope around his middle. He took the lead, and after a good deal of clumsiness and some anxious moments, we all managed to get over the first of the barriers. Then up the rocks again, in the mist. In this sort of climbing you use not only feet and hands, but knees, elbows, shoulders. The going got harder, and the healthy cold brook which tumbled down the gorge did not help. We were slower and slower. Every step was a problem to be puzzled out. And then the second chokestone intruded itself, a massive black wall almost over our heads—the end of the world—surely there could be nothing above that but mist! We looked back down; the way we had come dipped off and was as completely lost in clouds as the way above. We were on the precarious edge of everything concrete.

John, surprisingly, clung to a faith that there was really something beyond, and he began to figure out ways and means of getting to it. He was in favor of a desperate, improbable passage through the grim body of that chokestone and cut through a fissure at the top. There was a crude landing-place—a sort of shallow cave—part way up the side, and the brook ran through that. We began to straggle up to this gloomy ledge, only one of us moving at a time; but was no room when we got there—no rest—nothing for it but to straggle on through the rock. It looked very nasty, the next bit of climbing—up and around a wet black corner to an even more uncomfortable little cave, above the first one and completely out of sight. No room there, either; so I, who came last, had to wait at the first landing, while the rest of them took breath and considered matters. I was jammed in against damp rocks, and after a while became aware that I was also crouching in a waterfall—a small one, but very cold.

It was lonely. The others were scrambling about. I had

nothing for company except an end of rope. I waited—continued to sit in the waterfall, because there was nowhere else. It wasn't very comfortable. It was dripping down the back of my neck. Devilishly lonely. I was frightened, too. It was a precarious position, what with the waterfall, and the narrowness and slight downward angle of the ledge. If I so much as moved a toe, showers of loose pebbles and dirt went cavorting off down the mountain-side—bouncing and rattling and echoing disconsolately—farther and farther away until they were swallowed and hushed in the mist-filled gorge. Life was very cold and wet.

I waited. Sometimes they communicated from above. I couldn't hear very well, because they tended all to talk at once. But it seemed that they were having a dickens of a time. There would be silence, consultation, then desperate scrambles and showers of pebbles. They might have been in another world. I began to wonder if I should ever get off that ledge, or if I should presently fall off into the long steep gorge. I was stiff with cold by now; and that climb up to the next cave wasn't at all appealing. You had to swing outward, abandoning everything of any solidity, and wriggle up a slippery-looking tube of rock. The longer I waited, the worse it looked. Even at the end of a rope...

Even the rope was gone now. They needed the whole length of it up there. From the scraps of talk that came down to me, I realized that John had got out of the fissure at the top, and was trying to get Dinny out. Nick was crouching in a corner; she would "take off" from his shoulders, and then scramble desperately, while John held the rope from above, to make progress up a sheet of rock that not only was just about vertical, but also wet. And she couldn't quite make it. She would slide back and try again.

I shivered. Their comments and exclamations were anything but reassuring, and I didn't at all like the sound of the things that were happening to Dinny. I continued to balance in the waterfall on the edge of nothing, without even a rope for company, and tried to philosophize. The world was coming to an end, but there was chocolate in my jacket. I munched it and felt better. Chocolate was good even when the world was coming to an end.

My turn at last. I miracle had happened: Dinny was out. They slid the rope back to me—an anxious job, since it had to come around a corner, and I had to lean outward precariously to reach it—and then all three began calling instructions and encouragements at once. I asked them to say it over again, one at a time.

Nick's voice came out of the little cave above. "Tie a bowline! Your life depends on it."

"All right," I said. "I'll be glad to get out of this waterfall." But it was very hard to move. I was stiff, and anyway moving hardly seemed advisable. The mountain continued to slide out from beneath me.

"Are you O.K.?" asked Nick. His voice did not sound right.

"Oh, sure," I said, "only this here mountain's coming to pieces under me. I can't remember how to tie a bowline."

"Rabbit comes out of his hole, runs around a tree—back in hole," he reminded me.

I sat in the waterfall and thought it out quietly. "All right," I said at last. "Keep that rope good and tight, Nick, but for God's sake don't *pull* me. I want to come up under my own power, you understand."

He said: "Be careful. I can't stand much strain—things are pretty rickety up here."

"Nicky," said I, "isn't there anything firm and strong and solid left in life?"

"Let's hope the rope is," he said.

I clenched my teeth, and got off that horrible little ledge. Braced on the rope, I got a kind of foothold—lost it—got something with my hands—rested a minute. "All right up there?" I queried.

"Yup. You've got a knee-hold a wee bit higher up."

So I had. Knees and elbows. I suspended myself between the walls of the little dark passageway. The next crack was right above. Nick sat huddled in it, braced on nothing much. I rested again, heaved, and was up. And then I saw that I wasn't a bit better off than before, except that here there was no waterfall.

There's nothing amusing to tell about that next bit of climbing. Obviously, I got out at last through the fissure—mostly by dint of John's hauling me out by brute force. He hauled and I scrabbled like mad; but there were moments when I simply dangled in space by the arm-pits. The thing I was supposed to be climbing rose practically parallel to my helpless body, and offered not so much as a small fret or notch to grab it by. When finally I was out of there, standing on top of that beast of a chokestone, I discovered that I was rather banged up. Both knees and elbows were raw, and I was conscious of minor scrapes and bruises by the dozen. I shivered a little, and listened with a half-smile to Nick tying himself into the rope, humming to reassure himself. His voice was quavering badly.

After that progress was more possible, although there were bad times as we squeezed along too-narrow ledges, or shinned over slippery ridges, always with the mist blowing down cold from the Knife-Edge into our faces. Finally we passed underneath the last chokestone, which, suspended high between the walls of the gully, formed a sinister bridge. It was our gateway of triumph. The grade was a little less steep now—"rolling over"—the sky was close, full of its scudding mist....

We had climbed over that first bristling hump of the Knife-Edge, to see what it was like. It was very fierce and narrow. The sky was a blank of mist. The depths were a blank of mist. We walked on a narrow ragged edge of rock suspended in a space of clouds.

Back again over the first hump, into the gully below Pamola. And then—the lost foothold, the second or two of clinging, the little scrambling jump—and the falling, striking a ledge, and falling, falling....

I awoke with a start out of this racking daydream. I was picking my way in leisurely fashion over jumbled rocks. By now I had nearly reached the top of the Monument, and suddenly I knew that all the fear and trouble were ended. I was alone with the mountain, and the rocks were essentially friendly rocks. Mist was drifting in—not solidly, but in preliminary wisps and fragments.

I stood surrounded by wind on the Monument itself, and looked out over a Maine dappled with clouds. Lakes were a quick gleam of silver in distant sunlight between wraiths of mist. Patches of sunlight strayed about the mountain—alighted upon Pamola, went out, touched the little camp in the gulf, reappeared fleetingly on northern plateaus. In places the jagged line of the Knife-Edge, very sharp and black, pierced gray sinuous fragments of mist, looming above a restless obscure space. The drops into that abyss, with the spruces and firs in its depths—fuzzy little toy trees—were almost sheer, from Hamlin Ridge in the north clear around the huge circle to Pamola. Between the long slant of the Ridge, and the grim tower of the peak, was the only gateway to Chimney Pond—the only break in that stern wall. All this I saw brokenly between quiet clouds.

To walk from here down on to the Knife-Edge was like venturing out along the top edge of a gigantic jagged wall. The saying that in some places the Knife-Edge is so narrow that you can straddle it as if it were some mythical horse, is no exaggeration. On one side, the gulf of the North Basin—you can distinctly see pebble-like things that are big boulders at the bottom of Chimney Pond. On the other side, the vastness of Maine.

I munched my chocolate, there on the Monument, and felt and smelt of the wind, not very strong. And so I slipped along quietly on the Knife-Edge trail. I knew now that these rocks were not going to hurt me. The clouds were companionable, too. They wandered in, white and pearly gray, from the southeast, slipped through the jags of the Knife-Edge, and drifted off, unscratched, untorn, into the great basin. They came quietly, swiftly, not very dense, with breaks between them. They made the world infinitely more beautiful by keeping it half-secret. Looking southward, there would be a glimpse of tender purple hills, or the soft blues and greens of far-reaching forest, of a wonderful velvety texture, like a rich Persian rug on the floor of the earth. Then white curtains. Once a small, swift break showed me, between ephemeral pale streamers, a wide lake, burnished gold in a flood of sunlight. It was more a dream than reality—coveted glimpses in a rare and magical crystal.

Sometimes a gray cataract of cloud would stream across the jag I was on; then the wings of blue sky, and all light and shadow and color would be lost; it would be cold for a moment, and wet, and gray, and this cloud seemed to fill the whole world. Again, a cloud would sail through just ahead of me, leaving me on a pedestal in a clear pool of sky, with wetness and grayness and coldness streaming transitorily past, almost within reach.

I wasn't afraid. Only, when I came to the top of the Chimney, where the Knife-Edge dips into that sharp hollow under Pamola, where I had fallen, I worried a little. I though, what a devil of a nuisance it would be if I should pull that stunt again and really get smashed up, now that there was no one to rescue me! I came to the brink of the thing—the bristling hump—and looked over; and there was no doubt that it was bad—just as bad as before. I looked some more; and all of a sudden discovered another way to get down—an easy way around a corner and down a grassy crevice. I laughed aloud happily.

Pamola was smothered in mist. However, I picked the right

trail from several unmarked ones that diverge at the summit; and none of the great tumbled chaotic boulders, the narrow ledges, the difficult corners, the dark holes, seemed inimical. Quite a long way down I came into scrubby woods, where birches were growing at slants and angles and curves; some started horizontally, then suddenly changed their minds and grew upright. They were good things to hold on to. Farther down came ledges with rich deep moss covering them and spilling over the edges. Its greenness was striking after the gray pinnacles of a higher, more fantastic world.

This mountain and I had known a special and wondrous kindred solitude; and it was a culmination, a gigantic summing-up, of all adventure. There was no more haunting terror of gray rocks.... Exultant, I went to find the rest of the crowd. I was awhirl with things I wanted to say. I wanted to describe the peaks and clouds, gold lakes shining through the fingers of white....

Laughter—high-pitched voices—the crackle of a supper fire —the warm sleepy smell of cocoa brewing....

"Hi there, old bean! Get many?"

"Many? What?"

"Blueberries, of course!"

"Oh, that...! No, I—sort of forgot..."

"*Forgot—!*"

They looked at me silently; then laughed, as though going to Basin Pond for blueberries, and then forgetting to pick any, was just what they expected from anyone so scatterbrained.

And I didn't care at all.

APPENDIX 2: TRAVELS WITHOUT A DONKEY

"It's spring," Nick said.

In the very shadow of New York's skyline, one solitary white crocus had blossomed in a scrawny patch of grass.

"What shall we do about it?" he demanded.

"What does anybody in New York do about it? Grin and bear it."

"Come on, Bar—show a spark of life, old gal. I'm getting out of here this summer."

"But—"

"Getting out. Leaving the office. Going into the north woods. Mountains. It's spring, child!"

I looked at him to make sure he was serious. In these depressed times, one didn't leave good jobs in order to run away to the north woods. His brown eyes sparkled. But then, they always did. He was the one person in New York whose eyes always sparkled.

"All right—I wish you joy."

He fished in various pockets and finally produced a little square of white metal, with a monogram and the words: "Appalachian Trail – Maine to Georgia."

"That's what I'm going to do," he explained. "I haven't had a walk for ages. Well, I'm going to have a real one now."

"Not from Maine to Georgia!"

"Why not? It's only two thousand miles or so."

"It'll take all summer."

"Can you think of a pleasanter way to spend the summer?"

I looked at the solitary white crocus in the scrawny patch of grass. "No," I said. "I can't."

Over lunch that day, he told me about this Appalachian Trail. It is a footpath, starting at Katahdin, that grand old mountain in Maine, and ending at Mount Oglethorpe way down in Georgia, after having crossed the highest and handsomest country of all the states between. Now, owing to the diligence and energy of walking clubs in various parts of the country, only a few miles of trail remains to be broken. But two years ago, when Nick told me about it over our luncheon, a large part of the trail, especially in Maine, was still theory—a dream, an ambition. Where it had become an actuality, it was marked with metal squares like the one he had shown me.

Quite a grand project, it sounded. I just sat staring and smiling, while he talked.

"Bar," he began again, "I think I'd like you in shorts."

"Shorts!"

"With your hair cut, flying in the wind—your swell red hair."

"Cut my hair!"

"Your freckles are out-of-doorsy. You belong out-doors."

"I haven't got freckles," I protested.

"Yes you have—very swell ones."

"I know I belong out-doors," I agreed. "I get mountain-fever. Got it now—something awful. I want to climb Wildcat."

"We will," he said happily. "I didn't want to walk all the way to Georgia alone, anyway."

"Are you asking me to come with you?"

"Of course! What else?"

"But I can't—"

"Nonsense. We start up north the first of July. You give 'em notice."

"But, Nicky—"

"'But' isn't worthy of you, Bar. Not in spring."

Some friends had a camp on a New Hampshire lake. It was there that Nick met me, promptly on the first of July. He was sunburned and smiling, comfortable in old clothes. Without stopping a minute, he deposited me and my pack in a borrowed canoe.

We paddled vigorously into the sunlit lake—magic to someone parched from too much New York. After a while I saw white beach ahead of us, and the green canoe scraped sand gently.

A small green island. A pine dipping graceful branches over a flat boulder that stood half in the rippling lake, half on land. A tiny stone fireplace on top of the boulder. Golden rippled reflections wavered on the sand at the lake's edge; silver ones shimmered on the under sides of the pine branches. The world smelt of sun, and bay leaves, and pine-needles. The brightness was almost unreal. The sun wrapped us in gleaming shawls of warmth.

We drew the canoe up. Nick parted the bay-bushes and revealed a little path, hardly more than would be made by a rabbit. Five or six yards back, on a knoll screened with bushes, was our house—a brown tent, not more than six feet square.

"This is it," Nick announced. "This is home."

I wanted nothing so much as to swim, although I soon found that muscles that had been in the city for two years had forgotten some of their rhythms. Then I sat, dripping, on the big boulder, long hair cascading down my back. I felt very white in this summer-time world where the human body ought to be brown.

Nick brandished a pair of scissors. "Off with it!"

I put up my arms in self-defense. "No—no!"

"Yes! Absolutely! You can't walk two thousand miles with that yard of hair, child. It'll get wound up in the blackberries. It'll collect whole hay-ricks. Bats will nest in it."

"But, Nicky, I like my hair. And I don't object to bats."

"I like it, too. But I don't like what you do to it—tying your face to the back of your neck with it. I want to see it wave in the wind. That's really why I married you. And anyway, you can grow it again."

I wavered. "It would be more comfortable, of course...."

Snip!

"Don't, Nicky—!"

"Too late now. Got to go on with it."

Snip! Snip!

The air was full of flying fragments. Reddish fluff covered the boulder. A great weight was vanishing from my head. What hair I had left began to stand on end in the joy of its freedom. For the first time in years, it was waving in the wind.

We sat peacefully in the sunshine, then, and did some organizing of equipment. For instance, the tent needed a mosquito curtain. There were almost bound to be a few malevolent bugs somewhere between Maine and Georgia.

The tent itself, of the Baker type, was ideal for our purpose. It could be rolled up small enough to fit across the top of the pack; it weighed only a trifle over six pounds. The flap was the whole front side of the tent. In fine weather you could throw this back over the roof and out of the way—there you were, wide open to the skies. In rainy weather, you could stretch it horizontally six feet above the ground, so that you had a protected front yard, in which a fire could be built and kept dry. The simplest house in the world! And what more did anyone need, in the summer time?

The rest of our outfit was correspondingly simple. Two very light-weight sleeping-bags, adequate for summer weather; a light but man-sized ax; the minimum cooking-kit; some food bags to hold such things as flour, sugar, cereal, cocoa; a very few clothes....

A marvellous stillness pervaded the air. Even the breeze was basking in the sun; and the lake stretched itself, cat-like, content, almost purring. It sparkled with brightness that had been melting into it all day. Waves continued to sigh in rhythm —a sleepy stirring at the dazzling threshold of sand.

"When do we start, Nicky? To tell the truth, I could stay right here very happily all summer."

"Well, my hunch would be to stay here till we get you toughened up a bit, and the worst of the sunburn over. Swim—tear around—muscles working again. Say a couple of weeks. Then Katahdin—how about it? I admit I want to get to Katahdin."

"Swell."

"And in the mean time," he went on, "we can experiment with cooking. We've got some things to learn, too: how to cram the most nutrition into the least space and weight; whether it's worth while to carry powdered eggs; how much sugar to allow per day—things like that."

"Why don't we study up on the nutrition that grows wild?" I suggested. "Mushrooms, for instance. And there must be all kinds of stuff that would make swell spinach. I read somewhere that you can eat cat-tail roots. Cat-tail salad—that's a delightful thought!"

"The only thing that worries me," he said, "is whether we can carry on our backs even the minimum junk. What would you think of getting a donkey? Not an expensive one—a sort of second-hand one, you understand. He'd be companionable, and useful, and no trouble to keep, in the summer."

"Can't you see us?" I chuckled. "We might write a story about it. 'With a Donkey from Maine to Georgia'—something on that line."

D'you think he'd last that far? What's the average mileage of a donkey—second-hand?"

"Couldn't say."

We were quiet, while a small gray sandpiper, with an edging of white dots around his wings, went quaintly teetering down the beach.

"Another thought," I said. "And this one doesn't belong to the nutrition department, or the transportation department. It's more the philosophy of the thing."

"I'm all ears."

"I think we want to forget about Georgia. After all, Georgia will stay put. What we want to do is explore the country. Not stick too rigidly to this Appalachian Trail, if we happen to feel like wandering off the edges of it."

"Right," he agreed. "We aren't out to make records or cover lots of ground. We can get to Georgia next summer—or the next; in fact, we don't *ever* have to get there, when you come right down to it."

"Getting to Georgia is a nice idea," I said. "But the real aim of the expedition is to stay out-doors and try our best not to take the city with us, but—well, Kipling put it pretty well—'melt in the landscape.'"

Boy Scout parties may intrude into the lordly calm of Katahdin's Great Basin, where Chimney Pond lies shining; but even they cannot really harm the aloof mystery of the mountain—they can only scratch it slightly. The country is not nearly so wild as when Thoreau explored it, or when Indians gazed at the mountain from far off with trembling reverence and fear—still, it is wild. Bear and moose and big cat prowl about in it; there are long wildernesses of tangled, untracked swamp and forest; some of the trails on the mountain itself are faint and unmarked; and one still has to walk a good seven or eight miles to get in to Chimney Pond.

This Great Basin, except for one break, is encircled by a straight-sided wall of mountain, from Pamola Peak on the east clear around through south and west to the long downward slant of Hamlin Ridge on the north. Straight above the Pond the jagged Knife-Edge looms, top edge of the wall, joining Pamola to the Monument, highest of Katahdin's peaks. The headwall is gray, with patches of dark green where the most warped and stubborn little firs in the world cling. After a rain, this whole great headwall will be laced by a network of slender silver waterfalls.

For a week or so Nick and I had lived in one of the shelters at Chimney Pond. We had listened to the stories of Roy Dudley, who has been "guidin'" and running that camp for years. He is personally acquainted with an arrogant devil-spirit, Pamola, who boasts wings and claws, and guards a darksome lair in a secluded cave high on the storm-swept peak which bears his name. This old fellow causes Roy Dudley plenty of trouble. He resents intrusion into his lofty solitudes, and from time to time he hurls enormous windfalls in tangles across carefully cleared trails. He no longer can turn Roy round and round and get him mixed up in the fog; but he persists in gorging himself on bull moose every now and then, and sometimes comes late at night humbly begging for bicarbonate of soda. Another curious habit of his is that of sailing about Chimney Pond by moonlight on a raft of crowbars.

Roy knows a few likely stories, too. While he tells these and the others, Mrs. Dudley sits by the stove, deftly knitting thick red and gray socks. Her curly white hair falls to her shoulders; her girlish face is browned; and her eyes are clear bright blue. Every now and then she smiles ever so little; then you must be on the look-out: Roy is "stringing" you....

We had climbed Pamola Peak, making our way cautiously

over and around great boulders. We had crept across the Knife-Edge, in places so narrow you can straddle it. One one side, a sheer drop into Chimney Pond; on the other, a sheer drop into tangled Maine wilderness. Surrounded by wind, we had stood on the Monument itself, and far and wide the country was dappled with ponds and clouds, hard to tell apart. And we had ventured into the wild Northwest Basin, battling fierce underbrush, sliding down steep banks, and finally taking a very short swim in the coldest little pond in the world.

But now it was time to shoulder our packs, say goodbye to Katahdin and the Dudleys, and start our tramp toward—Georgia! Down the Appalachian Trail which here in Maine existed only in theory and as a dream.

"Have a cranberry," Nick said. "I want to sit down and think this thing out some more. It's worrying me."

"Don't let it. We'll get on all right."

"Yes—but I haven't even got a decent map of that country. I don't know that there is one."

He waved his arm off toward the southwest. We were sitting in a cranberry patch on one of Katahdin's enormous high plateaus. It dipped off toward a blue wilderness sprinkled with ponds and big haphazard lakes gleaming in the afternoon sun. Perhaps a temperamental giant had once stood here, carelessly flinging quicksilver until the countryside was strewn with shimmering pools of it.

Nick had pulled out a battered sketch given him by Mr. Dudley, and was for the hundredth time anxiously studying it. I looked over his shoulder at a jungle of six- and eight-syllable Indian names—unpronounceable concatenations which constituted nearly all we knew about this country to the southwest.

"We want to get to Moosehead Lake," he said. "That's the

whopping big one you can see just a bit of, way off."

Silver arms and bays, very faint in a distant haze, shone beckoningly across the unknown.

"I think it's exciting," I said, "taking off into nowhere."

"Exciting, all right," he agreed. "But I feel sort of—well, responsible. We may hit old tote roads, or we may not. We may have to bushwhack for miles."

"I don't mind bush-whacking."

"Strenuous—with a pack. Through raspberries, maybe."

"We can eat the raspberries—and as for the thorns—my dungarees—"

"Swamps, maybe," he went on.

"Well, where we can't wade we'll swim."

"Strenuous—with a pack. Suppose we get stuck in the mud? And suppose we under-estimate about provisions, and get stuck with miles of swamps and raspberries between us and sugar?"

"You're a nice cheerful person, I must say."

"And how the hell are we going to get across the wide roaring Penobscot River? The old dam above the Sourdnahunk has gone out, they tell me."

"Wait a minute! Why do we have to get across the Penobscot so soon? Aren't we going up it to Ripogenus Dam anyway?"

"Well, Roy says that on the other side we'll hit a little tote road in decent shape, and that this side would be awful. He knows—he's trapped around here for years."

"Might build a raft," I suggested hopefully.

"It's probably too swift to pole a raft across—if I could build one, that is."

"And even supposing we do escape all these various disasters," I put in, "the bears will get us, anyway."

"You're right—that's another possibility."

"Let's go home to the island in the sun," I said.

"Much more sensible," he agreed. "But who the hell wants to be sensible?... Come on, child, let's get going. We can easily enough get to York's Camp on Daicey Pond, and that's a beginning."

"Shall we stay there tonight?"

"No—I thought we'd stay in a—well, you'll see. Let's go—sun's going down."

This upper end of the Hunt Trail was rough. It fell off very steep, with nothing underfoot but edges and pinnacles and uncomfortable crannies. We scrambled over huge rocks, and squeezed cautiously through crevices between them. Two or three times we had to take off our packs and push, haul, or lift them through. Sometimes they got stuck—worse still, sometimes we did.

We were not yet used to those packs of ours. Eventually, we thought, when we got in training, we'd slide lightly over the countryside, all unconscious of the seventy pounds of worldly possessions which between us we were carrying on our backs. That time seemed distant; but already we had a feeling of triumph because of our complete self-sufficiency and independence: we could go anywhere and stay as long as it pleased us. All very gipsy-like; only right now we were a trifle more tired than first-class gipsies ought to be.

"Perhaps we should have brought along that second-hand donkey, after all," I suggested.

The trail dipped into woods, and remained very steep. We climbed down ladders formed by tangled roots. After a while we came out into a green clearing, velvety with moss, and here we found a sort of cave, a crude shelter made by one enormous rock leaning against another.

"Well, here we are," said Nick. "This is it. Our first night out on the A. T.—in a cave. Romantic enough—isn't it?"

We set to work, he getting firewood, I cutting fir boughs for a bed. We hauled out the food bags and cooked supper over a small crackling fire. Clouds were drifting in; it rained a little; the sunset came through rose-colored mist. But when we curled up for the night stars were to be seen through rifts in the clouds. They seemed friendly.

The morning was clear and warm. We got up rather after dawn—"too late for gipsies; we must do better," said Nick—built a fire, and cooked a large pot of corn meal mush with raisins, after which the trackless and mapless wilderness we felt ahead of us diminished a good deal in size and consequence. Who was afraid when the sun was so bright?

We struck the Millinocket Tote Road at Katahdin Stream, which came rollicking over rocks and sand-bars, whirling joyously in deep pools, sliding around green bends. It was too clear and cool to be resisted; off went packs and clothes, and in we plunged. Ripe cherries and raspberries overhung the stream. We feasted on them; we sat on a little sand island and observed the private lives of very small minnows and trout. Wonderful blazing dragonflies, all black velvet and gold plate, crackled by. We marveled at the verdure and luxuriance of this Maine countryside in the summer time. It was hard to reconcile with our first forebodings. Nothing difficult or even strenuous about this—standing knee-deep in a sparkling brook and eating berries on its banks!

After lunch we went at a good pace to York's Camp. Katahdin loomed gray-green and forbidding across Daicey Pond. Along the Sourdnahunk River there was an old tote road, and the going was easy and peaceful through evergreen woods—a contrast to the mountain's rocky trails. The big brook itself was entertaining, with swirling pot-holes, swift glides down smooth rocks, boiling rapids.

"What's the matter with this?" I teased. "Bring on your swamps and mud-holes!"

"All very fine, my dear girl, but how are we going to get across the Penobscot?"

"Oh, we'll worry about that when we get to it. Don't cross bridges—"

"That's just it. There isn't any bridge."

"Well, is the problem imminent?"

It was. And what's more, that wide river was going at a tremendous clip. Piles of dark water hurried along, breaking now and then into rapids, humping up in eddies. Much too deep to ford; much too swift to pole across on a raft. And no sign of humanity at all. And it was almost evening.

"No use," I said. "We'll only get headaches puzzling about it. Let's make camp and go to sleep."

The river rushed darksomely past our front door all night.

And in the morning, when we peered out of our front door, there was the river.

"Looks desperate," Nick said cheerfully. "But let's have breakfast, anyway."

A little path led along the river on the side of a steep bank. We brushed under low-drooping spruce and hemlock branches; and after half a mile or so came out into a clearing where several ruined gray buildings of an ancient lumber camp looked out desolately from raspberry bushes.

"Here's where the old dam used to be, I guess," Nick mumbled.

We heard noises now from one of the buildings, and found an old man building his breakfast fire in a rusty stove.

"Good morning!" we hailed.

He looked up sharply, and stared at us suspiciously for a few seconds. Then, slowly, his face relaxed and broke into a smile.

"Oh!" he exclaimed. "You folks wants t' git 'cross t' river, mebbe?"

His understanding and perception seemed so remarkable that we merely nodded and said nothing. But the old fellow apparently thought it a fine joke. He chuckled gleefully and recited, in a high singsong: "I be t' watchman of t' old dam, I be. Dam's out, but here I be—me 'n' my old boat—jest in case any folks wants t' git 'cross t' river. Charge 'em for it—dollar 'piece.

Not that there's many folks, mind you—but jest in case... and so you wants t' git 'cross t' river—well, well!"

He chuckled again, and rubbed his hands together; then went on about getting breakfast as if we weren't there, serene in his confidence that, since we couldn't get across in any other way, we must necessarily wait for him. Only once he stopped in the middle of a cup of black tea, and asked, with friendly curiosity: "Where you folks start from anyways?"

We told him about Katahdin.

He shook his head with sage disdain. "Ah—Katahdin!" he repeated. Then, mumbling: "Awful pile o' rocks."

We filed down to the gravel beach where a battered old boat lay half full of water. After much straining we tipped her over; then put our packs in, and shoved off. The river was not so swift at this point. We rowed, Nick at one long oar, the old man at the other. Safe across, we gave him his two dollars.

"And if you folks ever wants t' git back 'cross t' river," he said solemnly, "here I be—jest in case... me 'n' my old boat. Jest sing out—here I be."

"Will you give us back the two dollars if we come back across the river?" Nick could not help asking.

We spent the day tramping up the river to Ripogenus Dam; and the little road of which Roy had spoken was in fair shape, mostly. The woods were fresh and green and alive; and there were deer tracks in the mud. About sundown, when we were pretty weary, we pulled into Ripogenus; and the keeper of the dam let us sleep in a shack which, during the winter, served as schoolhouse for the four or five local children.

Next day, a friendly gravel-truck driver offered us a ride part of the way to that Moosehead Lake which had gleamed to us from so unattainably far away as we stood on Katahdin. This wasn't sticking to the proposed route of the Appalachian Trail, but it seemed like a good idea. Our shoulders were pretty lame by now.

"Oh, they'll toughen up all right in another day or so," Nick assured me. "But in the mean time, let's try a gravel truck."

We stood on the shore of Moosehead Lake, where we were getting ready to make camp. "This feels like home," Nick suddenly said. "Here's where we stay a while."

The lake is an endless jungle of islands and long peninsulas, deep bays and coves. The huge square rock they call Mt. Kineo seems at first to be a northern boundary, but north of it are miles more of those alluring silver arms and fingers of water, winding, weaving among the hills.

"We ought to have a canoe," I said. "It would be marvellous to explore the shore and the little islands."

Nick was staring out toward a peninsula that bristled with tall Norway pines, and a green island that stood in the mouth of the bay. "I don't see why we can't have one," he answered quietly.

"Buy an old second-hand one, you mean?"

"Sure. We'll go down to Greenville—only six miles or so. Got to have grub, anyhow, and we'll hunt up canoes. And if we get one, we'll paddle her back here to camp."

"And sell her after we get through exploring?"

He thought a while, then dug a map of Maine out of a pack pocket, and studied it. "I wonder—you know, I think I've got an idea. Maybe the Kennebec River's canoeable. I'll find out. If it is, we'll run down it to Indian Pond, and from there to The Forks." He followed the course of the Kennebec with one forefinger.

"So the A. T. becomes a waterway," I said.

"Sure. Give our legs a rest—use our arms for a change."

❄

Greenville was pretty depressing, just as any town is depressing after woods and hills, freedom and sunshine. But a couple of ice-cream cones fortified us; and we went to attend to the nautical business. A shrewd-looking old chap named Allen had canoes for sale. First he tackled us about a spick-and-span red-painted affair for forty-five dollars; but, seeing that we didn't bite, he decided he had made a mistake. After thinking it over for a minute, he introduced us to the most marvellous canoe in the world.

She was a strong and heavy eighteen-foot Oldtown, battered and patched and scraped and dented. She had no bow seat. Seven of her ribs were broken, and a couple of planks besides—apparently the thwarts were all that kept her gunwales from buckling together. She had the look of a very battle-scarred veteran who should be carefully put away to rest. We eyed her doubtfully, as she lay drawn up on the sand.

"Do you think she'd stand for hobnailed boots?" Nick queried.

For answer, Allen, who was wearing heavy hobnailed boots, jumped violently into the canoe and walked heavily up and down her bottom. We held our breath in horror. We thought we understood about canoes. We had always been taught that they were delicate and must be treated with respect.

"How about all those broken ribs?" we tried.

The old chap burst into a scornful laugh. "I tell you," he began, "round this country a guide that knows anything won't think o' takin' a canoe down a river unless she has at least four or five broken ribs. That softens her up, gives her a good flexible bottom, don't you see, and she don't get hung up on the rocks. That's why we shellac the bottoms o' canoes round here, 'stead o' paintin' 'em. If you have paint on your bottom and hit a rock, it'll scrape through the paint and tear the canvas; but if you have shellac, she jest slides over, jest as nice.... Yes, sirree, a flexible bottom's what you want. And the canvas on this canoe is sound as if she was new. She won't leak a drop."

He went on in an amazing stream of patter, expounding what was to us a new philosophy of canoeing.

"She won't leak, eh?"

"Not a drop," he said.

It seemed very unlikely. But in the end we bought her and her trappings—two enormous paddles, vastly heavier than the spruce ones we were used to; a setting-pole at least fifteen feet long to help us down-river; and an old stool to serve as bow seat. We put aboard some supplies we had bought at the local grocery, and started off, by sea, for our campground on the beach.

The canoe behaved astoundingly. She gathered momentum slowly, but once it was gathered there was no stopping her. She forged through the water with an immense, powerful swing. We were used to light sixteen-footers. Already our arms were aching from the weight of these tremendous paddles; and then and there we decided that we had never known anything about canoeing.

"I feel more like a man than I've ever felt before," said Nick from the stern. "She's immense."

At that moment a sporty motor-boat roared past. The people aboard her had to yell their conversation, and we distinctly heard someone say: "See that canoe? Well, those are the boys that are going down the Appalachian Trail."

"*You* feel like a man, do you?" I retorted to Nick.

Our arms ached and ached. "How many more of these long points do we have to go round?" I inquired. "And how are we going to recognize our own bay when we get to it?"

"I haven't the remotest notion."

"Well, I hope we don't have to paddle two or three miles into *every* bay, to see if our camp is at the end of it, and then two or three miles out again, when it isn't!"

"I'll consult the map," said Nick. We paused, in mid-sea, as it were, to compare hills and peninsulas with the brown contour lines of a topographic map. "I think it's pretty amusing, myself," he said. "Navigating homeward over unknown oceans. We ought to have a sextant. What do you suppose the compass variation is?" He was holding his compass in the palm of his hand, and lining up his chart with it.... "Plenty more long points," he said finally. "Courage, child!"

We dug in our paddles again. The wind was coming up, and there were hard choppy waves, through which we forged solidly. All of a sudden Nick gave a curious sort of cry. I whirled about. With a horror-struck stare, he was watching the pack in the middle of the canoe. As I looked, too, I saw that it was quivering, from the canoe's sharp impacts with the waves. And then, before our very eyes, that pack lifted—heaved upward a little, and settled back again.

"Wh-what...?"

"It's the 'flexible bottom!'" Nick fairly shouted. "Don't you see? She just lifts her belly and lets the waves slide under! It's the darnedest thing I ever saw!"

"Is it dangerous?"

"I don't know. Looks pretty bad. Wait and see."

"What else can I do?" I asked, and dug in again. But the old girl herself appeared not the least bit perturbed. She slid on solidly, leaking never a drop; except for that lifting and settling of her bottom, every now and then, she seemed as stable as some flat-bottomed tub of a row-boat. We wondered if the whole thing was a nightmare.

Moosehead is a romantic lake. Because it is so very big, the summer camps are not obtrusive and can be escaped. The shores are beautifully wooded with fine old spruce, hemlock, and pine; and every once in a while a stretch of grayish sand made us yearn to stop and swim. At times we would hear a weird, quavering cry, dismal and lonely over the ripples—a big black and white loon diving and gliding along the shore. Sometimes two or three of them would converse mournfully. But the loons belonged there, and we were not surprised to see them. What did surprise me, on this big lake ninety miles from the sea, were flocks of seagulls, who sat around on top of the waves, plunged for fish, flew and shrieked overhead very realistically, and acted quite at home.

We explored. The canoe took us everywhere, steadily, solidly, unfalteringly. Some nights we did not even pitch our tent, but simply stretched out on a fir bed under the open sky. Every morning, when mist was rising from the lake and the early sun made it gleam faintly golden, we wriggled out of our sleeping-bags and plunged into that cold soft water. Every day at high noon we would pull up in a quiet place and stretch out naked in the sun. Life was a long continuous being out-of-doors—which was just as we wanted it to be.

We had fun making culinary experiments; and here at Moosehead Lake was inaugurated the never-ending quest for an ideal pancake. We tried all possible combinations and proportions of flour, graham flour, corn meal, oat meal, sugar, baking powder, powdered milk, and powdered egg. Every morning we had a different kind of pancake, and they were all interesting. Gradually we evolved something almost cake-like, which could be eaten with no embellishments, and would stay fluffy till noon, when we ate a stack of them cold, along with the berries we picked.

One night, as we were about to settle into our sleeping-bags, it seemed that the lake was too beautiful to abandon in an abyss of sleep. A magic sliding sheet of moonlight covered it. Islands and headlands were soft velvety black. The wind was gentle, and rather warm. It was a tropical night.

"What shall we do about it?" Nick questioned. "We can't just—" he yawned slightly—"go to bed, can we?"

"How about climbing Kineo? The lake would look heavenly from Kineo tonight."

"That would be pretty romantic, I should think."

We slid the canoe out. The water was a strange, magical substance—quickgold. We dipped our paddles into semi-solid golden pools, which shattered, rippled, and dripped off the blades. Somewhere, in the midst of all this enchantment, a loon wailed.

It was a rather long paddle from the island to the foot of Kineo, and we had done a fair day's paddling already. By the time we had beached the canoe, and started out to find the trail up the mountain, we were yawning desperately, and our feet were incoherent—the white road swayed beneath them, and we were treading insubstantially upon air which misbehaved.

It was dark in the woods as we plodded up that trail. Now and then we stumbled or stepped into an unexpected hollow. We kept on yawning. The romance of the thing was pretty much lost upon us, and getting more lost every minute. We were ashamed of ourselves: it was such a grand night, and climbing Kineo by moonlight ought to be exciting... we tried to take a firm grip upon ourselves, but it was useless.... After a long time we came to a look-out place near the top. A confused version of a marvellous silver octopus of a lake spread out among black velvet hills.... We sat down in the grass, and sighed. Then we leaned a little against each other. Slowly we sank into that moon-silvered grass, and instantly fell asleep.

Dawn was breaking as we paddled back for breakfast to our unslept-in camp on the island. Afterwards we started for the east outlet of the Kennebec. But we found this the wrong outlet. A guide at the dam told us this was a mighty tough river. Only real old-timers ever ran it; he himself had once run the four miles to Indian Pond in one wild quarter-hour. The river *drops* nearly a hundred feet in those four miles, he said. And as for the Kennebec *below* Indian Pond—oh, no one even attempted it. He was horrified at the very idea. Go to pieces just like—that! He snapped his fingers.... But we could get to Indian Pond all right by the west outlet, an altogether nicer-mannered little river, which took its time and used twelve or fifteen miles to get where this one got in four. In fact, on the west outlet there was only one place where we might have trouble—a corner called the Devil's Elbow.

"So there," said Nick, "go our pleasant hopes of canoeing all the way down to The Forks. Shall we sell the canoe here, or try for Indian Pond?"

"We can't part with her yet," I protested. "Why, we're just getting used to her."

"I had another idea," Nick went on. "I think Indian Pond's on a railroad; and it isn't such a far cry from there to the Rangeley Lakes—five lakes in a string. We might ship the canoe to ourselves and pick her up at the Rangeleys, and explore them."

"Sounds good. We might even be glad to see the old girl," I said.

"But this business of running to Indian Pond has got me kind of worried," he said. "I ought to warn you. I don't know the first thing about river canoeing. I haven't the remotest notion of how to handle this magnificent setting-pole."

"Well, that old fellow said it was a quiet little river."

"Mm—the Devil's Elbow doesn't sound any too nice."

Of course in the end we set off for the west outlet, where we hove our belongings over a small dam, and had a wonderful feast of raspberries.

That guide was right: it was a nice quiet-looking river—

hardly more than a big brook. We could see that it started with a swirl just below the dam, but immediately flattened out and became peaceful. I climbed aboard, and crouched low in the bow, and the next moment there was a hair-raising quiet plunge —a rapid descending glide—and we came into deadwater with a rush, hardly knowing what had happened. That was the beginning.

We paddled through long stretches of shallow deadwater, and we had begun to wonder whether the river would ever show another spark of life, when, coming around a bend, we found ourselves in a slight current, with the thick grasses on the bottom all straining downstream; and then we heard an ominous rumble a little way off, increasing to a roar. Then the gleam of white water, with black jagged rocks sticking through it, the river seething and hissing. It was impossible to tell which was rock and which masses of water eddying high. We tried to hesitate on the brink, but there was no hesitating—down it all went, pell-mell. We hit a big, round rock full on; and Nick in the stern saw to his horror and despair an enormous bulge traveling rapidly down the bottom of the canoe toward him—much faster than it can be written—making a frightful racket of scraping and tearing on the canvas. When it got to the middle of the canoe, he saw the pack lift up several inches and then settle down again. And then, almost under his very feet, he heard a plank smash, and saw four ribs snap, one after another—prrrttt!—only much louder—the splintered ends sticking right up in the air. This was obviously the end, he thought—no boat built could stand it. In a minute water would be spurting in the whole length of her gashed bottom. But to his amazement, she ran down healthily into the quieter water below the rapids, and she seemed sound and tight as ever. He kept on going through the forms of guiding her, although he didn't believe in it.

"I guess Allen was right about the flexible bottom," he said, and his voice quavered.

Again and again we lived through this performance of coming around a bend—the preliminary rumble, the frightful rush of water, our headlong mad descent, slamming against rocks with loud crackings and tearings and destruction. After four or five of these places, we began to have a notion of how to avoid some of the rocks. And when we came to what we immediately recognized as the Devil's Elbow, where a mighty volume of water plunged down between two grim black jags, and went around a corner at the same time, Nick steered through faultlessly. However, at the next place we crashed some more. We were getting used to it by now, but we still didn't understand what was holding the old bones together.

We thanked heaven for stretches of deadwater between these rapids. During them we could rest and think, and look at the deer, of which there were many. They peered at us out of undergrowth by the river's edge, then galloped away with magnificent bounds. Once we came into a sort of pond with shallow, marshy shores, and here a big buck was swimming, browsing contentedly among water-lily pads, pulling them up by the roots. We stalked him, by sea, as quietly as we could; but when we were within fifty feet of him he decided he'd better get ashore, which he did in a hurry—then bounded off through the swamp, long-stemmed lily pads still dangling from his jaws.

Indian Pond was not so far away now. We were anxious to make camp and turn the canoe bottom-up to survey the damage. The river fell into that pond in a dickens of a hurry, and down we went so fast that a fleeting glimpse of a big sporting-camp on the shore was superimposed on a green island farther on. We struck out for that island as fast as weary arms would let us, took the packs out, and, lifting Old Bones tenderly, turned her upside down. She didn't fall to pieces.

We bent eagerly over her. And again we could not believe our eyes. The shellac, by which old Allen set so much store, was scratched in many places. The canvas itself was laid bare in one spot the size of a postage stamp. Old Bones was complete, whole, unharmed. Better than ever, because of course, with seven or eight more broken ribs, her bottom was still more flexible.

"Well, this is 'the bush,' all right," said Nick, next morning.

It was. The trail had started out well from Indian Pond, where we had put on our hobnailed boots and left Bones in the freight station. We had inquired about this trail, and heard that it was in fair shape right through to The Forks. "Might have one or two rough places, you know, but nothing to trouble you any."

So now we stood where the trail had petered out and abandoned us, in a shoulder-high jungle of raspberry bushes and half-rotten, charred windfalls lying in a tangle.

"I don't see that short shorts have much use here," I said.

We climbed into our dungarees and rolled our shirt-sleeves *down*. Then we fought raspberries and other undergrowth for a long time.

"Strenuous!" Nick said. He was wringing wet. "I move we stop and—well, we can't sit down, but we can eat raspberries. And you never saw raspberries any bigger and better than these —that's one consolation."

"Pretty gloomy country, though. I hate the remains of forest fires. Do you know how much of this there is?"

He shook his head. "Obviously, a few miles of it can hold us up for days. D'you see a trace of trail anywhere?"

"No, but I see an old broken-down telephone line, which is probably where the trail would be if there were one."

"We'll follow it if we can," he decided. "Funny, to get our bush-whacking here, where we didn't expect it, and none at all in that wild stretch just after Katahdin."

"Oh, well, life's like that."

We took turns breaking trail. Little by little we pounded ahead, shielding our faces, wrestling, battering, climbing over and under the wreckage left by fire.

"We aren't going to make The Forks tomorrow, that's a cinch," I said.

"No, we aren't—and food's kinder low, old girl."

"Lots of raspberries."

"Can't live on raspberries, and work like this. Sugar's almost gone. And that's the most uncomfortable thing to be without—wait and see."

The next three miles or so took us the rest of the day. And then, just as the first shadows of dark came, we found ourselves at the edge of an oasis which somehow the fire had missed—tall green firs and spruces on a steep bank high above the river, which roared and gleamed wickedly white below.

"It's a fine place to camp," said Nick.

A tiny narrow path led down through ferns and young trees. It was doubtless made by deer going to drink, and we liked the idea of sharing it with them. We built our fire on a gravel beach, and watched the river surge past.

"We're marooned," said Nick. "A green island with river on one side and raspberries on all the others."

"Think we'd better whack our way back to Indian Pond?"

"Well, I'd thought of it. But as a matter of fact, I'd like to try a little more, if you're game for it tomorrow. This stuff may not last, and I'm curious about it."

"I'm with you."

He looked at me gratefully. "You're as good as any gipsy going," he said. "And lots cleaner than most."

More raspberries, more desolate and tangled country. But a little less difficult. A few comparatively open spaces. Blueberries, big as Concord grapes. And then, like people walking out of a desert into a cool greenness, we came to the edge of woods—evergreen woods, glades of moss. But still no trail. We scrambled along the tops of ledges high above the river, with blueberries and spruces and gray reindeer moss growing on them.

Nightfall found us still more than half a day's walk from The Forks; and we had to build our supper fire in the rain. As for supplies, in the morning we saw the last of the cocoa boil up, without sugar, and the last of the flour go into a small batch of pancakes. I was heating the little frying-pan, when I remembered something else.

"We haven't any grease," I said.

"No bacon fat?"

"Not a scrap."

"Well...? There must be something greasy around somewhere."

We examined sky, trees...

"Boot grease!" I exclaimed.

"Haven't any."

"Ought to, then.... Well, never mind. I'll use a little salt. But they'll stick."

"I have it!" said Nick. He fished in a pack pocket, and held up a small stump of candle! "Rub that around on the pan," he suggested.

It worked....

We walked through a greenish drizzle of rain, waded across a troublesomely big tributary of the Kennebec, climbed over some more ledges, rich with moss of every conceivable green and gray, and the bright crimson and yellow-brown of sphagnum. Snowberries, with their tiny dark leaves and frost-white berries, grew in thick mats on the moss. We stopped in the rain and ate lunch, our last crumb or two of chocolate.

At last a path promised easier going. It led us into an old lumber camp where we ravaged a blackberry patch. Then we pushed on, still through misty rain, downhill and uphill, across swamps and fields and often among big trees. The trail got better. It developed into what had once been a lumber road—narrow and bumpy, to be sure, but perhaps once passable for a strong cart with a strong-minded driver. This we followed down into a cow pasture. Ahead of us now were a couple of houses—The Forks.

At this moment we were confronted by the blank back side of a large signboard on a tree. Curious, we passed it and turned to see what it was all about. It said in large black letters: CAUTION. NARROW ROAD.

Since it was raining and we pretty tired, we decided to be snooty tonight and sleep in town. A large white farmhouse announced rooms, and we went inquiring. An old farmer, very thin and tall, with scant gray hair and blue eyes, came to the door and asked us in. Yes, they had rooms. He called in a quavery voice: "Hattie! Hattie! Here's some boys wants a room for the night." We went into a warm, deliciously warm kitchen, and there was Hattie, with her white hair piled high on her head, and her inquisitive, half-startled smile. All this, the warmth and homeliness of the kitchen, the vague scents of hay and of apples, and the two old folks, were the essence of one part of New England, just as quiet woods and hills were the essence of another part.

Hattie was very much interested in what we were doing. She wanted to know the details of our life out-of-doors. Her voice was gentle, a little cracked and weary, but there was a ring of wisdom and understanding in it.

"I see," she said, "you just go where you want to, sleep when you want to..."

Gaily she mocked her husband because he had taken me for a boy. "Why, I could tell right away you warn't no boy," she said.

The old man wanted to know where we had come from; and when we told him about our trip through from Indian Pond, he shook his head cynically and murmured: "Aye, a bit o' fussy doon, that! Real fussy doon." We wanted his advice, as that of one to whom all this country was an open book, on the best way of getting up Dead River. He had logged hereabouts all his life. He pawed over our maps, marked them for us obligingly, but it was plain he felt scorn for these civilized trappings.

"You folks got a lot o' maps," he half protested. And then he admitted grudgingly: "Most of 'em's pretty near right, too."

There was scarcely any "fussy doon" at all along Dead River. A little shadow-flecked road; a deserted lumber camp the first night; next day the little road again. At noon we took a bath in a swirling rocky pool, along with some very young trout. The second night we camped beside a basin deep enough to swim in. The current was about as swift as we were, and we laughed at the sensation of swimming vigorously and staying in the same place, like fish that poise on flickering fins, heads upstream. The river slid under our naked bellies.

Dead River Dam, at about noon the third day. We ate lunch, and surveyed the country with mistrust. Above the dam were six long miles of deadwater, with frightful tangled marsh on each side.

"What did old Kennedy say we should do here?"

"He said we could find a trail over those hills—but that seems pretty roundabout. I think I've got a better idea."

"Another of your inspirations?"

He pointed to a curious object on the muddy bank: three logs nailed together with a plank across them at each end, lashed with rotten rope. "Remains of a raft," he observed. "We'll fix it up and paddle up this confounded deadwater!"

We looked around, and gathered together some more planks and a few rusty spikes; and with these unpromising materials

Nick contrived a very creditable raft. His performance was so deft and rapid that it had a touch of the black arts, and I eyed the craft with some suspicion.

"Handsome creature. What'll we call her?"

"'Quinquireme of Nineveh from distant Ophir,'" he chanted, "'Rowing home to haven…'"

"But she can't be a quinquireme," I protested, "with two paddles."

"Never mind—that's what we'll call her. Make us feel as if we had lots of power aboard."

We stood around and admired the quinquireme for a while; then put the duffle aboard, got aboard ourselves—she wabbled—and shoved off from the bank—she wabbled—paddling hard with some planks.

"She wabbles," I protested.

"Never mind about that," said Nick. "Paddle. See 'f we can make her move."

We couldn't. "We'll wear ourselves out before we get her any six miles," I mourned.

"Maybe poles would work better. We could get some traction on the bottom then."

Poles did work better. The bank, grayish mud, sloped off steep, so we were able to keep close to it without getting stuck too often. I stood forrad, Nick aft, and we pulled and shoved strenuously; but no matter how hard we labored, the quinquireme would not be hurried. Come nightfall we were still far from the end of the deadwater, so there was nothing for it but to camp. We picked a place where the bank was fairly high—a little above the swamp level.

"Sing me to sleep, lullaby of the—mosquitoes," Nick intoned drowsily, as vagrant airplanes howled outside the black netting. "Lord, I'm weary."

"Maybe it would have been less strenuous to go round over the hills, after all," I suggested.

"But not so much fun."

"Course not."

Early next evening, after a morning of poling and an afternoon of bush-whacking, we pulled into the town called Dead River Post Office.

It was just that—a post office. Half a mile or so down the road was a farm. Two miles the other way, another farm. That was the town.

We walked into the post office, and it seemed that the floor gave way giddily beneath our hobnailed boots. We slid a little, and regained balance. We wondered if being in the woods so long had somehow unfitted us for floors; then we saw that this floor sloped decidedly nor'-nor'-east.

The postmaster, having seen us go in, had come from his house next door and was busy unlocking the office. He fumbled with his keys, seemed unused to them. The office was festooned with cobwebs.

"You folks been hikin', I s'pose?"

We told him we had come down from Katahdin.

"My, that be some ways, that be," the old fellow commented, nodding his head.

"We've a great liking for the woods and hills," we confided.

A smile brightened his wrinkled face. "Wal, I've a likin' for 'em meself," he told us. "You know, one time I lived way down south in Floridy. Ever been to Floridy, you folks? Wal, there ain't a mountain in sight bigger 'n an ant-heap. Many's the time I've waked up in the mornin' wishin' I could look into the side of a mountain. There's somethin' about mountains—and the big trees. I been loggin' hereabouts most o' my life."

"You know Jim Kennedy at The Forks, don't you?" we asked. "If you're Sam Parsons, he wanted to be remembered to you."

"Sam Parsons I be. Let's see, now.... Jim Kennedy... sure, I remember! I used to log with Jim and all the rest o' them boys, years back. Sure!"

We said we'd like a couple of stamps—added apologetically that we hated to bother him, but we'd been in the woods a pretty long time now, and had some letters to get off. He nodded, and seemed to sympathize, but the whole problem evidently baffled him. He bent down out of sight behind the window of his little cage. We waited. We heard papers rattling; we ventured to look in. Sam Parsons was in the midst of a dusty wreckage of folders, cards, slips of different colors—all the post office paraphernalia in chaotic disorder.

"Wonder where I could have put them blessed things!" He unlocked drawers, peered into dim corners.

We were worried now—afraid we were imposing on him, asking altogether too much. "Oh, never mind," we said hastily. He reappeared from the depths.

"Sorry, folks, I can't think... guess I must be all sold out o' stamps."

We asked him if there was any chance of buying a little food somewhere hereabouts. He stood considering.

"Well, I guess my wife would sell you a few things—nothing fancy, you know."

"Oh, all we want is a little corn meal and some sugar," we assured him.

We bought these from a smiling, rosy-cheeked woman who consulted us conscientiously as to what we thought a pound of sugar ought to cost.

In the end we pitched our tent in Sam Parsons' apple orchard, and for supper brewed our largest pot full of apple-sauce. The next day we did the same. We could not bring ourselves to leave while there were still so many apples lying on the ground; so we rested our weary muscles, and mended our weary clothes, and ate apple-sauce all day.

Whenever we could, we camped on islands. Even if they consist of one rock, one bush, and one turtle sitting in the sun, there is always glamour about them. Which explains why we headed promptly for one as soon as we had collected Old Bones from the station at Oquossoc, and got her headed outward on the first of the Rangeley Lakes. This island was quite large, and had good spruce woods on it, also what looked like an abandoned house. And it had a beach to land on.... But was it a beach? We drew closer... it was artificial! Someone had cleared away all the rocks from a short strip of shore, and piled them high on either side, leaving a low sandy stretch. This was hemmed in not only by the piles, which must have amounted to tons and tons of rocks, but also by two enormous tree-trunks, one on either side —trunks such as only a whole gang of laborers could have put in place.

We wondered....

A neat path led back into the woods. Beside it was a curious shed, long and narrow and high, as if it meant to house a motor-launch. The trouble was, no motor-launch could possibly have gone through the narrow doorway. We studied the shed some more. Wide planks stood upright against a strange, rounded roof. As we stared, this roof gradually took on a familiar look; and suddenly it dawned upon us that it was simply a big dory upside-down!

A few yards further, we stopped to stare at another marvel. The front end of a motor-boat, which had been vertically sawed in half across the middle, stood upside-down on stilts two or three feet high. For no reason at all, apparently. It was just there.

Nick drew in his breath sharply, and passed a hand over his eyes, as if something was wrong with them. Neither of us said anything, but the farther we went, the more we doubted our senses. We saw the ruin of what had been a solid little house, with a pleasant lawn and birch trees around it; and we saw an unfinished three-sided log shelter like those in the White Mountains—but these were ordinary enough. We also saw an enormous hole in the ground with several huge beams laid across the top of it—beams such as only a good deal of power could have put there. We saw a block of stone about four feet square and two feet thick, set off from the ground on two chunks of stove wood. We found a deep passage into the ground, partly filled with sawdust. Ice might once have been kept there. We found a pile of old bed-springs. We found cages and chicken-coops. We found paths through shrubbery; and flowers, now uncared for—poppies, pansies, marigolds, peonies, red and white roses. We found cisterns—a deep iron tank sunk into the ground; and another one built of stones. Any number of strange holes, serving no apparent purpose. Rock-piles, corresponding with the holes. Old iron boiler tanks.

"What do you make of it?" I asked.

"It looks to me," said Nick, "as if at least ten persons, of gigantic strength and completely crazy, had been turned loose here and allowed to carry on for some years."

This idea was anything but reassuring. We explored cautiously toward the other end of the island, and found the remains of another garden. We were pretty scared now, so that ordinary currant bushes, carefully potted, had an air of mystery. There were also gooseberries, grape vines, raspberries. And a blackberry patch. But not a real one. This was going too far. This was Alice-in-Wonderland stuff. Enormous arching tentacles reached up and outward... thorns half an inch long... berries, just beginning to ripen, each berry as big as or bigger than a crab-apple.

It was like some fantastic, frightening dream, peopled with shapes and shadows—ludicrous, grotesquely distorted.

We fetched our canvas water-bucket. I crept in around the

outer fringes of that blackberry patch, a fit habitation for the Macbeth witches, or any other witches. Plunk, plunk—keplunk! I dropped the berries into the bucket. We tasted one, each taking a large bite out of it... sweet and juicy, and tasted like a blackberry. Plunk, plunk! In ten minutes that bucket was full.

Slowly the palpitating of our hearts grew less, as we began to adapt ourselves to these incongruous surroundings. We built a fire and ate supper on a dock affair—another of those giant tree-trunks on the shore—and we watched the moon rise, full, pale gold, while we ate enormous quantities of blackberries with Klim and brown sugar. No monsters descended or ascended. Life went calmly on. We cut the usual fir boughs, and spread them on the floor of the unfinished log shelter. A quiet talk, a long sleep. In the morning another bucket of blackberries, and a swim. Then we piled our belongings into Bones, and pushed off from that perhaps enchanted shore, leaving Mysterious Island wrapped in its sinister yet comic mystery.

The old canoe was full of grub. Nothing to worry about, then; nothing to do but paddle. When we came to a good place, we stopped and swam. It was a peaceful, swinging life, full of sunshine, without special adventure. It needed no adventure beyond itself.

Mooselookmeguntic narrowed and merged into Mollychunkamunk—a silver-gray lake when we came to it in late afternoon. And another island was ours that night—a very little island, just big enough for our tent, two spruces and a fir on a moss carpet, a fringe of rocks and a few blueberry bushes around the shore. It was not in the least mysterious, but very lovely in the lake's silver solitude.

We awoke to look out into mist rising densely off the water. Brush sticking through that mist looked witch-like, black and bare in a soft white infinity. A faint splashing, and a string of brown ducks slid by, just outside our front door. They were the sole inhabitants of this white world. They quacked, twisting their necks from side to side. They sculled along gracefully, the water edged with silver at the base of their slender necks. Now and then the vigorous kick of a yellow foot would send a ripple over into the hollow of a smoothly feathered back—a big drop would glisten there silvery and ephemeral, and roll off like quicksilver. They trailed out into the mist, little brown ghosts.

The last of the blackberries for breakfast, on top of our oatmeal. And then we glided on, past more good green woods, with occasional big fish-hawks perched on overhanging branches; now and then a fish leaping—a flash of silver scaled in swift sunlight; a loon crying his heart-broken cry along marshy shores. We swam—arched elbows and the slip of silver past brown shoulders. A seagull gliding—a shaft of white light.

Came a dam—Lower Dam—we hoisted Bones out of water, and carried her tenderly, with aching arms—heavy old gal!—up one bank and down another and set her into Welookbanticook, the next lake. And glided on.

Another sleep, and, next day, another dam. This was a more extensive affair. Bones would somehow have to be transported three miles overland before she could be put into Umbagog, the last of the Rangeley chain. There were a few houses at this Middle Dam, and one of them was a sporting camp, a semi-stylish place, with deer's antlers on the walls, and a shiny desk in one corner. Some fat old men sat in rockers on the porch. The proprietor was evoked. He was also old and fat; worse still, he was grumpy. He didn't like us; he didn't like the weather; he obviously hadn't had a good breakfast. Five dollars his price, and he couldn't be bothered talking about it, and the sooner we got out of there the better for everybody concerned.

We got out, and eventually struck a bargain with a jovial,

rosy-cheeked guide who said he would take us over to Umbagog, bag, baggage, and canoe, for three dollars.

His auto was one of the old Stars. To this he hitched a wabbly trailer only half as long as the canoe, and to this he lashed half of Bones over and under and around, with yards of rope. They piled the luggage and me into the back seat; Nick got in front, and with many squeaks and creakings the caravan set out.

"How's the road?" Nick inquired.

"Oh, it's a dandy little road," our guide told us proudly.

We pulled over a grassy bank, and were confronted by a gate. Nick hopped out and unfastened it, and it rolled smoothly open on a cart-wheel. We passed through on to what seemed a very fair specimen of a narrow country lane.

"Keep an eye on the canoe, won't you?" Nick warned me.

I peered through the small back window. Bones seemed to be following us smoothly enough.

Nick was interested to know how the old fellow had got his Star in to Middle Dam. No roads went to it, as far as he knew. By barge from South Arm, a landing-place across the lake, seemed the most likely way.

"Oh, no! There's a road."

"Where is that?" Nick asked.

"Through the woods from over by the Magalloway."

"What sort of a road is it?" Nick inquired.

"Wal, it's good enough. I got my car in seven years ago. 'Bout six miles, it is. Took four men and six horses to get me here; three-day job, it was."

We went over a little bounce. I peeked back anxiously just as the trailer also hit the bounce. As the trailer went up, the stern half of the canoe, overhanging behind, sagged abruptly downward, only to spring up again as the trailer went down. Bones waggled both ends limply a minute, and then subsided.

"Say, Nick—"

But he was lost in conversation. He was curious to know whether it was possible to run in a canoe the stretch of river between these two lakes. We had at first considered doing it.

"Wal, you might." The old guide was frank to admit the possibility. "One party tried it three years ago. They smashed up —went all to pieces."

This "dandy little road" we were on became narrower and ruttier, though I could see that it was a paved highway compared to the one through the woods from over by the Magalloway. Grass grew in the middle, and we scraped the brush on each side. I didn't like the way Bones was reacting, as if she had neither ribs nor planks—which, of course, was not far from the truth. I noticed now that she was lashed so tight that the rope drew her sides together a little—there was a sort of pucker in each gunwale—and the back edge of the trailer made a ridge across her bottom, like a mole tunnel. She waved her free hind end up and down, bending in the middle of her back. I expected at any moment to see her snap clean in two.

"Nicky, listen—"

We hit something in the road that must have been nearly the size of Katahdin. There was a back-breaking jar and crash; and car, trailer, canoe, and ourselves rode up in the air and down. My head hit the roof and I saw many stars. When I could see anything else, I looked back, fully expecting to see half a canoe on the trailer; but Bones was riding along at ease and whole, waggling from her middle, quite unperturbed. Such things were nothing to her. I know now that she was undefeatable, and bore a charmed life.

With horrible jarrings and crackings, we pulled up by the shore of Umbagog. The old guide unlashed Bones, and her gunwales resumed their normal curve. He and Nick lifted her down, and the mole-ridge in her bottom vanished. We put the packs in her, and the carton of grub, and our hobnailed boots.

"Got a good bow-man there?" the guide smiled.

"Sure have."

"Thought it was the young brother, first."

"Well, it is, in a way.... Here you are—thanks a lot."

And we were gliding down along the east shore of Umbagog in mid-afternoon sunlight, as serenely as if Middle Dam had been only a wild interlude in a peaceful dream. Except for a slight headache.... There were birch trees in the dream. Their reflections were a sinuous tangle of shifting black and white shadows in silky water.

A long, narrow arm of water, with a beach at the end of it—Tyler Cove. We pitched the tent on a hillock just back of the beach, then swam. It was not until we were cooking supper afterwards that we noticed the beginning of a majestic parade of thunderheads in the western sky. They were far away and hardly real. We went on cooking, unconcerned, over a dream of a little fire of white cedar. The thunderheads surged up, black with marvellous curled edges of light. They came fast, wind with them. The sky was slate-gray and tense around them; the lake reflected it. Gray waves edged with foam struck gloomily at the sand.

"Good Lord! That storm's coming a mile a minute. Let's get the grub under cover—quick!"

Over went the good old canoe, her solid back to the wind; and under her protecting wings went our carton of grub. Those thunderheads were shutting out the whole world, now; and they were pretty noisy about it—gashed and split and torn to black rags by spears of lightning.... We looked up from our job just in time to see an immense sheet of rain sweep the bay, eclipsing everything, and as we turned and ran for our little tent above the beach, the first drops struck like hailstones.

We buckled down the front flap at a sharp angle, and tested the lines. They seemed firm enough, although the tent shook and quivered as the trees to which it was moored thrashed in the wind. We had a dismal vision of that tent spreading sudden wings and taking flight in the middle of the storm, leaving us exposed to furious skies....

Storm? Where was it now, anyway? After that first flurry, wind and rain had both gone strangely still. They were hanging around somewhere, waiting and listening. Sly devils, leering out from behind cosmic tree-trunks, watching. It was very dark, an unnatural dark that rumbled and growled and was shot with fire. The storm was holding off, in ambush. We were frightened, and wished it would come and get done with it, and demolish us, if it was going to. Not so good to lie in our sleeping-bags just waiting to be demolished, and listen to the rumbling of celestial innards.

I recoiled from the floor of the tent as if it had exploded. A slight movement under me—a crackle that sounded, against my ear-drum, loud as a forest fire.

"Whatever is the matter with you?" asked Nick.

I wiped my forehead. The air was lifeless and hot. "Some damn bug," I said. "Crawling around under the tent—almost in my ear. How can I sleep with my head on a clawing beetle?"

I shifted ground, and tried again. Sleep? With that impending cataclysm thrashing around overhead? Besides, it was worth listening to! A livid blue-green flare lit up the forest, and out of it, as if evoked by lightning, came the deep-voiced melancholy cry of an owl, like a lost spirit without a body drifting among the trees. A crash of thunder buried the owl. But then, out of tense silence, a ghostly echo—an answer from far-away hills.

I shivered, and could have bristled like a cat. "Lord, what a chorus it is! Storm growling, *bass*; trees listening, *sotto voce*; and owls..."

"Wait till the loons hop on it, *mezzo-soprano*," said Nick.

They did. A long, quavering wail rose out of the lake—a wail, or was it a laugh?—insane, heart-broken; and its answer, two notes lower, a little farther off. A shaft of fire speared them, but their ghosts went on talking.

"This is almost too much for anybody," I said. "I wish it would rain—or something."

A mosquito overhead was louder than an airplane. He tormented one ear, while the subterranean scratchings went on below the other. The chorus was growing. Somewhere a dog howled desolately, as if he had just had the disappointment of his life. And the owls went on, and the thunder, and the trees, and every now and then the loons. A big bull-frog joined, and croaked raucously from the beach: "Awk! Awk!" And sly and wary movements and rustlings were all around us.

And then, just outside, one of the most disheartening sounds the woods know how to make—the jarring snap, half snarl and half grunt, of whatever breed of toad it is to whom that noise is a natural method of expression.

It was too much, even for Nick. He snapped on the flashlight, and shot a piece of night with it, but caught only a little porcupine ambling about outside the front flap.

"Imagine anything, even a toad, having the heart to do that on a night like this!" he mumbled. It went off again, with a horrid rasp.

"He would park right by us, too."

The owl again, the dog, the loons, and the toad. The porky rustling. Lightning... thunder... owl. Witches were abroad. The forest was an unearthly pandemonium.

Sunshine next morning seemed unreal and a mistake. We eyed it mistrustfully, and stepped into it without confidence. But it warmed us. It made fairies dance on the lake. The lake was enticing, and so we swam again. It was iridescent, over ripples of sand. We forgot to put our clothes on, and then it occurred to us that now was a good time to repair them again.

Voices, talking and laughing, at the other end of the beach. A slender man and his small daughter, both in bathing suits, came out of the woods, carrying pails and shovels, and a fish-net. I slipped into shorts and shirt, and strolled down the beach.

The man was absorbing sun on top of a big boulder, while the little girl, net in hand, paddled around after small minnows that chased up and down across a golden pattern of ripple reflections. I climbed to the top of a neighboring boulder, and said good morning.

"Why, good morning!" he exclaimed. "Are you the guardian mermaid, or naiad or dryad, of this beach?"

"I don't know. Do mermaids live in tents? I rather doubt it."

"Oh, that's your tent, is it?"

"Yes, and that—" I waved my arm down the beach, "is my husband. He's diligently sewing, but I can't be bothered—when the sun is shining. We've come down from Katahdin."

"On foot?"

"Partly—but partly in Bones. Bones is that overturned object you behold on the beach."

"Some might call it a canoe," he suggested.

"I'm not committing myself. She has a very flexible bottom," I explained.

His smile was pleasing, but just a little crooked, a little wistful. "Your husband," he remarked, "looks like Robinson Crusoe."

I looked at Nick impersonally for the first time in many weeks. I saw a solid figure, well-muscled and well-browned, sitting cross-legged on the sand, bent over his sewing. And I noticed especially the majestic red and black beard behind which he had been gradually disappearing for some time.

"Doesn't he, though?" I agreed. "But he's really rather nice."

"Because he does the family sewing?" my friend queried.

"That's part of it," I granted. "I loathe sewing."

"You know, I'd like to hear about that trip of yours—all the way from Katahdin. You must be stout pioneers."

"Come on down," I urged, "and meet Sir Robin."

We all sat in the sun and talked, while the brown-haired small daughter ran busily up and down. And it turned out that Mr. Jackson understood us. He was a New York insurance man on a vacation; he looked as though he had been chained to an office desk most of his life; and yet, mysteriously, he was one of us. He understood the joy of open places. He knew about packs and boots, tents and campfires, fir beds and stars, rough trails and dawn over mountain peaks. He nodded his head with quiet appreciation. His pleasing brown eyes were lit with vicarious excitement and pleasure, which changed to a look of intense desire, and then a stare of longing. The story came to an end—or rather, it got to Tyler Cove, and stopped there to bask in the sun.

But not for long. "Listen here, Mr. and Mrs. Crusoe. You're shifting camp tonight. Come on over and pitch in my back pasture. All the apples you want. I don't want to lose you. You make me feel young and sentimental again. Besides, I want my wife to know you—and her cake and coffee are of the best."

Mrs. Jackson came out on to the front porch to greet us. She was soft and round. She had a soft round rosy face, with too many chins, and gray hair of the wrong length that hung down straight. She looked older than Charlie by many years.

"Meet Mr. and Mrs. Crusoe," said Charlie.

She giggled. "Charlie says you're going to sleep in the pasture tonight," she began. "But won't you come and sleep in the house instead? We have plenty of room, and you'll be so much more comfortable."

I thanked her, but said we'd stick to the pasture—we really slept better out-doors. She looked at us in friendly vacancy, but Charlie's warm brown eyes registered comprehension.

"They're Romany Rye, Maggie," he explained. "Don't you see? They don't give a hoot for your nice clean comfortable bed. All they want is their stars." And he smiled again. "But they'll have some cake and coffee," he suggested. "Why don't you run and get it ready? From what they've been telling me, it's a dickens of a while since they've had anything resembling chocolate cake."

We sat around a cosy table in the dining-room, and there was a most magnificent cake. Maggie asked questions. She wanted to know what we did when it rained, what we ate and how we cooked it, if the bugs didn't bother us, and how we could stand all the funny noises in the woods at night. Charlie sat by in silence. When she had asked everything she could think of, she rested her elbows on the table, and began to talk about herself—to confide a long story.

"Charlie and I used to go on camping trips, too," she said. "When we were first married. Didn't we, Charlie? It's so long ago that I hardly remember it now, but we've still got a lot of old junk in the attic somewhere—pots and pans, tents, sleeping-bags—you never saw such a lot of useless old junk. We didn't go so strenuous as you people, because my health was never good. And then one time when we went, it just rained and rained, all the time. We stayed in the tent, waiting for it to clear up, and I got the fidgets, and the mosquitoes were something fierce. And I said then that that was the last time I'd go—I was done with it. And—" she recounted with pride— "I never did go again, either. Did I, Charlie? And then the baby came. Charlie wanted to go but he couldn't budge me." She giggled playfully. "I just had to have my hot baths and my gas stove. He wanted to go with an old college classmate of his, but I don't think a man should leave his family when he has such a short vacation anyway—do you? So we put all the old things away in the attic, and there I guess they'll stay." The fact satisfied her tremendously. She smiled with confidence.

So that was it!

I glanced toward Charlie's slender face. "Oh, no they won't!" he contradicted quietly. "They'll go with me and Joy, when she's old enough… a year or two more…. Won't they, pal?" he asked the little girl beside him.

"And what do you expect *me* to do then?" Mrs. Jackson queried grimly. There was a swift play of eyes….

It was sunset. "We must get along," said Nick, "and make camp. Fir boughs to get in… Thanks ever so…."

Charlie followed us out on to the cow trail to the back pasture. He was very quiet. We shook hands and said goodnight. Suddenly he waved his arm expansively toward house, woodshed, pond and dam and flower garden. In his sweeping gesture he included Maggie—he included the whole of his life, except perhaps his little daughter. "God, how I envy you!" he exclaimed. "I'd swap the whole of my outfit for yours—any day."

Canoe for sale! It was hard making up our minds to part with the old faithful. She had served us well. But now we were leaving behind us Maine and its network of lakes and rivers. Soon we would be crossing into New Hampshire, the next section of the Appalachian Trail. Soon we would be in familiar country that was much loved by both of us—the White Mountains.

So we peddled Bones. We put our possessions in her and nosed her along the shore of Umbagog. Whenever we passed a summer cottage, or a fisherman, or a solitary camper, or a sporting camp, we asked if they wanted a canoe—a good canoe, with a very flexible bottom.

For a long time nobody wanted to pay more than ten dollars for Bones, although we insisted that her bottom was one in a million. Her value, we thought, should have increased since we had bought her. This did not seem to be the case.

One elderly farmer wanted us to exchange her for a cow, but we couldn't quite see the use of that. Now, if it had been a donkey.... But a cow on the peaks of the White Mountains was a weird thought.

At last, somebody offered twelve dollars. Without further ado, we stepped out of the canoe and put on our packs, collected our money, and passed through to the road, foot-free. That was that!

It was raining slightly—a misty silent rain. The woods liked it. Leaves and needles were pearled with tiny drops, and moss was very green. We walked along slowly, humming.

"What's the date?" Nick asked me suddenly.

"Good Lord, how should I know?"

We reasoned quietly with this problem, and came to the conclusion that it was the first half of September.

"Which means," Nick said, "that the summer's getting on."

"We can't walk south fast enough to keep up with the summer, can we?"

"No, but we can stay out a good deal longer. Till November, say."

"And then...?"

"Well, then we've got to go back to work, haven't we?"

"You do think of the morbidest possibilities, Nicky. All the way from Katahdin you've shown absolute genius for it. Eaten by bears, stuck in the mud, starved to death—and now—back to work."

"Well, what else can we do?"

"Anything! Keep going to Georgia on snowshoes. Or, perhaps better, buy a sack of beans and some corn meal, and shack it out for the winter."

"Would you, Bar? Strenuous!"

"Course I would. The crunch of hobnails. The soft whispers of mist.

"And next summer," I continued, "we'll proceed on our interrupted way toward Georgia—Appalachian Trail."

"You know," Nick said, "we haven't got money enough to buy salt enough to put on a small sparrow's tail."

"You forget we've just collected twelve good dollars. At least, I hope they're good."

He thought it over. "You're right," he announced. "We'd better stay out if we possibly can—not let the machines and mothballs get us—the way they've got the Jacksons."

"We've melted too much into the landscape," I said. "We'll never again be able to unmelt."

"Well, you like it, don't you? Aren't you glad you decided to come with me?"

"I couldn't do anything else," I admitted. "You know, I'm even glad you cut my hair off."

"It's waving in the wind very pleasantly," he said.

"I almost think you married me just for the fun of cutting it off."

"Well, that was part of it, of course," he conceded. "But then, I didn't want to walk all the way to Georgia alone. And incidentally—I liked you a little, child."

"Oh!"

We came around a green bend, and I stooped to pick up a small object in the road.

"What've you got there?"

I held it up—a battered nickel.

"That settles it!" I said. "You see how luck is with us."

"We'll get to Georgia yet," said Nick. "Even without a donkey."

APPENDIX 3: WALKING THE MALLORCAN COAST

Mallorca, Thursday [April 1933]

Dear Helen:

This is already an expedition worth writing about, or at least taking notes about, so here I am, sitting in the sun in the middle of a little glade carpeted with flowers, in a sort of sand-dune country just back of the sea, with pine trees soughing quite realistically in the wind. I am writing shorthand—rather slowly and haltingly now, to be sure, but at least it is quicker than longhand.

In this letter I am not, as you will see, going to say much about the places of so-called historic interest. I may be cracked and all that, but that isn't my concern with life. To tell the truth, I am not interested in the insides of cathedrals or even monasteries, and I am not going to bother with them. I am interested in the country itself and in what I can do about it with arms and legs. Besides, plenty of people go to see cathedrals and write very dull books and articles about them. Did anyone ever glorify carabineros, though? You will just have to take this as it comes.

I am writing what seems good to me—what awakens a keen response in me.

This is the fourth day out. As you know, we did very little all winter except chum around in Palma with some amusing people we met, or sit in cafés to keep warm and read and write. I had begun to think we never should do anything much except that—just fall into the usual Spanish way of life. But now that is being changed with a vengeance.

We lit out very abruptly, because the Virginian with whom we had been staying suddenly got himself a new "wife"—he has already had several since he has been here—so there wasn't room for us any more. We borrowed a blanket from the picturesque "dueña" of our old pension, chucked some belongings in the pack and—started out. Just like that.

We are having a spell of very slick weather—clear blue sky all day, a growing moon at night, good sunshine but with enough wind to keep it from being too hot. Apparently this is just the right time of year for an excursion of this sort. It is spring. The bare, barren, rocky hills and valleys are much greener now, and there are flowers everywhere, very interesting ones. For instance, there are things that look something like wild roses, only a trifle more lavender in shade. They have curious crinkly petals, like tissue paper; no fragrance (also like tissue paper), and grow fairly high without thorns in glorious masses all over the place. There are scores of very tiny flowers, some little creeping ones growing close to the ground—yellow, and all shades of red, and a good rich blue. There are red lily-like things growing wild. There are extraordinary little orchids. And poppies! Masses of flagrant blazing poppies growing absolutely wild and uncared for among fields of lush green wheat! There are tall yellow flowers and small ones that look like buttercups that have gone a bit out of their heads, and yellow daisies, and things that look like daisies, and then things that really are daisies. And a climbing flower that grows thickly in places, that has thorns and looks and smells like a very small wild rose. But perhaps that is enough about the flowers—only it has been so cold and dank and dreary all winter, and we have been so rather discouraged about Mallorca and with a decided tendency to be cynical and "debunk" the whole thing, that these masses of wild flowers shooting up everywhere seem like the Garden of Eden come true.

The first night out from Palma we spent in a place that has almost a sacred significance to us. It was the Moorish watch-tower that we discovered shortly after we arrived here and wanted so much to live in, only we couldn't: the owner of the land wouldn't have it. It is a magnificent structure, maybe a thousand years old and certainly 750 years old. These towers are built at frequent intervals all around the coast, left over from the days when the Moors owned this island. (There's some history for you—about all you're likely to get, too!) Of all those we have seen, this particular one is by far the best. It is just a simple structure of big blocks of stone, with a door about halfway up it and a big room inside with a beautiful domed ceiling, a fireplace, and a well full of perfectly good rain water which runs down from the roof, to which there is the best little circular stairway you ever saw. You make two complete turns going up it, and the stairs themselves are not more than eighteen inches wide. Really delightful. It is a pretty hard job to get into this tower, because the old wooden stairway outside has been broken away, and there is nothing but a couple of ropes hanging from the doorway, together with what footholds can be found in the crumbly old sandstone. So we had a most amusing time of it. We cut our bed from a kind of bushy, piny, broomy thing that grows around there, and I passed the cuttings up to Nick in bundles, tying them on to one of the ropes, which he would then haul up. Then we passed our own traps up. Shortly after that, at sunset, we had our supper on the roof, overlooking coves and beaches and headlands and hills. It was all very romantic and picturesque. There will be pictures later, but for the present try to imagine that tower, almost on the tip of a high rocky bluff jutting out into the sea. We have seen it in silhouette against sunsets—the high black headland, and that old tower at the top of it. On each side of this headland are long curving white beaches, where we have swum "en cueros," as they say here.

Well, there we were, ready to spend the night in the beloved tower that someone's prejudice had denied us as a dwelling place. From the doorway we could look out over the curious betwixt and between vegetation characteristic of this island, consisting of pines, bushy stuff in clumps, flowers that tend to bushy and clumpy. The country is very rocky and humpy, and gives an odd appearance of being both barren and in its own way luxuriant at the same time.

There were tracks of little animals—probably rats—here and there in the dirt on the floor of the tower. We felt very swell when we closed the massive old door, first pulling up the ropes by which we had entered—a sort of drawbridge effect, you see, to keep pirates out. We could see the moonlight outside through a couple of big cracks down the middle of the door.

In the night we were awakened by a rustling which came suspiciously from the region of the pack containing tomorrow's food. A Moorish mouse, we speculated? We lit a candle and went exploring. The small flickerings of that little candle lit up the whole big domed room, casting eerie shadows. No mouse. It had become a ghost again. After a while the dawn came, and the sun thrust a ray through a hole in the eastern wall (by the way, the walls themselves are almost seven feet thick!); growing red spots appeared on the opposite wall, as if the sandstone were red-hot. We got up then. The sea was a soft misty blue, and a native fishing-boat, one of those with lateen rig, was becalmed out in the little eastern cove. The sea, the boat, and the circle of hills were all rather dreamy looking. The shadow of the tower itself stretched out for miles and miles, dark and menacing, over the countryside to the west. Nick tied one of the ropes around under my arms and let me down, and I walked around the old tower a couple of times, admiring how that little fragrant half-rose-like vine had climbed up it here and there. It was good to see those new, young flowers clinging against a wall that was maybe a thousand years old. Nick showed tremendous courage all of a sudden, and insisted on lowering himself into the old well—an idea that was fascinating in its horror—and exploring it to find out how big it was! He had a notion that it extended clear under the floor of the room—in fact, that the whole lower half of the tower was one gigantic cistern. However, this proved not to be the case. Our visions of Moorish ichthyosaurs lurking below were shattered.

We did not go far that day, partly because we were tired from the sudden work of the day before, and partly because we wanted to spend most of the day swimming and sunning. But first we needed grub, so we went exploring to find the nearest "fonda." This turned out to be a hell of a lot farther than we had expected; we ended by walking in a long winding circle all over the countryside. Then we found a little place where we had been once before, where the proprietress, although a lovely person, speaks not a word of anything but Mallorquin dialect—not even honest-to-God Spanish. So we had a most amusing time. For instance, we desired eggs. She understood "huevos" all right, but we could not make her understand that we wanted her to hard-boil them for us until she had called in all the farm hands from the fields and got them to help! We got our "boracha" (a swell kind of leather flask which you will see sometime) filled up with good black wine, and went off again over the fields toward the sea-coast and the long white beach that by now we were yearning for.

Later that day we picked up our traps and went a mile and a half or so to Cala Viña, where we spent that night sleeping out in front of an enormous cave. I ought to tell you a little more about the general character of the sea-coast of this region. It is for the most part very cliffy—spectacular sandstone cliffs of a tawny color, sometimes reddish, sometimes almost golden in the sun—cliffs that have been gouged out by sea and wind and rain into all sorts of fantastic shapes and caves. You walk along, usually quite high above the sea, which is so clear and bright that you can count the stones on the bottom of it and see every flickering fish or black sea-urchin. Then, where it is sandy, the sea has a wonderful greenish-blue color, darkened here and there by patches of sea-weed, and fading off in the distance into a bright but rather dreamy misty blue far out. The most inviting-looking water you ever saw in your life. You walk along on the top of the cliffs that partially overhang this, and you are in the middle of that sort of piny, bushy country sheep seem to like and thrive on, for you often meet vast flocks of them grazing, every one of them with a bell around his neck so that the whole landscape is a-tinkle, as if alive. Then every once in a while the little "senda" or footpath you are following dips down suddenly toward the sea, and you find yourself on a grand little cove with cliffs rising sharply at either end of it and a snug, swell little white beach between them—and the water so sparkling that you have to swim. This is a "cala." There are a good many of them along this part of the coast, sometimes three or four in a row, with only a narrow high ridge between them.

You see mostly two sorts of persons in country like that: fishermen, with their picturesque big black and brown nets, and their boats, lying quietly against the side of a cliff, perhaps; and carabineros. These last are all our friends, it would seem, and they are all pretty good guys. One of the good things about them is that they talk real Spanish—naturally enough, since they are Spanish. They are all eagerness to help one in any way they can—showing you the way to wherever you want to go, going far out of their own way to guide you, feeding you whenever they have a chance, letting you sleep in their places, share their blankets. They live by twos and threes at frequent intervals all around the coast, and their job is to watch out for "contrabandistas" of which there are apparently a tremendous number, because there are seven hundred and more carabineros in this island alone! The Mallorquins are greedy after money (they have learned a lot of bad habits from the influx of tourists) and to that end they smuggle tobacco like the dickens and all. These carabineros live sometimes in little huts, but also sometimes they just camp out primitively in open caves. They have a couple of old black cooking-pots, wooden spoons, some blankets, a boracha, baskets for food, fishing tackle, guns. They take turns, moving about from one place to another within a certain area, usually staying about three days, then moving on again.

Our two special friends among them are José Calvo and Vicente Flores. The first is fairly young, the second fairly old, and they make as amusing a pair of "compañeros" as one could wish for—always joshing each other, kicking each other in the pants, thumbing their noses at each other, making jokes at each other's expense. These two have been very good to us. It was José who tried hard to get us the tower to live in; and every time we have met them they have given us a meal or strong black coffee in the afternoon. At Cala Viña, where we spent that second night, we learned from some other carabineros that these two of ours were at the next station, Cala Figuera, so we decided we would spend the next night with them. At Cala Viña Nick amused himself very much by borrowing a big pick from a "guardabosque" and hacking some curious old pieces of fossilized coral out of the sandstone. You could almost expect to find dinosaur bones.

We never get tired of rocky winding paths along the tops of cliffs, and of the joy of coming suddenly to one of those delicious little white beaches at the end of a long sharp cove of bright water. The third day, from Cala Viña to Cala Figuera, we also took in a very leisurely fashion. The country was just too good to hurry through. In the morning we went back to the little inn and got some more food, then collected our luggage and went on over a hill, through sparse pine woods until we came to a path that went down abruptly into a good place called Cala Portales, which consists of four little coves and beaches right close together, and a cave which seems to be a sort of headquarters for fishermen, since there are great heaps of black tarry nets there. We stopped at the best and privatest of the little beaches and swam naked; and after that I sat on the beach and wrote until I had practically finished the Ktaadn story. I was quite inspired.

Later we pushed on to Cala Figuera, which is the very southern-most tip of this side of the island. And sure enough—there was our friend José himself in the cave. He welcomed us with a tremendous burst of hospitality, and we fell to talking Spanish in good style. A little later the older fellow, Flores, pulled in, and things were still better then, because neither of the two is quite as good alone as when with his compañero. We were a little startled when Flores said he had been out hunting rabbits very, very quietly so as not to scare them, and had seen us swimming "en cueros" at Cala Portales! And we had imagined ourselves so private! He pointed to his eye and said: "Carabineros see things!" Well, that's what they're for, and I guess they do. They served us "revoltillo" (spelling doubtful), which seems to be the Spanish equivalent of "gom"—a dish made of everything in general. With this went masses of Mallorquin bread, which is a magic bread, because it's the most horrible stale tasteless stuff imaginable most of the time, but becomes transformed into a thing of glory when you are hungry. And with all this, rich red wine. Then strong black coffee with wooden spoons. And we talked and laughed by the fire until it was time for us to go to bed and for them to shoulder their guns and go out on their ceaseless round of vigilance. Watch-fires along the coast.... The whole thing seemed inexpressibly romantic.

All this swimming has been excellent for me. Now I can almost swim the "crawl" proper, which is not only much faster, and prettier, than anything I have ever done, but also much more fun. It feels really mermaid-like and thrilling. Furthermore, the leg thrash is a specially strenuous affair which tends to improve the lines and curves, and all that. I am having fun in the water such as I haven't had since I was a kid at Sunapee. But for Nick this sea is still too cold. A minute in it sets him to shivering violently. I think we women have certain superiorities, and hardness to cold water is one of them. Floating is another art that few of them have acquired. I can lie in the sea perfectly calm and peaceful, without moving a toe. I have thought, in fact, how swell it would be to have a sort of wire frame to set on the tummy to hold a book or a writing pad, perhaps. Then you could lie out in delicious ease under a blue sky, floating, drifting idly. Rather good picture, what?

After Cala Figuera our indomitable José thought we had better go by the road at least for a way, saying that the paths along the coast were bad and circuitous. But these good carabineros of ours have a different point of view from us. They want to save us time and exertion. They don't like to walk themselves, and they don't see why anyone else should. They are continually trying to get us to go by the shortest way, whereas we want to go the most picturesque way. We went by the coast in spite of his warnings, and found ourselves well rewarded for scrambling over rather rough country, climbing a couple of hills, losing the path occasionally, and so on. For there were marvellous glimpses off the edges of the cliffs into a sea of a blue almost tense, strained—a slender peninsula of reddish rock with an island off its point and a small white lighthouse shining on that island; there were good passages through clumps of pine trees, and there was a good fresh green smell in the air. We went down fairly steeply again, and laboriously crossed a huge field of very green wheat—oh, it was the longest field of wheat in the world, like walking across the ocean; and then we came out on to a very desert rocky cala where there were few green things, rather desolate and strange except for the welcoming blue of the sea. Then on by way of a little road back country, until finally we found ourselves on a hill looking down over the beach of Santa Ponza. It was still forenoon, but this place looked so good, at least from the hill, that we had an idea we might spend the night there. This expedition is not to get places, but just to have a good time—to sit around and talk Spanish with agreeable souls, to swim, to write a little—to enjoy life generally. So if we only walk a few kilometers a day we do not mind.

We went down toward this good white beach that we saw gleaming in the distance, gleaming at the end of a strip of clear blue-green sea between us and a marvellous sheer headland with mountain peaks sticking up over it far away. And then, down on one side of the deep cala, we came to the most perfect little house in all the world. It was built into a small hillock, so that there were bushes growing beside the front door almost on a level with the roof. It was made of stones held together with brown mud—an earthy little hut, like part of the ground itself, and yet with an indefinable jauntiness, a cockiness all its own, especially in the angle of the snub round dirt chimney on one side. Its size was as utterly correct as its color. Although the walls were about two feet thick, the hut itself inside was not more than twelve feet long and nine or ten wide. You can stand up along the middle and a very little way on each side, but to go out of the wooden door you must stoop. Inside were two bunks with mattresses consisting of the usual matted grassy stuff; there was a little fireplace in a corner, cooking pots at hand; a tiny square window opposite the doorway, with a bird-cage hanging near it. The hut is built into the hillock in such a way that the ground is just at the level of the window-sill. But the roof! Its structure was simple: a beam of gnarled pine down the middle with one vertical support in the center of the hut; smaller gnarled beams running down at a fairly steep angle to the eaves. Above these beams the roof was thickly thatched with pine branches—a dense mat of twigs, needles that had turned brown, and little stubby pine cones in the generous abundance with which they grow on these pines. One of the side-beams was not like the others; it had a curious shape to it, and on looking at it again you saw that it was the blade and part of the handle of a big oar! That was the ceiling. Outside, the roof was covered with smoothly packed brown mud. Under the big center beam bamboo fish-rods were slung. It was the most home-like and comfortable little place I ever saw or dreamed of. And from the back, where it is built right into the earth, it is only a cocky little brown lump. From the front it is a dwarf house out of a fairytale. To tell the truth, I'm not sure about it yet, and I hope the pictures of it are good so that I can believe in it again.

The owner of the house appeared to be an elderly carabinero with a good smile. We asked him if we could take a picture of him and his perfect little house. He went inside and changed his hat, straightened his jacket a little, and called his compañero out too. They were both very friendly, and it ended by our being invited to sleep that night in the fairy-tale house. These two were moving on that afternoon, and the others who were coming to take their places would be living in the other larger house a few feet nearer the sea. The carabineros really have a delightful place here right by the sea under some pine trees, with a table and little benches out in the open, a fireplace and wood-pile, some old black cooking-pots, and two of the usual big Mallorquin water-jugs that have good lines to them. The roof of this larger house has been partly tiled, but the job is not finished yet, so there is grass, and even a long-legged flower or two, growing peacefully on the untiled half! They tell us that grass seed blows from across the cove.

One of the carabineros had been fishing, and showed me a bowlful of the prettiest little fish I ever saw—shining, many-colored, with brilliant stripes of flaming red and green and purple—beautiful, slender creatures. "Doncellas," they call them —"damsels."

Presently still another compañero pulled up on his bicycle. He took off the very business-like heavy belt that holds his ammunition, and took two little white eggs out of his business-like cartridge-box! And then, after we had talked a little more, nothing would do but that we must go up the road a way with them and have a cup of coffee at the telegrapher's house, this being a farm at the end of a cable line to another island. By this time we were chatting quite comfortably in not too bad Spanish, telling them about the things we liked to do, and what we had been doing so far, and finally one of them, without smiling, without looking in any way as if he were going to say something usual, asked: "¿Y no tienen bastante dinero para comprar un niño?" ("And haven't you money enough to buy a baby?") At that everyone burst out laughing: we shook our heads, and all stopped right in the little road and laughed together.

Later

We went swimming at the good beach at the end of the cove. After that we sat in the sun in the sandy pine woods back of the beach out of the wind. Later still we walked up the road to a sort of little shop to buy some of the necessities of life, consisting mainly of bread, eggs, and wine. When we got back at last to our little brown hut, it was late afternoon. We cooked a small supper over the carabineros' fire, drank plenty of most excellent wine (at four or five cents a litre!), and watched the sun go down behind that headland of purple cliffs that looked as if they had been chopped off square by a giant knife. A few birds called. The fire snapped. And oh, oh! La tranquilidad!

This expedition is costing us less than anything else so far.

We have been living for between three and four pesetas a day for both—which means somewhere between twenty-five and thirty-five cents! Nick is tremendously enthusiastic about it. I think he is really thrilled for the first time since the expedition last summer. I know that this is our life, that we fit into it and not into any other. Old clothes. Sunburn. Away from the silly tourists and the exasperating people, people, people.

Friday

We have got a pretty good system doped out now. We get up early—oh, I mean really early, six o'clock or even five-thirty—with the sun, almost. And so we have several hours to walk in the fresh coolth of the early day. Then, in late forenoon, when the sun's brightness begins to take it out of us too much, we stop in a good place and swim, eat, lie around, and write until the afternoon has cooled off a bit. Today, for instance, was rather severe. Just after leaving Santa Ponza we got into some awfully desert country, up-hill and down-hill, with hardly any paths that could be followed, and plenty of thorns—quite rough cross-country going—scrambling up sliding gravel banks, slithering down others, always with the sea below and tawny-red naked cliffs over it. It was very hot and very arid desert-like stuff. Nothing grew there except scraggly pines and even they didn't look as if they were enjoying life.

We came out again, however. We always do. After sliding on precarious ledgy little sheep-paths around the edges of some precipitous barren hills, we got down on to a big beach. Fairly tired we were, then, and the water looked very inviting. I plunged into big round swells, clear as glass, full of light, and the sun made a wavering golden mesh on the blue-green sand below. It was a mermaid world. After that we lay rather naked in the sun, and I burnt my tail. Very mermaid-like!

We went on again finally, a little better country this time. First a stretch on the main road (which we are avoiding as much as possible), then off toward the shore on small roads and paths near the tops of cliffs, as before. The country seems to be growing more and more hilly as we progress. This afternoon we passed near some very spectacular pinnacles and cliffs and sharp blue and purple headlands—all much the same character as the country before, middling dry and arid with a growth of pine, sometimes thick, almost like a pine grove but not quite, and sometimes very sparse and poor indeed. After a few miles of this sort of thing we dipped down to the sea and found ourselves in the little, little town of Puerto Andraitx, where we found a bed for two pesetas. The town is on one side of a narrow deep harbor in the hills. A lighthouse stands in the mouth of it, and several native boats are moored peacefully at the quay. It isn't so good to be spending a night in a town, even when it is only a little one, as to sleep in a carabinero's casita on the side of a delicious little blue-green cala. Still, I like to see the sunset through the rigging of native ketches.

Saturday

Today has been strenuous. Ye gods and little red fish-hooks, how it has been strenuous! We started out early from Puerto Andraitx, walked round to the other side of the harbor, and then started up a small footpath that looked as if it would lead along the coast on top of the cliffs, same as we had been doing before. We had faith by now in these little paths, you see. We thought we understood their ways. We thought that when we lost one we knew how to push on without worrying and pick it up again mysteriously. But this time the going got rougher and rougher, till it was a hands-and-knees job to get over the ground. We got to the top of one steep rocky hill, which was trying its damnedest to slide into the sea, only to find ourselves looking down into a ponderous gully with another worse and rockier hill on the other side of it—this apparently to go on ad infinitum. The good thing was that that same gully had a crack of bright sea in it. Just outside the crack were some black jagged rocks with the waves foaming around them, and on these in dignified rows sat a whole regiment of sea-gulls with the sun on their backs—still and gleaming snow-white against the picturesque turrets and pinnacles of black rock in the blue-green sea below. As we came over the hill, they rose up in a wild crying flock.

We thought we would take some little back-road cut across inland for a way; and to that end we followed what looked like a practicable path inland. The whole island is thickly seamed with paths and small roads, which lead round in circles, apparently, joining and rejoining and splitting and coming together, entirely without reason. Many of them are made just by sheep, others by people out for the lower branches of pines for firewood, of which there is more or less a scarcity, I guess. You can follow what looks like a perfectly clear-cut little road, and suddenly it will not be there any more—it has sort of petered out and stopped, and you are left standing in the middle of a thorn thicket, or on the top of a mountain, or the edge of a cliff. Sometimes all this works out to one's advantage—you go on a little way, and pick up another, and eventually you get where you want to go without too much work or worry. I guess knowing this technique made us over-confident, because this morning we got into an awful mess. We followed a little winding road up a long steep hill very circuitously until we were overlooking a great green basin that dropped off almost sheer below. It was surrounded on three sides by high rocky barren hills, with the sun striking them rather fiercely. And on the other side it was divided from the sea by impassible cliffs. And there we were.

We left our little road because it now seemed to be going utterly in the wrong direction. And we toiled down a little way into the upper end of that green gulf, and we toiled all the way out of it again on the other side, and it was strenuous—I mean strenuous. Cruel sun, and rough steep going—big boulders and thorns, not much else. When we got out of it we saw a sight that made our hearts very sick—we saw that if we had only stuck to our original little road it would have taken us out quite easily, although, to be sure, very circuitously. So we drank some wine on that.

We decided now that we really would stick to that little road and try to have faith in it. But behold! This whole countryside, that had once been so friendly and helpful to us, offering us little roads at every turn, now became hostile and inimical. The little roads were malevolent demons. This one led us up on to an awful ridge and—stopped. And again there we were. We could see a swell beach miles down the other side, and our tongues were fairly hanging out of our mouths with longing for a swim, and we had to figure this thing out. We were drenched with sweat, and so weary and scorched that we were positively swaying on our pins; and how were we to get down? Desperate-looking cliffs, a stretch of wild and woolly country separated us from that shining sand. We made our way step by step along the top of that ridge that seemed more like the Knife-Edge on Ktaadn than anything else. A narrow ridge made of big boulders jutting up among a few pine trees, the whole thing looking like the back-bone of an armored dinosaur towering over the country on each side. A devil of a thing for a harmless-looking little road to desert you on! And terrifying glimpses down between boulders on either side. We edged along this thing for several hundred feet, until we reached a lower point from which we thought there was a chance of making our way down toward the sea. After that nothing much happened except that eventually we did make our way to the sea, but only after having all sorts of trouble with the roads again, and shinning down through some country that not even a goat or sheep would have attempted if he was sober; and we weren't sure we were on the road to that beach until we were actually on the beach, and even then I had to touch the water to be really sure. If I don't wake up, I am sitting on that self-same little white beach at this very moment.

We have agreed that for a while now we will stick to the main road. The country is just getting too wild to be handled the way we handled the first part of it. And the heat is intense in the middle of the day. It gets as hot, even now in April, as it ever does all summer in New Hampshire, although, ridiculously enough, the nights are much too cold for comfort! And as well as getting more hilly, the country is getting always more dry and desert-like. Sometimes we come to the side of a hill absolutely golden with low bushy bright yellow flowers—and the most awful thorns you ever got into! Right out opposite this beach there is an island picturesquely named Dragonera. It has mountains on it, but so far as I can see not a single tree of any size. It is like this coast here, only worse. Some of the country we came through this morning, especially that Knife-edge job, reminded us of the peaks of our own mountains after you get almost up to tree-line. That would be all right if there were good green woods at the feet of them. The trouble is the whole country is like that. They don't understand about real woods, here. And yet, if you can imagine such a thing, even this seems like a sort of verdurous paradise compared with some of the country just around Madrid!

There are little green figs now on the fig-trees; and the almonds are beginning to ripen too—you see them by the thousand on the trees in their fuzzy green skins. It is curious to come upon a place where the hillside is terraced off with stone walls, and fine fruit trees there, and a small hut making a little scrap of cultivation in the middle of the arid wilderness. In the most outrageously difficult and unpromising-looking places, too.

The sun is gradually burning off our ears and noses.

There are a lot of perfectly good birds here, although not many that I recognize the songs of. They sing all the time, too, which makes it seem a little less of a desert when you are stuck in those wild high places. There are bugs, too. Later they say that one can't live here on account of mosquitoes. Now they are mostly in the larval stage, but they could be easily exterminated in no time. It's simply a question of draining a few pathetic little beach pools and watching out for reservoirs. But that is Spain. Don't get annoyed with children—it doesn't pay. Plenty of fleas, too. But in general I think we are taking this walking trip at exactly the right time of year—after the worst of the cold weather has gone, yet before it gets unbearably hot; also before the mosquitoes amount to anything. Also while it still rains now and then, and freshens up the ground. It must be awful here in the summer, when it doesn't rain for months.

I say all these things so you won't get to believing all the ridiculous tourist patter about this paradise of the Mediterranean and all that. While it has its points, it also has things wrong with it, and I've seen better places. However, enough of that—and now for a swim.

Sunday

In a way Mallorca gypped us today. It left us at noon-time high and dry on a rocky shore without even a bit of a beach to swim at. Son of a gun!

Last night we walked up along a white dirt road from the beach where we swam yesterday, and as we walked, the thirst that had been growing all day became a full-fledged demon of a thirst. We pulled into a small town, and, stopping in the first café we saw, we sat down at a table and drank beer. One bottle did no good whatever, so great was that thirst of ours, and we didn't know how to get hold of soft drinks, which so far as we could see they had none of, and the water round here isn't supposed to be quite safe; so we drank beer, and we continued to drink beer. When we left that town, we had to begin a long way off to avoid donkey-carts, bicycles, and similar impediments of the road. What do you think of that? A country where you can't quench a thirst got up through an honest day's hard work, without getting stewed!

We slept that night at the next town up the road, Andraitx proper, which is only a couple of miles from Puerto Andraitx, where we had been the night before. We had wandered over all kinds of cliffs and mountains and backbones of giant dinosaurs just to get round in a circle to within a few kilometers of our starting-place. It was rather ridiculous; but anyway, we had had an exciting time of it.

Then this morning we started bright and early out of Andraitx, hoping to do better today. This time the main road for us! And it was a most astonishing main road. Farther on it gets almost too much like a highway, but along this part of the coast it's like a little country back-road. First of all, out of Andraitx, it went up and up and up, winding somewhat but not unreasonably, up out of the big valley. Then it began to loop itself around the shoulders of big cliffy hills, amazing hills with sheer sides that fell off sometimes into the sea and sometimes into cataclysmic ravines and gulfs. Some of them were covered with pine trees (the pine with which this island is covered looks a little like our white pine, but it isn't), some of them were nearly bare, and some had great clumps of the golden thorn flowers shining out between the green pines—and that was gay. As we went on the road got more and more windy, doubling back upon itself in double and triple and even quadruple hair-pin bends, until it beat anything I ever saw in New Hampshire. And, as you know, that is going some. It seems to me that when poets and similar riffraff have mentioned "winding roads," as they do so often, they don't really know what they are talking about. I can't tell you how spectacular and wild some of those mountains are. There are great purple cliffs of fretted rock, rough and ragged against the sky, almost above you—then ahead there may be a long ridge with a breath-taking slant to it and pines growing stiffly down its edge. And as we went on the chaos increased.

I pity the poor peasants who have to keep their farms on land such as this. Yet, you know, somehow they manage it. They build terraces and terraces—oh, scores of them in dreary giant stairs up a whole huge hillside. There may be just olive trees growing on them, or there may be good green wheat. The walls are stone, of course. That's one thing there is plenty of here—stones. The olive trees themselves are worth looking at. You see some that must be three thousand years old at least—that certainly look as if they were about the first things created. Gnarled and twisted fantastically—grotesque, distorted old trunks out of which young shoots are growing. Their leaves are narrow and grayish-green, sometimes a sort of silvery gray—hoary with age.

We walked in all more than sixteen kilometers on that road. By that time we were descending into the big valley where the next town is. We expect to stay up there tonight—Estallenchs, it is called. I don't suppose that means anything. The trouble is, that when we came down to the seashore trustingly, to find our little cala and beach for swimming, there was nothing but a frightful old rockpile and some pebbles. If I swam here I am afraid I would bang and scrape my tail on the barnacles, like the whale in *The Treasure of the Isle of Mist*. Furthermore, the shore here is positively strewn with pieces of a native schooner that was wrecked awhile ago. Little pitiful scraps of sail are mingled with the incredible mess of splintered wood. I'm disillusioned. I'm going back to Cala Portales where there are four perfect little beaches in four separate little coves, one right after another.

In all this island so far I have seen nothing I would call woods. There are pines, and a kind of bushy growth that ranges from very thin to moderately thick, that's all. But there aren't any real honest-to-God bushes. Suppose you are taking a walk in New Hampshire, and the desire for a bush comes upon you. Well, there are bushes at every step—good, dense, luxuriant ones. Here if you want a bush you have sometimes a heart-rending search. It makes it all very difficult. You see something up a little way on a hillside that looks like a bush and ought by all rights to be a bush—but when you get to it you find that there is an admirable view all over the countryside up and down, right and left. It just isn't there, to speak of, any more. Which is, to say the least, discouraging.

I sit here on this pile of rocks and think of what a gorgeous swim I had yesterday. Toward the latter part of it a little boy came along the beach and sat watching me (I had my bathing-suit on though). I guess he had never seen anybody swim before, or something, because he was open-mouthed with astonishment. Especially when I swam under water. Then Nick came out and we swam under water between each other's legs, turned somersaults, and such things. The kid had probably never had such a good show in his life. There were little tide pools at the edge of the beach, where the water was almost hot from the sun. We had fun making corrals and driving or trying to drive curious little fish into them, just as I used to do thousands of years ago at Sunapee.

Monday

Today we landed at a slightly better place. There is a beach about so long (gesture of arms) and I think I can swim here unless I step on some sea-urchins, which would be distinctly bad. So here I sit dangling my feet in the cold sea to rest them from the morning's walk. Although it can hardly be called a real walk at that. It was only about nine kilometers, and we dawdled —absolutely dawdled all the way. It was because of the scenery ("Scen'ry? I've druv across these hills for forty year, and I ain't never seen no scen'ry")—taking pictures and one thing and another. For instance, one good thing was a small tower, one of the old Moorish ones, standing on a nubbin of cliff with a sheer drop to the sea, and above this tower the ridge of the hill went up at a sharp angle with pine trees—odd-shaped ones such as grow in such difficult places—against the sky-line in a procession upwards. Then we saw some fine examples of the art of farming on a steep hillside—a wheat field growing on terraces, and a horse ploughing on one of them! Also there was a complicated system of irrigation with big tanks and old stone aqueducts and all. Gosh, the work that has gone into the building of a place like that! Years and years, I suppose—passed on through generations. Every stone of every one of those numberless high walls was laid by hand, one at a time; soil was transported by means of the shallow baskets that all the laborers use here. A sort of Mallorquin *Growth of the Soil*.

The mountains are grand. They get always higher and sharper and more rugged as we progress up the coast. We are now at the cala of a town called Bañalbufar, which I think a good name. It sounds rather like a bath that ended in a bull-fight. The trouble with mountains like these is that they aren't quite real. You are too near the peaks of them, and they haven't any normal bottoms. You are up among them and the sea is below. But mountains they are, without a doubt. If you don't think so, just try climbing one.

Saw a lot of goats this morning. They are all over the island. I think they are made to be clowns. They are the funniest animals going. Ridiculous lines to them, to begin with—too thin necks and too thick haunches and too stiff legs. And their backs tilt upwards toward the stern. And their ears and mouths are funny. And they are in general bumpy, knobbly. They stand looking at you with their body pointed in a direction that is entirely uncoordinated with the direction they are looking in, and they make ridiculous noises at you and then start gamboling stiffly—absolutely, literally bouncing over the ground with a slightly see-saw motion. Sure-footed little critters, too. For all their apparent recklessness they never seem to miss fire. There are plenty of sheep, too, and quite a lot of black ones. I guess the black sheep tend to come to Mallorca, anyway. Furthermore, a lot of sheep have reddish patches on their backs, or sometimes their whole back is red—strawberry blondes, I suppose. There are fowls, of course, and the roosters here are very distressing. They have no sense of time or propriety, but crow in the darkest, deepest watches of the night. All night. Lots of rabbits, too, go bounding and skittering over the hillsides. You see, as I have said so many times, it is rocky country, bumpy country. And rabbits are supposed to go in for that sort of thing. And then there is a bird (I haven't seen him yet and don't know what he is or what he looks like, but I think he is one of the long-legged wading birds) who lives along the coast and cries mournfully and loudly "O-eep! O-eep! O-eep!" all night. The natives call him the "carabinero" bird, because he is quiet and sleeps in the day-time, but watches at night. There are dogs of all kinds. Frogs, with a special Spanish croak. Horses, mules, and donkeys. Oh, the donkeys! Little shaggy wonderful creatures with big ears and eyes. And cats. Apparently they don't ever drown kittens here at all, which is in its way good—but there are cats. All over the roof-tops and everywhere else. Black predominates, but there is everything. Sometimes when you are walking home late at night up a narrow empty street, void of life, you happen to turn your head and look back, and there will be no less than five black cats sitting there glaring at you with green eyes shining in the light of a nearby street lamp—sitting in Hallowe'enish attitudes and poses—five cats all of a sudden where there weren't any before. It makes one wonder a little. When we were in Palma, they went courting every night right outside our window. Sounds that would make the strongest man's hair stand straight on end like quills upon a very fretful porpentine. I guess that will do for the live-stock of Mallorca. Except for the children, of which there is a certain superfluity.

The weather has held absolutely perfect for a whole week now! We have seen but one small cloud in all that time. About four days more, and we will be in Sóller, where we think we will end this expedition, since that just about ends practicable roads in that direction. And as time goes on we get progressively browner and thinner and firmer. We have been living on Mallorquin bread (which comes in thick disks ranging all the way from six inches to three feet in diameter), figs, cheese, chocolate, wine, with an occasional glass of coffee at towns, or a supper consisting of green stuff and oil, which one gets to crave. The night at Estallenchs, we bought four heads of lettuce and some oil, swiped some salt from the dining-room table, and retired to our room! The last several nights—in fact, since the carabinero hang-out back at Santa Ponza, we have been sleeping at the little "fondas" in towns.

It is the darnedest language they speak here. It is a dialect which mixes Italian, Moorish, Spanish, French, and other miscellaneous languages, corrupting all of them; and it has curious harsh sounds and some intonations that remind one of the Oriental tongues. A Spaniard from Madrid would get along here very little better than we do. It is just hopeless. They say it very much resembles the dialect they speak in Catalunya, which is by the French frontier. But I imagine it has ramifications of its own, besides.

Nick is growing a beard again. I don't know how long this one will last. It is little more than a week old, and pretty good.

Tuesday

We didn't stay at Bañalbufar after all. They wanted two pesetas apiece out of us at the inn (they have apparently caught on to the tourist racket), so we decided we would sleep out in the bush instead. We left the little town an hour or so before sunset, and pulled our way gradually out of the big valley, not knowing where we would stop or why, but liking the adventure of the thing—much more pleased with ourselves, of course, than if we had gotten a cheap room in the town. We went slowly higher and higher, sometimes following the road all the way around its astonishing bends, sometimes taking the rough paths which serve as occasional short-cuts, and which cut off whole kilometers. After a while we began to wonder whether we should ever get out of this immense round gulf. The little town, with the low sun shining on the white of its houses, was perched precariously up and down the slope of the valley floor; it looked as though a good landslide would precipitate town and mountains into the sea. At last we thought we saw sky between the pines on the crest above us, and sure enough, we were at the rim. Then, as we went on up, nothing happened. The sky grew and grew, but that was all. There seemed to be positively no other side of the thing. It just fell off. We were quite excited, but when we got to the top at last, and looked down on the other side, the view was a let-down. Down below was something we thought was coast. It looked as if cliffs fell off into the sea, and even as if there was an edge of breaking surf against red rocks, but it was so far away we could not be sure. And the bottom of the valley itself—well, Nick said it was impossible to take a picture of it—it was all too far away—vertically, you understand —to show up! So there we were on the edge of hell itself—so deep, straight down, we couldn't see properly to the bottom. So we just went on.

Off beyond, great barracks of bare mountain ridges stood up. Some parts of this drop below were not so sheer that olive orchards could cling to them—but olive trees can cling to most anything, anyway. All sorts of curious noises came out of these orchards—and the noises made by the peasants themselves were almost as funny as those of the sheep and goats baa-ing in chorus and separately to one another—a complete conversation of "baa's"—high, low, quavering, or prolonged—out from among the olive trees. And the peasants were singing—singing heartily and happily at their work, which was good. It sounded like a mixture of Japanese folk-song, grand opera, and religious anthem. In reality I believe it is pieces of Moorish influence that got left over.

We walked on. And, having once looked at that coast in the distance—the long tiers of headlands in folds as far as we could see—we decided that we certainly would not take a chance on being able to make our way over that sort of thing, and that we would be very civilized and keep on following the road. We were going away from the sea now, but we had hopes. Farther on we stopped and asked some questions of a group of carabineros; still farther, just as the big orange globe of the sun was sinking into a curiously ephemeral sea that had no definite horizon, we stopped again and had a somewhat more hearty supper than we had meant to.

It was darkening fast now, and there was a small, almost pathetically small, cluster of lights in a green bowl away southward—a tiny village down there—a casual handful of tiny people trusting themselves in a deep bowl in the hills. And then a pale silverly glow began to come over a long ridge in the east—the full moon getting up behind it. It was magic. And here and there sheep-bells tinkled tranquilly over the landscape. The road was white in the moonlight, and the fantastic peaks around us were half-lighted by it. We wound on and on until we were tired, then we rested and wound on again. The moon was shining over thousands and thousands of olive trees. We began tentatively looking for a place to curl up for the night, but saw nothing but olive trees growing in freshly ploughed fields, with stiff ruts and ridges—impossible. We kept on going, sang songs, took a few swallows of "clarete." It affected us and made us wondrously happy. Olive trees and freshly ploughed fields! But we really wanted to sleep now. My God, is there never an end to this olive orchard? Apparently there wasn't, so we went on. Our feet got tired: we rested, consulted the map by the light of four or five matches, went on. We walked through olive trees for days—weeks. We cursed the bloody olive trees in earnest.

At long last we turned off on to another little road that supposedly wound down to a small town on the coast, Puerto de Valldemossa, where we would go next day. This road took us out of those olive trees that had been haunting us so persistently. We came to piny slopes again, the kind of rough, rocky pasture stuff that there is such a lot of round these parts, and that goats and sheep seem to enjoy. And now the question began to be acute as to where we were going to find even a reasonably smooth level place to lie down in. In this country it is often devilishly difficult to find even a decent place to sit down, let alone lie down! A country like that ought to have something done to it! Maybe that is why the goats are so knobbly—from trying to curl around rock—and the sheep so thickly padded with wool. I should think even the rabbits might get tired, but there's no accounting for taste. Anyway, at last we found a place that was rather leveler than the rest of the country, although far from being level. We chucked about a ton of small rocks out of it, and then went cutting bushes to pad it with. At last, very weary, we stretched out under the open sky and the full moon that had by now risen high.

We awoke in the middle of a golden whirlpool of bird-songs —light-hearted songs from every tree, every corner of the sky, every bush and twig. The air itself had simply burst into song. So we got up, munched breakfast, and packed the pack. At this point Nick noticed a curious thing: that is, that there was a sort of blister on the inside of the sole of one sneaker. From the long march the day before, doubtless—but imagine a country where you raise blisters not only on your feet but on your shoes as well!

Afterwards

We pushed on then, and after we had gone a few paces down the road, we saw that we had been sleeping peacefully on the very edge, almost, of a greenish gulf set in between the sea on one side and a colossal wall of mountain ridge on the other three—a ridge so sheer and gray and high that it made us think of Ktaadn with its Knife-Edge towering over the bowl in which Chimney Pond lies; only here there were occasional hardy pines that managed to find footing in crevices up the wall. Right beside the sea, so small it looked like a bunch of fly-specks, was a tiny fishing village, Puerto de Valldemossa—a mere microscopic handful of houses packed together beside a strip of white shingle that promised the good swim we hadn't found for two days. And the road—a reasonable road that an automobile could drive down—went down the side of this sheer wall, winding diabolically back and forth against itself, making a distance of many kilometers out of what could be accomplished in one wild leap from the cliff. Masses of yellow thorn-bushes shone in the sun among the pines on the upper slopes where the drop was less sheer. Our knees were a little weak when we looked down into that enormous valley or up at that enormous gray wall of cliffs around it; and we felt a tingle of joy at the idea of that perfect white beach where we would presently be swimming—after we had walked around some miles of hair-pin turns. In fact, the scenery was awe-inspiring, don't you know—it was something to be amazed at and to stand in rather serious silence before. And at that moment, all of a sudden out of that monstrous valley came strange preliminary raucous squeaks, growing louder, increasing in speed, until it sounded like a French automobile horn with asthma and whooping-cough—and then another joined the first, and this went on for some seconds until the mountains were reverberating—a couple of burros conversing in the fields below! Apparently there is no real solemnity in nature.

We went on down, still pretty much keyed up about that beach. When we got down there the town itself looked more picturesque than ever, with its fishing nets draped over the sea-wall, its tile-roof houses bunched up snugly together, with cliffs and sea behind them. But oh, that beach! The smallest grain of sand we could find on it was the size of an egg! Things are not what they seem when you look at them from mountain-tops. We swam a little, and hurt our feet.

Then we climbed part of the way out of the valley again, and took a little road along the coast which was supposed to go to a town called Deyá, where we were thinking of spending the night. This road started off admirably—in fact, Nick said how pleasant it would be to drive a car through it—Aunt Edith when she arrived—it could be done quite easily. But after a while we began to go through a gate or two into farms where pigs were kept in this road, along with a good many bumps and pebbles. At this point Nick remarked that he would take his own car through all right, but it wouldn't be such a good idea to take somebody else's. All the time this little road was sliding along almost surreptitiously between two cliffs—one that dipped off to the sea below it, and another, higher and steeper, above it. Presently we came to where a big boulder had slid down the mountain into the road, and the road had been turned aside and went around it. And a little further on we saw where a whole great landslide had come tearing down the mountain right across the road, and completely squelched its last little sparks of life. From then on it was hard enough even to go over it afoot. At this point we decided it was about time we got up out of that mess and on to the main road again, which ran along near the top of the upper cliffs, a hell of a long way straight up. We came to what looked like a graded footpath up the wall, but it looked at the same time too steep to be anything but chimerical. You understand that this cliff above us on top of which the main road went was another of those sheer straight birds that are found in great abundance in this island.

We had lunch, we took breath, and started. Well, I have done some fairly strenuous climbing in my life, and so has Nick, but by gorry, neither of us ever got into anything so exhausting as this. It was hot, to start with—we were breaking our usual rule and climbing during the bad part of the day when we should have been swimming if there had been any place to swim. I carried the pack at first. Later we changed. And we plodded up, one step at a time—one—step—at—a—time.... The thing was sheer over us, and yet there was a perfectly good footpath up it, switching back and forth—and it looked as if it had been a fair road at one time. Really these people here have done some of the most amazing things! And you'd never suspect it, to look at 'em. We plodded on. Presently we were directly above the place where we had had lunch. Overhanging the sea, almost. One misstep... And the going was none too good, because it was that loose pebbly slidy stuff that rolls with frightful ease when at such a grade. It was a pretty dangerous trail unless one were very careful. I wouldn't recommend anyone ever go down it. We plodded up. We continued to overhang the sea. I never saw anything so God-damned steep in my life. Down below us there was a big cliffy hunk of rock that stuck out into the sea with never a leaf growing on it, but it was interesting from up here in that it had a big hole in it, so that you could see right through it to the sea on the other side. But to tell the truth, we weren't bothering too much about the scenery. We were just plodding on. We climbed over a thousand feet, step by step—and when we ended we were still right over the place where we had had lunch. So we sat down to rest and think it over.

But presently, noticing a flock of big black buzzards swooping and circling around overhead, we wondered if they were waiting for us, so we got up again and, after wading through some terraced olive orchards for a while, we found ourselves on the main road, which was rather dusty and most amazingly level. We walked on and on to Deyá in a sort of daze. We were pretty thirsty and wondered if we would have to get stewed again that night....

The first five days of the trip were by far the best. This

walking on the main road is never much fun, especially when it is through country like this—fairly steep hills, dry as dust—in fact, composed of just rocks and dust—terraced with high stone walls and planted with olive trees. You look at a hillside in the distance, and you can see the bare dusty ground between the trees. And close to, it is worse. It is a desert. Deyá is just another of those small towns in a hole under beetling bare crags. I don't like towns anyway. I like woods and beaches and carabinero caves and camp-fires.

Sóller was sort of another disappointment, too, although it is tremendously talked up. It sits in the best hole of them all, and has the tallest, barest, and beetlingest crags around it. It holds the record in that respect. The much-talked-of beach at its Puerto is not one tenth so good as some of the tiny, unknown ones at the other end of the island; although the little harbor itself, considered as a harbor, is corking.

We came back from Sóller to Palma by train, still partly in a daze. The last two or three days of the trip are already pretty much faded in my mind. I have dim recollections of a succession of terraced olive orchards. But the first days! One never forgets nights such as we spent in that old tower on the headland, with the moonlight outside, and the carabinero bird calling mournfully: "O-eep! O-eep!" all night along the coast.

Love,

Bar

ACKNOWLEDGMENTS

I am grateful to Maryka Biaggio, Nile Cappello, Paul Collins, Brenda Guiberson, Ann Hulbert, Francesca McCaffrey, Hannah McCarthy, Sarah Meuleman, Jackie Morris, Abby Norman, Margherita Orsi, Lynn Schmeidler, and all who keep Barbara's light shining.

Thank you to the Rare Book & Manuscript Library at Columbia University for sheltering the Follett archives and making them available to everyone. Thank you to Courtney Abud for sharing her Ture Schoultz clippings. Thank you to Ekrulila for his evocative photograph used on the cover, generously shared on pexels.com.

Extra big thanks to Daniel Mills for his unflagging detective work; to Laura Smith for *The Art of Vanishing* and camaraderie; and to Resa Blatman for her enduring love.

Stefan Cooke
Somerville, Mass.
February 2020

www.ingramcontent.com/pod-product-compliance
Lightning Source LLC
Chambersburg PA
CBHW032112110726
47902CB00003B/558

* 9 7 8 0 9 9 6 2 4 3 1 4 8 *